COURAGEOUS BOOKS

RETURN TO WENT

Book three of the Planet Walkers series

A. V. Shackleton

Published by Courageous Books 1081 Wallaces Gap Rd
Ballalaba NSW
Australia 2622

ISBN 978-0-9925814-9-7

A.V. Shackleton

Thank you to my family and friends for your tireless support, and to my intrepid fellow Planet Walkers - I'd be lost without you. Also, thanks to Elisabetta Faenza for her help with Imperial communiques.

Planet Walkers

GLOSSARY

(Go to www.avshackleton.com for more detailed information)

Annangi: the dimorphic race of angels and archangels.

Djan'rū: the point at which a planet can be joined by a navigator's song.

El: Deity. Annangi believe that the Breath of El blows through all. **Asheru** is El's consort.

Great House: There are ten Great Houses, each with a home planet and a leader accepted by El.

Haze: easily visible aspects of an individual's aura. **Mark:** the soul mark granted by El to those who become proficient in a particular psychic gift. The Mark appears as a symbol shining through the skin.

Qalān:

- **Personal Qalān** is a sub-dimensional space that surrounds every individual. Annangi access this space for storage of personal items.

- **Planetary Qalān** surrounds every planetary body in a web of interconnected wormholes. Skilled Annangi can create portals in this Qalān for instantaneous travel between locations on a given planet.

- **Galactic Qalān** connects the stars and planets of the galaxy. It merges with **planetary Qalān** at specific points known as Djan'rū. **Navigators** travel between Djan'rū.

Sajhar: both Mark and title of one who has mastered all powers entailed with the working of metal.

Screen: internally, a psychic construction that hides private information; or externally, a shield that hides one's presence.

Shamkar: the Mark of one who is a master of the power of voice.

Shamkarun: the title of one who bears the Shamkar. **Tiamät:** the Imperial House; the God-Emperor and Empress are of House Tiamät. The three clans of Tiamät are Gok, Enna and Ashik.

Tsemkar: the Mark of a master of mind power. This ability is often strong in those of clan Ashik.

Tsemkarun: the title of one who bears the Tsemkar. Although the current God-Emperor is a Tsemkarun, not all God-Emperors are Marked.

Veil: a psychic construction that hides thoughts and feelings from the perception of others.

Ziquarra: the Mark of one who can leave their body at will and send their soul to far distant locations.

Ziquarra is also the name of this skill.

Ziquarudjan: the title of one who bears the Ziquarra.

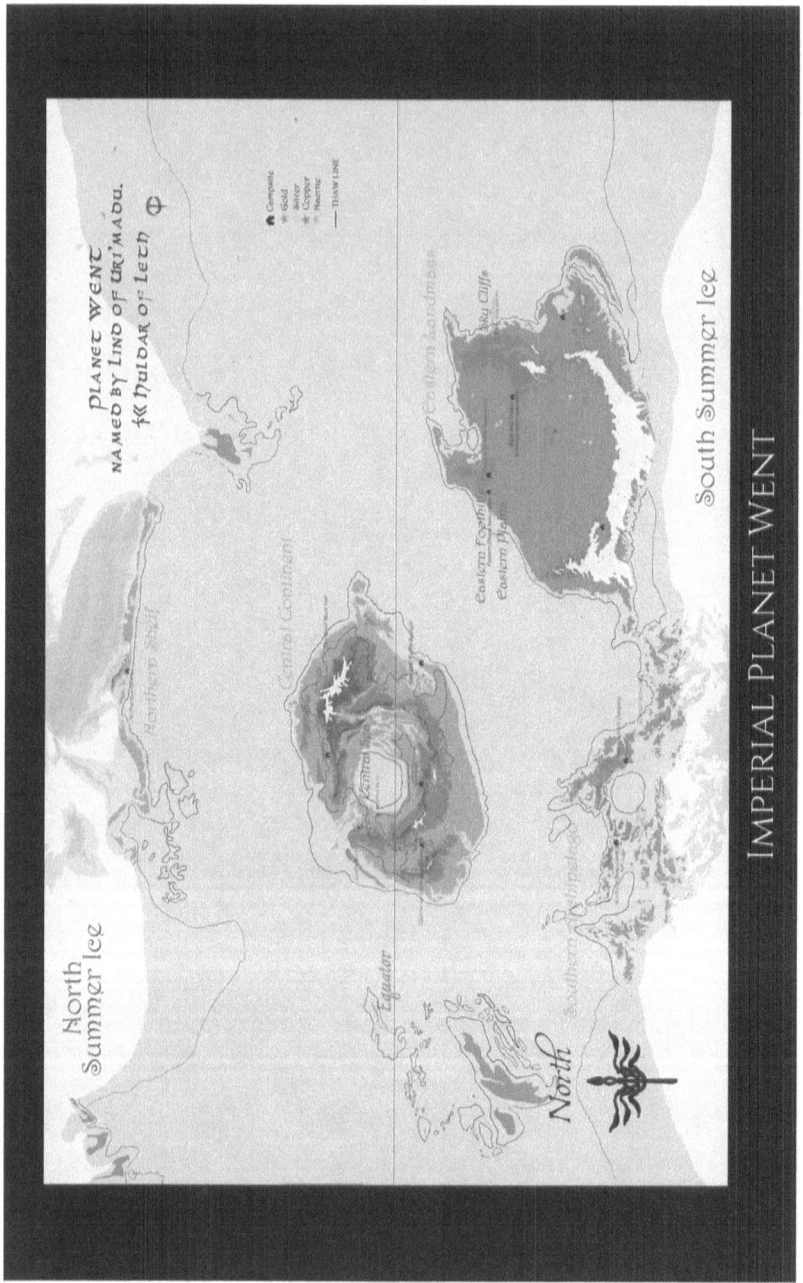

A.V. Shackleton

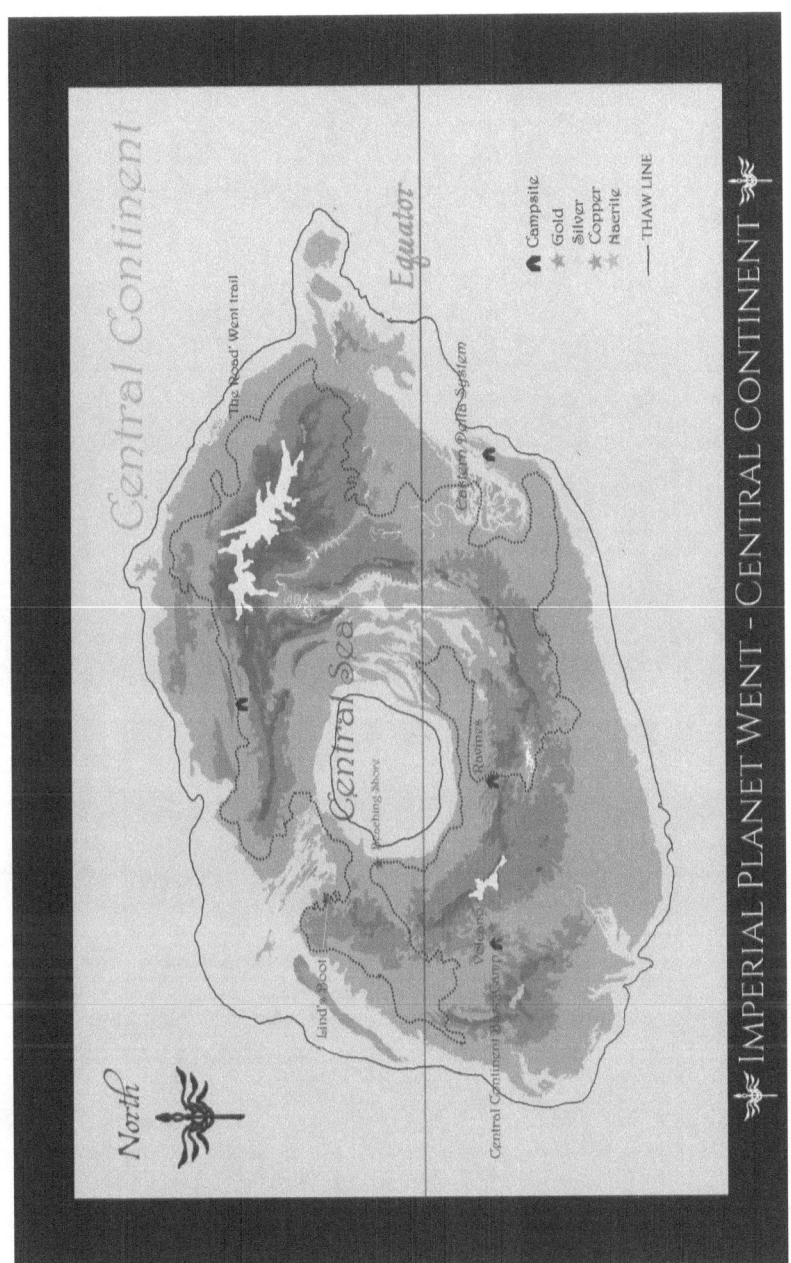

Planet Walkers

The following papers were liberated from the private desk of Tsemkarun Ishät Ashik, 26th Chosen of El – Reproduced by permission of the Library of Maatu.

IMPERIAL COMMUNIQUE 790KQZ

Regarding:

Report to His Imperial Majesty Tsemkarun Ishät Tiamät 26th God Emperor Chosen of El

Regarding: Imperial planet 5149P – also known as Went

Urgency Priority /5: 5

Summary:

Presence of **nacrite** deposits confirmed to be richest ever discovered. Large quantities of gold, tin and other precious metals easily available including:

- Rare minerals
- Blue calcite
- Rare and unique gems

Recommendations: Increase exploratory resources to enable mining to begin at earliest possible after full assessment and ecological sign-off.

Dendar Gok

Dated/RAPEN 5 7/38

Planet Walkers

HIS IMPERIAL HIGHNESS
TSEMKARUN ISHÄT TIAMÄT, 26TH
CHOSEN OF EL

To Explorers Guild,

URGENCY PRIORITY 5:5

Directive:

Mining of planet **5149T** must be expedited to commence immediately. It is vital no other house is permitted access to the planet or its reserves of nacrite.

Conditions:

1. Faytha has been granted exclusive mining rights over **5149T** to be rewarded accordingly for this service.

2. All products of such activities remain the property of Tiamät including all nacrite, precious gems, and, in particular, all Eyes of Bel Nishani.

Status:

Secrecy absolute.

Threat Level:

Maximum. Galactic insurrection risk high. Nacrite necessary to establish war footing.

Imperial Secrecy Order:

No approvals to be sought from House Leth, House Maatu, or any other House or agency. No environmental assessments to be sought or communications to be engaged with on pain of death.

All miners and exploratory crew to be terminated on completion of mining cycle.

Planet Walkers

ON HAAS

In Haaseen, well-ordered capital city of Haas, homeworld of the Rukh, the shine of the mid-morning sun gained strength on a timeworn mid-city training ground. Under its watchful eye, eighteen doughty Rukh, a whippy Enna and another of uncertain heritage whirled body and sword through the movements of "Rope and Rada".

The master, Embar of Rukh, watched them intently. "Two!" he shouted. "Twist the Rope!"

The smell of sweat thickened with the dust. Casco's sinews bunched and flexed as he flowed by rote through the exercises. The low-stance form of Twist the Rope progressed to Three, Arch of Faris, then Four, Pelar's Dive.

Bare feet danced in synchronized tread. Metal flashed in the haze.

"Five!" Embar called. "Race the Rada!"

Casco raised his sword and crabbed forward, relieved to feel no pain. The work the healer had done on his shoulder was holding up well.

Embar of Rukh continued to bark corrections with harsh economy. Casco was thankful none were aimed at him. Completion of the series required the discharge of a stun charm – the release of voice and tsemkar with split-second timing. He gathered the sequence to mind and held it ready, wary of the painful backlash if he got it wrong.

The next call came. "Six: Run for Mama!"

Casco ducked and rolled and then it was time. The percussive shout bent the ether around them. It was followed by groans from those who had misfired, but no one actually collapsed – a vast improvement on the group's last effort.

"Seven!" Embar barked. "Rope the Rada!"

As the series lunged to its conclusion, those still capable held their stance. Sweat dripped from Casco's entire body but as he waited to be released, he was proud that the low posture no longer felt awkward.

Embar surveyed their lines with a hard gaze. When he came to Casco he gave a nod. Casco fought to retain a neutral aspect as a quiet thrill raced through him. Embar gave compliments as rarely as Faythans gave away coin.

Beside him, Daric Enna was also breathing hard. He'd gained muscle from the regular drill but his light frame was still far more agile than any of his classmates'. He'd always been deadly, Casco mused. Now he looked it.

Ye's vizzin starry too, sho la, Daric whispered. Humor danced in his thought.

Casco kept his mind on the charm they'd been set to learn. It was not worth risking Embar's wrath if their exchange was sensed.

Without warning, a sword swept toward his head. In less than a heartbeat he'd blocked the downward thrust, landed a swinging round-house kick and activated the charm. Embar reeled and went down. The point of Casco's sword rested against his throat.

Daric smirked as eighteen Rukhish warriors struggled to reconcile the sight of their master laid low by a half-breed.

A little dazed by what he'd accomplished, Casco moved his sword aside and bowed low. He stepped back, still bowing, as Embar got to his feet and dusted himself off. Blood ran from a deep slash on the instructor's cheek.

He motioned Casco to straighten up. "Are you sure there's no Rukh in your heritage?"

"None I know of, sir," Casco assured him.

"Must be Maatu, then." The towering archangel dabbed at his wound and signaled for the healer.

"Step forward," he said to Casco.

Casco's heart raced. Blood dripped steadily from Embar's face, staining his shirt red.

"Face the class."

Nineteen pairs of eyes fastened on him.

The healer arrived but stopped outside the group at Embar's brusque hand movement.

"Despite the differences in our weight and height," Embar said to the class, "Casco is the victor here today, and do you know why?"

"He didn't pause to think," Daric answered boldly. "He let his body think for him."

Embar nodded. "Remember this. The repetitions you moan about? Attention to detail! This is what training is for. Muscle memory gave Casco the brain-space he needed to coordinate voice and mind effectively. Remember this also," he continued. "*Never* turn your back on your enemy. If Casco had lost concentration, he'd be the one needing the healer now. On these grounds, between these walls, I tell you when it's over. Out there?" His steely gaze narrowed. "Things are different." He bowed. "Class dismissed."

As the group began to dissipate he indicated for Casco and Daric to remain.

The healer approached. Embar bent his head so his injury could be assessed. Casco winced as the elderly Naghari probed the split flesh on Embar's cheek.

"Fractured," he murmured. "You'll need to sit down."

They followed to a bench on the edge of the practice ground, stepping over fresh bloodstains on the way. One patch seemed larger than the others and Casco wondered what had happened there. Had someone died in training? It wouldn't be the first time.

The massive fighter stared stoically at the middle distance while the healer repaired his face, but fresh sweat beaded his brow. Casco had trouble watching, but felt, as a budding warrior, he should.

Afterward, he and Daric waited while Embar gathered his wits. Suddenly the Rukh's eyes cleared. Dilated pupils returned to archangelic slits.

"You two off tomorrow?"

"Mid-morning," Casco replied.

Ambar looked at them speculatively. "My two enigmas fly free," he said. "Let us hope it is on the wind of the Breath." He turned to Daric. "What brought one of clan Enna to train with the Rukh?"

"Came with him." Daric's eyebrows flashed upward. "Didn't want to be left out."

Embar snorted. "And you, Casco, have shown your kind can be trained as well as any other. You are welcome to rejoin us whenever you return." He beckoned him closer and Casco watched in amazement as he pinned a silver badge to his shoulder, a triangle with the outstretched wings of Rukh.

"Draga," the warrior said. "Third stage on the path. Wear it with pride."

Casco bowed. "I will," he stammered. He tried to keep his elation politely contained but beneath his veil wonderment refused to abate. Daric's look of admiration was also seasoned by startlement.

"And as to the task at hand?" Embar continued. His voice lowered. "My advice is to watch yourselves. I've had word about an Ashik contingent signed with your particular Host. I fear their function will be to subdue Lethian outrage."

"They're serious then," Daric said quietly.

"You knew?" Casco said. "Why didn't you say?

Daric shrugged. "I only heard this morning."

"You hear far more than you should, Daric Enna," Embar murmured.

Daric made no reply.

Embar's brow twitched. He returned to Casco. "Logistics?"

Casco nodded.

"A busy time ahead in preparation for your next deployment. Any trouble, call on Colmar." Embar flashed him an image. "Works in the palace."

Casco nodded. "The Guild-Lord has taken steps. I have permission to return to Giahn, but must stay under Guild supervision at all times."

"And Daric here is a Guild-member?"

Daric gave a slight smile. "As it happens …"

Embar snorted. "They say there's good in everyone. But remember, both of you, the blade itself has no morals."

Dismissed, they made for the Imperial Arms, an ale-house placed strategically near the academy entrance, and settled into their customary nook. "Besh." Casco lifted his stoneware jar and swilled the cool brown contents. "Still can't believe they make it here, and nearly as good."

A chair-leg squeaked on the floor as it was pushed aside.

"Better!" a low voice rumbled.

Casco paused mid-draft and looked up at two familiar faces. "Gento! Cobar! Didn't think we'd see you till tomorrow."

The two sidled in beside himself and Daric.

"I see your paws are still empty?" Casco laughed, and signaled for two more drinks.

"What's this bit of glitter here?" Gento dusted the badge on his shoulder. "See this, Cobar?"

"Embar's going soft," Cobar teased.

"He earned it." Daric bristled. "Laid him out well and truly."

Cobar frowned down on Daric as if surprised to hear him speak.

Gento raised his eyebrows.

Casco grinned. "This is my friend, Daric Enna. Daric, this big lump squashing me against the wall is Cobar, and," he waved his ale at the other, "this one's Gento."

"I'm the brains," Gento said.

"Daric will be joining us on Went," Casco told them.

"Ahh. So that's you, is it?" said Gento. "Looks like he can handle himself, eh Cobar? At least he has real hands. No blue polish."

"Thought I'd brush up when I get home to Giahn," Daric answered.

"An Enna slumming it on Haaseen?" Gento jibed. "You 'n' our lad Casco must be pretty tight?"

"Dinna fash yourself," Daric replied with a thick Rukhish accent. "I barely made it inda is wee trousers an still decidin tworth the fight."

Casco's drink sputtered over the table.

"Now look." Gento laughed. "You made him choke."

Daric rolled his eyes. "Again!"

Beside him, Cobar patted his back with a little more force than expected.

"You're not helping!" Casco wheezed.

Daric shook his head. "See? That's why I'm here," he said cheerfully. "Don't get this level of entertainment in the hallowed halls of Enna. Best order another round, good sirs!"

By the time Casco had recovered his breath, their second round was on the table. Daric muttered something to Cobar and the normally reticent Rukh let out a shocked bray that turned the heads of nearby tables.

You're in fine form, Casco said.

Daric winked. *These good Rukh will be sharing space with me for the next few years. At least if they start out with a good opinion …*

That'll wash off soon enough, Casco laughed, but he felt Daric's sudden contraction. There was unintended weight to his comment. Traditionally, Rukh despised assassins. Daric had left that life behind, but eventually they would find out.

"Heard from Sari?" Gento asked.

"From Sari?" Cobar echoed, and Casco chuckled again.

"Our Sari always repeats what we say," Gento explained to Daric. "Loveliest angel that ever there was."

"That she does," Cobar agreed. "And that she is. Heard from her just the other day."

Casco nodded. "She's been in touch with most of us, but she's having trouble tracking down Bush and Topper."

"Moonlighting as spinners again," Gento said, "and good luck to them! Wish I could."

"What, spin?"

Gento shrugged. "Wouldn't you?"

Casco shook his head.

"They're doing a passenger run to Hesh with Emmiel of Maatu," Daric said.

The others looked at him.

"How'd you know that?"

"Sister's a navigator. Said she'd run into these two Lethian tricksters. Casco's told me a bit about them and I put two and two together." Daric lifted his glass. "Simple."

"How'd you two meet?" Gento waved his finger between them.

"Helped me out with a rescue operation," Casco said.

"Couldn't resist my astonishing good looks," Daric quipped.

Cobar studied Casco intently. "Half-breed crisis? You?"

"Kareski," Daric corrected.

"That's what brought us here, really," Casco said. "And when things calmed down, I decided I needed to continue my training."

Daric shook his head. "They told him to leave town for his own safety's sake. He's an outlaw, you know. Very famous."

"Outlaw?"

"Don't believe him," Casco assured them. "It's not that bad."

"No reward then?"

"No!"

He gave Daric a hard look.

Daric gave the hint of a wink. *Payback!*

"Anyway," Casco continued. "Even though we're not Rukh, for some reason the academy let us in. I think Daric here's the first Enna to ever walk the sacred grounds."

Someone from a nearby table grunted. "Sullied 'em, I'd say."

"So, what happened?" asked Gento.

Casco envisaged Tess and Kana with little Kisha between them. "A couple I know from home. Kana was already working here. Wife and daughter got into trouble. We managed to reunite them."

"Enna couldn't save himself from swarm a' zilla." The heckler sniggered again. "Soft as saroo."

Casco glanced around.

"Friend of yours?" said Gento.

"Aula," he answered. Around her table, six warrior companions nodded darkly. "And no, not exactly."

"What's her problem?"

"Danar's bunch. Danar of Rukh …"

"Rival group at the academy," Daric filled in.

"Ahh," Gento said. "Danar. A little less open-minded than some – or so I've heard."

"Exactly," Daric replied. "Pupils follow like fled of a color."

Aula tipped her head back to swig the last of her drink. The jar clunked back onto the table.

Daric rolled his eyes.

Casco gave him a look and imaged the door.

"Well then, friends," Daric said. "Maybe it's time we moved on?"

Aula sneered. "Yeah, shove off, prince la-di-da, "she spat on the floor, "an take yon cheatin mongrel with. How much did shiny badge cost eh? Ol' Embar short a coin?"

Like a cloud across the sun, Daric's congenial demeanor changed. He stood up, his gaze strangely remote.

Cobar and Gento started to stand also, but Daric motioned them back.

"Little Enna come to play?" Their antagonist's chair scraped the flagstones. "Gonna let your pet splitter play too? Or is he just for show?"

Cobar and Gento pushed to their feet.

Casco sighed. *Just let it be!* But his friends weren't listening. He climbed out of the booth also. "No need for this," he said, "I'm not offended …" But beneath his veils, his blood seethed.

"Huh!" Aula turned to her cohort and chuckled. "Splitter speaks!"

Embar's words flashed through Casco's mind: *Never turn your back on your enemy.* He tapped her shoulder. She spun but he was ready. There was a crunch as his blow found its mark. A crash and clatter as she fell.

Her tablemates launched at him, but Daric stepped in and the first of them went down.

Gento nodded to Cobar. "Good hands. Told you so."

Cobar grunted as he grabbed the nearest brawler by the shoulders, drove his knee up hard, and finished him with a double-fisted wallop to the back of the head.

Aula groaned as someone stepped on her. Her posse glanced at the carnage so far and hesitated.

"Come on!" Gento cried, "I want a turn!" But their opponents backed away.

A bar attendant came to drag the bodies aside while another summoned a healer.

Casco looked around, but the other patron's conversations seemed barely interrupted.

Gento gestured to their booth. Their drinks remained as they'd been left.

He shrugged and returned to his seat, then watched his companions settle back into place.

The proprietor hurried forward. "Such rudeness!" he muttered. "Breath be sweet, that lot will never drink here again." He plonked a basket of snack food onto the table and bowed to Casco. "We welcome our new arrivals. You aided my sister's safe return. There will be no charge for your drinks tonight."

He bowed again, and motioned to the bartender for a fresh round.

Gento and Cobar eyed Casco with new respect.

"Training's paid off," Gento said.

Cobar turned to Daric and gave a wry nod. "Tidy."

"A shame you missed out," Daric said to Gento. "Maybe they'll wait for us outside?"

"Not that disappointed …" The big Rukh grinned and lifted his ale, "but you never know."

Hours later, beneath the light of Haas's two enormous moons, they staggered toward a sturdy wooden terrace on the outskirts of the city.

"This is it," Casco said.

A small girl stood inside the door as it opened. She gave them a look then turned her head. "Mama, mama! Una Casco an de Badun's home an dey's be bringen dem oders wid-un."

Casco put his finger to his lips and whispered loudly. "Shh, bless. Doan wake de folks!"

She waved him closer. "Be savin some bikkies on de table for ye."

"Ta, Kisha," Daric said quietly. "Be hopin dere's some for us too?"

"Be stashin extra," she said, and with a grin she led them toward the kitchen

SACRED TO LETH

In the Imperial City of Giahn, baking summer days were occasionally relieved by afternoon storms, but more often it stayed hot until midnight, when cool air from the mountains wound its way slowly through the maze of streets.

Bare to the waist, Huldar leaned against the window frame and gazed up at the sky. Perspiration chilled against his chest as the alpine gusts finally arrived. He recalled a night very like this one – had it really been only ten years? – waking from a recurring nightmare in which he relived the death of Joumelät Enna. Thankfully, those dreams no longer bothered him, and although her end had been gruesome and at the time he'd been devastated, her passing had brought Andel into his life, and for that he was most grateful. He glanced back at his wife, sound asleep on the bed, sheets strewn aside. So much had changed since then.

He moved back as a black-clad patrol passed below. Where once there might once have been a cosmopolitan mix of people walking to and fro, now there were only the so-called peacekeepers, patrolling, so they said, for illegal half-breeds. It was not illegal for others to walk at night, not yet, but if anyone *was* out, the peacekeepers would want to know why.

There were extra taxes for employing a half-breed, the Explorers Guild's paperwork for Casco had been checked more than once, and an exorbitant additional fee had had to be paid to the Navigators Guild. Casco had taken to wearing a sash around his head with the Guild badge pinned to it, and always carried a spare in case the one on show was "confiscated" by an overzealous officer or even, as in one incident, a particularly bigoted archangel. However, if he was accompanied by an archangel, trouble was minimal. It was as if he had to be owned. The situation made Huldar's blood boil, but Casco had asked him to ignore it as best he could, claiming the attention just made things worse. Apparently, his involvement in the Kareski uprising – an event Huldar had only heard of in passing – had made him a particular target, but that was something else they'd not discussed. He felt guilty, not knowing, but with the passing of Andel's mother to the Breath, Andel's subsequent break-down, and nursing Inshogi through the terrible pain of his loss, news of the Realm had seemed of little consequence.

You all right? Andel asked. He hadn't even sensed her waking.

Can't sleep, he said.

Truly? She sent him a warm dash of humor.

Casco, peacekeepers, everything's changed, he said darkly. *And why does Pieru want a private meeting tomorrow? Something's going on, I know it. As if there's not enough to contend with already! Leaving six weeks early? It's madness. Breath knows what conditions on Went will be like, but Faytha has spoken*, he said sarcastically. *Coin rules the Imperium now: coin and greed. El's representative my ass!*

Huldar!

He sighed an apology. *I'll be glad to be gone. Always am.*

Come back to bed. She stroked the space beside her. *I'll make it worth your while … comfy mattress … warm … clean …*

He nodded. *It'll be bedrolls and icicles soon enough.*

No icicles here …

Cool air followed him back to the bed. The sheets rustled softly as he lay down and wrapped her in the crook of his body.

Not too cold? he asked. *Should I pull the covers up?*

Hardly!

She wriggled around to face him and drew his forehead down to touch her own.

Are you all right? he asked. A fleeting image of her mother passed between them. *Are you sure you want to go back?*

Three years on my own? Beyond contact? I don't think so.

You'd have your father …

She buried her head against his chest. *I'm trying – you know I am, but Mother …*

He kissed the top of her head. *I know,* he said gently. *Ubaid and Alis will be here in a day or so. Maybe they can help?*

She lifted her face back to his. *Maybe.*

Their lips touched. A jolt of excitement flooded his limbs.

He raised his eyebrows.

She answered with a shy smile. *Clean sheets? Soft mattress …*

You're right. He smiled. *Shouldn't let them go to waste.*

———————

Huldar's brows contracted. He studied Pieru incredulously. "An assassin?"

Had he misheard? But the word resounded in his mind and he knew he hadn't.

"The Cantori hasn't admitted as much, of course," Pieru continued, "but there are several sides to the coin that is Mirashael, and one of them is dark indeed."

There was an awkward pause. "Why?" Huldar asked.

"Why would I approve this?" For a moment, Pieru wouldn't meet his gaze.

Huldar's head tilted. "There's danger enough in what we do without a trained killer in our midst!"

"You'll find Daric Enna has superlative abilities when it comes to screens and veils, and portals too," Pieru added smoothly. "As to his professional skills, of course, I can only surmise. He has made it known that he wishes to embrace a new lifestyle and leave the old behind – and I believe him."

Huldar waited, his thoughts a blur.

Pieru frowned. "Huldar. Perhaps you haven't thought of it this way, but soldiers are trained killers too. Maatu are famed for their martial abilities, yet that doesn't stop us using them as navigators. Cobar and Gento are Rukh. Efficient killing for them is a matter of pride."

"You know what I mean!"

"I sensed nothing out of kilter with him." Pieru had the good grace to allow somewhat of an apology to cross his veil. "There are shadows to be sure, but he is fast friends with Casco and that gives me reassurance. I'm surprised you don't know him already."

"I've haven't met him," Huldar rubbed his neck. "Casco and I …" He searched for words to explain. "We've lost touch. What with getting married and the trouble with Andel's health after her mother died … and now the whole issue with the Faythans and the mining – breaking all the rules." He looked vaguely around the room. "I'm looking forward to getting away, I really am, but another, more realistic part of me is dreading it. What am I supposed to do? Why will no one listen to me? This whole situation is wrong."

"Maybe Daric Enna will be a greater asset than you imagine," the Guild-Lord said softly.

Huldar looked at him, aghast.

"I hope you understand, Huldar, that you are sacred to Leth."

"For all the good it's done so far," he said bitterly. "I didn't ask to be!"

"As if that matters! You are chosen by Went and, despite the difficulties, or perhaps because of them, it is your duty to protect her. You *are* the guild in this instance. Arien Leth himself has acknowledged your status – never forget it! But I know you … However hard it seems, you must keep this power any way you can. The Host's superintendent, Olatu of Faytha, fancies himself overmuch for my liking and isn't one I would have selected for such an isolated posting. Things may go bad."

"Bad? What does that mean? Things are bad already. And what of the new Overlord? Isn't it his job to deal with such issues?"

"Radätel Gok seems decent enough, but whether he'll be able to stand up to a seasoned rogue like Kashmät … All I'm saying is that if worse comes to worst, well, maybe Daric's special gifts will prove somewhat of a boon."

"A boon?" He raised his shoulders in disbelief. "What are you suggesting?"

Pieru's gaze pinched. "In survival situations one must be prepared to make sacrifices."

"Surely it won't come to that! But the Faythans? The miners? I doubt they'll care if I've spoken to El himself just so long as they get what they came for."

"Exactly. I know it's hard to accept, but don't be shy about it, Huldar. You are the authority on Went, no one has rank to surpass you, and She will rely on you to protect her – She has no one else."

Huldar's mind flashed back to his time in the Heart of the Planet. '… *Creator and destroyer … the circle must be broken …*' The frantic search for answers and the enormity of her presence, yet vast as She was, he'd sensed her vulnerability. '… *I weep for my people*,' She'd said, but who were her people? How could he protect them?

"A heavy burden," Pieru admitted. "Only you can inhabit the worth she has placed upon you."

More words floated through his head. '…*The sacrifice foretold – already the flames dance in your heart.*' At first he'd thought Lind had been the sacrifice, but now he wasn't so sure. The reference felt more personal.

"I have also spoken with a planet," Pieru offered. "How can one frame such an experience? Even our recollections … overwhelm."

Huldar looked at him in understanding. "Which one – if I may ask?"

Pieru smiled. "Giahn herself."

"Giahn? But she is the Imperial planet. Surely the God-Emperor –"

"Does not know."

It took a moment for this sink in. "What does She say?" he asked eventually.

"She? He?" Pieru shrugged. "I doubt such distinctions are relevant to the souls of planets. I call her 'She' in my own mind, the mother of us all. Our first home."

"Went is definitely a 'She' … I think. Does Giahn share with you? Has She spoken with you again?"

"Not in actual words, but I can feel Her – in here." He pointed loosely to his heart. "And I can tell you … she senses a storm building – violent change." He looked at the walls around them as if they were windows to the Realm beyond. "The troubles with Karesk? This … greed for coin, this sickness – a God-Emperor who flaunts El's most basic of tenets?" He held Huldar's gaze. "The harbingers are already here."

Huldar recalled Ninjay's vision of blood in the streets and panic in the Imperial Bays and shuddered. With her dying breath she'd warned Andel of a dark road ahead, and now this from the Guild-Lord – from Giahn herself? He sighed. Why couldn't prophecies be of good things to come, or at least be uplifting? "An assassin on the team, uneasy planets, and I'm in charge – except it's unlikely anyone will listen and there'll be no one to back me up … except this assassin of course. Anything else I should know?"

Pieru gave a rueful smile. "I think that's it. The other new team members are experienced – steady natures, exemplary records. They won't be swayed by blustering Faythans, especially with you to lead them ... and all have at least some military experience."

Huldar stood up. "Military experience? Since when has that been a selection criteria?" His jaw clenched shut. He tried to take steady breaths, but to no avail. "A war? You think I'll be fighting a war? On a planet where that if anything should happen – if we all got killed – no one would even know until it was all over! I'm an ecologist. An explorer. I do not fight wars. For Breath's sake! I wouldn't know one end of a sword from the other!"

Pieru raised his hands. "Please, Huldar ..."

"My wife – people I love!" He paced the room. "The Uri'madu, they'll be under my care, my responsibility, and now you're advising me to take measures that no one in their right mind ... no one should have to! In defence of helpless creatures, and – and a world that ... that ..." He felt for more words, but none would come.

"Arien Leth himself could not stop him sending the miners early," Pieru said. "The God-Emperor ..." he added softly, *there are whispers.* He looked around. *Many believe he's insane. That Tiamät itself rules him. I myself have seen it – the spirit that lives within him. What would such a being want?* His feeling of dread shocked Huldar to the core. *Take care, my friend. I fear we are pieces in a game with consequences we can't yet understand.*

BRIEFING

The room in the Explorers Guild smelled of old wood and stale adventures, but as the team began to arrive there was nothing stale about Huldar's nerves.

He rearranged his notes again.

Andel's pulse of reassurance was spiced with a little humor.

Their marriage bond was a wondrous thing, a constant two-way conversation of the mind, but although it had been some weeks since his meeting with Pieru, he still had not shared with her his knowledge of Daric Enna's past, nor Pieru's fears.

His reply was a self-deprecating image implying his preference to deal with cyclones or even tectonic upheavals rather than a round of briefings and introductions. Despite everything, he was surprised to sense overtones of excitement in the thread of his sending, and mind itself could not lie – that was what veils and screens were for.

She countered with a vision of the Uri'madu, battered and worn, the last ones standing before a pristine planet still untouched by greed.

And the rest of the host?

Fed to the Went? she suggested.

They're vegetarian.

We don't know enough about them …

She paused as the door opened. Casco and Daric gave half-hearted waves.

"I see they've recovered from last night," she said.

Huldar grinned. "Only just, by the look of it."

"The others aren't far behind," Casco said.

True to his word, it was not long before Cobar and Gento sauntered in, followed by Sari, Bush, Topper and Tam. When the Naghari, Alis and Ubaid, arrived, Ubaid studied her with wise eyes, brushed her haze with knowing care and searched the veils beneath.

"Your healing has progressed," he said.

She nodded. "Since working with you and Alis, things do seem easier."

"No more nightmares?" Alis asked gently.

Andel shook her head and made a small bow. "Ready for the next challenge."

"No need for that," Ubaid smiled. "We are family – remember?" He looked around as if counting heads. "Arko?"

"Still a wee bit delicate after that Tiamäti swill!" joked Bush.

"As if!" Tam retorted. "You've forgotten, haven't you – or maybe it's your own constitution that's suffering." He raised his eyebrows and waited. "With Nachiel and Ronnin, remember …?"

"Oh yes," Andel said. "A new tea-house in Sirdar?"

"The Beach House," Tam said. "All done up with an ocean theme. Wonderful seafood in little containers so you can eat wherever you choose – like a little picnic."

"Any good?" Sari asked him.

"You'll find out soon enough," Casco said, and gave her a wry smile. "I've been working with him."

"With who?"

"Mirashael of Cantori. Provisioning ... and you'd never believe who he's married." His mind furnished an image of an archangel with a plain yet sensible face.

"No," Sari exclaimed. "It can't be!"

"Yes it is," he assured her. "Leahät Gok, once wife to a certain Overlord."

"Really?" said Tam.

"The very same," Casco assured them. "Chief in charge of catering for the Host."

"So, may we hope that Duvät Gok has rejoined the Breath?"

"He has." Casco gave Daric a quick glance. "Justice blown to some, at least."

"Host?" A suspicious frown formed on Topper's face. "What Host?"

"Ahh." Casco nodded. "I'll leave that for the boss to explain."

Huldar had been observing Daric Enna during the exchange. There was a certain reticence about him. He was constantly attuned to Casco's whereabouts, almost as if they were lovers – but Huldar was fairly certain they were not. And that was it, he realised. Fairly certain? Once, he would have known.

You're just jealous, Andel said.

Huldar sighed. *Maybe a little.* But concerned was closer to the mark.

He looked around as Nachiel flounced in with Ronnin and Arko close behind. Between them were several trays with rows of small, steaming packages, and above those, heat radiated from the contents of a large brown paper bag.

There was a dash to clear space on a table at the side of the room, then Arko ripped open the bag and a mound of curly-fried kosh spilled out.

"Come and get it!" Nachiel crowed.

The Uri'madu dived in like a pack of hunting zek.

You'd better hurry! Andel said to Huldar.

Not hungry, he replied, but even as the thought left him, Topper approached with a folded-paper bowl of steaming fishy morsels garnished with a fist-full of kosh.

"Here ya go, boss," he said. "Get your choppers round this lot, eh!"

"Enjoy good eatin while we can, mates." Bush grinned. "Be downin Tam's efforts soon enough!"

The spinner's comradery was impossible to resist, but anxiety still wound tightly in his chest. The majority of the team had yet to find out about Duvät Gok and the Eyes of Bel Nishani, or even the circumstances of their return, and he hated to be the one to tell them. So many things would change.

He'd met the new Overlord, Radätel Gok – pedantic as only a Gok could be, and doubted he'd see his role as a token one. According to Pieru, he'd worked with remote assignments before, but nothing as primitive and isolated as Went. How he would cope remained to be seen – and how would they cope with him coping?

"Uri'madu! Listen up!" The team turned to him in surprise. "We've got a lot of ground to cover before the others get here, so pay attention."

"Right you are, boss," said Bush with a good-humored wink. "We can eat and listen, eh, mates?"

"Others?" Sari echoed.

"Three things," said Huldar, "then we'll take time for questions … Firstly, the Imperium has ignored normal protocols regarding Went. Our mission parameters have altered. The major part of this assignment will be to shepherd an advance Host as they set up for several fully functional mining operations."

The Uri'madu looked at each other. Eating slowed.

"It's the nacrite, isn't it?" Tam said dourly.

Huldar held up his hand. "Questions in a moment. Secondly, we've been allocated several new team members to help with the pressure: some Lethians, a Rukh, and our Enna here to take Lind's place in the team. All are experienced and extremely well qualified. They'll be joining us later this morning and I know you'll make them welcome. We'll meet the new Overlord, Radätel Gok, at a special briefing tomorrow. Something to look forward to," he added wryly.

Daric bowed. "I know of Lind's death," he said, "and of the circumstances." He turned to the others. "I realize I can't replace her in your hearts, but I hope to be a valuable member for the Uri'madu, just the same."

Huldar returned his bow. "I'm sure you will be." He returned to the Uri'madu. "Daric Enna's not one to sing his own song, so be aware that he is especially gifted with personal screens and knowledgeable about the manipulation of portals. He's also a more-than-competent charm-singer and comes highly recommended by our Guild-Lord."

"So what's the third thing?" Tam asked.

"Now we get to it." Huldar sighed. "Duvät Gok had a secret – he was more evil than we knew. During our time on Went, somehow he managed to kill some sea-creatures and take their eyes."

"Their eyes?" The Uri'madu looked at each other. "Real eyes?"

Huldar grimaced. "Yes, it is as gruesome as it sounds," he said. "The eyes ... removed ... become gems of immense beauty. Lind discovered what he'd been up to, and that's what spurred his behavior toward her."

His friends sat for a moment, faces grey or flushed with shock.

"How did he keep that from us?"

"'Duvät Gok has eyes' ... her death cry" Sari said hesitantly "... that's what it meant?"

"That's what it meant," Huldar said.

"What it meant ..." There were tears on her cheeks. "We thought it was because he'd been watching her."

"As did I."

He saw Andel reach for her hand, but hesitate at the last moment. A pulse of self-loathing slipped through her defences and he sent a surge of sympathy. They both knew she would not inadvertently harm anyone, but after the terrible events in the cave on Frith, her psyche had suffered.

"These artefacts, the so-called Eyes of Bel Nishani," he continued, "have become the property of the Imperium, and it is my deepest concern there will be an attempt to harvest more."

"Kill more creatures – for their eyes?" Tam said.

"Exactly … except that the creatures won't necessarily be killed. The eyes make brighter gems if taken while their owners still live," Huldar said flatly.

The room went silent.

Fried kosh spilled from the bag and skittered to the floor.

As if a screen had been lifted, the uproar began. Huldar stood back and waited. Eventually the din subsided.

Casco glanced at Daric. "I should tell you, there'll be Ashik among the secondary host."

"Where did you hear this?" Huldar asked him.

"Haaseen," Casco replied. "A sort of parting gift from Embar of Rukh."

Huldar paused to think. If it came from a Rukh, and Casco repeated it, the intelligence was likely to be valid. He gave a nod. At least they'd be prepared. "They're not listed for the first phase," he told the others. "I'll do some checking, see exactly who's on the manifest for the second. No need to panic just yet. In the meantime, Cobar and Gento, can you please make sure we have capability to defend ourselves – should it come to that?"

The Rukh nodded soberly.

"Weaponry?" Tam scratched his head.

"Ashik?" Sari said. "Why would they send Ashik? The God-Emperor is the protector of the Realm, the direct representative of El. There's no way he could condone ... anything like what you've been saying. I don't believe it."

"He's already spurned eons of tradition," said Tam. "Who knows what else is for the scrap heap?"

"Scrap heap?" Sari echoed. "I'm not so silly that I can't see there might be problems. And if there's a risk of permanent damage we'll have to ... to go against them. I can see that. But ..."

Her eyes searched Huldar's face. He wished he could tell her it wasn't true. "Peace, Sari," he soothed. "I will find out what I can, and remember, we won't be alone. There are four new team members besides Daric Enna. We'll meet them a little later on. Also, the navigator and her spinners will be remaining with us for the duration; they've also been assigned to us."

"What about the new Overlord?" Tam asked. "Have you met him? What's his stance likely to be – us or them?"

"I have met Radätel Gok." Huldar pictured their new Overlord's craggy face. He was tall and lean with a gravelly tone. "There's more depth to him than there was to Duvät ... but he is a Gok. You'll have time enough to make up your own minds. And as to his loyalty? One can only hope at this stage."

Bush nudged his brother. "Jolly times ahead to be sure!" He threw a twist of kosh in the air, caught it in his mouth and crunched down with relish.

"Kisha's favorite," Daric muttered.

Casco gave a gentle smile and reached for a handful also.

Huldar saw the smile pass between them and wondered who Kisha was, then a saying came to him – *Breath gives time its voice* … he could almost hear it on Inshogi's lips. He let go his regret and let pride tighten his chest. The Uri'madu had taken the changes in their stride, as if new Overlords and greedy miners were everyday occurrences. He only hoped their new members would come to feel as confident.

JOURNEYMAN

Daric Enna slipped into an unobtrusive corner and settled on a padded chair, thankful to be sidelined for the moment. Even during the previous night's get-together he'd managed to keep to himself. Confronted by a crowd of strangers his first instinct was to screen himself to invisibility, and it was hard to let old habits go.

Sensing his moment of anxiety, Casco flashed him a glance. Daric laughed at himself. Their situation was quite a reversal. It was usually him being supportive, especially here on Giahn where half-breeds were despised. But for the Uri'madu Casco's ancestry simply wasn't an issue: Daric was glad. During their travels together, every time his friend had been disrespected Daric had felt the honor of the Realm slip just a little more.

Tam offered Casco more kosh. Daric tuned in to their conversation.

"So, Casco," Tam asked, "you didn't seem surprised about the Eyes."

Gento moved closer, interested to hear his answer.

Casco's nod was a shade guilty. "After we got back from Went, Duvät Gok stayed with me for a short time." He raised his hands. "I know, I know, but by that time he was in pretty bad shape."

For a fraction of a second Tam's gaze narrowed. "In your house?" He winced. "I don't care how tragic he was, you've a kinder soul than mine!"

"Breath knows I was pleased to see the back of him when he left." Casco said. "So, what do you think of the goranda? Should be a nice base for stews and the like. I was told it stores well if prepared properly."

"It does, but we'll still have to use it within the first quarter. Is it on the resupply list?"

As the discussion turned to food, Gento joined in conversation with Andel, and Daric relaxed. However it wasn't long before the cook noticed him alone in the background and came to talk.

"Daric Enna." Tam smiled at him. "I hope you don't feel left out?"

"Not at all," he said. "Still feeling my way."

"You'll get to know us all too well soon enough."

"No doubt!" He smiled politely in return.

"And this business with Duvät Gok? The eyes?" Tam went on. "Terrible! Not the usual sort of thing we Uri'madu have to deal with."

"Ghastly!" Daric agreed. "And I don't doubt it. Astonishing what people will do for coin. And you? How do you feel about it? The Faythans, the mines, and new team members proliferating like zilla?"

Tam grinned. "It's a challenge, to be sure." He looked Daric up and down in a not unkindly way. "Have you ever been to a wild planet?"

Daric shook his head.

"Amazing experience," Tam said. "Especially the first time. I suppose it's the silence that's hardest for beginners to come to grips with." He circled his finger in the air. "No buzz. Nothing. Takes some getting used to. Joumelät Enna struggled for a bit when she first signed up."

"Silence? I think I'll welcome that most … But that's not what killed her."

Tam blinked. Clearly this was not the comment he'd expected. There was a slight pause. "No," he answered more slowly. "It was complacency – or Tiamäti arrogance, maybe. She didn't scan for predators and one got her."

Daric tipped his head. So, the cook had teeth. Tam looked at him expectantly. This was an opportunity to be likeable, but what should he say?

"I'm sorry, Tam. I'll admit, I'm a tad overwhelmed," he said at last. "I'm hoping that if I just sit quiet and listen, I'll learn some things and not make a fool of myself." He gave a rueful smile and was pleased to see the cook warm to him.

"You'll be fine," Tam said. "An attitude like that is a relief, to be sure, especially from one of your lot. We've had others – so full of their own song they're deaf to anything else. They're the ones who find it toughest." His direct smile, innocent as a child's, touched Daric unexpectedly. "Just ask," he continued, "that would be my advice. If you don't know how to do something or feel unsure, we Uri'madu are a team and that's how we operate."

Daric nodded. "Thanks, Tam. Casco has told me a lot about you. Says you've been a good friend to him."

"We're all friends!" Tam laughed. "No ceremony here. You'll get used to it."

Casco joined them. "Just don't knock his cooking," he said. "Then you'll see how far the friendship goes."

"I'll remember that." Daric held out his hands as if to tick an imaginary list. "Cook must get his daily dose of adoration."

"You'll do well!" said Tam. "I like you already."

Daric was surprised to sense it was true. Casco liked him, of course, but he worked hard to be sure that remained the case – teaching him, supporting him … not that it was a chore. Casco soaked up all he had to offer with disarming ease. He'd never had a friend before, not one who was just a friend, and he found he liked it very much. There was Mirashael, of course … Mirashael claimed he was like a son to him, but if you stripped away the business considerations, would the love remain?

The usher arrived with water for tea and a few plates of nibbles.

"Just time for a quick dose of Guild-food before the new lot get here," Tam said sourly. "Cheese on little sticks again?"

The usher turned and walked away.

Nachiel gave an ostentatious eye roll. "How many years now?"

"I hate to think," Tam replied.

"Well, that's the truth," Nachiel said archly. "Leave thinking to likes of our Huldar here!"

Tam gave a soft snort and continued to set the cups in order. Galano twigs rattled into a round-bodied mug with the rune of Trianog on its side.

"Well, just so long as we've got some of that gorgeous pink paste they had last time," Nachiel said.

"Pink?" Tam glanced up at him.

"Well, pinky red then." Nachiel shrugged. "Who cares? It's divine. You should get the recipe." He sidled closer to Daric. "A word to the wise, Daric Enna: you'll be sick of the sight of little attar by the time we get back!"

Daric winked. "I introduced Casco to some new contacts, and I think you'll find that for this rotation, a few more of our excellent cook's desires have been met."

"Ooh!" Nachiel said. "I love surprises."

"Excellent cook?" Tam repeated. "Learns fast!"

Casco glanced toward the outside corridor. "Here come the new team members," he said. "Lord Pieru's with them."

"The Guild-Lord?" said Sari. She looked for somewhere to put down her tea and quickly straightened her outfit.

There was a clatter as Tam put out extra cups.

Huldar moved to the center of the floor and the Uri'madu gathered behind him, veils tuned to polite neutrality. Moments later the door swung open and Pieru entered, followed by two archangels and three angels. All appeared Lethian bar one doughty Rukh. Daric eyed her discreetly. When things got sticky would she be loyal to the Imperium or the Uri'madu?

Pieru stopped Huldar from bowing. "Please, there's no need."

Casco gave a subtle nod and Daric cocked his head. The Uri'madu's regard for their leader ran strong, but to Casco he was more like a brother – or had been.

Daric listened with half an ear to the Guild-Lord's preamble, a reiteration of the troubling task before them, the pressure to do the right thing, etc. etc. He knew, perhaps better than any, exactly who they were dealing with and what lay ahead. He bowed as expected when Lord Pieru spoke about him, and looked thoughtful when Lind's death was mentioned, but it was more enlightening, as usual, to watch those around him.

Gento and Cobar glanced at each other then back to Rosheen, the new Rukh – an alpine survival specialist and clearly not one to be trifled with. Maybe it was a Rukh thing.

One of the archangels, Calen of Leth, seemed to be studying the woodwork of the walls, but he could sense her covert study of Huldar's face.

Daric felt a tingle of shock when she turned to look directly at him. He smiled pleasantly and made a mental note to be more careful.

The other new archangel's spiky haze kept others from crowding him. He was nuggety and tough with brown hair and a bit of a scowl, but Daric knew Shamkarun Ariben of Leth to be one of the finest substrate specialists in the Realm. The Mark on his face was not extensive but conferred status just the same.

He detected tones of farewell in the Guild-Lord's speech and returned his attention to the front. "… an excellent leader, and he'll look after you all," Shamkarun Pieru was saying, "but the dangers of Went are poorly understood as yet, so please, be extremely careful. As yet, no additional healers have been assigned to the Host, so Alis and Ubaid will have their work cut out for them. I'll say it again: there will be no contact with the outer Realm until the quarterly navigational link. The second phase of the Host will arrive with the first of those visits. At that time, you may send letters and requests for extra kit and the like. Beyond that there'll be no opportunity for communication until the summer solstice, as you already know. So, I'll leave you with that sobering thought. Do the best you can and stay safe." He bowed to them all. "Breath blow good fortune."

They watched him depart.

Nachiel held out a tray to the newcomers. "Cheese on a stick, anyone? The pink paste is lovely." He gave the remains of their seafood a guilty glance.

Ariben of Leth held up his hand. "I have a question, Shamkarun Huldar."

"Please, it is our custom to use familiar names, at least among ourselves," Huldar said. "From now until we return to Giahn, we are the Uri'madu, our own entity, and we make no such distinctions."

"Refreshing," one of the newcomers remarked. Her name was Van– a Lethian of unremarkable build and height, but her speaking voice was pleasant to listen to and her eyes showed intelligence.

Ariben shuffled impatiently. "What's prompted the Imperial high and mighty to go against a hundred thousand years of protocol?" he continued. "Have El's tenets ceased to have meaning?"

As Huldar began his reply, Daric dipped his cheese-on-a-stick into the bowl of pink paste and settled down to enjoy. Tam grinned at him and he found himself grinning back.

Already the social protocols were slipping, and no doubt they would slip even more as everyday life in the Realm became a thing of the past.

He made another note to himself. *Be careful not to mistake temporary interdependence for genuine affection.*

THE PROJECT

Dwarfed within their vast new warehouse on the edge of Crafters, Leahät studied pile after pile of produce as she searched for the last thing on Mirashael's list. He was very fond of lists, she had discovered.

Green labels, he reminded her. *Are you looking for green labels?* Her husband's head bobbed up from behind a carefully balanced tower – three thousand plump sacks of little attar.

I am, she assured him.

It doesn't look like it.

That's because I'm using my mind as well as my eyes … There they are.

???

Underneath the semi-dried guerdi. She shared an image of flattened silvery blobs bound into a bale with wide raffia straps.

Ahh! He hurried toward the place she'd shown him, threading between the ordered piles in a manner very similar to the way he danced between chairs in their restaurant.

Beneath the stack she had indicated he found the errant item, a cache of well-wrapped galano twigs.

He pulled one of the bundles slightly forward and imaged its bright green label back to her. *You are such a treasure – you know that, don't you?*

She smiled.

But I mean it, he insisted. *A real gem.* "That's the lot then?" As he made his way toward her, the bounce in his step was somewhat muted and the hug, although heartfelt, had elements of drape. He held a long list, each entry meticulously marked. "I'll get this off to the Bays. The Uri'madu's goods each have a little circle – it's very easy to see. Do you think they'll see it?"

"And they're stacked separately too," she assured him. "There'll be no mix-up."

He took her board and eyed a second, even larger list. "We'll give this to Shen, when he gets here." He turned his head for a last look at the enormous project they'd undertaken, then back to her. The satisfaction in his gaze made her smile.

"I'll call the spinners then," he said. "We're right on time." He frowned at the door. "Where is Shen?"

"On his way I expect. He'll want a last check too. It's not as if he can come back if he runs out of something."

"Or make an exchange if it's the wrong item." He turned to her again, and a sense of wonderment came through their bond. "Business in the city may be down, but this will make all the difference. Such an undertaking, dear lady, so much at stake, and you have managed it all." His lips touched her forehead. "So cool, so calm." He kissed her again. "I am in awe."

She drew him close. "I've had the best of teachers."

I know you never expected such value in this lifetime, he said. *I feel it every day. But dearest of ladies, look what Breath has blown. Where would I be without you?*

Still searching for the galano, she laughed.

He looked toward the street and shared an image of a non-descript angel of medium height and build, hurrying through a narrow laneway, his shoulders damp from a summer storm.

Your protégé, she smiled. *Clean Giahni accent, looks pure at a glance ... his haze seems completely natural, and with a ready-made identity as the Host's cook, no one will question him.*

He smiled in admiration. "Soon you'll be taking over the other side of my business as well and I'll have nothing better to do with my days than to gather bright seashells on the sunny Pannias coast."

"Not likely," she retorted. "And knowing you, you'd sell what you gathered for a tidy profit."

Leahät felt a brief tickle as Shen scanned and located them. The door creaked open, and with a last fond squeeze they stepped apart.

"Ah, my star pupil! How are you holding up?" Mirashael asked him.

Shen relaxed his veil and excitement bled through. It worried Leahät that he was not at all nervous. Surely he should be. She was.

He held out his hand for the lading list and tucked it into Qalãn.

"You don't want to check?" Mirashael's voice was a little scandalized.

"That's your job this time and no one could be more thorough," Shen said. "In my state, I don't think I should even try." He grinned. "My life has changed beyond recognition, my friends, and all thanks to you."

"We'll miss you," Leahät said.

"Ja," Shen said drily. "Who'll be moanin at ye now, sho la, complainin all's beyond un?"

"You never stopped trying, Shen," Leahät said. "And I don't remember too many complaints."

"And now, the next part," Mirashael said proudly. "Stretch your culinary wings! Astound the Host with your vast abilities, then come home and regale us with enthusiastic tales of momentous adventures and salacious gossip, and we'll be amazed by all you've learned."

"Salacious gossip?" Shen laughed. "How much intrigue can a pack of miners and explorers get up to? But on the other hand, it can get pretty cold where we're going. A body might have to stay close to keep warm and it's possible confidences may be shared."

"They may indeed!" Mirashael winked. *Best leave us now, my love*, he said to Leahät.

She nodded. "I'll meet you back at the shop."

After surprising Shen with a farewell kiss on the cheek, she made her way through the steamy streets to Mirashael's café. It still didn't have a name, but it didn't need one. That was part of its charm.

An hour or so later she sensed her husband's return and lifted her head from the ledgers. His mood was somber, and she wondered what had happened to dampen his spirits.

He sat heavily in his chair. "Yes, not so much dampened as struck with the realization of the enormity of what we have done ... the potential ramifications of the project in which we are enmeshed."

But we have fulfilled our contract, delivered on time and to the letter. Even Lucaät of Faytha has no complaints. Is it something to do with Shen?

Something he said.

Mirashael retreated into himself, but she could feel his thoughts churning.

After a short pause she ventured, *May I ask?*

His gaze met hers, and for the slightest of moments, she sensed a whiff of fear. It was covered by an upwelling of love and a sense of bittersweet success.

We have done exceedingly well my dearest one, yes? But there was a last-minute change to Lucaät's manifest. A clandestine addition. He pictured two styles of bag: one larger, open-weave and stain resistant; the other black and silk-lined – the sort one might use for the presentation of jewels. *Four hundred large and one thousand of the smaller ones, separate to the sample bags and containers already supplied to the Uri'madu. He had Shen source them.*

"Shen?"

"Shen knows nothing of the Eyes, only that they exist – the same as anyone else who follows court gossip and has seen the Empress Ishiquel's fabulous headdress."

A stone formed in the pit of Leahät's stomach. Since their deal had been struck, Lucaät had not mentioned the Eyes of Bel Nishani, but she knew he'd been forced to surrender the ones he'd got from her to the Imperium.

Ishiquel's sensational headdress had made its first appearance at the sun-return festivities some months later. Speculation was rife as to what the gems were and where they had come from – she had even heard a rumor they were the petrified spawn of a long-extinct amphibian.

A single tear scrolled down her cheek.

Mirashael took her hand. "And now it is confirmed. There will be Ashik in the second wave. I fear we both know what the bags are for."

We must stop them! How can we stop them?

"I don't think we can," Mirashael replied gently.

Leahät took his hand in both of hers. "But what of the Guild-Lord? Can't he do something?"

Mirashael shook his head. "He couldn't stop them from mining the planet too soon, and neither could Arien Leth himself." *It is as if our God-Emperor has gone a little mad*, he thought quietly. *How else does one explain such avarice?*

And we are part of it ...

He drew her hands to his lips. "We are business people, my lady. We have done no wrong. Had we not undertaken to supply the contract, another would have.

"What of the laborers? The ones we've signed up? Will they be forced to attack those creatures? Surely they would not do so by choice?"

"They must act as their conscience directs," Mirashael said. "But I fear that even were they warned, many depend upon this income to feed their families."

"Then we'll find them other work! What of your cousin's new factory on Cantor, the water-plant venture?"

Mirashael frowned. "He's not too bright, I'll admit, although a good employer when it comes to it. But my lady, would we want the Imperium to know of our involvement in the movements of the gems?"

Leahät's impassioned plea to warn their employees stalled. "What of the Uri'madu, or their new Overlord?" she asked more quietly. "Surely they will not stand for it."

"They will abhor the plunder and I'm sure they will do all they can to prevent it but they are few against many, and Radätel Gok owes a long-standing debt to Lucaät."

"Is there nothing we can do?" she asked. "To harvest the eyes … it's horrible! I've seen it. My soul cried out against it. How can the God-Emperor want such a thing?"

"Gentle lady, you have gone to the heart of this awful dilemma. There will be an aftermath, I am sure of it. We must be prepared – yes, and ready to help where we can."

"As we have with the Kareski?"

"Indeed, you are the most savvy of students."

She thought for a moment. Mirashael was right to be somber. These days, those who opposed the God-Emperor in thought or deed were in danger of imprisonment and death. "And what of Shen?" she asked. "With the Ashik? Will he be safe?"

"Shen is not alone," Mirashael assured her.

She nodded slowly. "I might have guessed." With her husband, there were always plans within plans. He would never leave one of his employees out on a limb – it was not his way. Her love for him spread fresh warmth through their bond and he blinked in surprise.

"Mirashael of Cantori," she said, "I thank the Breath each day for what it has blown me."

"You do?"

"Every day," she said. "This road of ours has many challenges, and it may be that this particular evil can't be stopped, but I know you will do whatever you can, and I will be there with you."

THE PROBLEM WITH LOVERS

Malena of Maatu caught her lover's hand as he traced the Shamkar on her cheek, and smiled into the lively brown eyes above her.

"I can think of a better use for that," she purred.

"So it's true what they say?" His redirected fingers trailed lazily toward her loins. "That you navigators have paramours waiting on every world?"

"Not every world …" She gasped a little as a wandering digit found its mark. "There may be a few I've missed."

Her hips began to rock in time with his slow caress.

Malena of Maatu! Are you coming to this meeting or not!

The rocking stopped as a familiar voice pushed into her mind – Mael of Maatu, Lord of the Navigators Guild. The way he'd used her name was a definite sign of annoyance.

Her companion hesitated. "What is it?"

"I'm supposed to be at a meeting," she said, "but for some reason I forgot."

She made a moue with her lips and pushed him aside. He watched appreciatively as she slithered into tawny buckskin pants – the unofficial uniform of the navigator, and laced the front of her shirt.

"It's been fun," she said and gave him a lingering kiss on the lips, "but I've got to go."

"See you when you get back?"

She took a last look around the opulent apartment and made a promise to herself. If she could remember his name before she got to the Imperial Bays, she'd bed him again when her contract was done.

It wasn't far, only a few steps and a bit of a walk through Sirdar, but not far enough. As she looked up at the glittering dome and passed beneath the navigator's sigil above the Guild's entrance his name still eluded her.

Shamkarun Mael of Maatu's glare met her before she'd even reached his door, and she conceded he had a right to be cross. As she entered his office, his flat gaze made her feel like a first-year apprentice about to be disciplined.

"I'm sorry," she started, but heavy disappointment crept through his veil. He'd come all the way from Hesh to negotiate for her. He had not only dug her out of trouble – the new contract was worth a fortune.

He indicated the chair opposite. "I know you're not thrilled about this, Malena," he started.

Again, no nickname. All navigators had a nickname shared only between themselves. It was part of belonging.

"I understand how difficult it will be for you to be tied to one place for three years. No doubt you see it as some kind of penance."

"Navigators don't marry," she replied sullenly.

"Thanks to a lot of fast talking, his offer is still open for when you return," Mael continued. "Shamkarun Erelät Enna is related to the Empress, and a navigator too," he pointed out.

"Yes, but not a very good one," she retorted. "He's barely Marked. And that la-di-da voice – like sandpaper. If we were Blessed, it would be born with ready-painted blue fingernails."

"Kattíst!"

"Well it would," she said sullenly.

"You must marry," Mael said. "You are the daughter of our House Leader's sister and as such it is your duty ..."

She wobbled her head in time with the words. "... Because Shak'ri hasn't married and he's Maatu's First."

He narrowed his eyes. "If Anu has not yet agreed to wed, all the more reason you should. The Empress chides me constantly about your cousin's marital status, and now she can add you to her list of grievances. Think about it while you are off-world. Think about how it might seem – the damage you are doing to our House."

"Anu's already singing that one!" she snapped.

Mael rolled his gaze skyward.

"And I don't blame him!" she said. "Although, he will marry – when he's ready. He's too noble not to. Overachiever. Drives me nuts."

"Think about it, Kattíst, that's all I ask."

"Three years stranded in the utter wilderness?" she retorted. "No amenities – surrounded by a bunch of biome geeks and semi-literate miners? Don't suppose there'll be much else *to* think about! Why did I agree to this?"

Mael snorted. "You know why," he explained over-patiently. "Damage control. This goes some way toward keeping House Maatu in the Imperial good graces. Shows loyalty."

"Huh!" She sniggered. "And my only contact with reality will be Bai'ah, Ishät's very own eyes-and-ears in the Guild."

"Shamkarun Kandät Enna is one of the most accomplished navigators in the Realm. You could learn a lot from him. Anu did."

"Funny thing I heard about Anu …" She leaned forward. "His nickname – Shak'ri … funniest thing. Should be Shak'alu instead." She waggled her finger up and down and grinned knowingly. "Just a bit too slow where it counts – if you know what I mean?"

Mael grimaced. "Really, Malena? No one could say that about you – or so I've heard." His frown deepened. "Stop this childishness. Anu will be Maatu one day."

She sighed and reined in her psychic emissions. Mael was right to some extent. And she still couldn't remember her lover's name.

"You've studied the Went chord thoroughly?" he asked. "It's a difficult entry."

"Typical Kandät. He's not *that* great."

"Have you studied it?" he snapped.

"Of course I have!" She struggled again with her anger. "Just because I don't want to marry and just because I let you sign me up for the shittiest contract ever doesn't mean I want to die."

"That's something, then," he said sourly. "While you're there, try and locate a better Djan'rū site. Make sure it's loud enough for Bai'ah to pick it up in the final pass." He looked her in the eye. "You might be a pain, but at least you're a talented one."

She felt suddenly awkward and looked away.

"While you're on Went," he continued, "you remain under contract and the Faythans want you to work."

"Coin-grubbing bastards. Not enough that I should get them there safely."

"They've paid well for your time," he said shortly. "You've been assigned to the Uri'madu. You will assist them with their investigations under the direction of Shamkarun Huldar."

"The Uri – what? Planet walkers?"

"The exploratory team – 'biome geeks' as you so eloquently put it. Good bunch. Be nice to them."

"Well, so long as they don't make me dig holes."

"What, and ruin your pretty fingernails?" he said archly. "Try and behave. Your crew, whom, I might add, are a lot more positive about their new assignment than you are – will also be deployed by Huldar to where they are most needed. I've already spoken to them."

"You spoke to my crew?"

"Yes. They were here at the date and time I actually set. It seems their lives are not so 'busy' as yours."

"I'll miss you too," she said tartly.

Mael stood and bowed. "Kattíst. Breath blow fair Chime and safe journey."

At last he'd used her Guild-name. "Dahj," she said, using his, and bowed in return. "See you when I get back. I'll report straight to Hesh?"

"That would be wise." He looked out the window toward the distant turrets of the Imperial Palace. "This used to be my home, but I hate it here now."

As Mael's office door closed, her latest lover's name still tantalized her. It was almost within reach. He was Cantori – but was he some sort of relative to one of her spinners … or was that Hamid of Nhadu? Hamid's eyes were blue. She pictured the Nhadu's hands, strong crafter's fingers, dexterous and with just the right amount of callus. Hamid lived on Hesh. Yes, that's who she'd spend time with when she got back. At least she could remember his name.

TO WENT

The rhythmic echo of Malena's stride bounced back and forth through the warren of inner passageways until it dwindled to who knew where. The vast complex of the Imperial Bays was so ancient it was hard to imagine how it was still standing, yet here it was, in the place where the first archangels had built it, turning on the skin of Giahn as if linked to eternity itself.

She paused when she reached the final hall. An image of Mael of Maatu's disapproving gaze flashed an overlay to her memories of this place – but that was yesterday. Today she would be back in the Chime and the whole sorry issue left behind.

The last layer between her and her contract was a carved stone wall punctuated by long row of doors. Each carried a number written in a style as ancient as the building. She doubted anyone except a few navigators who had studied the old tongue actually understood what they saw. Most learned just enough words and phrases to work out nicknames. Hers, 'Kattíst', meant 'the weaver'.

She took a deep breath and went to door fifty-six. It opened onto one hundred and sixty-five souls waiting to be sung through to the mysterious planet Went.

Her crew already had the massive load of cargo in balance. Four held the envelope and three stood by. Even without engagement, she could sense the weight of it. Compared to the average load even a full Host would require, it was huge. But on this assignment there would be no hopping back and forth to top up supplies. The trip was arduous and cost-prohibitive, and the organizers had budgeted for the minimum permissible: four quarterly runs over the three-year period.

Banga, the crew boss, skirted the main press of travelers. He'd been with her for eons. She held out her hand for the passenger list. "All checked in?"

He gave her a look. "Just one or two who couldn't get out of bed on time."

Something about the way he moved jogged a memory and suddenly her most recent lover's name came back to her. Cotael of Cantori. How had Banga reminded her of him? Banga was Maatu, like her.

She turned and her gaze settled on Huldar of Leth. He was tall for one of his house, maybe as tall as she was. With slightly sharpened focus she could see his Shamkarun's Mark spread across his cheek to halfway down his neck, a rare occurrence even among navigators. Broad shoulders, long legs, tight bum, huge status … eminently beddable – but then he gave his wife's hand a surreptitious squeeze and her eyes roved on. There were plenty more to choose from, after all.

The rest of the biome geeks, her workmates for the duration of her exile, were clustered nearby. They seemed excited, even boisterous, although from variations in their consonance she could tell some were more familiar than others. She recognized Bush and Topper as spinners she'd seen working for Omar a'tello, or Shamkarun Emmiel of Maatu as he was known to the outer world. 'Hands of Silk' was right – he was a known go-to for shifty dealings, and not too bad in the bedroll either.

The Rukh caught her attention next. She'd need something with stamina for the letdown after she'd done with the Chime. Rukh were often conservative in their physical tastes, but endurance was rarely in shortfall. Maybe on a wild world she could tempt them to wilder deeds?

When the Overlord came into view she stifled a sense of distaste. Despite his pleasing ruggedness, he was a Gok, and Tiamäti were definitely off the list.

No one else among the Uri'madu took her fancy but as she began to search the rest of the Host for talent, Huldar waved to a late arrival, another Lethian. He stopped to talk with Huldar. An archangel. Shamkar ... Darkish hair – she liked dark hair. He walked with confidence, even a touch of swagger.

She started toward them. "Permit for the half-breed?"

Shamkarun Huldar bowed slightly and handed her the necessary paperwork.

"Four minutes," she said. "See that your people are ready. First six weeks, we'll be following familiar routes, but then ..." She caught the gaze of the newcomer. "Well ... I hope your crew are seasoned travelers." She thrilled to think of it. A whole new chord in the vast unknown? That's when the true challenge would begin.

"We've seen a few things," Huldar assured her, but his wife was all eyes. The dark-haired one met her gaze with interest. His Shamkar was no match for Huldar's, of course, or her own, but his features stayed in her mind.

Standing with the half-breed was an Enna. Her eyes slid past him but, just by chance, she caught one of the catering contingent giving them a clandestine nod. As she made her way toward the center of the bay she took a moment to study the nodding one more closely. It was hard to place his ethnicity. Nhadu, maybe, but his accent was upper Cantori. Then she smiled. The clues were tiny - something about the quality of his hair and slightest of accents, but navigators were trained to be aware of minute variations in pitch and tone. This was another half-breed, undeclared.

Should she say anything? There were fees involved. Who would pick up the tab, and the reprimand, if this one was found out?

The crowd parted as a shard-thin Faythan came toward her. She recognized the Host's superintendent and, with a slight smile, turned her back on the questionable caterer.

"Shamkarun Malena of Maatu?"

He waited as if expecting some kind of acknowledgement, but she enjoyed baiting Faythans, and in truth, he was so far beneath her …

Begrudgingly he bowed. "Olatu of Faytha … my lady."

She inclined her head in the slenderest of gestures.

"What reason for the delay?" he asked crossly, abandoning any semblance of courtesy. "I have been waiting for hours."

To her, his question meant nothing. Within moments, his life – all their lives – would be cradled in her song. Family and friends of the passengers had already begun to filter to the outskirts. The Uri'madu spread cushions and rugs in a gap between piles of cargo and seemed to be preparing for an ashut tournament.

"Is all in readiness now?" the Faythan insisted, annoying as zilla-flies.

All checked in, Banga?

The crew boss winked an affirmative.

Then let's get this party sung.

There was a burst of noise as the last of the well-wishers were cleared away and a tingle of anticipation as her travelers realised their journey was about to begin.

Sound swelled as the envelope was committed. She took her place between the spinners. A deep breath triggered her descent within herself and she thrilled to the call of the Chime. Her Shamkar warmed. Passengers and cargo became visible as pure vibration. There were a few nervous jangles among the miners, but overall a pleasing keenness. With a light touch, she caught their threads and wove them into loose harmony with the envelope. Only then was it safe to bring the Song of Passage fully to mind.

Ready? she cried.

A familiar elation possessed her when she opened herself to the spinners. With an orgasmic rush, she released the chord and, as the envelope surged smoothly into the Chime, she took joy in the steely discipline required to speed it through the vast emptiness toward its goal.

THE WALL

Down! Now! Huldar threw his arm over Andel's back. The envelope bucked with unprecedented violence. The Uri'madu hit the floor, but many of the Host seemed shocked beyond reaction. Around them, the voices of all seven spinners and their navigator raged in deafening, desperate harmony.

"Wasn't this bad last time!" Tam muttered.

Huldar shook his head and wished him to silence. It was imperative nothing interrupt the delicate contract between sound and matter – all that kept them from the bitter dark of the Chime.

A block of cargo slipped its bonds, careened across the envelope and smashed into a knot of miners. Injured and terrified, their cries caused a section of wall to rip. Stars flashed as the fissure spread. One slid back and dangled like a kite in the dark. With clawed fingers he scrabbled for purchase. Gelatinous gouts tore from his grip and dissolved into nothing.

Help me! he whispered, but even that small vibration made the shaking worse.

Bush anchored Topper's legs as he lunged for the miner's hand, but before they could touch him the envelope snapped

72

shut. The wall melded, seamless as if it had never been breached.

The brothers stared dumbly at where the hole had been while the chord raged on, triumphant against the void.

Huldar felt Andel's shock as well as his own and pulled her close. Their surroundings gave another tremendous jerk. He battled to hide his deep disquiet. Should the navigator's chord fail, they would all die as the miner just had, lost to the songless waste.

It's as if she doesn't want us back, Andel whispered, and as they swooped through another violent upset he had to agree.

Finally the chord roared to resolution. Malena stood with bowed head, breathing deeply while exhausted spinners maintained the envelope. In that silence and the stillness, they began to realize their journey had come to an end.

"Let it go," she said tiredly. "Just let it go."

"Wait!" Huldar cried. "We don't know what's out there –"
But the song cut off and the envelope dissipated into the teeth of a raging snowstorm.

Already numbed, the Host stood like statues in the screaming wind.

Huldar reached for his coat, wrapped a scarf around his face and pulled the hood over his head. Frantically he signaled Andel to do the same. "Huddle together!" he cried. "Extremities! Leave nothing exposed."

Malena's exhaustion was forgotten. "Quickly!" she yelled. "Blankets. Warm clothing!" The spinners scurried to obey.

Casco ducked against the onslaught and fought his way toward the dark shapes of their stores. Gento and Cobar followed, barely visible in the white-out. They quickly identified the container labeled *Tents*, but as Gento prized the lid off it was ripped from his grasp. White snow blasted against dark leathers. Cobar grabbed the top-most tent before the wind could snatch it too.

We'll never get these up in this, Casco said.

A particularly strong blast rocked Huldar on his feet. Their lives depended on the creation of adequate shelter.

Rosheen stepped forward. Only her eyes were visible. Frost already caked the fabric around her head. "Put blocks of ice between the cargo containers and we'll have a wall in no time," she yelled.

"You heard!" Huldar barked to his team. *Shift crates. Make blocks!*

Gento banged the lid back over the tents and with Cobar and Casco started to shift containers. At Malena's signal, spinners hurried to help.

As the wall grew, the Host gathered in the lee, huddled beneath blankets. Ubaid and Alis of Naghar hunkered down in one corner to tend those injured during the final hours of travel. There was no sign of the new Overlord.

Daric Enna tapped Huldar's arm. "I also have an idea, if I may? Quicker than snow-blocks."

"Anything that will help keep us alive," Huldar replied.

The Enna nodded toward Malena. "Problem is, I need her help."

"What's the issue?"

"I'm Tiamäti."

Malena! Huldar called.

The navigator continued as if she hadn't heard.

Malena of Maatu! he barked.

She turned as if startled.

Our journey is over, he shouted. *I am your team leader. If you had listened to my warning, this situation would have been avoided, and now you won't work with my charm-singer because he's Enna?*

"Tiamäti." She turned away again. *I hate them.*

Here, we are Uri'madu! He stabbed his finger toward Daric. *Work with him.*

She opened her mouth as if to argue then seemed to think the better of it. Daric closed his eyes. She nodded stiffly and went with him to the leeward side of a mountain of supplies, where he described a circle roughly ten body-lengths in diameter. He then levitated some small but heavy boxes to points in the perimeter and arranged several smaller ones in a simple arch. He surveyed the set up one last time, then he and Malena joined voices.

The charm they sang tingled against Huldar's senses. It seemed familiar but before he could identify it, a heavy window sprang up from the circle in the snow. It buckled and bowed in the gale, but when the top closed, it stabilized into a transparent dome anchored to the boxes.

As their singing stopped, Malena shook her head in disbelief.

Huldar was stunned by the genius of the idea. No wonder Daric hadn't tried to explain.

A fresh blast reminded him of the urgency of their situation. He sent a wordless request to the Rukh, then said to the healers, *Ubaid, Alis, we have somewhere for you.*

Cobar made a fire inside the new shelter. Bush and Topper arranged stretcher-bearers and helped Banga usher healers and patients toward the warmth.

The remainder of the Host peered at their activity through slits in their blankets. He tipped his chin toward them. *Casco, Arko, get them moving.*

Right you are, boss! Casco replied.

Daric and Malena marked out another circle.

Pace yourselves, Huldar warned them. *Especially you, Malena. Exhaustion under these conditions may be fatal.*

She gave him a tired nod. Shortly afterward, a group of miners trudged forward to help Daric set anchors in place.

Huldar nodded in satisfaction. *Once the wall is under way, locate the smaller tents. If you show them where they are*, he added, *they can put them up themselves.*

Andel looked at him over the blocks of ice held fast in her mind's grip. Admiration for Daric's quick thinking gushed through their bond, then anger for Malena's rudeness. *What a hide that navigator has!*

She's used to leading a team, not being part of one, he replied.

Sari came to his elbow. *What can I do?*

He pointed toward Casco. *Help distribute tents once the wall is high enough, and remind people to tramp the snow flat before they try sleeping on it.*

She nodded. *I remember that from last time.*

As Sari started for the crates, Huldar called to Tam. *Get kitchen staff together. Hot food, quick as you can.*

The wind screamed as if in protest at their small successes. Huldar turned his back and tramped his feet up and down to keep the blood circulating. Many miners had answered the call for block-makers and as fast as the chunks of ice could be fashioned, those strong in tsemkar hurled them into place. The first dark leather roof-top soon poked above the shelter of the wall, and several huge pots were carried toward tenuous cook fires sparked in its lee.

Huldar made for the dome where the healers were stationed and crawled through the low doorway. Inside, the fire beat back the cold, but when Ubaid looked up his expression was bleak.

Losses?

The Naghari glanced at a row of mounds in the snow. *Six so far. Four more in the balance.*

Six!

We're doing our best!

Of course, it's just ... so many?

Imagery of the hole in the void was shared. The miner's last despairing cry rang in their minds. Alis shared her sense of sorrow. How the cold, grey body she worked on clung to life, Huldar did not know. Her haze drooped with weariness.

Ubaid returned his attention to his patients. Huldar asked Ronnin to stay with them and tend the fire, then left them to it.

Casco and Ariben requisitioned superfluous wall-builders and began to supervise the positioning of stores left free of the wall.

Daric and Malena beckoned him over.

The Host have their tents, Daric said, *and the wall's nearly complete.* He tapped a snow-covered crate. *Our own marquee. Before the adrenaline fades – what do you think?*

Huldar looked up. There was a break in the snowfall, but it wouldn't last, and for all their hard work, the Uri'madu themselves still had no shelter.

You're right, he agreed. *Put it right here. Curve the wall around us to cut the wind. Snow's already trampled flat. All in together and worry about individual tents when the weather clears. Call the others.* Even in good conditions it would take a full team to put it up.

With respect, Daric said, *we have several powerful archangels with us, and if Malena is still willing to help …*

The navigator nodded tiredly.

Have either of you set up a tent like this before? Huldar asked.

Daric glanced at Malena. *No,* he admitted, *but I'm a quick study.*

No doubt of that! When the rest get here I'll show you all at the same time, just to be sure. Can't risk any accidents at this point.

He sent word to the rest of the Uri'madu and between them they dragged the new, larger marquee into position.

Let's do this, Huldar cried.

Rosheen, Daric and Andel united in tsemkar to hold the flapping leathers firm against the wind while Huldar and Malena sang the supports into position. Casco, Ariben and the Rukh sang the guys secure, rope by rope.

Check the stays one last time, Huldar ordered.

Casco and Ariben set off in opposite directions and soon returned inside. *Done,* Ariben said, *and no thanks to the Host. All gone for a feed and left us to it!*

Wouldn't want to be with that lot anyway, said Van.

We need food, Huldar said to Casco. *Can you organize what's necessary?*

Crates 338 and 347 will do for a few weeks, Casco replied. *Kitchen's stowed in 49.*

Huldar turned to the crew. *Topper, Bush and Ariben, go with Casco and get those crates inside this tent. Gento, Cobar, fires! Ronin and Nachiel, while Tam's off feeding the Host, you and Arko get the kitchen set up. Everyone else start digging out snow and getting the space livable. Rugs on the floor! Something to collapse on beside raw ice.*

With the supplies installed and the fires going, Huldar finally allowed himself to relax a little.

Tam shoved his way through the door and after a brief battle fastened it firmly behind him. "What, started without me?" He hurried toward the kitchen fires and while the others continued setting up he soon had a couple of cauldrons bubbling. Hands clasped mugs of tea, soaking up the warmth. Clouds of breath faded as sounds of chatter rose.

Ubaid and Alis came in and headed directly for the fire. They stood close together, shrouded in silence. In short order Tam delivered two more hot drinks and the healers cradled them close.

"Survivors?" Huldar asked quietly.

Without looking up, Ubaid shook his head. Conversation faded.

"Anyone sighted the new Overlord?" asked Topper.

Bush barked a laugh. "Just like old times, eh?" He looked to their new team members. "Never saw the last Gok either, not unless he wanted something."

Huldar studied the mug in his hands as if the steam were somehow oracular. "Ten dead already, plus the one lost to the chime."

Andel watched him with huge eyes. Their sense of victory slipped away.

"This is terrible news," he said. "Ubaid and Alis, I'm sure you did all you could."

"Hypothermia stole what little resistance they had," Ubaid replied. "But I must admit, I'm relieved none of us were among them."

Huldar nodded his head in agreement. "Is there any besh in that crate, Casco? I think we've earned it. A celebration of survival."

The company put up a ragged cheer as a case of the alcoholic beverage was opened.

He noticed Daric Enna standing back and beckoned him closer. "The domes ... Your idea?"

Daric nodded slightly. "But I needed another strong singer to power the charm. My sister's a navigator – I'm used to working with them."

"Very creative."

Daric gave a wry shrug. "Adversity brings out the best in one."

"Can you show me how you did it?" Huldar asked. "Not now, of course. We're all too tired for that, but perhaps we could put one here ..." He pointed to the ceiling. "What do you think?"

"It's a much bigger area," Daric replied thoughtfully, "and the charm may be unstable in the longer term. I'll do some work and let you know."

"Shamkarun Ariben's a substrates expert," he suggested. "Perhaps he could help."

"How long before the storm passes?" asked Calen.

"I don't know. Hopefully some time tomorrow," Huldar answered.

Malena gestured upward. "Is it often like this?" She gave him a level look. Her eyes had lost their spark. "I had no idea. I should have listened."

"A briefing on Giahn couldn't possibly prepare you, I know."

"And it'll get worse," said Ariben. "No doubt about it."

"Weather reader?" Huldar asked hopefully, but Ariben shook his head.

"Aching arm," he admitted. "Not quite so reliable. Got cut off below the elbow. Took months for the healers to re-grow it and more to make it useful."

Ubaid lifted his head. "Fortunate for you a healer was present," he said. "The sequence is difficult to apply unless there's good initial consonance with the subject."

"No picnic, I can tell you!"

The healer nodded. "I've heard the discomfort is considerable."

"Discomfort?" Ariben snorted. "But better than bleeding out – or one of those prosthetic things. The charm to knit them to your stump …"

"Not an ideal outcome," Ubaid agreed.

"Not ideal?" asked Sari.

Ubaid gave her a quick smile. "The charm is complex and somewhat painful to apply. When successful, the replacement limb responds as if it was your own, but daily maintenance is necessary to keep it functional."

"Accident on assignment?" Huldar asked.

Ariben shook his head. "Got involved in a turf war with the Ashik – years back. The things you do!"

"The Cara incident," Daric murmured.

Ariben nodded. "Bunch of Faythans, back when Ishät Ashik was new to the throne. If you don't know, Cara was a village on Juna Leth," he explained to the rest of the group.

"I remember hearing something about this," Huldar said. "The Faythans petitioned the God-Emperor for mining rights, and he agreed?"

"At first, farmers left peacefully," Ariben continued. "Resigned to Imperial ruling – but then we saw the damage they were doing. Arien Leth himself appealed, first to Faytha then to the God-Emperor, but they would not be stopped. So we farmers refused to move. Made our stand at Cara. Faythans hired Ashik. I lost an arm."

"Gold?" Rosheen asked.

Ariben shook his head. "Carusite. Essential ingredient in slave chains. Rare as furry fish. If we'd known, we would've fought harder."

"Slave chains …" Calen shuddered.

"Furry fish?" said Van. "A Maatu saying."

"Spent some time there," said Ariben. "Fine people."

Malena inclined her head. "There's good and bad in all Houses," she said.

"That may be," Ariben replied, "but to my mind, the majority of bad got scraped into the Faythan barrel, and any leftovers got guzzled up by the Ashik."

Daric nodded.

Huldar spent a moment observing him. He was tired and disheveled as the rest, but there was a glow of life now in a haze that had once seemed muted. Had he ever worked as part of a team before? Perhaps not. During their many weeks of travel he'd made sure Daric had been given opportunities to speak, but his background remained undisclosed.

"The happenings at Cara are rarely spoken of," Huldar said.

Daric's haze gave a ripple of contraction, but as if on cue the wind reignited, shrieking in new levels of torment. Tent guys creaked. Instinctively, the Uri'madu ducked. Their breath steamed in the intense chill.

Huldar blew into his cupped hands and rubbed them together. "Glad we sung those stays down tight," he said. "Thanks everyone."

"Move away," Gento said as Rosheen pushed closer to the fire. "Give her some room."

When she crouched and sang to the blaze, it gave a whoof and doubled in size.

Bush and Topper gave a cheer and clinked the necks of their bottles.

Ariben loosened his jacket. "Too hot now," he joked.

Huldar turned to watch Andel, silhouetted with Sari by the hearth. Her sadness was harder for her to control when she was tired, but Sari was foremost on her mind.

It's Lind, she said to him. *Coming back here, she's haunted by memories.*

He shrugged and sent his own feelings of regret. *She's not alone*, he said. *The best we can do is stay with her.*

"At least when the snow's covered the tent, wind can't blow it down," Rosheen said.

Gento and Cobar nodded and Huldar had to smile. If she'd said it was sunny and fine outside those two would have found a way to agree. He only hoped their attraction wouldn't lead to trouble down the track.

"She's right," said Tam. "We'll be lucky if we can dig ourselves out of here by morning, but here we are, warm again and safe so far."

"Not so warm and safe as those who've left us," Calen murmured. "May they rest sweetly in the Breath."

"Aye," others agreed sadly, "may they rest sweet," but before the mood could dip further, Arko lifted his hands and cried, *Done!* Tam took the lid from a steaming cauldron and the delicious aroma of hot hamarsi stole through the air.

"Bowls here, mugs there, boiling water and tea-things beside it … and these bottles here," Arko picked one up from the row on the kitchen trestle and waggled it, "just that little extra something to keep the cold at bay." He grinned. "After you, boss!"

Huldar led the charge but Andel and Sari remained close to the flames. He signaled Andel with a lifted bowl and a tilt of his head.

Yes, please, she replied. *And for Sari too. If she eats, she may feel better.*

So might you, he noted.

While he ladled stew into bowls, he noticed Casco hunker down beside them, and even though he knew he shouldn't, he tuned his ear to listen.

"Everything all right?" Casco asked.

Andel nodded unconvincingly.

"Sari?" Casco asked gently.

Sari stared fixedly at the flames. "She's not here," she said. "When we got back to Giahn, with everything going on, I could push it aside – and on the journey back, well there was lots else to think about. But now ..." She looked up at Casco. Through Andel's eyes, Huldar saw Sari's tears fall silently to the floor. "Could we have stopped her? What did we do wrong? We tried so hard ... and so did she."

Casco bowed his head. "I miss her too," he said. "I miss her snapping at me in the morning, and the way she walked – as if nothing in the Known would ever get in her way."

"And her smile ..." Andel added.

"Her whole face changed." Casco nodded slowly. "From someone you wouldn't want to mess with into something beautiful and bright."

Huldar wished there was more he could do, but although healers could help with the physical trauma of loss, other wounds would only heal at their own pace.

He returned with the extra bowls and handed one to Andel. Gentle love passed through their fingers as they touched.

Sari accepted her bowl but could only stare silently at the contents.

"Try to eat something," Huldar said kindly.

"Yes, please try," said Andel. "What with the weather and the terrible journey, you need food."

Sari nodded, but her haze was dark and her veils ragged.

"Tam has worked so hard," Andel added. She took a mouthful. "And hmm! It's really excellent. The love he's put into it will bolster our spirits."

She smiled as Sari selected a small portion and raised it to her lips.

"I'd best get some for myself," Casco said, "if you will excuse me?"

Huldar watched him leave and stifled a fresh sadness. Although he missed Lind, the state of his friendship with Casco hurt him more.

THE NEW OVERLORD

Huldar's internal clock told him it was midafternoon, but little light penetrated the walls of the marquee. Overnight, more wild storms had covered everything in yet another layer of snow. However, thanks to the most recent version of Daric's window charm, a transparent dome kept a layer of open space between leather and ice, the winds hadn't touched them, and, although dingy, their home was warm.

Partying had been well under way by lunchtime. Now two teams had formed, spinners versus Uri'madu.

Seated on a plump cushion, Malena of Maatu tipped her head back to drain the last besh from the bottle. When it was empty, she wiped her lips with the back of her hand and inclined her head toward Ariben, the Uri'madu contender, who sat in an equally rowdy group across the floor.

When he nodded, she turned to the kitchen and gave a florid wave. "Arko! Again!"

With an ostentatious flourish, the impromptu barkeeper took another by the neck and tossed it somersaulting in a neat parabola above their heads.

With the lightning reflexes of a well-schooled fighter the navigator snatched it from the air.

To raucous support she opened the drink and sculled it in a single draft.

"Seven!" she crowed, and lifted the empty toward Ariben. "Beat that, old-timer – if you can."

"Old-timer?" Ariben scowled hugely and held his hands up for quiet.

At his signal, another ale was tossed, but the Uri'madu gasped as Arko stumbled mid-throw. The missile tumbled off course and wide of its mark. With loud cry, Ariben flung himself into its path and caught it right before it hit the floor.

He rolled onto his back and raised his trophy.

Huldar grinned at Andel. "Has to be the winning catch!" he murmured.

As the ale vanished down Ariben's neck, the Uri'madu erupted in a massive cheer.

Malena swayed to her feet and saluted his victory. "Breath blow truth!"

"Bleath brow true," Ariben echoed. He stumbled across the cushions and clinked the neck of his empty against hers. "Till nex round."

Tam lifted the lid on a crock and released the smell of fresh honey-cakes, but the party hushed a short time later as Huldar sensed their new Overlord's approach, tramping laboriously through the snow.

Radätel Gok made his way down the icy entry ramp with care and pushed through the

door. "Huldar, may we speak?"

"Certainly." Huldar picked up a honey cake and offered it but the Overlord frowned.

"Two days have passed with no work accomplished!"

Andel laughed privately through their bond. *Déjà vu?*

Huldar looked down into Radätel's face. He certainly had more appealing features than Duvät had owned, but he was a Tiamäti none the less. He was reminded of Pieru's parting admonition about superior rank. Already it seemed an event from the distant past.

He pulled his heavy jacket from Qalān and wrapped a thick scarf over his face.

Radätel watched, slightly puzzled.

"Come with me," Huldar said, and led him back outdoors.

Beyond the comfort of their tent the world was very different. Huldar narrowed his eyes to slits against the ferocious glare. Even through the scarf, the air was so cold it hurt to breathe. Deep snow rendered the landscape featureless but for the semi-circular hummock above their marquee, the bump of the snow-wall and the ploughed trail of the Overlord's path from his tent with the Host's shelters.

He waved his hand at their surroundings. "Do you see this?"

"See what?" The Overlord squinted. "It's not snowing any more. The sun is even shining."

"Let's walk a little further."

Huldar trudged toward the west gate, glad his grid-work of portals had stood the test of time. Away from camp, they were enveloped in a cloak of gelid silence. Andel's smile followed him and his mind relaxed as it never did in the Realm.

He drew Radätel Gok's attention to the shimmer of Qalān.

"We could step through here to the potential copper mine in the valley, but snows on site are over ten feet thick. I've been there. It's a wasteland, and will remain so for several weeks at least." He pointed East. "Flying Slug Reef, where the gold is. Warmed by geothermal activity and almost clear, except for endless rivers of slush. Even so, the strap trees and heart palms are showing signs of life, larval slugs emerging ..."

"Well, why can't you start work there?"

Huldar sighed. "Every morning, Andel or Ariben and I join forces to scan and assess the weather. At this time of the Wentish year – early spring, I think you'd call it – the climate is extremely volatile – even more so than usual. Although the snow has almost cleared from the reef, the winds are appalling, and because the vegetation has not yet grown there is nothing to shield us."

"Set up a tent." Radätel said. "We have plenty."

"Of course," Huldar replied. "And that is exactly what we'll do – as soon as the winds have subsided."

"When will that be?"

"Depends on how the air masses interact with the rising sea surface temperatures. Since this is only our second visit to this planet we have little knowledge to guide us. There seems to be less volcanic activity in the ranges here compared to last cycle, but we've noticed a large eruption in an island chain to the west, and an area clear of sea-ice. Volcanically warmed currents are fueling the winds – or that's what we think. It's all very turbulent. We are lucky not to have been worse affected – except for the massive snow dump – and the winds of course."

Radätel rubbed frost from his hood with one gloved mitt and glanced at Huldar's Mark. "You can't cool the offending waters to rectify the climate?" he ventured.

Huldar caught an unexpected glint of humor in the Overlord's eye and a small smile formed beneath his scarf. He shook his head.

"Are there other sites we could be preparing?" the Overlord asked.

"As soon as the weather permits." Huldar nodded. "Once it starts, the thaw should gain momentum quickly."

A spark of anger replaced Radätel's amusement. "This is outrageous! If we had known, we could have delayed our departure. Saved thousands. Why weren't we told?"

"And saved lives," Huldar pointed out. "The variables of Wentish climate were discussed at length during several briefing sessions. Not enough is yet known to predict the progress of the thaw or what is 'normal'," he said. "I recommended we wait, but Olatu of Faytha insisted we leave earlier. His employer has funded the Host and also a large percentage of the Guild's contribution."

Radätel scowled.

Huldar tucked his hands beneath his armpits. A faint cheer from their tent reminded him of what he was missing. There was no such noise from the other, much larger marquee in the distance, and when he looked at Radätel's firmly correct veil, he almost felt sorry for him.

"Preparations must commence as soon as possible," Radätel said. "Olatu will not stand for unnecessary delays."

"Of course," Huldar agreed. "And, as usual, you will have my full report on your desk by nightfall."

"Very well." Radätel sighed. "I know you are doing your best, Shamkarun Huldar, but you must understand – Olatu of Faytha is on my back already. Snapping and snarling: he doesn't even have the decency to veil his frustration. His first time away from the Realm, you see. He thinks the normal rules of conduct don't apply."

They looked toward a faint gust of laughter.

"Nothing like that in our dwellings, I can assure you," Radätel said miserably.

"You are welcome to join us," Huldar suggested. "Get to know the team a little better?"

Radätel snorted. "Olatu of Faytha thinks it 'unseemly'. Ha! From him!"

Huldar grimaced in commiseration. "Well, the offer stands – and rest assured we will commence our duties as soon as the weather permits."

The overlord bowed. "Thank you, Shamkarun Huldar. I am certain you are doing your best … Is something wrong?"

"My apologies, Radätel Gok," Huldar said carefully. "Your approach surprises me. It's somewhat different from that of your predecessor."

"It is?" Radätel turned and they started back toward the tents. "Well then, it is early in our assignment. Perhaps the strains of wilderness existence have yet to affect me."

"Let's hope they never do," Huldar replied.

FLYING SLUG REEF

Over the following weeks the weather warmed as predicted and snow-storms became less frequent. At Flying Slug Reef, Huldar waited as Nachiel squelched across barren ground toward him. Thickets of emergent strap trees surrounded them as if the space they'd prepared for the miners' camp had been cut with a stamp from wild green dough.

"Four hundred and twenty-seven slugs accounted for," Nachiel said. "Slimy little darlings are much easier to handle before they grow wings! I've delivered them to the next canyon over, as you suggested, but there's overcrowding … and some there can already fly."

"They'll form flocks soon. I know they're territorial, but hopefully the difference in developmental stages will avert too much aggression. They're vital to the ecosystem," Huldar said. "It's important we save as many as we can. I'll warn the miners to watch out for them – for all the good it might do."

"They don't share our respect for life, do they?" Nachiel said. "I thought, with the slugs, if they could just see how pretty they are, especially when they get their wings."

Huldar shook his head glumly. "They're here for one thing, and one thing only. Is everything up to standard otherwise?"

"My word, yes," Nachiel answered. "Food's good, better than I can ever remember. Casco tells me it's because Daric Enna introduced him to a whole new set of, shall we say, more open-minded suppliers outside of the Guild-sanctioned lot. Made a big difference to what we could afford."

"I agree," Huldar replied, "but that's not exactly what I meant."

Nachiel looked around the large square. "I'll admit I didn't want the winds to ease," he said at last. "I wanted things to stay the same, to be like normal. Me, cataloging and recording … you deciphering ecological relationships and bickering with the Gok. But it's not the same. Not at all."

Huldar sighed. Nachiel merely voiced what the rest of them felt. Even the newcomers were finding conditions stressful, and it wasn't just the weather.

Nachiel moved a withered frond with the toe of his boot. "It hurt to kill so many strap-trees," he said plaintively. "Who knows how long it will take the area to recover? And all those poor beasties and critters – they have no home now. And how many will hatch or crawl out of the ground and there'll be nothing here to sustain them and they'll die?"

"I know," said Huldar. "And there's no precedent, none of the usual trial plots. No time. It's disgraceful! But at least we've cleared as sensitively as we could," he added "The miners would just hack their way in, regardless."

"Try telling that to the locals," said Nachiel. "They don't understand."

Huldar sat on a nearby boulder and invited Nachiel to join him. "At least we've worked out a charm to keep them away once the tents are up," he said.

"So long as the grubbers maintain it."

"I'll make sure of it."

Huldar felt the sun warm his back. He remembered his first look at the seams of gold in the nearby rock face. How excited they'd been …

"Ronnin and the others?" he asked.

Nachiel waved loosely at the portal. "Gone with Calen to get the tents. At least this isn't *our* old campsite," he continued, "the one where the planet first spoke to you. And nowhere near the Went. They won't even know they're there, with any luck."

"You don't think the miners would hurt them?"

"They might," he said diffidently. "Who knows? They're not like us … and the Went, they're so trusting – there're something really special. I know it."

"I've been watching for them," Huldar said. "It's vital we understand their role … but whether I can convince Radätel Gok or Olatu of Faytha of that is another matter. They want all our time spent on projects like this one."

"I know," Nachiel replied. "I haven't even opened my folio yet, and I have such lovely new paper and a stylus crafted by Mamet of Nhadu herself! I bought it with my share of Lind's bequest … a way of remembering her. I'm sure she wouldn't mind."

"She loved your drawings," Huldar assured him. "Remember the one you did of her? It was stowed in her Qalän."

"I have it with me." He patted his chest. "Ronnin scoffs, but sometimes I feel like she's still with us, looking through her image, seeing what I see."

"He understands. Everyone deals with grief in their own way."

Nachiel bowed his head. "We've been together so long … how would I cope if he were the one who was gone?"

Huldar nodded sadly and gazed westward to where Andel worked with the copper miners. They were deciding on the best place to open their pit. Another habitat scarred.

The portal quivered and Calen stepped through ahead of Ronnin and three spinners: Tague, Minna and Tala. Although the spinners were experienced load-bearers, their burden of crates and boxes seemed quite unwieldy. With brusque movements, Calen directed them toward the square.

Ronnin paused to wipe his forehead.

"Keep moving!" she said firmly, "or we'll never get this done."

Huldar stood up. "Calen!" he called. "What's going on?"

As Calen turned to him, the spinners juggled the rest of the cargo to the ground.

"She's always like this," Nachiel murmured.

Huldar walked toward them.

Calen have an affable snort. "A few weeks lazing about waiting for the weather and they've gone all soft on me."

He turned to Ronnin and the spinners and cast his eye over the disorganized heap of stores and supplies.

Minna, one of the spinners, glanced quickly at Calen.

"This load seems over-large," Huldar said. "Why is it so …?"

"Unbalanced?" Minna finished for him. She looked at Calen again.

Huldar tuned his voice to reach Minna alone. *Tell me.*

She just kept pointing and wouldn't listen! the spinner said. *We tried to tell her – then when we wanted to balance the load properly and bring Ronnin into the mix, she told us to stop wasting time – as if we were lazy! If Malena had been there …!*

And why is the load so heavy? Huldar asked, but he thought he already knew.

We thought she was going to help, Minna said, confirming his suspicions.

He turned to the archangel. "These people are very experienced in the bearing and transport of cargo. Yet they tell me you wouldn't allow time for correct preparation. Is that the case?"

She frowned back at him. *Someone needs to direct them.*

"Words please."

Calen hesitated. "We have a large amount of goods to shift in as short as possible time," she said reasonably. "They were laughing and joking. It seemed to me they could have been working harder."

"We always joke about," Minna said. "Doesn't mean we're not working."

"Calen, we have a long contract ahead of us," Huldar said. "Listen to the spinners when it comes to this sort of work – perhaps even learn from them. The need for safety can't be stressed enough. And in future, I expect to see you carrying your weight as well." *You are stronger,* he added to her mind alone.

But I –

Yes, Huldar finished for her. *You're an archangel – and so am I, but our strategy here is to share the labor without regard to hierarchy. That way it's done quicker and with less stress on the overall team. Greater safety – you understand?*

Ronnin gave the nearest spinner a surreptitious nudge as if he'd heard what Huldar had said.

Calen bowed. "I apologize."

"It's these people who deserve the apology," Huldar said. "Work quickly by all means, but don't hurt yourself or others in the process."

Ronnin thanks you! Nachiel whispered. *She's a bit of a bully – not used to our ways.*

Tell me if there are further problems, Huldar said. *The quicker they get used to how we –*

Shock resounded through his marriage bond. He turned toward the source – the copper mine.

Moments later, a call came from Ubaid. *I think you should see this …*

Are you with her?

Yes. The healer sent an impression of their location. *Hurry.*

Andel's shock devolved to grief.

He started to run. Already the quickest route was mapped in his mind. He calmed himself before each step and made certain the song was firm. She was not injured, but whatever she'd witnessed had turned her thoughts to pure emotion.

He stepped through the final portal and ran to the mine. She stood, waiting for him. Her arms were wrapped tightly around her ribs. Nearby, a stocky angel hugged his knees and rocked back and forth.

He fell, he hit his head, and then …

Ubaid squatted at the injured one's side, murmuring calmly as he tried to examine his head. The miner's eyes were squeezed shut. His free hand worked across the toe of his boot. His lips mumbled softly, "… three, four, five …" then he moved to the other foot, "one, two, three …"

With effort, his gaze found Ubaid's. "What's happening to me?" he whispered. *Why am I doing this?* But as if of their own volition, his fingers began their task again.

Ubaid looked up. *I'm at a loss to explain,* he said to Huldar. *The injury itself isn't severe.*

Andel gazed at the miner fearfully, then quickly turned away. *He was just there,* she said, *and he fell and knocked himself out and Ubaid ran to him and then he started counting like … like … Lind.*

Huldar gathered her into his arms. A morass of fresh-stirred fear streamed from her heart to his. On a good day, she could accept that her guilt over her mother's death and their captor's terrible fate was baseless, but now, confronted by this inexplicable echo of Lind's torment …

How can this be? he asked bleakly.

Ubaid handed the miner a small glass of thick green fluid and watched as he drank. *Dreamless sleep – enough to knock him out for a full day,* he said privately to Huldar. *Hopefully by then the symptoms will have run their course.*

I did this, Andel cried. *There's something wrong inside me. I can feel it.*

You did not do this, he said firmly. "I love you," he whispered into her hair. *I will always love you. It wasn't your fault*, he soothed. *You defended yourself, that's all. You didn't kill your mother; your captor was the evil one and he's gone now, Andel. He's gone.*

But in her mind Andel relived the moment when Ninjay's eyes turned to emptiness. A litany of images subsumed her, a bitter path he knew too well. There was no answer. All he could do was open his heart and hope her torment passed quickly.

"Lady Andel?" Ubaid offered her a cup of the same green liquid. "It's diluted – not as strong as what I gave the miner. Let it soothe you."

She shook her head. "I won't be able to find the ore," she said brokenly, "and we have deadlines."

A new fear came from her, that she should not have come. That they would suffer because her inadequacies, and he would begin to hate her – yet she knew beyond doubt of his love. His own head began to flounder.

"Take the samik," he suggested kindly. "You're ahead of schedule, and even if you weren't, your health is far more important than the desires of one greedy Faythan." With another part of his mind he called Sari, hoping her presence would help.

The miner's mumbling slowed. His eyes sagged shut, then watched without true comprehension as several nervous workmates hoisted him onto a litter.

Andel turned away.

I'll find out why this happened, Huldar promised her. *Perhaps the planet herself has answers.*

The planet? she said. *But you'll need me to keep you safe – and I'm useless like this! Mother was right …*

You know that's not true. He was relieved to sense the portal's activation. *Look, here comes Sari …*

He reached for her hand and let love try to ease the pain they shared.

When she returned Sari's wave, he smiled at her bravery. He felt the tide of another battle turn and knew that as her score of victories increased so would her confidence. It was just a matter of time – or so the healers assured him.

Ubaid presented the sedative again and this time she took it.

"Let's go back, Lady Andel," Sari said. Her eyes met Huldar's and he gave a tiny nod of appreciation. "We can relax over a nice cup of galano," she continued smoothly, "and Tam has fresh honey-cakes with sweet-rash topping."

"Sweet-rash?" Andel asked.

"Sweet-rash, yes. A new thing he's trying. Smells lovely. Not sure about the look of it though. Did I tell you about my cousin Enadia? At my nephew's coming of age party? No? Well it was the funniest thing …"

Huldar watched until they vanished through the portal. Around them, the miners ceased operations for the day. Their movements as they tidied up were unusually hurried.

"She will be all right," Ubaid said. "But I'm glad she chose to work with us before we left Giahn, things being as they are. What happened was terrible. To inflict pain on another is very far from her natural inclinations, yet a deeper part of her rejoices at the vengeance she took. A terrible dilemma, and difficult to own."

Huldar nodded tiredly. "Since we started traveling, and especially since we've been here on Went she's been much better, but ... She doesn't know how she did it, and no one else seems to know – and now this?" He hunched his shoulders. "Perhaps you can get to the bottom of it? There's not much you and Alis haven't encountered."

Ubaid inhaled slowly then huffed a breath through his lips. "Except for what just happened here."

"Toe counting ..." Huldar shook his head. "Breath knows we listened to Lind doing it often enough," he said sadly. "Even the cadence of this one's voice ... I know it's impossible, but does Qalān remember?"

"Well, something does," Ubaid said thoughtfully, "and whatever it is, I'm afraid it's not our friend."

SARI'S STORY

A gust of warmth brushed Sari's face as she pushed aside the marquee door. The bittersweet aroma of Tam's latest cooking experiment – the sweet-rash honey-cakes, was enticing.

Andel staggered a little. "Oh! I feel quite giddy."

"Giddy?" She caught her elbow. "It must be that potion Ubaid gave you. Here, let's sit by the fire." She helped Andel lower herself onto the same durable strap-tree bole they'd often used during their last stay – broad enough for comfort and just long enough for three.

Tam caught her eye and glanced across to the tea-making things on the counter.

She gave a quick smile then returned her attention to her charge. Soon she heard the clatter of twigs and the gurgle of simmering water poured into cups.

When the tea arrived, she tried to seem unconcerned as she guided Andel's chill fingers safely to the handle.

"The tea might make you feel better," she said gently.

She thought she saw Lady Andel move her head in a slight nod, but it was hard to be sure. "Are you all right?" she asked. "Would you like something to eat? … Cobar and Gento put a slug in Rosheen's lunch-box yesterday, did you hear? I was there when she opened it." She gave an inner chuckle, remembering the rugged Rukh's expression as the glittering wings burst from the leather wrapping. "It took ages to catch it again, then we had to work twice as hard to make up for it. She made them return it to its home canyon that afternoon before dusk, so it could nestle back with its flock before it got too cold. They're so pretty when they get their wings … all those colors. Like the glass in the navigators dome, a bit … don't you think …?

She smiled, but Andel held the cup numbly, her gaze lost to the fascination of the flames.

There was a sharp crack: sparks puffed from the coals. Andel turned to her mug as if seeing it for the first time. She blinked in the rising steam, then blew on its surface and concentrated on getting her lips neatly to the edge.

"How are you feeling?" Sari asked, then her cheeks colored. It was not the first time she had asked the question and she didn't want to seem foolish. "Do you need to lie down?"

Andel shook her head.

Sari looked at the tea. It must be lukewarm by now. "Would you like a fresh cup?"

"Mustn't waste the twig," Andel replied vaguely.

"The twig? Yes, the twig," Sari assured her, even though she knew they had plenty.

"Galano is very good for your eyesight," she said, remembering her training with Alis, "and for hair and fingernail growth."

"Oh?"

"And it's good for pregnancy, too, did you know? My sister's friend was blessed – she announced it after my nephew's party. She swears by it."

"Pregnancy?"

"Pregnancy – yes." She tilted her head. "Sometimes the newly blessed feel quite nauseated, especially in the morning. Galano helps." She patted Andel's arm. "You and Huldar are so happy; you'll be blessed soon, too, I know it! Maybe even while we're here."

"Blessed?" Andel gave her a startled look. "Not yet, I hope."

Sari smiled and wondered what it might be like to birth a child so far from home – or even to birth one at all. "But it would be exciting, wouldn't it? A baby born here, on Went. A Wentling!" She gave a light chuckle and was pleased to see Lady Andel's hesitant smile.

She tried to imagine how Andel would look, gazing into the eyes of her very own bless, then turned away as an old sadness fought for air. She moved her fingers softly over the grooves and gullies of the log and tried to dispel her emotions before Lady Andel noticed. But her friend looked at her hands, then at her face, and she knew she'd failed.

"Why did you never marry?" Andel asked. Her manner was dreamy, still held by the samik, but Sari could feel the care behind her words. "You're so kind and you'd be such a wonderful mother," Andel continued, then she turned away. "I'm sorry. I shouldn't have asked such a personal question."

"Personal? … Oh no. It's all right," Sari said. "Really." But her sadness persisted.

"I don't know what came over me," Andel said. "So thoughtless! Please, forget I said anything."

"Thoughtless? You, Lady Andel? Never."

Tam covered his cakes and started for the door. He gave a small nod as he passed and left them quite alone.

"No, it's all right," Sari said again. "It's just not something I'm used to talking about, that's all."

"Then don't," Andel said gently. "Not unless you want to."

"Unless I want to," Sari repeated. Maybe it was the warmth of the fire that had brought it on, or the empty space at the end of the log, where Lind used to sit. She flinched when Andel took her hand, and despite her best efforts, a melancholy, deep and old, seeped through their touch.

"Blessings only come from a male–female union," Sari said at last. "And I can't … with a male."

"Can't have sex with …" Andel paused. "Well, some people do find it distasteful with the opposite gender."

"It's not that," Sari said. "Not really. Some males I find quite attractive. Take that spinner, Silar, for instance, or even our Casco. He's very handsome, and although he's a bit gruff at times it's only because he cares, and he has a marvelous sense of humor … and when he smiles, he … well, anyway, but he seems quite taken with Daric Enna at the moment, doesn't he?"

"Yes. I hear they've had quite a few adventures together."

"Adventures. Yes … No." She fiddled with the wood-grain some more. Why was it so difficult to speak about this? Especially with lady Andel, the kindest person she knew. "… It's just that I can't bear for them to touch me – not in that way." She looked deeply into Andel's face. The diviner's gaze held her. It seemed as lost and sad as she was. She knew Andel and her mother had been captured by someone who wished them harm, and her mother had lost her life as they escaped. A terrible experience, and no doubt the source of her turmoil. Perhaps if she shared her own story, Andel would find it easier to tell her what had happened, and that might help her.

"Adventures? … Well, I'll tell you a story," she said bravely. "There was a little girl, barely one hundred and twenty summers, but tall for her age, or so I was told. She lived on Lentath, on Purd, a large island off the Marinas coast in the northern hemisphere. A pretty place in spring. Ma, the mother, was cooking … delicious cakes with honey and caluma and little squishy blade berries inside."

In her hidden mind she saw the small house again, built from the soil and timber around them, and thatched with huge slabs of bark her da had taken from the sides of trees. One slab per tree. The bark grew back, but the scars remained.

"I've never had blade berries," said Andel. "What are they like?"

"Blade berries." Sari smiled softly. "They only grow for a week or two when the weather begins to warm. Haven't had them in years, but my word, they are good! A little bite to them, but sweet and juicy."

Her gaze came to rest on Tam's kitchen things and the ever-simmering pot above the cook fire. How different her life was now, yet there she was, back in a warm kitchen with the smell of cooking all around.

Andel looked at her expectantly, and she started again. "She'd nearly run out of milk – the mother had – and we'd need some for when the father came home from the fields. 'Run and get some from Bett's next door,' she said, and so I did, but it was such a lovely day and the sun was shining – not a cloud in the sky. I knew I should've stepped through the portal – I was just old enough to make it work and very proud of it, as Ma knew, but the smell of spring was so strong and a puff of baby summer sprites bubbled up from the grass … and I decided to go the long way. A walk across the fields. Ma was annoyed, but she said it was all right so long as I hurried home."

"And did you?"

"No … it didn't go like that."

The wave of distress that followed was difficult to suppress. Her veil rippled with the effort.

"You don't have to tell me," Andel said softly.

"Tell me?" Sari murmured. "But perhaps it's time I did." She smoothed the log and continued. "I'd seen him at Bett's – but he stayed out of the way. She never introduced him, but it turned out he was a relation of some sort. Light brown hair. Pale eyes. Smelly breath …"

The smell of his breath? Andel frowned. "What happened, Sari?"

"What happened?" She looked around the empty marquee. Should she really burden her friend with this? She had grief of her own. Her gaze lingered on an untidy pile of bedding, then moved on.

"Please, Sari." Andel offered her hand. "You can tell me anything, and I want to know … if you feel you can."

Sari nodded. She had never even told Lind, but under the gentle gaze of lady Andel, the threads of her ancient shame seemed drawn to the light.

"I told Ma I was on my way home," she continued. "The portal was just outside, not far at all. He must have sneaked around because I didn't see him. I just looked up and there he was.

"'I have an orphan kressie,' he said. 'Such big eyes, so sad.' He asked if I'd like to see her. Said it might make her feel better." She shrugged. "I'd never seen a real live kressie before, but I'd seen vision of them in Da's stories of Haaseen. He was a Rukh, you know, my da."

A memory of his face came to her. She hadn't thought of him in ever such a long time – but there he was. Buried deep – not lost after all.

"He used to light up when he smiled at me." She paused, remembering. "But he never said much, or it was more he didn't believe in chit-chat – like most Rukh.

"The stranger smiled. 'It won't take long,' he said. 'Your mother won't mind … if we don't tell her.'

"His haze seemed odd, but," Sari bowed her head, "I so wanted to see the little baby kressie. As we stepped through the portal I listened carefully, thinking perhaps I'd be able to sneak back and see the baby again, but on the other side it was dark – night time – and I knew we'd come a very long way. I tried to step straight back home, but he grabbed me." She rubbed her arm as if it were still bruised. "He pulled me toward another portal, then another, and I was so frightened. Ma heard me screaming but I was too far away. I didn't know where I was or how we'd gotten there.

"He took me to a hut, an old timber hut. There was a light. And a bed.

She turned to look at Andel. "I didn't want to take off my clothes, but he hit me. I'd never been hit before, not like that. I saw stars. I couldn't think. "Take them off!" he said so I took them off. I could feel my Ma ... terror. Outrage. But me? ... I felt nothing. Nothing, that is, until the pain when he ..."

Images flittered through her defenses. Andel's hand flew to her mouth.

And then ... others came.

Fear returned as if it were yesterday. The shame was overwhelming. Tears washed her cheek, but she felt they belonged to someone else.

"I took my clothes off ..." she whispered. "I should have run away."

"How did you survive?" Andel asked. "What happened?"

"Da." Sari's fingers picked at the log. "Da found me." She turned briefly to meet Andel's gaze, then had to turn away. "He killed them. All of them. With his bare hands. I've never seen such rage. I was terrified. Their eyes ... staring." She ran her hands down her arms and saw smaller arms with blood spattered on them. "I couldn't stop screaming."

Tears ran from her eyes as if they would never stop, and she realized they hadn't – not the ones inside. She just didn't look at them any more.

"They took me to a healer, then another one ..."

Andel took a sobbing breath. "Your parents?"

She nodded. "Then later, when I realized I had a problem, I spent time in a Naghari Chapter House." Recalling the kindness she'd encountered there, she felt her strength returning. "But it was no good." She sighed brokenly. "It's never been any good. And it dawned on me – no matter how

110

much I wanted a child, I could never be blessed." She gave a rueful smile. "It's why I eventually joined the Guild, so long ago now. A complete break. Time to come to terms with myself – and I feel safer when there's not so many people about."

"But I've seen males of the Uri'madu hug you – I've even seen Cobar lift you off your feet and carry you ..."

"I know!" She smiled a little. "Isn't it wonderful? I trust them, I think. And that's very different from the kind of touch I can't allow."

"Other females?"

"Not a problem. I've been in love – more than once ..." She hesitated then went on, "When my sister gave birth for the first time, I was there. It was a miracle, a blessing indeed. And that little mind, so strong! So demanding! She let me hold him, and I looked into his eyes, and he grabbed my finger, held on so tight. We'll always have a special connection ..."

But it's not the same, Andel finished for her. "Oh, Sari."

She wiped her cheeks with a small white handkerchief. "But Lady Andel, here you are, so unwell, and here I am prattling on." Her sadness funneled back inward, where it belonged. "How can you forgive me?"

"There's nothing to forgive," Andel assured her. "You're so loving to us all. We depend on you – lean on you." She offered her hand. "I wish I could be so strong."

Sari looked quickly around as Tam returned, then smiled. *The Naghari say true love requires self-acceptance, and that by giving love, one learns to accept it from others.*

Skin to skin, the care they felt for each other was amplified. Another face swam to mind and a sorrow shared.

Fresh tears moistened their eyes.

I saw in her the echo of what had happened to me, Sari said. *When she took her own life … I understood.*

A pang of fear tightened Andel's hold. *Please, tell me if ever you face that temptation again. You are not alone. You are loved.*

Sari glanced at Tam again. *But if they knew?*

Andel's grip firmed again. *They would love you even more fiercely for your courage.*

For my courage? She shook her head. Courageous was not what she felt. *I am not special, Lady Andel. Just scratch the surface of any one of us and you'll find misfortune – it's what's brought most of us here, to this life … even your Huldar, I expect. The challenge and the isolation – it's how we cope. That, and our strength in each other.*

Andel nodded.

Their hands let go but the specter of Lind remained. Why had the injured miner started counting his toes?

Andel's sorrow rose again, and together they let grief run its course.

COOK'S KITCHEN

With the spinners Banga and Kira beside him, Huldar took the last step home and squinted through thick mist at the warmth of their marquee. Daric's dome was holding up well and had made a great difference to their level of comfort.

"Quiet tonight," Banga remarked.

"Little wonder," Huldar murmured. From outside, the mood was hard to decipher, but there was more than a whiff of fear.

Huldar pushed aside the door. Andel and Sari sat at their usual place by the fire. Andel returned his smile brightly, but grief whispered like smoke from the well of her soul.

Behind the kitchen bench, Tam and Shen, the Host's head cook, were deep in conversation. Tam took a sprig from Shen's hand and said something about it.

"The Host might have to start cooking for themselves," Kira said.

"He's here more often than he's there," Banga agreed.

Without meeting Huldar's gaze, Sari got to her feet. "I made sure Tam saved some for you," she said, and started for the kitchen.

Huldar thanked her and took her place beside Andel.

She reached for his hand and murmured, "Look at those two." *Malena and Ariben.*

She dug him softly in the ribs ... *Don't actually look! Sari thinks they'll have sex together tonight. I thought they wouldn't be so rude – that they'd wait for a little privacy, but look at their hazes. Maybe she's right!*

Malena giggled at something Ariben said. Ariben fed her a sweet-cake. Kira rolled her eyes.

Maybe she is, Huldar agreed. The navigator's rampant sexuality was another worry he didn't need. He waited a moment then said carefully, *I'm going to have to talk to everyone about what happened today.*

She looked at their clasped hands. *I know. They expect it,* she said. *I'm all right ...*

He looked down as something tickled his calf and saw the end of a multi-legged creature disappearing up the leg of his trousers. A quick song stopped it, but as he stood to shake it free, all conversation ceased.

"Rope bug," he announced. He picked up the wanderer up and walked it self-consciously to the door. Even Shen watched in silence. He returned to the fire. It seemed the time to discuss the miner's strange condition had come.

"I can see you all know what happened today," he began. "I spoke to the Host not long ago and the injured miner is still sleeping. Ubaid is monitoring the situation and hopefully by tomorrow we'll be able to ask questions."

"But what does this mean?" Nachiel asked. "Was he really counting his toes?"

"Bizarre," Ariben murmured, and Malena nodded in agreement.

"If this *is* a repetition of your former team-mate's condition," said Calen, "perhaps Lind wasn't stuck in Qalān at all. Perhaps something else happened, some other threat unknown."

"Of course she was stuck in Qalān!" Casco snapped. "I was there when the boss pulled them out, she and Andel both. Bravest thing I've ever seen."

"But you found her boots *here*, on *this* plane ..."

"Although it's very rare, inanimate objects have been ejected before." Heads turned as Daric Enna spoke. "But never people," he continued. "As I understand it, Lind and Lady Andel are the first to have seen the inside of Qalān and survived."

"Huldar," said Casco. "I remember you explaining that to make new gates in wild Qalān was not so much a mechanical imposition as a negotiation ..."

"Yes, that's correct," Huldar said. "Portals can be forced, but the quality is different."

"In what way?" asked Ariben.

"Negotiated portals are easier to use. They allow a wider range of exit points and are more accepting of change."

Fire crackled in the hearth. The air was thick with questions that had yet to morph into words.

Daric lifted his shoulders. "So Qalān ... is alive?"

Huldar paused, struck by the enormity of this idea ... Could it be true? He had always taken due time when forging pathways across planets, treated it as a concession Qalān allowed him. There was a feel, a connection made during the process, as if each major branch – even each world – had its own character. He remembered his arrival on Trianog Frith, how its personality had confounded him at first, but then they seemed to settle into one another, as if they had registered each other's vibration. But there were so many people, and each so small when compared to the bulk of a planet, how could it even notice? How could one person make a difference?

The attention of the Uri'madu pressed in on him.

He turned to Daric. "You have great skill with portals …"

Daric inclined his head. "But I have never forged a new one, only worked with what's already there."

"Yes, but when you work with them, is there a moment of connection?"

"I … suppose so," he admitted. "It's as if voice and mind hit a sweet spot and suddenly many things are possible. I only have to ask."

"Exactly! And you, Malena?"

The navigator knitted her brow. "I have very little skill with planetary Qalān," she said at last. "But as for the Chime: yes, it has moods, storms even, and those can be violent – as we saw on our way here … may they rest sweetly in the Breath." Slowly, she looked up. Her head tilted as if she were listening to the skies. "But it's so vast. How could it be a living thing? … A living matrix, singing its own, all-encompassing song?" She met his gaze, fiery green eyes full of more questions. "And if all Qalān has consciousness, what of our own personal space? What is it that we use to store things in? That Shamkaruns with skills such as your own sing to release when we, ourselves have rejoined the Breath?"

"A mirror, maybe? A shadow self?" Daric mused.

"If that's the case," said Ariben, "what is it that is mirrored by the Chime?"

"The Chime?" Sari said. "I don't know about the Chime, but I know this planet is alive. We all do. It spoke to Huldar."

"Yes, but that's not Qalān."

"Qalān – no. It trapped Lind and held her, and now, when that poor angel hit his head … it found a way in. It's fighting back!"

"Against us?"

"After what our last Overlord did, who can blame it?"

"But are the planet and its portals one and the same?" Banga asked.

"It's as if she doesn't want us here," Andel said. "I felt that when we went through that last stage and everything was so violent."

Malena nodded. "I'll admit it was a struggle."

"I don't think it's us." Ariben's hands opened inclusively. "It's just that there's too many annangi here all at once, making changes, and maybe she wasn't prepared."

"And more's to come," said Shen.

Huldar turned, surprised to hear him speak. He'd almost forgotten he was there.

"An I'm just saying, the conversation over here is certainly mind-blowing." Shen tipped his head toward the Host's marquee. "All they speak of over there is muscle, metal and coin – oh, and complaints about the food, of course!"

"Of course." Huldar smiled. "Well, you are welcome here any time."

"Yeah," said Topper. He looked around suspiciously. "Any time you want to hear stuff that's gonna bend your head an keep you awake at night!"

Bush grinned. "Crook tucker'll do the job just as well."

"Is he insulting us, Tam?" Shen laughed.

"No dessert for you two!" Tam said with mock severity. "A pity. I've made sweet-rash cakes and barberry pies."

Bush raised his hands. "Just my luck. I take it back, whoever I was insulting."

Huldar laughed with the rest, but the greater part of him was lost to the overwhelming proposition that Qalān in one or all of its forms might be a living force. Was this the reason the planet had spoken to him? Was his connection with Qalān also a gateway to the heart of the world? … or even more, the key to the heart of every world?

Andel reached up and took his hand again. *Ask her,* she said. *You're the only one who can.*

He remembered his frightening experiences from their previous cycle on Went. Any attempt to deliberately communicate should not be undertaken lightly, and he admitted to a deeper fear … perhaps his special status – Sacred to Leth – would prove undeserved.

She gave his fingers a gentle squeeze. *I'll go with you.*

To the volcano?

If we replicate our last approach … I think we must.

He let his senses range. Beyond the glow of their fires was a night of impenetrable dark. "Cold" didn't begin to describe the conditions.

It won't be tonight, he said.

Of course not! she said. *We don't want to die in the attempt. But soon, my love, as soon as we can. I need to know. I think we all do.*

For a short time, as he thought about the journey they had planned, his inner mind calmed, but long into the night he lay quietly as Andel slept, and watched small flames in the fire-pit flicker across the coals.

VOLCANO

Huldar woke knowing this was a designated rest day and, after a week of bad weather, their best chance for an excursion to the volcano. While some sat chatting over breakfast and others remained cocooned in their bedrolls, Huldar took his cup outside. He squinted at the sun through an early morning fog. By midday there might be enough heat to turn snow into slush, but until then the going would be passable.

He swigged the last of his tea and started back.

Let's go now, he whispered to Andel.

Her surge of amusement surprised him. He thought dread might have been more appropriate. But when he stepped back into the tent she directed his gaze to a lumpy pile of bedding at the rear of the marquee.

Malena and Ariben?

Banga saw him looking and shook his head. "Once she's set her sights on someone …" he muttered.

Kira laughed quietly. "Six weeks? Must be a tough nut to crack."

"So to speak …"

"Let's hope they *are* tough," Minna said snidely. "He'll not last otherwise!"

She's already followed the rules with a couple of the Host ... Sari whispered.

Andel seemed mystified.

Huldar raised his shoulders. *The twenty-seven rules?*

Sari blushed. *You haven't heard that one before?*

Andel's cheeks flamed. She stifled an embarrassed giggle.

Come on, Huldar said. *Out of there and get dressed. We can go now while they're distracted.*

Maybe I'm hoping for a few rules to be read for myself! She wiggled her eyebrows suggestively and pulled the bedroll higher.

He shook his head. *Today's the day.*

She made a moue of disappointment. While she pulled on warm clothes, Huldar went to speak to Casco.

"We're going to the volcano," he said quietly.

Casco frowned. "Why are you telling me?"

"Because I trust you. I need to talk to the planet and that's where we spoke to her last."

"Foolish idea." Casco glanced to where Ariben was emerging from Malena's spacious bedroll. "You know how unpredictable the weather is."

Foolish?

Casco returned to him. A spark of anger lit his haze. *What? So anyone can speak their mind except me?*

Of course not. Huldar struggled to maintain a neutral aspect. *Are you angry with me?*

Of course not, Casco echoed, a tad too courteously.

Huldar stopped himself from making an irritated retort. Casco was no doubt still upset that some of the miners had refused to work with him. The gang-leaders had been disciplined, and he and Casco would talk about it when Casco was ready, but until then there was no use digging for it. He looked briefly at Daric Enna. He suspected he hadn't taken the miner's attitude too well either.

If we're not back by mid-afternoon, he said levelly, *best come looking.*

Casco bowed with exaggerated respect.

Huldar scowled, then Daric glanced their way and he stifled another flash of annoyance. If Casco was upset about something – something to do with him – why couldn't he just say?

What's happened? Andel asked.

Nothing to worry about, he replied, glad all eyes were elsewhere.

She gave him an arch look.

As they slipped from the tent, Ariben left his bed and another round of ribald comments began.

Their first step across the valley lifted Huldar's spirits. Spellbound by the beauty of the wilderness, he didn't notice the faint shimmer of the expert screen that followed. As they moved on, it waited a short time before stepping through the gate behind them.

"Phew!" Andel paused to take a breath as they climbed. *I thought the weather had warmed, but if this wasn't such hard work we'd be frozen already.*

Huldar looked up from the rock-strewn ridge before them. He knew they were going in the right direction – but how accurately was another thing. *After that last eruption … everything looks different.*

Andel started again, hiking steadily behind him.

It's probably not critical that we find the exact site, he went on, *or at least I don't think so. Just so long as we're in the same area.*

A flash of annoyance stung his mind.

What now?

And if you don't make contact? she said. *It's colder than I thought. I don't want to wait around all day while you keep trying.*

You wanted to come, Huldar snapped. *You suggested it in the first place.*

Silly me.

One foot followed another as they toiled up ridge. At last he felt a hint of familiarity and closed his eyes to listen. A light breeze sifted ice crystals downslope. Life was slow to get going where the freeze held sway, but he could sense a certain hum.

What now? Andel asked.

He took a small shelter from Qalān, a new design with an outer skin charmed to prevent ice and snow from sticking. *Wouldn't these have been handy last time? Here, you take this corner.*

They drew the leather sheet over flexible supports and sang it tightly down. He conjured a small fire but the warmth was slow to take effect.

You're no Rukh, are you? Andel said.

I can't be good at everything, he said crossly.

Here, let me …

With a deft flick of her mind, Andel turned his feeble effort into a respectable blaze.

Something Rosheen showed me, she said proudly. *Pretty good, don't you think?*

Excellent, he agreed. *Somehow, I can never get my head around the trick of it.*

Never mind, she said magnanimously. *There are other things you do reasonably well.*

She shared a wicked grin and he snorted a laugh. She shuffled around to get under his arm and he held her close.

You seem … better, he said. *Smoother inside …?*

I am, a little. Something Sari said – it helped me gain perspective.

She's old and wise.

Not that old! Andel said. *If you're nice to me, I won't tell her you said that!*

Please, don't! We'd be lost without her.

Lost without her, Andel echoed cheekily.

They laughed together and for the first time in a long while he felt everything would be all right.

I love you, she said. *Now go. Do what you came to do. Be strong. I'll be here, watching over you until you return.*

He gave her a last fond kiss. *I love you too.* Then, taking strength from the warmth of their small, private world, he stilled his soul. A long exhalation triggered his drift, and soon their tiny tent was a small spark of brightness, like a star in the dark, as he sank toward the planet's core.

Be nothing so that I may see your shape, she had said at their last meeting. With effort, he let his wants and desires dissipate.

124

The sound of his heartbeat faded. The rhythmic roar of his body's breathing receded until the sound was little more than the wash of a distant ocean against a long, curving shore.

Please – once more I need your help ... he whispered.

Another phrase circled his mind – *Love is the one true beacon* ...

He filled himself with love – his feelings for his wife, his feelings for the planet itself, and let it shine like a beacon from his soul.

I am here ... he said, amazed at how complete and truly present he felt.

She arrived without warning. A rush of psychic wind set him adrift in her vastness, and he fought to keep his awareness anchored.

Her words came in short verses and he clutched at them like falling gems ... *What is born must die ... The Breath of El, a tapestry of which I am but a single thread ... you ask for my help, yet it is I who will suffer ... Breath's hub is unbalanced. The broken circle comes near ... songs of life cease ... the heart is empty ... Watchers lost ...*

The lines flowed faster until he could not hold them. Fear rose like ale in a glass, but the fear was not his. He fought to stay afloat. To put his questions into words seemed impossible, so he drew forth an image of Lind. He saw her smile again, and his heart clenched. He had not known the extent of the sorrow he still held. In life, her smile had seemed a badge of eternal confidence. He now knew it had been merely a protective shell.

As the planet absorbed her image, the question he needed to ask finally coalesced ... *Is Qalān a living force?*

The planet slowed and seemed to consider.

You ask the impossible, she replied at last. *The weight of thought, the tapestry of threads … All are one in the Breath. We fight. Darkness comes, my dear friend. Treasure the light until the light of knowing blows through you. Lind has gone … One, two, three … measurements of time remaining …*

Is there danger?

Danger? El breathes and we roll, tumbling on the path he has blown. What then is danger? The white reborn … The Black held in the grip of time …

What should I do? How can I protect my team, my loved ones?

Beloved, yes … and such they will be. She mused for a time then a gust of anger rocked his being. He was buffeted by images of the host, the Uri'madu, and others he did not know.

Go! Get away! Flee now, she cried. He saw a mean-eyed Ashik with a terrible scar, a navigator's face twisted in pain, and ethereal beauty clad in a glorious mask of glowing Marks whom he recognised as the current Kaskarudjan, Kariiel Enna. *We fight although the battle is lost,* the Marked one murmured, *but what of the war?*

As if from a great distance, he heard Andel's call, *Huldar! Come back!*

But how will I keep them safe? he cried. *How will I know what to do?*

A bell chimed and his confusion came to rest, carried away on that one pure note. Perhaps his question had been the correct one.

I will be with you, she said. *I will never leave you. Listen and I will guide you. I will be your shield you when there is no one else, and give you strength to do what must be done.*

Huldar! Please – wake up.

He could hear Andel, feel her anxiety, but the planet's bell still rang in his soul and he couldn't respond – not yet.

"Wrap him in a blanket," another voice said. Was the voice familiar? Who else was there? Was this part of the danger? He struggled to surface.

"We'll have to carry him back."

"No, wait," Andel murmured. "I felt something."

There was a long sigh, an exhalation of pent anxiety, then, "Breath be praised!"

"Finally!"

When he recognized Daric Enna's voice his first response was alarm, but inside him, the bell toned calmly. Reassured, he released his fear and the way to full consciousness opened.

The planet's presence receded. He gazed into Andel's eyes and her love flooded in, warming him right to his toes.

Daric gave a delicate cough.

Huldar let go a soft sigh. *How did he get here?* The connection between himself and his wife was so strong at that moment it was hard to divorce thought from speech, so he mouthed the words as he sent them.

"I don't rightly know," she replied.

His body ached. Outside, he sensed lengthened shadows. It had been late morning when they'd set up the shelter, but now it was afternoon.

She stroked his face. "You were gone so long. Your body was cold and stiff. I started to panic. I was just about to call for help when Daric turned up. Gave me quite a start."

He struggled into an upright position and turned to Daric. "You followed us?"

The Enna looked away as if composing a reply, then seemed to think the better of it. He returned his gaze clearly. "I did."

"Why?"

"I wondered what you were doing," he admitted.

"You could have asked," Huldar said. "Does Casco know?"

"I haven't said anything."

"He didn't ask you to follow us?"

"Of course not!" Daric said. "There are some things we don't share. There are times when I need space. It's testing to be with the same people every minute of every day … when you're not accustomed to it."

"It's a trial sometimes even when you are," Huldar conceded.

"Don't be too hard on him," Andel said. "He was willing to do whatever he could to save your life. He has some healing ability – did you know?"

Huldar shook his head. *Full of surprises*, he said privately.

"We are a team now," Daric said. "Whatever is necessary, I will do. Did you speak with her?"

"Yes," Huldar said cautiously, "but it will take time to process."

"Is Qalān alive?"

Huldar tried to process the planet's words, but the effort was beyond him. "I still don't know." He turned to Andel. "She mentioned Lind."

"Lind?" Andel said. "She knew who she was?"

"She remembers," he said sadly. "She remembers everything."

Andel gave him a long look then pushed herself toward the door. "Time to get home," she said briskly.

Daric collapsed the tent. Cold hit him with bone-chilling intensity.

"A little more warning would have been nice," he complained.

Daric extended his arm. "Can you walk?"

Huldar nodded, but he accepted Daric's help in getting to his feet. "It's all downhill from here. I think I'll be all right – just need to get the circulation going."

Thick layers of clothing kept them from actually touching, but in the moment they faced each other it was as if he could see the darkness hidden beneath the assassin's expert veils.

Daric nodded as if a message had passed between them.

Andel started down the ridge. "Come on! Bad weather coming."

"There always is," Daric murmured.

As they threaded down the slope every step Huldar took was clumsy and painful. He listened for the sound the planet had implanted in him, but all he could hear was his own rasping breath and the crunch of snow.

THE TROUBLE WITH RULES

Huldar's legs stumbled at the limit of endurance as they labored through slush. Exhausted by his ordeal in the heart of the planet, and with Andel supporting him so closely, it made sense to let Daric sing them through the portals. There was a difference in style but the steps were confidently read and pitch perfect.

Huldar's relief at the sight of their marquee was difficult to hide, but after a short way he paused. Something was different. Then he noticed a broad trail in the melting snow and a screen set to cover the mouth of a nearby gully.

"Are you all right?" Andel murmured.

"Of course," he answered.

"Nearly home," Daric said.

"What's happening over there?" he asked.

"A few more paces and we're done," Daric said smoothly. "I've alerted the Naghari."

"There's probably no need," he said irritably. "I'm just tired."

He lurched from their support and went toward the disturbance.

What are you doing? Andel said crossly.

"The Rukh train every day," Daric said hurriedly.

"Yes, I know that," Huldar said. "So why the screen?"

He pushed through into the impromptu practice area. In the shelter of the rocks was a small flat area with a sandy floor cleared of snow. Near the entrance, Malena of Maatu sparred hand-to-hand with Ariben. Despite the intense cold she was clad only in loose pants with a tight sleeve around her upper torso to keep her breasts in place. It was clear her abilities far outstripped Ariben's and although what they were doing might have been in some way instructive, there was a lot of body contact involved.

Beyond them, three swordsmen, also naked to the waist, followed Rosheen's movements through a series of exercises. "Progressing the forms", he thought it was called. One of the participants was smaller and less massive than the Rukh, but barefoot in the slush, no foot misplaced, Casco had his own, deadly grace. There was no sign of the close-held apology or self-doubt that had always seemed the governors of his life.

Looks like he's done that before, Andel said appreciatively. *Sari said he was handsome, but I don't think I've seen it till now.*

He shouldn't be here.

Why not? He's trained with Gento and Cobar before.

He'd known that Casco had a blade, and while they were on assignment the Rukh had given him a little education with it. When it was just them, the Uri'madu, it didn't matter, but now, with the Host's encampment right on their doorstep …

The Host! It's forbidden for a half-breed to own a sword or train in any sort of combat.

Daric touched his arm.

He turned to snap, but the Enna's expression held an anger so deep it transcended insult and was instead a gift – an insight into the hidden soul Huldar thought he'd glimpsed earlier.

"We trained together on Haas." Daric's jaw clenched as if the decision to speak had been a difficult one. "Rukh have relaxed the rules." He stripped off his heavy coat. "Casco is a hero."

"A hero?"

"To those who matter."

To those who matter? Huldar repeated. What hadn't Casco told him? Were they no longer friends? Surely the many years and dangers faced together could not be discounted so easily?

Daric shed the rest of his upper clothing. As he turned to join the workout, Huldar was struck by the many faint scars that seamed his back. Malena eyed him also but he strode past without acknowledgment. After a short bow to Rosheen, the assassin took a fine-bladed sword from Qalān and entered the line. The disciplined progression continued without a glitch.

Huldar was not sure whether to be sad or angry … or both.

What should I do? he asked Andel.

Leave them, she urged. *You're too tired to think straight. Talk about it later, when you've rested.*

He bowed his head and followed her back to the marquee. Daric's dark expression remained like a shadow on his mind. Where had the anger – and the tangled invitation to know him better – come from? What did it mean? But in the recesses of his soul, the bell tolled peace, and when Andel led him to their blankets, its soft tones carried him swiftly to sleep.

The next morning, he woke before the sun. A quick scan told him Casco was also awake. The need to say something tormented him. Their friendship was fragile, but Casco had already been targeted by bigoted members of the Host, and if Olatu discovered he'd been training with the Rukh the backlash would be hard to control.

He slithered from his bedroll without waking Andel.

Casco's eyes glinted in the light of the coals.

Could we have a moment, please? he asked. It was too cold to go outside, so he indicated the far corner of marquee, where their current workstation was set up.

With a sigh of annoyance, his friend left the warmth of his bedroll. He sat at the end of the bench and studied him with narrowed gaze. *What's this about?*

Huldar was certain he was well aware. *I need to talk to you about rules.* He pictured what he had seen. *If it was just us – why would I mind? You are my friend ... more than just a friend. But if any of the Host see you or catch on to what you're doing ...*

You'll look bad?

No! That's not what I meant. They'll imprison you, shave your head – who knows what – They're an ignorant lot and that's for sure. But when we get home? The penalty? People – your people – have been killed.

Indignation sparked in Casco's eyes.

It's not fair, I know...

What do you know? Casco stood up. *How could you even begin to know?*

All right, Huldar pleaded. *I'm not considered a half-breed, but technically I sort of am one. And I do know right from wrong, and right now it's wrong for you to be involved in martial training.*

Casco's haze bristled. It was a shock to see such anger. He tried to project understanding but he could not back down. Casco's safety depended on it. At least he'd been favored with some show of emotion. He would have felt even worse if his friend had veiled it.

Am I clear? he pressed.

Yes. Perfectly clear, Casco snarled. *I'm done with being your pet aberration, the token you use to demonstrate Lethian 'open mindedness'! No so open now, is it!*

Huldar let his hurt show. *I thought you'd understand ...* but Casco seemed impervious.

I've learned more in seven years with Daric than I learned in five hundred with you, he cried. *And ask yourself why. Is it because you know less? I don't think so, Sir Sacred to Leth! He wants me to learn. He wants me to be someone, to realize my potential.* He glowered at Huldar. *Be all a dis time an barely even speakin de lingo true.*

I want you to achieve things too. I've never held you back!

Casco's expression was unconvinced. Memories of Huldar's caution when it came to bending increasingly draconian edicts flitted across his veil.

But it's not my law! Huldar cried. *It's not me making the rules. It's the Imperium. The Tiamäti. And Daric's one of them.*

As soon as the words were out, he wished he could take them back.

"I shouldn't have said that," he said humbly, but Casco withdrew his anger behind a perfect veil. His haze lost its ruddy glare – a feat Huldar was not sure even he could replicate.

"I apologize," Huldar said again. "Whatever else he is, Daric Enna is a brilliant thinker and a valuable member of the Uri'madu."

Casco fixed his gaze on a point slightly below Huldar's face. "Is there anything else, sir?"

He sighed. "As it turns out, there is something else," he said awkwardly. "I want to organize a memorial for Lind. I thought that we should meet at the place she died – among the stones. I – I was hoping to hear your thoughts."

His mind reached out, hopeful of a shred, some small concession.

"My thoughts?" Casco said stonily.

Briefly, Huldar feared he would turn and leave without reply, but after a long moment he took a breath and said, "It will mean more to the originals than the newcomers."

"What about some time next week?" Huldar suggested. Outside, the first rays of dawn drew steam from the frost that encased the marquee. "If the weather clears we'll be ahead of schedule."

Casco nodded sharply. "Will that be all?"

"No, I mean, yes. That's it."

For a moment Casco studied him. Almost, there was a touch of leeway, but then he returned to his bed and yanked his covers up.

Inside, Huldar felt like crying. Casco had been through a lot – so much he had yet to learn of, more than enough to fuel lasting rage. Was it just that he was a safe target to vent at? Their friendship had once been the mainstay of his life. Now, it seemed lost forever.

MEMORY AND HONOR

On the morning of the visit to the place of Lind's last song, Huldar woke to the sound of Tam and Arko's hushed discussion as they labored over the cook fires. He disentangled himself from Andel's arms and went to see what they were making. At the end of the long bench Arko doled out another tray of honey-cakes into a bowl already near full. An array of containers filled the space beyond it. By the cook fire, Tam flicked a whisk through a creamy, sweet-smelling mixture while it simmered.

"What's this?" Huldar asked.

"Onder-kush," Tam replied. His whisk never slowed.

Arko lifted the lid of a shallow blue crock and the air was filled with fragrant steam. "Hamarsi rolls with strips of grilled kanth," he said. He pointed to a plump red bowl. "This one's merindi, and this one here is talemgal seasoned with caluma."

"We've done poached cansheys," Tam added, "easanberry sauce, and the onder-kush is to go with the saroo tartlets."

Huldar's eyes prickled with sudden tears. "You planned this before we left, didn't you? All Lind's favorites …"

"And not a fragment of little attar to be seen," said Tam.

Arko handed him one of the rolls. "Here, try one."

His teeth bit into crust with a perfect crunch. The kanth lifted the last of the morning fog from his head, but it was difficult to swallow past the lump in his throat.

"I can't think too much about it," Tam said, "or I'll start crying too." He pointed to a large pot at the other end of the bench. "That's breakfast."

Huldar filled his bowl with soft cooked grains, drizzled it with honey and runny cheese and went outside to wait for the sunrise. He could feel Andel nestled in his mind and knew she was dreaming.

Slowly the song of the day began – first the piping undernotes of myriad small creatures, then the cautious unfurling of green life as it cracked through frost, awakened by the call of the light. For a wonder, there was no fog, and red-gold skies faded through yellow to the crisp blue of a perfect spring morning. The planet's bell was faint but clear, as if all was in harmony with its desires.

At last, Andel stirred. He answered her query with a sense of his location, but there was no rush for them to join each other. Today was to be a day of peace dedicated to the memory of their fallen sister.

I've never heard you call her that before, Andel said.

Maybe I never truly understood it till now.

He let his senses range for a feel of what the weather might bring. To the west, a storm was brewing, and with the sun's power on the increase, it might become quite fierce – but he didn't feel it would strike until later in the afternoon.

To the east, the sleeping volcano glistened. It seemed amazing that only six days earlier they'd climbed her side and he'd spoken to the planet. He certainly didn't feel more sacred.

In the valley below, snow cover was reduced to occasional blobs between fast-growing clumps of vegetation. Closer to home, snow-drifts remained between the weathered boulders on the plateau's edge, but not so deep that they couldn't enjoy today's picnic. He recalled the scene when they'd found Lind's body – the shock of grief, the navigator's late arrival. So cold, and so very sad.

Andel emerged from the marquee and slipped her arm beneath his coat.

Listen … He cocked his head. *Can you hear it?*

Hear what?

He directed her senses toward a staccato concert of tiny snaps and pops.

She smiled. *What is it?*

New shoots. They gather energy as the warmth hits them, then crack through the frost. I don't know of another world where it makes that noise.

By late morning, the feast was ready. Tam and Arko loaded everyone with food and drink and led them in solemn procession to the clearing by the rocks. Huldar and Andel spread rugs and cushions around a long low trestle. When all was in order the company gathered in a loose semi-circle around the monolith where Lind had chosen to end her life's song.

Remnant drifts glittered blue and white in the shadows. The aroma of Lind's favorite foods mixed with the fresh fragrance of small pink flowers that nodded shyly through the snow. Clicker-bugs made their first experimental clacks in sheltered, sun-warmed places.

Huldar turned to Sari. In her hands she cradled Lind's work-worn boots.

Are you ready? he asked gently.

After a long glance skyward, she nodded.

With her eyes on the rock, she went toward it, step by step, but then she looked down at the boots and stopped. The Uri'madu waited for her to continue, but she hugged them close and seemed unable to move.

Andel went to stand at her side, then Casco followed. One by one, the rest of the company followed suit.

"You can put them down now, Sari," Casco murmured gently.

"… When you're ready," Andel said through tears.

Sari took the last steps and slowly lowered the boots into place at the foot of the rock, then she stood up and gave them a deep bow before returning to Andel's side.

Huldar gave a sad smile as a clicker-bug crawled across one toe and went to explore inside. "So, you think we've left you a nice new home?"

He bent to remove the invader, but Sari stopped him. "It's all right. She liked the clickers."

Tam crouched to touch the broken clip. "I should have fixed it for her."

Casco sighed. "I think about it sometimes, how strange it was we found them."

"Shoes clothe the foot as the body clothes the soul," Daric said thoughtfully. "Maybe by the time she was found, her spirit was already tied to the Breath too strongly … torn between two states of being. Perhaps the loss of her boots symbolized the purification already under way."

Andel turned to him. "If that's what purification involves … the price is unbearable."

"Are you saying we shouldn't have found her?" said Huldar.

"Not at all!" said Daric. "But from the little I know, it just strikes me as sad … to be so alone."

They moved back while Gento and Cobar made seven small fires to encircle the area.

Huldar stepped between the flames and looked up at the infinite skies. Memories of her final song filled him. He saw her again, a smile and a wave as she tramped into the unknown, the special look she had when studying a new specimen, and the pain in her heart when he told her he wasn't in love with her. He placed his forehead against the rock. "Lind," he breathed against it. "I'm so sorry."

He turned to the crew. "Lind was our friend and comrade. We loved her and cared for her, but she is gone." He faced the skies once more. "I loved you for your spirit. Keep safe in the Breath until you are ready to face life again. You will not be forgotten."

He left the circle and Cobar took his place. "You saved my life on Karga-An – but you always cheated at ashut." He took a small carved piece from his pocket and placed it by the boots. "I loved you for that."

Nachiel left a drawing of a flower, and whispered something to the stone, then Tam left a gift of honey-cakes. Slowly, others took their place among the fires and paid their respects.

When all were done, there was a lengthy silence.

Rosheen cleared her throat. "I ... have a short poem," she said, "in the style of Nomen Rukh, an ancient leader of our House ... If you don't think it inappropriate?"

"Of course not," Huldar said.

She took her place within the circle, bowed to the boots and turned.

"*Frost coats the shadows,*" she said solemnly. "*Bright stains ripple our dreaming hearts ... A lost song finds Breath.*" On a small paper, she had written out the poem with meticulous care. This she placed with the other gifts left by the rock. "I wish I'd had the opportunity to know you," she said, then with another ceremonious bow, she rejoined the onlookers.

Slowly, the Uri'madu drifted away until only Huldar and Casco remained.

"Remember the time you put creeper-vine in her bedroll?" Huldar said.

Casco smiled sadly. "Never seen someone move so fast. But what sticks with me most is that time we took her to see the Went."

Huldar nodded. "I'll never forget it ... when they bowed to her." He shared his memory of the huge shaggy beast rearing up to display its colored underbelly.

"Her face," Casco said. "No fear, only wonder."

"Then it bent down as if it was bowing and began to drone. Remember that sound?"

"It was as if they knew," Casco agreed. "Maybe Daric is right. There was a purity to her when she was returned to us …" He turned to laughter and the clink of bottles. "Come on. She'd be horrified if we let this feast go to waste."

"Or the besh."

Casco gave him a smile, and Huldar was suddenly happier than he thought he should be.

"Saroo tartlets?" he said. "She'd think it a wish come true."

THE WENT

After a rare string of fine days, it was another bright morning. Tam emerged from the dome that still covered their marquee and joined Huldar outside.

Huldar smiled in greeting. "Nice to see you out of doors."

"Couldn't resist." Tam looked up at a china-blue sky. "Weather turning at last?"

"I think so."

"Are you enjoying the new menu?" the cook said. "I haven't had a chance to ask."

"Since you're interested," Huldar started solemnly. "About last night's goranda stew ..."

"Casserole," Tam interjected.

"Casserole, then ... it was a triumph."

Tam's face lit up. "Really?"

He nodded.

"Well! That's good isn't it?" Tam rubbed his hands together. "It was a bit of a break with tradition, ordering all that variety, but Casco asked me to be a bit creative with my meal plans and it's certainly made things more interesting. You don't miss little attar?"

"Sometimes." He winced. "But don't tell anyone. I think I'm the only one."

Tam winked. "We do have some. I'll see what I can do." He looked at Huldar's empty hands. "Where are you off to today? You don't need a lunch-pack?"

There's a valley I'm keeping an eye on, to the north. I suspect it may be where the Went are hibernating, but no sign of them yet."

"Going alone?" Tam seemed rightly scandalized.

Huldar gave him a rueful smile. "On my own more often than not right now, with everyone so busy. I won't take any undue risks, and Andel always knows where I am. Expect me back about midday."

Ten minutes later, he stepped from a windy valley onto an undulating plain hidden among the mountains of the Central Continent and walked briskly to his favorite vantage point – a low hill overlooking a picturesque lake. Its surface had thawed more quickly than expected and he'd since discovered a region of geothermal activity further along the river's course, although as far as he could tell there were no active volcanos nearby. As the thaw progressed, snow-melt boosted the flow, but the waterfalls pouring down the rugged mountainside still steamed hot from the springs above.

A little further north, over a jutting ridge and just beyond natural sight, lay another valley, broad and flat. In overview, the area seemed no more than another flood-plain, however, its northern edge was seamed with vein-like canyons, slotted like a maze of roads into steep foothills, and it was only from the ground its true grandeur was evident.

The canyon walls themselves were pock-marked with caves – honeycombed with them – some so vast they must have their own internal weather systems. But there were smaller ones that resembled tunnels and he wondered if perhaps they were.

Huldar pictured the Went trail. It began as a wide swathe leading from the Circular Sea into the mountains, then meandered unbroken around the entire continent until it reached the valley of caves. The trail narrowed as it progressed, most markedly after it crossed the mouth of the Circular Sea – a feat only achievable in early spring or late autumn when falling sea-levels cut it off from the outer oceans.

One of the larger tunnels from the valley of caves showed signs of wear around its edges, and on the other side of the ranges he'd discovered a narrow trail that led from a similarly worn opening down to the circular sea, where the bel nishani beached. This fueled his suspicion the sea creatures were a larval form of Went. Andel had not had time to assess the tunnels on either side of the ranges yet, but when she did, he was sure she'd find the two were linked and the trail led in an unbroken circuit from this valley.

Another very small branch led from the valley of caves to this one and terminated at the waterfall before him. It was the only time the path diverged.

Maybe the lake was a destination for the Went too, if the valley of caves was indeed their home. With the thaw gaining pace, surely they would show themselves soon.

With a last look at the lake and its spectacular falls, he retraced his steps to the portal and stepped through to a cold and windy position on a mountainside above the valley of caves. The position had a commanding view of the terrain, and happened to be right above the mouth of the tunnel with suspiciously polished sides.

He shaded his eyes to do a visual scan. The snow at the canyon mouths seemed undisturbed, but when he listened carefully, the local song had developed distinct variations. *At last!* His inner smile blossomed. The change could only have come from the presence of sizable creatures. They were there, and beginning to stir!

The strongest emanations came from the southern flank of the valley wall, almost a mile away.

He scrambled down the slope, keen to get a closer look.

As he swished through the hardy vegetation on the valley floor, his trouser-legs were soon sodden to the knee.

Closer to the southern edge, the microclimate was more temperate. The green tendrils pushing sunward with such enthusiasm were already under attack from a clicker-bug variant. Perhaps as the melt progressed there would be flying slugs there too. There was a sting on his cheek and he flicked a blood-sucking insect from his face. The Went must definitely be about to emerge – there would be little else for the tiny parasites to feed on.

As he neared the source of the vibrations, what had seemed to be a solid valley wall turned out to be a warren of ravines and grottos. Some were open and empty, but within the gully-sides he sensed many chambers sealed shut with rocks and mud. The Went were tantalizingly close, but after seven years of freeze, their dens were difficult to see.

Eight days later, Huldar asked Andel to make a breathing-space in her schedule and stepped her through to the vantage point above the lava-tube entrance.

His heart leaped to see shaggy backs filling the valley.

Look! Andel cried. *How many do you think there are?*

Five or six hundred? No! There's another group over there. Maybe a thousand. More than I thought there'd be. There must be groups apart from the one we saw last time.

The Went used their long noses as well as their prehensile fore-feet to tear fronds from the trees and stuff them into their mouths. By the intensity of their focus he guessed they must be hungry indeed.

Do you think this is the entire population?

As far as I can tell, he answered. *Do you see how they're grouped according to coat-color?*

On the boundary between the ginger group and the browns, a huge ginger reared up to show its under-belly. The largest brown pushed forward and stood to face it.

"Wae-e-e-en't!" the creatures bellowed to each other, then they touched noses in what seemed for all the world like a joyful reunion.

Andel laughed aloud and the brown one turned. Its trunk poked the air as if searching for her scent, then it dropped to its knees, placed its forehead on the ground and began to drone. When she stood to get a better look, a wave of copy-cat behavior ensued. The Went bent like a field of grain in the wind and the sound they made filled the valley with a sound so deep they could feel it through their feet.

His spine tingled. *I think they've seen us.* He smiled.

What's the display of patterns all about? she asked. *And that noise …*

Thrilling, isn't it? he said. Through their bond he could feel she was also moved by the display.

Do you think it's a sexual thing? she asked.

I'm not sure. It seems to be more about status, and the droning might be a herd thing, a bonding behavior.

After a time, the Went resumed feeding, but although they seemed settled he fancied he could feel their attention, noting every move.

I haven't seen anything that looks like mating, he said, *have you?*

Andel watched as avidly as he did. *No, but over there, see the ones with a blue tinge to their fur?*

Oh yes, he said. *It's a much smaller group than the rest. Possibly some still in hibernation?*

They seem awfully round compared to the others. Perhaps they're pregnant.

He sharpened his vision and saw that the blue-tinged faction were indeed quite plump.

Well spotted! he said. *These could be females. We'll make an ecologist of you yet.*

She grinned. *Must be the Lethian influence. See how the others move aside to give them the best food? Isn't that sweet?*

Maybe, but social etiquette must have survival value. The blues must have great importance. He turned to her excitedly. *Perhaps they are the only females … that might explain it.*

One of the blues lifted her trunk and made a plaintive call. This seemed to be a signal for her sisters to separate from the others, and with much droning and display the small group started for mountains.

The leader seems thinner than the others, Andel noted.

She smiled when he studied more closely and saw she was right.

They are so beautiful, she said. Her overwhelming surge of affection for the enigmatic creatures filled him also, but it sparked a wave of fear. He visualized Duvät Gok and the long beach.

With so few mothers, their breeding patterns may be fragile. We can't let any more be killed.

And if you're wrong and the sea-creatures are not related to the Went?

To wear the eyes of a living being as ornaments? He didn't bother to stifle his disgust. *I know they'll try. But I've been watching the portal to the beach and no one's been there yet.*

Let's hope it stays that way.

I wish I could close the area down, he said, *but I don't think it's possible to un-make a portal.*

Entranced by the curiously gliding movement of the Went, they watched the blues wander slowly down the mountain path until they disappeared beneath an overhang. Huldar glanced up at the sun. It was getting late and they had things to do. With a last look at the placid herd, they turned and stepped through the portal behind them.

Andel followed as Huldar picked his way over emergent vegetation. The next portal shimmered in the distance, clearly visible to him over the stubbled ground, but more distant than it appeared.

He picked up his pace.

So much still to do before the rest of the Host arrive! said Andel. *I'm glad the miners have decided to relocate to that eastern site with the new Djan'rū. Cooler now but when the summer comes on they'll be glad of it.*

More room for them, Huldar said, *and since we're staying put, more room for us. Topper and Bush are there now. The Host's so-called water-finders are hopeless. Then there's the latrines and waste management – subbed out to a Cantori concern with no experience whatsoever. Sari and Casco are familiar enough with the local ecology to guide them, but after the trouble with that mine-boss I might have to send Ronnin in his place.*

Could one or two of the spinners do the job?

They've had about as much experience as the Cantori mob. And besides, I'm not sure how far they'd follow my authority. They still look to Malena for leadership.

Understandable, I suppose, but really it's up to you. You should be more forceful.

He grunted. *Easier said than done. And Alis and Ubaid? Completely overwhelmed.* "It's ludicrous. I have no idea how the Faythans got away with it. There should be a whole posse of healers to their Host."

"Lucky Sari knows a bit about food and medicinals," Andel said. "Isn't she taking a team out some time next week? Some of the local herbs are staring to emerge. I hope they send a few more Healers with the next wave. They'll have to!" She paused to pick her way over a rough piece of ground. "There's Daric, of course, although he's no Naghari. And perhaps you should ask Malena. The Maatu are often multi-talented. Maybe she has some healing skills."

Huldar nodded, but the thought of asking Malena for anything was daunting.

"I'm taking Daric with me to assess the thaw on the Eastern Continent," he said. "He wants to learn about making new portals."

Andel glanced across her shoulder at him. "He's been with you on a few assignments now."

"Feel better if I know what he's up to."

"It hurts me to see you and Casco at odds."

"I thought – at the ceremony at the stones ..." Huldar said. "He seemed not so angry."

A surge of mixed emotions flooded between them.

"Perhaps if you get Daric onside," she suggested. "He and Casco are so close."

"It's hard to see someone take your place," he said ruefully.

"Maybe that's it," she said, "or part of it. Maybe when we got together he felt left out. You'd been friends for so long ..."

"He was the one who insisted on 'giving us space'!" Huldar said crossly.

"Hmm," she mused. "But think, Huldar, the system that supports us oppresses Casco. Somehow, Daric is closer to that oppression – as if he's been directly disadvantaged by it. I don't know for sure, but there's something about his manner. They share an anger. A seed splits its shell in order to grow ... Maybe his friendship with Daric has given him confidence to speak his mind – to seek to understand where he fits and no longer simply accept."

Huldar recalled the glimpse of black rage Daric had shared. Could Casco harbor an equal anger? If so, his inner shell must be deep and thick indeed, because he'd never suspected it. Did that make him a bad friend ...?

The portal hummed before them. *Perhaps you're right,* he sighed.

Andel shrugged. "Of course I'm right. Sari thinks so too. She's very wise, you know."

"Is everyone talking about it?"

Andel snorted. "They would be, but Malena makes brisk competition. She and Ariben – I heard Banga's organizing bets on how long it'll last. Two golds and you're in, winner takes all."

"Gambling?" He looked up, grimacing at the sky. "What next! What will the Overlord have to say about that!"

"Ask him," she said pertly. "He's an optimist. Put his coin on the full three years."

He shook his head. Of course, the Overlord was Gok, but how had the rest of his crew been infected with this disease?

"It's a joke," Andel said. "It's not real … and I haven't yet," she answered his unspoken question, "but I'd like to. You should too. Bonding and all that? Might help with the spinners?"

"Is that what Sari says?" he said sarcastically.

"It's what I say!"

She caught his hands and drew him in for a quick hug. Affection surged between them but before it could become full-fledged desire she pushed him away. "I'd best get back. And don't you have an appointment to keep?"

He kissed her goodbye and watched as she vanished. It still sent shivers through him to see her disappear into Qalān, but that was something he chose not to share.

SECRETS

On the Eastern Continent, Huldar hunched himself against the wind that flew unimpeded across the barren plain. Ice crystals swept the surface in feathered patterns. A dark figure crouched a short distance away as if feeling for a song of place. It stood and lifted a mitt-covered hand in greeting. He wondered how long Daric Enna had been there. He was keen to learn if nothing else.

"Easier to feel with bare skin," Huldar said. "Sometimes the mind is not enough on its own … even yours."

Daric conceded the point with a small snort. "There's a hub here, of course, and I think I see one about two hundred paces over there." He pointed east.

"Show me what you see."

With a short nod, Daric shared his view of several faint lines of force converging on the area he'd indicated.

"That's good," Huldar said, "but what color are they? What tone? Such variations can tell you a lot about what's going on – how the chains are linked, what load the gate can bear and whether it will be resistant to manipulation. Let your awareness drift when you look, then half-close your eyes or even close them all together. Eventually, if you let it, your mind will assign color and pitch."

He turned his back to the wind and watched his pupil for progress.

After a while, Daric's haze lost some of its habitual tightness and showed signs of flow, but Huldar knew that unless he could relax and let the vibrations penetrate, the necessary refinement would not come.

Eventually Daric's shoulders slumped. Loose strands of his normally tight-braided hair streamed in the wind. He didn't turn. "I can't do it."

"Yes you can," Huldar said. "But you have to let go. Loosen up. Open yourself to the forces."

Daric looked at him. "It's all right for you."

"Would you like me to show you what I see?" Huldar offered.

You'd trust me?

Is there a reason I shouldn't?

As Daric contemplated a deeper level of sharing, Huldar remembered his astonishing, rage-filled glance. He thought he knew what the problem was, but until his pupil could bring himself to trust another with his secret, he would not advance.

"Normally your business would be your own," Huldar said, "but in this case it has to do with the way your energies interact with those of the immediate environment. Your training can't progress. No amount of personal power can change this. I'm sorry, Daric … Your choice."

"I'm not used to sharing," Daric said at last. "Some things in my past …"

Huldar nodded slowly. "Pieru mentioned as much."

"You know?"

"About your past?" He nodded. "If you're not comfortable talking to me, maybe there's someone else you could discuss it with … Casco?"

"Casco already knows."

Huldar hugged his hands beneath his arms and waited. Daric's stance changed when he'd reached a decision. He seemed taller. His chin lifted. But his veil, normally impenetrably smooth, was marred with turmoil.

"Whatever you think you know …" Daric started, then he paused. "You never said anything."

An icy gust buffeted Huldar's back. "Would you like to go someplace less bitter?"

Daric replaced his mitts and followed him back to the portal.

Moments later, they were back on the temperate central continent and Huldar sighed with relief. They walked a short way to a group of granite boulders, where he shed his heavy-weather gear and settled onto a sun-warmed rock.

After an awkward moment, Daric joined him. He lowered his head into his hands. "I don't know how to start."

"You're an assassin," Huldar said evenly. "Apart from me, is Casco the only one else who knows?"

"Pretty much." He shrugged. "My sister … one or two others. No one here."

"Just start at the beginning," Huldar suggested. "I wouldn't have agreed to have you with us if I thought you posed a danger to my team."

"But you never said – I thought no one knew."

"I hoped you'd tell me in your own time, perhaps when you'd learned more about us." When Daric still floundered, he added, "Just start where the words want to come."

"My mother was a half-breed," Daric said eventually.

"There's no shame in that."

"And I feel none," he said firmly. "She was proud and beautiful, a Marked Shamkarun, claimed by Enna. My father was also Enna. A pure. They fell afoul of a group of Ashik bigots. It didn't end well. My sister and I had to fend for ourselves. Shera – she's a Kareski – was the closest thing to a mother I had after that, apart from my sister. Then Mirashael of Cantori caught me stealing."

"Ahh … so there's more to our new supplier than meets the eye?"

"He looked after me." Daric nodded. "Saw my rage and turned it to good use. Gave me the best of tutors, and when she died I took her place."

"What was her name?" Huldar asked gently.

"You wouldn't know it," he said gruffly. "I'm an assassin, Huldar. So was she." His tawny gaze turned direct. "I'd like to say I *was* but the training never leaves you."

"Why did you join us?"

"Something had to change. The life had lost its challenge. Lesson number one; complacency leads to death. And Casco is the first real friend I've ever had." Daric stood and faced him. "I'm not going to apologize for myself. I'm good at my job – one of the best … but here? I mean no one any harm. I have no reason to hurt you – but if any of the team were threatened …"

"Threatened?"

"I know about Duvät Gok. I know everything. I'm one of the few people who do."

"How?"

"I know about the Eyes of Bel Nishani and what the Imperium will do to get them. Or anyone with a hunger for profit and the God-Emperor's favor. It's a travesty, an abomination, but that won't stop them."

A realization reverberated through Huldar's psyche. He wasn't sure where it came from, but he knew it to be true. *It was you who killed him?*

Daric's eyebrows twitched.

"And now you're on some sort of mission? A crusade? Is that why you're here?"

"I thought my particular skills might make a difference."

Daric's eyes pleaded with him to understand – and here was another gift of truth ... but of all things, an assassin on a quest for some sort of redemption was not what Huldar had expected. He tried to clear his mind. When Daric started to speak again he held up his hand. I'm sorry, Daric. I'm honored by your confidence, but – "

"Enough to process for the minute?"

"Afraid so."

He let his thoughts run until they gathered themselves. "Given your talent, I'd wondered why you aren't Marked, but with such heavy secrets – perhaps too much of your energy has been subverted to their keeping."

Andel's voice came to him, *Is something wrong?*

He replied with a negative and the suggestion she ignore his emotional state for the moment.

"The safety of the Uri'madu is my primary responsibility," he said to Daric at last.

Daric's gaze slipped sideways. He frowned. "I would never hurt you – or any of the Uri'madu. I saved your life on the volcano – or would've."

"I know, and I thank you for it. But I'm still not sure why you followed us in the first place."

"When I first met you and the team, in a way, it was just like another job. I studied and categorized all of you, and most of the Host as well. I already knew what the circumstances would be. I tried to help Casco find the best resources in part because I wanted him to think well of me – as I said, he's the only friend I've ever had. But also because I knew how hard it would be and didn't want to suffer any more than absolutely necessary." He looked around him. "Now?" He raised his shoulders. "I'm part of something. I see much more is possible. I want to belong. Please, give me a chance."

"I will not lie for you," Huldar said firmly.

"The Host are the danger," Daric said. "They'll go for the Eyes; you'll try and stop them. It will get ugly. I'll be of greater use if they don't know about my … other skills."

"As I said, if anyone asks me a direct question, I won't lie … but I won't broadcast it either. It is up to you to tell the Uri'madu, and when you do I'll expect the same from them."

"Thank you, Shamkarun Huldar." Daric bowed low.

Huldar's inner bell chimed as if in approval, but had he done the right thing? He couldn't deny that if the Host tried to harvest more Eyes of Bel Nishani he would do his best to stop them, but the idea that an assassin might be useful in such case made him shudder.

He sensed a fresh lightness in Daric's spirit and looked up to check the position of the sun. The day was wearing on but he couldn't face the return to camp just yet. "Rug up," he said. "Let's go back to the plains. If there's any deeper, darker secrets you haven't yet shared and need to ...?"

The Enna shook his head and began to pull his coat on, ready for their return to the ice.

"If there's any further impediment, it will have to be cleared," Huldar said.

Daric gave him a short bow. "Understood."

Huldar studied the assassin for a moment more. They had definitely made progress, at least on a personal level, and as they stepped back to the unthawed winds of the Eastern Continent he found his enthusiasm for the task ahead had reignited.

HNARSE AND NEETHA

Through the dark of another night, the herd grazed steadily. Hnarse Stargazer watched the movement of the stars and waited. An elder now, it was responsible for many important decisions. The Went's most sacred had shed their burden. The Last Mother had taken up their souls for safekeeping and the Old Mothers had been duly mourned. Now day followed day in restless progression.

When the strange two-legs had been sighted again, Went had sung their presence to the Heart. Hnarse wondered if they were there because the Heart had made it so. They had been sung last cycle, and now again in this one. Did this mean they were now to be regenerated every cycle? Part of Heart's Truth?

Hnarse shook its fur to clear its thoughts – far too deep for so early on the path – and headed for a clump of fresh shoots spied earlier. It plunged its nose among them and breathed deeply. After it had been so long asleep, the spicy green aroma induced light-headed excitement. Small leaves tickled the hairs on its nose in a most delightful way. Then it could wait no longer. With fore-feet and trunk it savaged the bush, pushing food into its mouth as fast as it could chew. Within minutes, the find was denuded, but barely three strides to the left another bunch of fronds awaited.

Over the following weeks, as the lunar progression advanced, Hnarse kept its attention on the skies. First, the shining trail speckled the Web of Ombath, then it moved to the pale cluster of Rufa's Eyes. Hnarse shifted focus to the Roving Star. When the Roving Star had completed its transit of Rufa's Eyes, the season of storms was imminent, and the time of New Purpose was near.

At the evening gathering, Hnarse placed its head on the ground and sang these observations to the Heart.

Wentish excitement grew. Grassmovers followed the patterns of wind and leaves with increased vigilance, and at last it was announced; the Circle of Skies would descend within two turns of Arga, the greater light in the night.

When Neetha, Eldest Grassmover, approached Hnarse, they touched snouts fondly before standing to show the patterns on their underbellies.

When they had given each other's markings due examination, Hnarse waited for the Grassmover's hair to lift. The time was nigh, it was certain. The trail of trials must begin. As elders they must gather the Went for the trek to the sacred shore. This would be their first such duty in this lifetime: a great honor, but also a great responsibility.

Neetha Grassmover's hair rose and fell with crisp animation. "The snouts of the Circle of Winds, Hnarse, they thrill my heart. The first touch on shore – the spume flying up to be embraced by the sun. Such moments I sing to the Heart with greater love." Its hair movement softened. "Such moments take my mind from the confusion I feel concerning the alien two-legs."

The wind blew more strongly and Neetha's expression of sentiment was almost lost. Hnarse replied with a lift of hair it knew would raise the Grassmover's spirits. "May the moments that sing to your soul never be lost, Neetha Grassmover. Such songs bring warmth to the Heart. May you survive this trail and guide the New Purpose to abundant maturity."

"If this next trail completes my circle, yet I will be content," Neetha said. "Although I will miss the beauty of the world while I wait within a mother's care – and I will miss you, my friend."

Hnarse waved its hair in a way that was both melancholy and affectionate. "Come, let us gather the herd and begin the trek. I wonder what joys we will find among the New Purpose this cycle? I remember the last ones, full of grace and resolve."

Humor resonated through Neetha's nose. "Your memory is kind, Hnarse, and my affection flows for you, yet there are always those who will not listen, who do not learn, and face the end of their cycles too soon. Will they never advance?"

"Such ones have their own purpose," said Hnarse. "They show us where we came from, and set an example by teaching others what not to do." The Went's hair lifted in an expression of great amusement. Neetha brushed noses with the longtime friend of its cycles, and together they began to round up the survivors of the previous trail and purification.

Neetha and Hnarse walked side by side on the path as the trek began. There was no rush, but the herd moved forward with clear intent. They must reach the sacred shores in time for the most important event in the Wentish calendar – the New Purpose.

Inside the tunnel they walked between formations polished by the beginnings of countless migrations. There were many new sounds to share and discuss. A river flowed over sandy banks, dimly lit in places through ice that covered a deep crevasse in the mountains above. Water trickled as the ice melted, forming trails in the sand.

Once they'd cleared the darkness there were many tasty herbs and fruits to eat. Elders paused often to sing observations to younger ones, sharing the beauty of their surroundings so no detail would be lost.

Hnarse paused as a paddle-waving clicker-bug leaped clean over its head.

"They are exuberant at this time of year," said Neetha. "Examine the colors on that one. Imagine living with such richness."

"You have such richness, Neetha," Hnarse replied. "Your markings are strong and clear, and your voice shiny indeed."

Neetha's crown-tufts lifted. "Really?"

"Of course. You are an Elder now. One is as one should be."

It gazed at the herd, foraging as it walked. It was important that those in front gave way to those behind, or only the fore-runners would be properly fed. But today, everyone behaved appropriately.

"We have kept a good pace," Neetha said.

"All look forward to the engenderment," Hnarse replied.

"Such a thrill," said Neetha. "We have such good fortune to see it again. A fresh batch of New Purpose to guide and teach?"

Hnarse swirled its hair to mirror Neetha's excitement. "Yet I feel a sense of portent," it added thoughtfully. "The clouds build, the storms come …"

Neetha's hair flattened somewhat. "Yet their force is …"

A sudden gust combed words free.

"The circle is impatient," Hnarse started, but an eddy distorted the shape of its words also. "See how it toys with our ideas? They are blown beyond recapture."

"Ever the thinker!" Neetha said. Its crown-tufts spiked with amusement, but the gesture was softened by the touch of its trunk against Hnarse's side. "Come. We have traveled well so far, but there is much of the trail left to complete before we reach the sacred shores."

"You are right." Hnarse acknowledged Neetha's affection with a caress of its own. "We must be sure to arrive before the Circle of Winds touches the sacred shore, or New Purpose may wander and die unfound."

"Let us hope it will never be so," Neetha replied, and Hnarse agreed. To be lost to the circle was the most terrible of fates.

IT'S A RUKH THING

Although the sun had yet to rise, Tam was already at work in the kitchen preparing breakfast.

On the other side of the marquee, two pairs of eyes shone in the light of the coals. One glanced at the other as Rosheen's consciousness started to rise. Her face moved fitfully, as if already half aware of the leathery strap-tree frond that covered it.

Gento and Cobar grinned in anticipation.

Tam shook his head.

The Rukh ducked for cover as Rosheen leaped from her bed, whispered her sword to hand, and sliced the frond in two. The halves caught alight. Slowly they drifted downward.

Breath's design! she swore.

Gento slapped Cobar's shoulder.

As the flaming fronds landed, she threw her blanket over them, but seconds later two smoldering holes appeared.

"Cobaaar! Gennto!" she bellowed, and with a florid snarl, set upon the embers with her bare feet. At first it appeared she'd been successful, but seconds later they flared again.

The Uri'madu woke to the sight of a naked, sword-wielding Rukh dancing on the floor while Cobar brayed with laughter.

The pungent smell of charred wool filled the tent.

"Enough!" Huldar roared.

Gento could barely work the anti-charm and had to make a second attempt before the flames were snuffed.

"The flying socks were bad enough," Huldar said crossly, "but flames?"

Rosheen wrapped herself in a fresh blanket and glowered.

"Sorry, boss," Gento said, but his grin was poorly hidden. He motioned Cobar and the pair of them bowed to Rosheen.

She held them in a steely gaze. "It's as well to stay sharp in this world of dangers," she said. "I'll be paying extra attention to your own acuity at training, later today." With her free hand she threw the damaged cover at Cobar. "Fix it!"

Gento groaned.

"Breakfast's ready for those who are," Tam announced. He raised his brows at the two male Rukh. "And it might be wise for you two to take an extra helping. Sounds like you'll need to keep your strength up."

"By the look on her face, there might not be much left of them by tonight." Banga chortled.

Moments later the tent flap swept aside and Malena entered. She headed straight for the kitchen. "What did I miss?"

"Nothing," Rosheen said stonily.

Malena eyed the singed blanket then the grin still playing on Gento's face. "Gone for five minutes and miss all the fun."

Ariben gave a cynical grunt.

Tam plopped a ladle-full of thick, slightly lumpy porridge into a bowl and pushed it toward her. "Couldn't wait to get back for a real breakfast, eh?"

"Shen's pretty good," she laughed, "but I need proper sustenance after all that exercise."

"Stewed fruit? Honey?" he offered.

"'Honey' is it now?" she said teasingly. "I'll have both." She took the bowl and proceeded to fill it to the brim.

Huldar made his way to the bench. "So, how's the new site coming along?" he asked.

She sucked in a piece of yellow fruit and wiped her mouth. "Their Djan'rū's much, much bigger than ours," she glanced at Ariben, "and far more stable. Coming along nicely, thanks. You're welcome to accompany me later if you want? Learn a bit more about it?"

"How about the one here?" Huldar said. "Can you teach me anything with this one?"

"I could, but … Ask me about that when the new one's done. How about tomorrow? You too, Daric. Ever wanted to know how to configure a Djan'rū? I'm feeling somewhat generous this morning."

She picked up another bowl and waved it at Ariben. "Want some?"

He scowled. "I can get my own, thanks."

"Grumpy!" She put the spare bowl back onto the bench and sashayed toward Cobar and Gento. "Have you two been giving Rosheen a hard time?"

"They'll keep," Rosheen murmured.

"No more flames," Huldar said.

Gento bowed. "Yes, boss. No more flames."

Andel sidled up to Huldar and took his hand. *It was funny though.*

He shared his vision of the wild-eyed, naked Rukh swinging her sword at the flames and their chests contracted in a silent, mutual laugh.

I thought we might go over to the Went settlement today – see how they're faring? he asked.

Her sandy-brown eyes smiled into his. *We could take some food with us – take our time …?*

Good idea. "Tam, could you pack us some lunch, please?" Huldar said. "Andel and I are going to survey a new site."

Malena gave an arch lift of her brows. "Have fun!"

Huldar turned to address the entire crew. "I know it's a lay-day, but if everyone could think about where they're going to set their individual tents, please? It's getting warmer, and now the Host have gone I think it's time we had some space."

As Andel and Huldar started on their way, the crew spilled out onto the plain and, under Casco's direction, began to choose spots to pitch camp.

Where are we going to put ours? Andel asked.

Over there. He pointed. *Sheltered from the wind and gets the sun in the morning. Far enough from the marquee to be private, but not too far to get breakfast when it rains.*

Suits me, she said. *Nice view too! Does Casco know?*

I've marked it out. Put our stuff there late yesterday.

Ahh! So it wasn't the pranking that triggered this?

Merely a symptom, he said with a laugh. *We'll set up when we get back.*

Andel's hand stayed in his as they crossed the plains to the Went-valley portal. The day was still and bright. Small carnivorous plants waved sticky droplets on fine stalks, and drifts of pink and pale yellow flowers opened wide to invite their chosen pollinators.

There's almost a path here now, Andel said. *Maybe we're turning into Went.*

I didn't realize I'd been here so often, Huldar replied.

At the end of the winding trail they stepped through to the hillside where they'd last seen the herd, but the wide plain was empty.

Where have they gone? Andel asked.

I don't know, he said, then a fresh thought cheered him up. *But they won't be hard for you to find.* He swirled his finger in the air. *Just follow the road. I've been meaning to ask you to see where this tunnel leads. I think that's where they've gone.*

With a happy nod she closed her eyes. Her brows knit for a moment, then she smiled. "There they are – just emerging on the other side." She shared her vision of a sea of hairy backs. "The tunnel is quite wide for most of the way – winds around a bit and crosses an underground stream – shallow but fast-flowing. I wonder where they're going, and why? … They seem … happy."

She opened her eyes again.

He stared into their sandy depths, caught, as he often was, by the beauty of the soul they housed.

"Show me the waterfall?" she said. "You love it so much, but I haven't seen it yet."

"Not much more we can do here, I suppose."

In the valley of the falls, gushing veils of water thundered through a veil of spume into a lake now covered by a carpet of dark-green leaves. He pointed out a broad flat-topped boulder emerging from the water not too far from the shore and sat down to take off his boots. When he climbed onto the rock the legs of his trousers were wet to the knee.

Deeper than I thought, he said.

But no nasties?

None I can sense.

Andel left her shoes beside his and waded out. When she reached the rock, he helped her from the water.

She stood beside him and gazed up at the cataract. Dark shapes swooped through the spray. Wings flashed emerald where they caught the sun.

Birds?

Lizards, Huldar said. *Similar to some on an island in the south.* He shared a memory of cerulean wings lit by a storm-laden dawn. *I wanted so badly to show you at the time. The way they soared – like little bits of sky.*

She turned to him. *Like your eyes ...*

He smiled and drew her in for a kiss. *Best get these wet things off before we get cold. Perhaps I could ...?*

She turned to let him help her from her fur-lined coat. As he laid it on the stone beside his own, she began to unlace her over-shirt.

He took her hands. *Let me ...*

Beneath the next layer, his fingers found their way to her small firm breasts. He caressed her sensitive nipples with his thumbs and kissed her again.

Your turn, she said.

He lifted his arms for her to remove his shirt. *Impatient?*

More afraid that I'll freeze to death before we get to the good stuff. There's another shirt, a jumper and a fleecy vest to go!

Oh – I won't let you freeze.

The next layers came off with greater speed. Using discarded clothing as a bed, Huldar drew a warm blanket from Qalān and wrapped it around them like a cocoon. Skin to skin with his wife in his arms, warm and safe in the utmost wilderness, the joy of the moment spread through them both. The thunder of the falls drummed all around. Heat grew where they touched. He let his forehead rest against hers, closed his eyes, and let their hazes merge.

We are gifted, he said.

Yes, she replied. *In this moment, we are.*

She reached down and his penis sprang erect as if it had a life of its own. He laughed in apology. It had been some time since they'd had any privacy and he didn't want to rush her, but she met his laugh with a long kiss.

Later, there'll be time for play, she whispered, and, taking him in a firm grip, she turned him on his back and straddled his loins, thrusting her wet vagina onto him. The pleasure of it made him gasp.

His answering thrust slid hard through her tight confines. His arms drew her face down. Mouths fastened together. Rhythmic breathing mingled. She ground herself against him and he thrust up again and again in a desperate, joyous search for paradise.

Moments before climax, she stopped him. He hovered on an agonizing brink. Desperate for distraction, he raised his head to her breasts, but even that small movement almost brought him undone. Like smoke from a forest fire, her psychic projection entered his body and stroked his deep meridians. The pleasure was indescribable. Then her mouth came close to his ear and she murmured, "Now."

Their shared orgasm ripped through body and mind and did not stop. He screamed in ecstasy. If this was death, he welcomed it. Sensation rose in a spiraling updraft as if reaching for the Breath itself. For a timeless moment it peaked, then slowly began to fall.

His heartbeat banged in his ears. Breathing resumed. Utterly spent, they lay wrapped in the echoes of their experience, each resting in the other and reluctant to draw their minds apart.

Slowly, inevitable as the tide, Andel's sorrow rose. His chest was moistened by tears as she wept for her mother, for Lind, for the one whose mind she'd maimed, and for fear such happiness as theirs could not last. *I killed her*, she cried. *I killed my own mother. I wasn't strong enough – I'm never strong enough!*

He sorrowed for her pain, and for his helplessness to heal her until eventually, emotion drained and only the thunder of the falls remained.

Oh, my love, she said sadly. *Here we are in this most beautiful place and all I can do is cry.*

He pushed her back so he could see her face. Within their thick-lashed wall, her eyes were red and puffy. He gave her a handkerchief to wipe her nose. "That's certainly not all you can do," he murmured gently.

He kissed her forehead and she smiled a little.

I think we've just been as close to Asheru's Seventh as is possible this side of the Breath.

It was spectacular, wasn't it? she said, and her small smile became a grin.

Where did you learn how to do that? he asked. *The Naghari?*

She shook her head.

Well, perhaps you should share it with them. I'm sure it would help them in their quest.

He folded his arms around her again, warm and close in their woolen cocoon. Deep within him, the planet's bell tolled peace. The endless rush of the falls seeped through body and soul, and if he listened closely, Huldar could hear the faint piping cries of emerald lizards as they soared in diamond spray …

He woke suddenly from a golden sleep and squinted sunward. Green enamel wings swooped overhead – an errant lizard darting after prey. The space beside him was empty and cold. He stifled his panic and sat up to look around. White blooms had opened in the noon warmth and the rock was now an island adrift in a fragrant sea.

Andel hailed him from the bank. *Ready for lunch?*

Behind her, his clothes lay spread out in the sun. Above a small flame, the kettle simmered. Steam drifted from two bowls of stew. She lifted his mug. *Tea?*

His stomach rumbled. *Yes please!*

He slipped from the rock into a bed of shining, saucer-shaped flowers. Soft mud squished between his toes. As he waded to the shore, heavy stems fought his passage and although the water was warm it did little to ease the chill on his upper body.

When he reached dry land, Andel tossed him his trousers. He pulled them on, and she looked him up and down.

Seems a shame, really ... she said with wicked grin, and handed him a mug and a bowl.

"We should bring the others here," he said around a mouthful of stew. "Picnic and a swim? It's so beautiful. Before the flowers fade."

"Maybe ..."

He sensed her reluctance and smiled. "You feel this should be our own special place, but it's also a significant place for the Went. Maybe if we bring the Overlord, and the Faythan too, we might be able to convince them that the herds deserve our respect."

She looked around. "But there are no Went here."

"Not right now," he agreed. "But if they associate the natural beauty of this place with the creatures themselves ... first impressions and all that?"

"Devious!" She laughed. "But I'm not sure it will work."

"Maybe not, but a day out? After the sadness of Lind's commemoration, it would be good for morale."

"I'll think about it," she said. "But honestly, things have been a bit strained since ... well, for a while. I feel as if there's something I don't know, just beneath the surface. You've been keeping something important from me ... Am I right?"

He nodded. "There is something I should share with you – two things actually." He hesitated, wondering where this conversation would lead.

She sat more upright. *Go on ...*

"When I returned from talking with the planet, she gave me a gift – of sorts. A sound, something like a bell. She said I should listen and it would guide me."

"Guide you?"

"She senses trouble coming," Huldar said reluctantly. "It's not good."

"You said you needed time to process ..."

"And I do. I haven't said anything because I don't know for certain what she's warning me about, only that she fears it. The bell will help me to do the right thing – she says."

"Well. That's some consolation."

Andel sat quietly for a moment then looked up again. "The other thing?"

He dreaded his next admission. It was difficult to know how she would react, but they'd agreed there should be no secrets between them.

She nodded encouragingly.

"It's Daric Enna," he said. "His past – his history. He's ... an assassin." He shrugged in the face of her disbelief. "And a spy. Pieru told me before we left. Now he's admitted it to me himself. Qalān wouldn't open to him. It takes too much energy to hide some things. I explained what was wrong and he told me it was he who killed Duvät Gok, and that he'd been paid to do it."

Andel frowned. "That's why he's so good with screens." He could feel her emotions tumbling. There was more than a whiff of the cave where she and her mother had been captured. "But he seems so nice. A little reserved, but helpful. Funny ..."

"He is. It was a job to him, a skill – an excellence. But he wants a new life now, a fresh start."

"Do you believe him?" She contemplated the lake of flowers. "Does Casco know?"

"Yes, he does, and he believes in Daric wholeheartedly." He followed her gaze to look at the falls, where the lizards still flashed in the spray. "I'm inclined to trust him – Pieru approved his appointment – but either way, what choice do we have?"

She seemed to come to a decision. "If things deteriorate as the planet warns, maybe his skills will be more useful than you think."

"That's what he said."

"You told him what the planet gave you before you told me?" Her voice was sharp.

"No, of course not," he soothed. "He warned me about the Faythan's intentions. He thinks the trouble will start with the Bel Nishani."

Still thoughtful, she began to pack their things. He stood to help her fold the rug. Her grief remained, but it seemed more distant and she was stronger in herself. It was as if the catharsis on the rock had triggered inner healing.

"Let's go for a walk," she said. *I need to clear my head.*

He followed in silence as she started for the falls. Emotions fluttered across their bond without structure or intent: a wordless conversation that bypassed structured thoughts.

He learned that she did indeed feel better in herself. The news about Daric troubled her, but she was more worried for him than about him. She felt she understood his confusion of spirit – a good person at heart, but one who had done bad things.

Unlike you, he chose to do those things, Huldar pointed out.

Yes, but why? she responded. *There is more to this story.*

They began their climb to the head of the falls, but paused when they sensed a cave.

She peered beneath the plunging waters. *There's a path. Should we follow it? Maybe it's where the Went go.*

He shook her head. *It's getting late. Even the lizards have retired for the day.* He joined her as she turned to look back. Despite the relatively low elevation, the view was stupendous.

"We should bring the others here," she conceded. "I think it would be fun – so long as the weather doesn't muck it up."

Across the lake, flowers moved in sluggish patterns, stirred by the rising breeze.

"Next week some time," he suggested. "It would be a shame if the flowers had faded."

"Sounds perfect!" She smiled. "We can spread rugs, get Tam and Arko to make another feast – and maybe even go for a swim."

"Sounds perfect," he echoed. He peered toward the valley of caves. "I wonder if the Went will return?"

"It'd be even better if they did," she said. "But they seemed pretty determined about where they were off to. As if it was important. You could see it in their step."

On the way back they paused at the spot where their blanket had been. A rainbow shone in the spray above the falls, bright against the shadows, but even as he watched, the sun dipped lower and it began to fade.

Time to go, he said. And hand in hand once more, they set off toward the portal on the plains.

MIND GAMES

On Giahn, winter in the Imperial City was almost over, but there were still days when a jacket was necessary when out-of-doors.

Lucaät of Faytha looked up as fresh rain showered the windows of his luxurious residence. Outside, the ends of the gardener's scarf blew forward in a sudden gale. Apparently, the Imperial palace planned to feature red-purple sun-bells in their gardens this season, but his sun-bells would flower a few days earlier – another small way to insinuate House Faytha set the trend.

He stepped closer to the fire and sipped a glass of warm spiced wine. Perhaps the wind would jeopardize the survival of his new plantings, but if they knew how much coin he'd thrown at them surely they would make an extra effort to live.

The gate alarm buzzed inside his head and he scanned Tsemkarun Jaldan of Trianog, the mind specialist, right on time. His enjoyment of the wine dulled. He hoped Jaldan had come to tell him he'd found a way to ease the Agent's suffering, but if not … he gave a slight shrug. If his plans on the planet Went were progressing as planned, his old employee's potential for usefulness would soon be at an end. Perhaps it would be best to release him from his misery at last.

He turned as Jaldan's waxy features appeared at his door. Sender bowed and left them.

"Tsemkarun Jaldan of Trianog," he began. "What news of my Agent's condition?"

Jaldan sketched a bow. "No change, I'm afraid." He looked pointedly at the wine.

Lucaät almost summoned the slave, then remembered one of his Ashik had accidentally killed her. He had wanted to collar the perpetrator as a replacement, but could not risk the affront to the Imperium. Sadly, sun-bells were the best he could hope to get away with. His dresser had agreed to fill in as a servant until a replacement could be bought. She hurried in with a steaming pitcher and two fresh glasses, but made nowhere near the impact his former girl would have.

"The work progresses regardless," Jaldan continued. "You will be most interested to know that during my investigations into your agent's psychological state, which I have pursued most diligently, I have discovered a pattern of manipulation which, if used correctly, can be applied to others to initiate hallucinations so strong that the subject actually believes they are reality."

"You've found this while you've been trying to heal him?"

"Yes, of course," Jaldan assured him.

Lucaät wondered what it would be like to truly believe something had happened only to discover the whole experience had been a lie. "And can this induced reality be manipulated?"

The specialist nodded. "But the process must begin with a location or perhaps an event which the subject remembers in truth – that is, an authentic event that happened to them. Thus it is reliant on the skill of the practitioner – or so I envisage, since no other has as yet attempted the process – to discover relevant associations to trigger the state into, as it were, and then to guide the mind to experience the false memory through the subject's own imagination of what may have been variables in the outcome of the existing memory."

Fortunately, Jaldan paused to take breath.

While Lucaät tried to sift his words for their actual meaning, the mind specialist nodded rapidly, a gesture reminiscent of certain reptilian mating rituals.

"Oh yes indeed," the Trianogi continued. His head bobbed again.

Lucaät prepared himself for a fresh onslaught.

"The technique is most complex and requires careful yet completely spontaneous direction to be undertaken with considerable power, a difficult feat even for a powerful and learned Tsemkarun such as myself. Hence no other practitioner has been trusted to perform the procedure as yet … and there is one aspect which remains to be resolved." He bobbed. "Yes, a slight complication, but rest assured, Lucaät of Faytha, I am working on this issue most assiduously."

Lucaät stared blankly at the flames for a moment while his brain tried to process.

"What complication?" he said at last.

Jaldan hesitated. "It may be difficult to bring them back."

"How difficult?"

"Very."

"Can it be done?" Lucaät squinted at him. "Have you done it? Will false memories somehow ease the agent from his current state"

Jaldan paused again as if considering how to frame his reply. "Ah, no, not yet. But study continues. With funding to purchase more slaves I can assure you the prognosis will be more favorable," he said hopefully. "Slaves, of course, are ideal because their mind's barriers have already been destroyed."

"Will it work on archangels?"

"Given a suitably powerful Tsemkarun to hold them I see no reason why it wouldn't, but I have not attempted it as yet since the outcome at this stage would most likely be either death or madness ... followed by death of course, and I have no more disposable archangels on which to perform the experiment. As I have said, without an increase in funding ..."

"How do you see this as being of benefit to me?" Lucaät said.

Jaldan of Trianog peered at him as if he was an idiot. "Once the state is triggered, you see, the subject has absolute recall of the memory they are locked into." Jaldan opened his hands as if it would help Lucaät to understand. "They can be guided to live the experience in every detail as if it were real, but, as in a dream, relative time may be altered. An adept observer then has opportunity to study those details from their own perspective, but find results most rapidly. Because time has been altered, you see?" He tapped his forehead with one finger. "Let's say someone has stolen from you. You could relive the event alongside the culprit and also see fine detail that the thief barely registers themselves – the background noise, as it were – who else was there, what other factors were in play. This is a far more directed approach than normal interrogation, and there is no way the subject can hide or disguise anything because at this point they don't realize you are watching. It is as if they are there as they were when it happened, and the scene can be replayed any number of times without the subject even realizing this is the case. I see future applications such as the gathering of intelligence, of course, as well as the implantation of false memories as decoys from sensitive situations, and the secure delivery of extremely complex messages without the necessity for engaging a Hermes."

Lucaät cradled his wine. The glass felt warm and full in his hands. The Tsemkarun watched him with uncomfortable intensity. All this had been gleaned from his agent's misfortune? Should he continue to fund the Tsemkarun's research? It was ground-breaking to be sure, but the body-count was rising, and in the end, his agent had not been helped. Instead, he had been kept alive, locked in a terror so profound that at times he was rendered catatonic. The truth slowly dawned on him – Jaldan was a true monster.

"Yet you could not save the Agent?"

"As I have said, the key is almost within my grasp. I just need more –"

"Coin!" Lucaät snapped. "Yes. Believe it or not, I can understand that much."

Jaldan studied him again. His haze showed great interest, but other emotions were either extremely well hidden or non-existent. Lucaät turned to watch the flames and sipped his wine before returning to his guest.

"Get out."

Jaldan blinked.

"You can have a one-time increase," he conceded, "but if the Agent is not cured within three months, your funding ends – understand?"

Jaldan clasped his hands together and looked down. At last Lucaät saw emotions beyond mere interest.

"It may be that your factor cannot … is beyond …"

"Three months, or it's over," Lucaät barked. *Sender, show him out.*

ANOTHER PICNIC

"Gather round, people, gather round," Huldar announced. "The first quarter draws to a close. Within six or seven weeks the rest of the Host will arrive and we'll have fresh supplies and new people on the ground. They'll take time to get used to conditions here, but hopefully there won't be the fatalities."

"Getting it easy," said Topper.

"Now the weather is on the improve and we've done all the work," Banga replied.

"They'll have work enough," Huldar said.

Casco shared an image of Olatu of Faytha, red-faced and yelling. He smiled as others took it up and started to add their own embellishments, some less polite than others.

Huldar put up his hand. "If I could have your attention, please?" The sniggering came to a halt. "Thank you. Now, the Eastern continent has warmed sufficiently to begin setting up for mining operations to commence over there. Some time within the next few days, as weather permits, Topper, you and your brother will go with Casco to set up our new headquarters over there. However, this base-camp will remain operative after the move as mining operations on this continent still need to be closely monitored."

"Can't take our eyes off them for a moment," said Nachiel.

Huldar rubbed his hands together. "As a reward for your efforts, the day after tomorrow – if the weather holds – there will be a picnic at the lake of flowers."

"The lake of flowers?" Sari asked.

"You'll love it!" Andel said. "There's a waterfall. It's ice-melt, but warmed by geothermal springs, and the lake itself is warm as a bath, and simply covered in flowers. We can bathe even if it snows!"

"There'll be plenty of food," Huldar continued, "so if there are friends from the Host you'd like to invite, feel free …"

Tam raised his hand. "Just let me know beforehand so I can be sure to make enough."

"And if the weather goes to pieces we'll have our spare marquee set up just in case."

———

On the morning of the picnic, Huldar and Andel looked up at a sky dotted with scudding grey clouds.

Ariben emerged from his tent and looked up also. He rubbed his arm.

"What do you think?" Huldar asked him.

"About what?"

"Is it going to rain?"

"Nope," he said, and stumped back inside.

"Malena's bringing her new lover," Andel explained quietly. "Another miner."

Huldar shook his head. "That's sure to add to the fun," he said dourly.

They turned as the Overlord arrived.

"You're early!" Andel said with a smile.

"Good morning, good morning!" he replied cheerfully. "I'm so looking forward to this. I hope you don't mind, but I've informed Olatu of Faytha about our little outing and he said he'd like to come too."

"Too much fun for me," Andel said quietly. *I'll go help with the preparations.*

"No, not at all, Radätel Gok," Huldar lied. "So long as you both remember that this is supposed to be a day of relaxation."

"Of course," Radätel said. "I must say, I can't wait to see this so-called lake of flowers. I'm sorry, Huldar, if you think our presence will dampen things, but an opportunity to escape, just for a few hours – I couldn't pass it up."

"There's to be no talk of reports." He glanced at Casco. "And, please, ask the Faythan to respect our ways."

"Yes, I'll make sure he understands – tactfully of course. This will be a day when we can put aside the normal protocols and get to know each other."

"Exactly."

"Even more welcome after the loss of another of our miners the other day …"

"Terrible thing," Huldar said. "What exactly happened?"

"An accident. Falling rock."

"They know we have a rescue team? We are all well versed in handling emergency situations."

"I can imagine!" Radätel said.

"They only have to call."

The Overlord made a small bow. "I'll pass that on – again. In this case, they were moving rock aside to make an opening. It seems the singer lost control. It was the strangest thing. The victim was in the wrong place at the wrong time, I'm afraid. We're hoping for a replacement among the second half of the Host, if they can find one at such short notice." He raised his gaze skyward. "Breathless nuisance this inability to contact the Realm."

"Yes, it takes some getting used to," Huldar agreed, "but we are much better supplied than we were on our first visit, and with the quarterly navigator runs – feels quite luxurious."

"Luxurious? You Uri'madu are certainly are a hardened lot."

"Technically, you're one of us, Radätel Gok."

"Must make a better show of it!" Radätel chuckled. "Well, I've just contacted Olatu of Faytha and he's on his way …"

"If I could ask you both to wait at camp while our crew goes through with supplies, I'll be happy to lead the way when they're done. We don't want anyone getting lost."

"Good point, Huldar. We'll do as you suggest." He turned to the portal. "Ah, here he comes now. I'll give him your words."

Huldar bowed as the Overlord scurried off. Andel returned to stand with him, her haze abuzz with excitement.

Bush and Topper sauntered by with several crates of Besh and another which was unlabeled but clinked just the same.

"Will we be able to drink all that?" Andel asked.

"Sure gonna try!" Topper laughed.

Next, Tam and Arco came by with an unwieldy mountain of food between them. Noticing the bench with the casserole dishes seemed about to fall, Andel stepped in to help, but the cooks gave up and the whole ensemble was lowered to the ground. "Banga! Kira?" she called. "Why didn't you ask them to help?" she said to Tam.

"You go on ahead," Huldar said to her. "Make sure Tam's masterpieces get there safely."

She grinned as the two spinners strolled toward them. "Better hurry or it might be gone before you get there."

When all the food and drink was on its way, Huldar signaled their special guests. Radätel Gok waved briskly and hurried over. The Faythan followed at a more dignified pace.

"All set?" the Overlord said.

With his best long-suffering expression, Olatu brushed imaginary dust from his sleeves. "I hope it's not too far," he said. "I am unused to walking great distances."

"This way," Huldar said, and turned for the portal.

"You say it's beautiful?" Olatu said to Radätel. He looked around doubtfully. "But all I see is wilderness. Every day the same."

"If you left the camp you might see more," Radätel suggested.

"Leave the camp?" The Faythan snorted. "Prey to whatever lurks out there, waiting to eat me? I only came today because I'm curious. If it's as pretty as you say, maybe there's tourism potential. Usage in the long term beyond mere mining."

"Usage?" Huldar felt as if a stone had dropped into his stomach.

"Yes, of course," the Faythan continued. "You may not believe it but there are people who would pay handsomely for a 'wilderness adventure', so long as the so-called wilderness is somewhat tamed. A restaurant, a guest house …"

"No such building would survive the ice," Huldar said flatly.

"Just an idea. You don't approve?"

"No. I do not."

"Overlord?"

"I doubt such a scheme could be profitable, Olatu … not that I'm a Faythan, of course! But the expense of such a journey – especially after the terrible entry we had. And don't forget we are completely out of contact with the Realm."

"For some fools that alone would be enticement enough," Olatu said dourly.

As they began the trek to the lake, Huldar relished the warmth of the morning. With the emergence of many new species, the local song was gaining momentum, but the waving hands of the Overlord and his companion was distracting.

"I knew I shouldn't have come!" the Faythan said crossly as he fended off a growing assembly of micro-lizard pests. One group of the tiny creatures seemed particularly entranced by his hair.

Radätel had followers of his own. He glanced pointedly at Huldar's free airspace. "Care to share?"

"No problem." Huldar passed a small stick to Radätel and the majority of his pesky attendants de-camped to join Olatu's already vigorous cloud. He tried not to smile. "The charm integrates well with wooden substrates. Has to be specific to the area though."

"Where's mine?" Olatu asked.

"I'm sorry, I don't have another with me – though I made some for your miners. Maybe they'll have spares."

He winced as Olatu clapped his hands to squash one of the fliers.

"They won't hurt you," he said sharply.

"What are they doing here then?" Olatu snapped.

Radätel gave his stick to Olatu and the Faythan waved it around like a swat.

Huldar pointed to the lake. "Look, we're almost there. The marquee is fully protected, I can assure you."

"Breath be praised!" the Faythan said, and hurried forward with more energy than Huldar had seen from him at any time before.

———————

Andel smiled at Huldar's image of a grandiose guest house being crushed by snows and a last glimpse of the Faythan buried with it. She added some Went trampling over the top as if the structure had never existed and sent it back to him.

She turned as Topper waved enthusiastically at two new arrivals.

"The spinner sisters," Sari said, and winked. "Taken a bit of a shine to our boys. But that one there?" She tipped her head toward the taller of the two.

"Tala?"

Sari nodded. "Our Topper's just too shy to say."

"Shy?" Andel said. "I would never have thought of him as shy … Oh, look. Shen's here!"

The Host's cook strode over, several laden trays suspended in his wake. Not far behind, Malena sauntered in with her latest conquest on her arm.

"Here's trouble," Sari muttered.

"Lady Andel!" Shen waved his hand over a heaping platter. "Seafood parcels. Finest on the planet."

"Where did you get the fish?" she asked.

"They're *seafood*." He grinned. "Single word be singen a broad tune, ja – yes – doesn't it?" he corrected himself. "But there's an inlet on the west coast, reminds me a bit of Pannias. Shellfish – of sorts – on the rocks. Alis said it was all right to eat them, so …"

She smiled back at him. "Well, they won't have to work too hard to be the finest on this planet, but they do smell wonderful. Can't wait to try one."

"I'll be surprised if you can stop at one! Tam's jealous, but the recipe's a secret I'm sworn never to tell – and don't worry," he added, "there's plenty for all."

By the time Huldar and his two companions rounded the corner to the lake-side, the marquee was up, fires were going, and Ronnin and Nachiel were already swimming, but the wave her husband gave her seemed more than a little desperate.

She looked around as Ubaid called out, "Where's these vaunted flowers?"

Olatu and Radätel moved on. Huldar looked skyward in relief. "Not till the sun warms the buds," he answered. "Ubaid, Alis! Good to see you."

Ubaid clapped Huldar's shoulders. "This was a splendid idea!" He turned to Nachiel and called, "What's the water like?"

"Wonderful!" Nachiel replied. "I haven't felt so clean in ages."

Ronnin laughed and jetted water at Nachiel's head. "You? Clean?"

"Come on, Alis! Before someone needs us back at base," Ubaid said. He took off running for the shore and left a trail of clothing in his wake.

As the two splashed naked into the lake, Alis shrieked with delight. Andel found herself sharing a wide grin with Huldar. *Never thought I'd see that!*

Tam wandered over with a plate in one hand and a half-eaten seafood parcel in the other. "Shen's omosa, Lady Andel." He popped the rest of the parcel into his mouth. "Try one. They really are very good."

She selected a crispy-skinned morsel and bit into it. The juicy flavor filled her mouth – distinctively fishy, yet unique. She reached for another. "Where *is* Shen? These are marvelous!"

"He's wandered off to explore. Apparently there's a cave behind the falls."

"Yes, Huldar and I were up here the other week. That's when we had the idea for the picnic."

He gave the swimmers a wistful look. "Well everyone seems to be enjoying themselves, and there isn't even any frost."

"But you must enjoy yourself too," she said. "Why not go for a swim?"

"I might, later." He gestured with the plate toward Ariben, who was watching Malena cavort in the lake with her new friend. "She's a dreadful hussy."

"I'll keep an eye on him," said Andel. She found Huldar already trapped in fresh conversation with the Faythan. "If I may borrow my husband for a moment?"

"Of course," Olatu said. "We were merely discussing the weather."

Thank you, Huldar whispered.

She popped the last of the omosa into her mouth. "I was going to save this for you, but ..."

"Too late," he grinned.

They looked up as Alis and Ubaid waded over to see something Shen had in his hands. The three came back to shore, where the healers began to dress again.

When Ubaid came to talk to them, Andel smiled to see him so relaxed.

"Shen's found some golden wheel fruit," he said, "and a new kind of berry in the caves. We're going with him to check them out and maybe get some more – just in time for lunch."

"Wonderful," Andel replied. "I love the golden wheels! They must be the first of the season."

She waved as they left, then returned to Huldar. "Tam's worried about Ariben."

He put his arm over her shoulders and led her toward a tray of omosa. "They'll sort it out."

BERRY SURPRISE

By noon, the lake was a sea of fragrant white, small green dragons plied the falls and there was laughter in the air, but as Olatu of Faytha wandered toward him, Huldar sighed.

Look at him, he whispered to Andel. *Still sour.* He pictured the remains of their wonderful meal, the trestle littered with empty liquor bottles.

Maybe that scowl is just the way his face is arranged, she replied. Her twinkle of humor was infectious.

Well it's coming my way, he said. *Again!*

You're the only one with status enough to make him feel important.

He gave a cynical grunt, but before Olatu could come close enough to speak, Shen and Tam placed two large bowls covered with checkered cloth among the ravaged remains on the table. With great drama, they whipped the covers aside to reveal golden wheel fruit in Tam's bowl and, in Shen's, a mound of maroon globes, each a nice size to fit in the palm of one's hand.

"Dig in!" Shen cried. "The berries – or whatever they truly be – are luscious. Tam tried one just now and it hasn't done him any harm."

Tam grabbed the angel next to him and gave her a kiss. "Never felt better!"

"There may be a little euphoria and a mild aphrodisiac effect," Ubaid said lightly. "Enjoy!" He took a fruit for himself and gave another to Alis.

Shen passed the bowl around. "There's one each," he said. "We didn't like to take more without proper assessment."

"Mother's milk, they are good," said Topper.

As if that was a signal, everyone dived in at once. Only the Faythan hesitated.

"If you don't try it now, you'll miss out," Shen said.

Olatu's eyes narrowed. He picked up the last one and put it to his nose. "Interesting smell."

"It's up to you …"

The Faythan made a show of steeling himself, then bit through the outer skin. His eyes widened. "They *are* good!"

Shen grinned. "We thought it might make a nice treat – something special to mark the occasion."

Huldar peeled back the purplish skin and sucked the pulp from inside. His teeth closed on a small kernel and crushed it open. The wave of exhilaration it released made him reel. His inner bell tolled sadly, but he felt wonderful.

When Andel bit down on hers, surprise flickered through their bond.

"My goodness," she said breathlessly. "I wasn't expecting that."

He turned as Sari giggled. He could hear the fabric of her clothing rustle as she moved. Her haze seemed little different … it had definitely brightened. He wondered if the same thing had happened to his, but when he turned to ask Andel about it, he was taken by the beauty of her Mark and forgot what he meant to say.

The Faythan gave an oily chuckle and sidled up to Shen.

That's funny, Huldar laughed. *He hates half-breeds.*

Andel's eyes widened. *Shen's a half-breed?*

Of course he is. Huldar replied, then he blinked. Why hadn't he seen it before? *Shh*, he said, and reached out to stroke her face. *I think it's a secret!*

Over her shoulder he saw Casco strip off as if his clothes were somehow poisoned. Daric moved close to help him and they kissed, long and slow. The movement showed off the beauty of Casco's jawline.

Should he be shocked? Huldar wasn't sure. Andel gazed at him with pupils round and soft. When he ran his palms down her shoulders and cupped her breasts, her haze blazed into a full-blown aura, alive with lust.

She undid his pants with telekinetic fingers and they slithered down his legs. Hers were already at her ankles. Impatiently he removed her shirt, anxious to touch her. His fingers trailed over her torso, entranced by the texture of her skin. As they circled her nipples, the darker flesh crinkled and the aura around them swirled in matching tornadoes.

He bent to kiss them, then closed his hands around her buttocks and in one easy movement lifted her up. As her legs parted he drove himself inside. She clung to his shoulders and locked her legs round him. Their auras merged in an intoxicating rush. Slowly, carefully, he lowered her to the ground, each movement negotiated, her body throbbing over his. Once she was down, he thrust with a steady rhythm. Her breath was warm as she crushed her lips over his. He left her mouth to tease her nipples with teeth and tongue then traveled, inch by inch down her torso. The salty taste of her body inflamed his craving further.

She arched her back, moaning as his fingers slid inside her, and again as he tongued her, swirling and sucking. To fulfil her shared image of desire he moved so his hips were closer to her face. When her mouth latched onto him, the intensity of their connection drowned every movement in ecstasy.

Other bodies seethed beside them. Fingers and lips explored every surface in a gentle mass of shameless indulgence. At one stage he found himself face to face with Olatu of Faytha. He gave him a lingering kiss, then moved on. The planet tolled in his soul, but its dark message was lost against the urgency of need, the thrust of hips and the taste of sex …

Sleep left him suddenly. The fires had gone out. He shivered in the chill pre-dawn air. Around him, naked bodies lay in a jumble. He found his wife curled in the arms of the navigator. To see her so peaceful made him smile.

Even the planet's bell was quiet, as if it lay sleeping too. Careful to disturb no one, he left the tent and wandered to the gently steaming lake to immerse himself in its warm and undemanding embrace. He set his hair loose and let the water comb through it, prizing the last shreds of worry from his mind. He swam beneath flotillas of dormant flowers, then lay back with arms and legs akimbo and let himself float among them. Above him stars and moons blazed in glory, so close he reached up as if to touch them. In his ears, the suck and flow of his breathing and the slow la-lump, la-lump of his heartbeat gave measure to the distant roar of the falls.

Back on the shore, he sensed Andel's rise from sleep.

Over here, he said lazily. *Come join me.*

I'm all sticky, she said.

You won't be if you have a swim. Come on – it's warmer in here than out there.

With her arms hugged tight against her chest, she picked her way over the frost. Her pale body glimmered in the starlight. Shrouded by wisps of steam on the dark surface, its ghostly reflection broke and rippled.

As the water deepened, she lowered herself in and began to swim.

You're right, she said. *It's like a bath. Only the bits sticking out are cold.*

Then don't stick any bits out. He chuckled.

With confident strokes, she joined him in the deeper water, but hesitated when he suggested she float beside him.

It's worth it, he said. *We can turn over every now and then to make sure our top halves don't freeze.*

Maybe I've got more to lose than you, she retorted.

Is that so? You didn't seem too dissatisfied this afternoon.

It was good to feel genuine laughter flow between them. For the first time since Ninjay's death there no hint of sadness. Despite her misgivings, Andel stretched out and let the water buoy her. Her breasts rose like small white islands from her lean torso. Her Tsemkar glowed as she worked her hair free, like his. It flared around her head in a halo and brown and blond mingled like fabric woven with strands of finest silk.

He reached for her hand and let the question flow between them. *What if we were Blessed?*

I don't know, she mused. *Our lives would change, that's for sure.*

Would you be happy?

Of course! But it's not something I dream about – not like some. It will happen when it happens. We are *giving El every opportunity*, she said archly.

He snorted and ripples distorted the starry reflection. *I think I remember the Faythan's face far too clearly for comfort.*

Oh dear, she laughed. *And I woke up next to Malena – but did you see? Sari was with Casco.*

He sensed her deep approval and sent a query.

How much do you know about her past? she asked him.

Just that her family came from Purd and grew crops and shuna, same as most. I know that her father was Rukh. They didn't have much, and life was hard, but she loves her sister.

Yes, she does.

And …?

Let's just say that what happened earlier might be life-changing for her, and I'm pleased because she's had a sweet spot for Casco all these years.

I thought she and Lind had a special bond.

They did, but it was a loving friendship more than a romance, and now she's gone.

The thread of conversation closed. She shut her eyes and he wondered what it was he didn't know, but all he could sense was that the matter was intensely private.

Alis and Ubaid were gone by the time I woke, he said conversationally. *It must be hectic for them with so many to care for.*

She responded in agreement, then formed the query, *The miner that died in the accident with the falling stone – the crew boss – that was the same one Casco had trouble with, wasn't it?*

He sent an affirmative.

She retreated into her own thoughts again, and he wondered what had brought that particular incident to mind.

His muscles were tired with a new kind of exhaustion. There'd be precious little work accomplished for the next day or two, but he wouldn't have traded their experience for anything. *Lucky there's not enough of those berries to do it again. If they were plentiful we'd never get anything done! I wonder what they are and how they got there …?*

Anchored together by their hands, they drifted between sleep and wakefulness. Tepid water cradled them like a womb among the stars. A string of moons arced overhead like a trail, just grazing the Great Wheel constellation that would eventually come to dominate the sky. A lonely shooting star streaked the night with a flash of green, but he could hardly find the energy for his gaze to follow it.

A little later, the faint smell of cooking roused him.

Come on, Andel said. She turned and dragged him shoreward. *There's a fire going, food heating, and I can feel my skin wrinkling.*

With a burst of renewed energy he dove beneath the water lilies and pulled her under.

Race you! he cried, and while she sputtered at the surface he swam past in long even strokes.

Cheat! she yelled, and flailed after him with surprising speed.

Malena sauntered to the shore with a towel in hand, and, as Andel clambered from the water, she draped it over her shoulders.

"What about me?" Huldar said.

With a grin, the lanky navigator put her arm around Andel and shepherded her to the fire.

I must have made an impression, Andel laughed privately.

He wandered back to the marquee to find his clothes.

By the time he'd dressed, his wife stood by the fire between Malena and Daric, a warm mug cradled in her hands. As he made his way to join her, he saw Sari catch her eye and with the slightest of movements, tip her head toward Casco. The smile on her face was shy but luminous and his wife's answering surge of joy lifted his already lightened heart.

CASCO AND DARIC

Casco ate and drank with his friends, but inside him, everything had changed. It had happened with Daric's kiss. He felt as if his life had been hurtling toward this point for years, yet he'd only just realized.

Their sexual encounter had been drug-induced – but in reality, the effect of the fruit had released a part of him long suppressed. Occasional loves had colored his life, but there had been nothing lasting – how could there be when he had so little to offer? He'd always felt a deep fondness for Sari … and memories of Saphela of Hermes' smile still held a pang of loss; but Daric was welded to his heart with an intensity he would not have thought possible. Was this what it was like for Huldar and Andel? No wonder he'd felt excluded at the time – he had been. There was room for no other.

He watched him laugh and chat. Every movement was beautiful, every sound a gift. He longed to work his fingers through that mussed-up braid and see the hair flow free around his face … over his shoulders … down his back.

Daric felt his attention and gave him a quick smile, all the more endearing because their wonderful confusion was shared.

Huldar had been a good friend to him – he understood that now. But Huldar could never understand what it was like to be Kareski – to be reviled simply for the circumstances of your birth.

Daric completely understood.

Huldar had been a true companion, and had never treated him with disrespect, but he had never taught him much about his craft. To be fair, Casco admitted, he hadn't asked. It was a place few Kareski explored, seeing no hope of fulfilment. But Daric had seen past his reticence to the hunger he'd buried. He'd fed his desire to learn with a casual ease that had initially seemed condescending – he wasn't used to being taken at face value.

At first he'd been horrified by the fact that Daric was one of the best assassins in the business and proud of his accomplishments, but slowly he'd grown to trust his new friend and over time he'd come to see that the work was not dishonorable in itself. His choice of profession had been in answer to an unjust society – a way he could take charge – circumvent unjust laws.

He remembered him in training with the Rukh, each movement flowing into the next, precise and agile. How he'd wanted to touch those muscles, yet he hadn't. He'd been unable to bear the thought of rejection.

This evening when he'd woken, the first thing he'd seen was Daric's face, his eyes closed in a deep and trusting sleep – another thing he'd never expected. Daric never slept – not fully.

Sari's arms had been around his waist. He remembered her crying while they made love. Sari and Daric, two people he loved most in the world. He felt a fleeting sadness this experience would not be shared with Huldar, then shook his head. Old habits were hard to kill.

He remembered this morning, when Daric's eyes had opened without warning – instantly alert. They'd gazed into Casco's for a long moment, intense and searching … then softened.

I will never let anyone hurt you, Daric had said, and Casco believed him.

RECOVERY

Olatu of Faytha looked up at the waterfall shining in the early morning light and rubbed his hands together, thinking of the innocuous-seeming maroon berry that had given him such an incredible experience. A find that would win Imperial good will and coin by the bucket load.

There was no need to claim the berries for the Imperium since the planet already belonged to Tiamät. Lucaät of Faytha had exclusive rights to anything mined there, and he, Olatu, was sworn to protect those interests – but there was nothing in any of the contracts about ownership of food-stuffs or medicinal herbs, so the berries were his.

Once word got out, everyone would want them, but Shen had said there weren't very many in the cave to start with.

He saw the Overlord stand to wrap himself in a blanket. Most fortuitous …

"Radätel Gok, a moment of your time?"

"Olatu?"

The Faythan put aside his discomfort at being addressed so casually, though it was certainly less worrisome than living alongside a half-breed, papers or no. He led the Overlord away from the tent and made sure no one could listen. As the screen closed around them, Radätel gave him a doubtful look.

"It strikes me that I foresee a problem brewing," Olatu explained. "Those berries ... fruit ... whatever they are – if I am not mistaken there will be excessive demand on a limited resource. Given your station as Overlord of our ecological assessment team, it will be up to you to control this. What do you propose?"

"Now? After ..." Radätel looked back at the tent. "The sun's only just coming up."

"Exactly!" Olatu hissed. "This is the time, before word becomes fire."

Radätel's face twisted in protest, but Olatu said quickly, "Communicate your plans to me as soon as possible. Perhaps it would be advisable to involve the good Shamkarun Huldar. I'm sure he'll be as anxious as you to prevent an ecological disaster."

"Ecological disaster? What are you up to?" The Overlord looked toward the falls for a moment, then nodded. "You want them for yourself."

Olatu gave him a stern glance. "I am the leader of this entire operation. Faytha's representative in this desolate prison of a place."

Radätel held his gaze.

Olatu tried not to look away.

"So that's how it is?" Radätel said. "Very well, but as *Imperial* representative, I have my own responsibilities." He bowed shortly. "Enjoy the rest of your evening, Olatu of Faytha. Have no doubt I will do all I can to follow your ... suggestions."

Olatu hesitated before following the Gok back to the party. Isolation could have strange effects on people. He wondered how far he would have to go to get this Overlord back under control.

THE CAVE

Huldar glanced up as the midday sun and stifled a yawn. Somehow they had managed to tidy up the lake-side before lunch, but the rest of the day would no doubt be spent in semi-convalescence without any meaningful work accomplished at all. He had stayed to make a final check of their picnic spot, but before he could finish assessing the damage, he was startled to see the Overlord returning down the bank.

"Radätel." He held up his hand. "is there a problem?"

The overlord shook his head. He seemed out of breath, as if he'd hurried.

"Apologies for the rest of the day," Huldar said. "I've told the Uri'madu to take it easy, but I'm sure we'll be able to catch up once we are all rested."

"Yes, yes. I'm sure you will," Radätel replied. "But that's not why I've come back. I thought I'd catch you here so we could be sure to be alone. It's Olatu of Faytha, you see. He thinks we should we should come up with a way to limit access to the berries until we find out more about them … And I think he has a good point."

"Yes," Huldar said firmly. "These were my thoughts too."

"Word will spread, of course," the Overlord said. "It's only a matter of time before the Host begins to return to the site – on a treasure-hunt of sorts!"

Huldar gave the distant portal that would take him back to camp a regretful look, but Radätel Gok was right. The sooner measures were taken, the better. He started for the cave. "Let's go and assess the situation. Shen and Ubaid are the only ones who know exactly where the eggs came from, and they, at least, are already sworn to secrecy, and the only way through to the valley is from the portal at our camp-site."

"An alarm there might be impractical, but at least I can be somewhat reassured."

He gave an absent-minded nod and gazed across the lake of flowers. They'd left barely a mark, just a few disturbed lilies where they'd swum and played, and it brought to mind something he'd first seen on a fresco while on his way to Frith with Andel and her parents – a disappearance charm.

"Maybe the cave can be blocked off and no harm done," he said. "We should take a closer look."

Radätel peered doubtfully at the cliff beside the falls.

"The track is a short way up the side," Huldar assured him.

"There's a track?"

"I believe the creatures, the Went, use it, though I'm not sure why."

"Very well," Radätel sighed. "But bear in mind I have a fear of caves and what might lurk inside them."

"Most wise," Huldar nodded, "but in this case, it's likely the only inhabitants are the small flying lizards, those ones – see?" He pointed out the green flashing wings that darted through the spray. "Nowhere near as frightening as the red runners on the Southern Archipelago."

"Red runners?"

As they set off through the low scrub, Huldar began to tell Radätel about their first experience with the savage red hunters. He adjusted his pace to suit the Overlord's level of fitness, and sensed thankfulness and embarrassment in equal measure.

"Perhaps you should come out with us more often?" he suggested. "We do a lot of walking. It's a good way to connect with your surroundings."

"As you know, this is not my first exploratory assignment," Radätel replied stiffly. "And if you assess our relative stature, you'll no doubt ascertain that your legs are much longer than mine."

"Of course." Huldar stifled a grin. "My apologies."

The slope angled upward. Huldar paused, ostensibly to study the pinnate leaf of a new kind of strap tree.

"My goodness, it is steep, isn't it?" Radätel asked plaintively.

"Getting that way," Huldar replied. He waited while the Overlord caught his breath. "Ready?"

Radätel nodded and he continued more slowly. When they reached the track that wound around the cliff-face, Huldar paused to looked ahead where the trail vanished beneath braided sheets of melt-water. The noise was deafening.

Radätel looked back the way they'd come. "More of an adventure than I anticipated," he shouted.

Huldar snorted affably.

They followed the trail toward the falls then hugged the cliff-face to slip beneath them into a world of noise and darkness. Spray made every surface slick. Moss and fungi knobbled the walls. Algal slime greased the path. Further in there was enough room for them to walk abreast but he could sense the Overlord's fear.

With one hand he pointed out that the track didn't stop at the first cave, but went on to a second.

Radätel tapped the side of his head. *Do you mind?*

Not at all, Huldar replied. *See through there? Almost a mirror to this one.*

By the entrance to the first cave he ran his fingers over smooth stone, edges rounded as if worn and polished with use. It was tall enough that there was no need for Huldar to duck his head, but the Overlord hesitated.

… Tell me if you find anything, he said.

Huldar nodded and went on alone.

Dim light wavered, coating the walls in watery patterns that confused the eye. With sharpened vision he saw Shen's footprints tracking back and forth on gritty mud. Deeper inside, he found a natural rock partition, and beyond it a flat, sandy floor. Cold air issued from a narrow crevice, and when he filtered the sounds he could hear the faint echoes of an underground stream. Nine mounds of berries grew among the pebbles on either side of the cleft, each culminated at about mid-shin height. The globular structures were covered in a lacework of whitish fibers, maybe fungal? On one mound the material had been pulled apart to reveal a nest of plum-colored fruit: Shen's doing, no doubt.

There was no other life in the cave, and he wondered how these had come to grow there. Had there been flowers –

perhaps pollinated by the green lizards? Or were they asexual reproducers … but if so, why make such large fruit, and what distributers were likely to find them, hidden as they were in the dark? Did they have a distinctive odor imperceptible to his annangi senses? Clearly, a great deal more study was necessary. The Went trail led there. Was this where the small group of what looked to be pregnant females had come? Perhaps the berries were a special food for them also. The idea was tantalizing. He wished he'd had time to follow that particular group more closely.

He turned as the light dimmed, and found the Overlord had ventured inside.

It's quite safe, Huldar assured him. *See, here they are, just as Shen said.*

They don't look like much, do they? the Overlord said. *I wonder what gave him the idea they might be edible?*

Cooks! Huldar chuckled. *Always looking for new flavors.* He turned to leave. *Let's see what's in the next one.*

The Overlord stood just beyond the mouth of the neighboring cave and waited as he went inside. This one also opened out onto a sandy floor, but the far edge was filled with a rushing torrent that plunged over a dark cataract into unknown depths.

Huldar found no evidence of more berries, but as he came to the shore of the underground river he was shocked to see the remains of several large carcasses caught on the rocks by the lip of the precipice. Hair waved in the current. It had the same bluish color as the small group of Went he'd seen coming that way. His mind reeled. Had they died as a result of eating the fruit? He was glad the Overlord had stayed outside. It was best this remained secret until he'd had time to study the situation properly.

Can we wall it up? the Overlord said. *There's plenty of rock to work with.*

That's a bit extreme.

Radätel turned, keen to leave. *Maybe, but the berries would be safe.*

Huldar stood without moving. Battered on the lip of oblivion, the sad remains jostled as if longing to be free to plunge to their fate. Their fruit deserved protection, more so now that annangi had discovered such a seductive use for them. Then a small smile started as he considered again the disappearing blood-bug hidden in the charm-laden fresco on Lisbo. While he and Andel holidayed on Hesh he'd gone to great lengths to find the artist, Bethan of Nhadu. The charm she'd taught him was wildly complex. He'd felt a sense of accomplishment when he'd been able to sing it effectively. With a bit more work to upscale the effect, he could use it here to disguise a real cave rather than one merely painted on plaster.

As he left the cavern he sang a short string to clear the entrance of tracks – at least he'd be able to tell if any other creatures entered it.

The Overlord waited out on the path, beyond the edge of the spray. His face was paler than usual and beaded with small droplets, but Huldar could see they were sweat and not mist from the falls.

"I'll need to allocate more time for study," he said.

"Study?" the Overlord grunted. "You are joking, aren't you? Those things need to be forgotten."

"Not much chance of that," Huldar scoffed.

"You must make it happen! The Faythan requires it."

"The fruit may be crucial to the life-cycle of the Went."

The Overlord snorted mockingly. It seemed challenging his fear of caves had done his temper no good. "A handful of berries essential to a small population of creatures so elusive that you didn't even know they existed until you'd been here for a full three years? There's no shortage of rock nearby. Wall it off."

After a heavy tramp back across the plain, Huldar paused by the portal.

Radätel scowled. "Is there a problem?"

Huldar shook his head softly. "If I return to camp now, there will be things that need my attention. Work to be done. These caves must be properly examined."

"I can't find my way home alone," the Overlord said shortly.

Huldar waited. His stomach rumbled, and not for the first time. The sun, already low on the horizon, faded as storm clouds raced toward them.

Radätel slumped. "I apologize, Huldar. It's caves – even enclosed spaces sometimes. It's why I decided to join the Guild. At least I'm not stuck inside an office. Even a small room can sometimes make me sweat."

"I'm sorry to hear that," Huldar said, "but glad it brought you to us."

"Really?"

"You seem surprised, but you are the best Overlord we've had so far. Sensible and approachable, yet able to keep us all on track." Huldar made a short bow. "Thank you for your efforts, Radätel Gok. And don't be embarrassed. Bad things do happen in caves sometimes."

"Are you ever afraid?"

"Often, but when a job needs doing, I've learned to put it aside."

"Wise words. I will think on them." He returned Huldar's bow, then turned to look back the way they'd come. "I can see that a little more study regarding the berries may be a valid use of your time," he said eventually. "After all, we did eat them. But this little jaunt has taken up most of the afternoon and there are other matters I must attend to."

"My apologies, Overlord." Huldar gestured to the gate. "Shall we?"

THE VANISHING CHARM

It had been almost a week since Huldar had agreed to seal the cave beneath the falls, but the weather had deteriorated to such an extent that this would be his first opportunity to go back.

Andel stood beside him, far-searching the position of the Went herd. When she opened her eyes she took him by the hand and shared an image of a thousand shaggy backs plodding through the rain. *Another few days and they'll converge on the long beach where …* Her stream of thought momentarily dimmed. The vision zoomed up and down the long column. *Can't see any stragglers … and it seems there's only one blue one – I wonder what happened to them? But perhaps there's more. They're so wet it's hard to tell.*

She withdrew her vision. Huldar looked up at the sun, relieved not to have to admit what he knew of the Went females. If all but one died every cycle, where did the new ones come from? *Not a cloud in the sky on this side of the ranges,* he said, *a nice change after all that rain!* And now he knew the herd was far from here and still moving away he felt more comfortable about what he was about to do.

Malena and Daric waited nearby, their expressions wary. He turned to them. "If you're ready?"

"I'm intrigued," Malena said.

"Secrecy?" Daric shook his head. "You continue to amaze, Shamkarun Huldar."

They started for the southern portal. "You'll understand when we get there."

As they arrived on the plains, the roar of the falls was already audible.

"Can you hear it?" he asked. "There's been so much rain it's accelerated the thaw."

"Hear it?" Malena replied. "I can feel it! So that's where we're going?"

"Yes," he agreed, "to the falls themselves, but by the sound of it, we might not be able to get in."

"In?" Daric asked, then he nodded. "The berries."

Their squelch across the plain paused as they topped the rise and caught their first sight of the waterfall. A wide crescent of spume plummeted from the black lava cliffs in a never-ending crescendo. Their picnic spot was well and truly submerged, their rock buried beneath the waters, and even if they could reach the cave, he wondered what effect the deafening roar would have on the charm he had in mind.

He turned to the others.

"Olatu wants the cave walled up."

Daric nodded as if this was expected.

"You knew?"

"Makes sense." Daric tipped his head. "Don't want the Host distracted by a series of mass love-ins now, do we?"

Malena laughed. "It'd play havoc with schedules."

"So why bring us?" Daric asked him.

"You two are my strongest singers, and there's a charm I want to try. From Bethan of Nhadu."

Malena tipped her head. "Lisbo?" An image of the Bays crossed her mind.

"Yes, it's from the fresco," Huldar replied. "They want the cave sealed, but we know nothing about those berries – except their effect on us, of course. So I want to leave a hidden entrance so we can continue our studies and no one the wiser, and also let the Went in if they need to return for any reason, although Andel viewed them on the trail heading west this morning."

"What does this charm do?"

"It will close off the opening as if it never existed."

"You want a screen?" Daric opened his palm in a graceful motion.

"No," Huldar said. "Done correctly, it will be as if the opening doesn't exist – no residue, not even a hint."

"And you learned this from a Nhadu?"

"An artist?" Malena added.

He nodded. "I did indeed. The blood-bug charm. I've been working on a scale-up, and I think that with your help …"

Daric squinted across the lake, suddenly keen. "Along that ridgeline, our feet will be dry enough." He pointed out the potential path. "There's a track once we scale the mountainside, is there not?"

Huldar's brows twitched. How did the Enna get his information?

One side of Daric's mouth tightened in a tiny grin.

"And because it's wide enough for the Went," Huldar continued, "there's a good chance we may still be able to access the cave-mouth despite the increased volume of the falls."

They made their way along the high ground then scrambled up the slope to the trail. As they rounded the last corner, the noise of the flood hit them with brute force. Daric covered his ears. Flattened against the cliff, they sidled beneath churning brown thunder into spray-filled gloom. Huldar looked down as they crossed the cave's threshold, but the trackless strip he'd left across its mouth had washed away.

While he and Daric studied the area they'd have to close off, Malena sang a globe to life and wandered to the back.

You said there weren't many, she said, *but I thought there'd be more than this.*

The bell inside Huldar tolled. Of the nine web-covered piles, only eight remained. Maybe they had been eaten by something, but he doubted it. There were boot prints further inside, and some seemed fresh. He poked among the empty strands of membrane and made a rough count of the fruits that were left – one hundred or so per pile.

I take it there were more? Malena asked.

Someone's made a stash, Daric said.

But very few people knew exactly where they were, and the weather's been shocking. Shen?

Daric shook his head. *And it's not one of us.*

Word's spread. Malena said. *The miners find it difficult to understand the ban.*

Huldar sighed. *We'll close up what's left*, he said at last. *Hopefully we'll recover them before they're put to use.* He led them back to the entrance. *So, the charm. Hold hands and I'll pass it along.*

Interesting! said Daric. *The base structure is completely different to anything I've seen. Malena?*

I'm not that sort of Shamkarun, but yes, it does seem to be a novel approach.

I spent some time trying to get my head – and voice – around the original piece, but I've simplified where I could, and this is the result. Huldar said. *If you notice the deeper structure? Almost crystalline? I think that's where it swallows itself. Any thoughts?*

And the problem is that it needs to be stretched? Malena offered.

Exactly.

This is a shortcut we use in rough transits – when the Chime is more fluid than usual. She showed him a complex chord structure. *Could it work here?*

Daric shared a wave of excitement. *Yes! Look – if we insert that part of the string there, and modify the undertone there, the vibrational consonance in this area here will not only maintain the illusion indefinitely, it can be switched on and off with relative simplicity.*

Well done! said Huldar. *I think I see where you're going … If we adjust this section … so – unless the key is known, virtual solidity! It will look and feel like the surface it reflects with no residues to indicate otherwise.*

Brilliant, Daric said admiringly.

Breath! Malena snorted. *Of more than average value to one such as yourself, Daric Enna.*

Huldar and Daric turned to look at her.

She shrugged. *I've had my suspicions. You're quite notorious, in some circles at least … and I know your sister vaguely. And then I saw something in Andel's mind when we …* She turned to Huldar and shook her head. *You're a very lucky person. Showed me a thing or two!*

Huldar's train of thought was thrown completely askew.

Daric winced. *There is more to a relationship than sex, Malena.*

Malena made a pitying face. *She's married to Huldar, in case you've forgotten. And what would an Enna know about sex anyway – all a bit too mucky for your lot.*

Please! Huldar interjected. *You can continue this discussion in your own time, and leave my wife out of it!*

Daric bowed. *My apologies.*

Malena took a breath. *Daric, I'd tell the Rukh sooner rather than later. You know how they can be.*

Again, Malena, Huldar said firmly. *If we could return to the matter at hand?*

She turned to him. *Of course. Are we ready to try this thing?*

No. Daric gazed up the path. His haze seemed no different than usual, but Huldar could see tightness in his posture. Seconds later he turned back to them. *We need a bit of a rock-fall first, something for the surface of the charm to reflect.* He looked at Huldar. *Correct?*

Yes. He pointed out an area of loose stone above the cave mouth. *Just a small one. Remember, we don't want the whole thing buried.*

Daric fluttered his hands for them to stand aside, then with a deft twist of mind, wiggled a modest boulder free. As it thudded to the ground, he held it firmly in place while a slide of debris built up around it. Huldar waited while he cleared a space, then together the three of them shored the opening with stay-charms similar to those used by the miners.

We should cover the debris as well, otherwise the stabilizing charms will show, Malena said.

Not necessarily, Daric said. *We can tie the new charm to those we've just put in place and hide the whole construct together.*

How? Huldar asked.

Daric passed his idea around … *Here, and just there, where there's the possibility of a bridge?*

Very effective! Huldar said admiringly. *Let's take a moment to fix the sequences in our heads. If we each take a turn – sing the charm, make sure it works, then collapse it?*

The other two nodded and retreated into their own mind-space. The roaring water filled the air with noise but he barely noticed. It was crucial the sounds were made correctly and with power enough to override the ambient vibration.

Malena lifted her head. The steel in her veil was a far cry from the coquettish outer shell she normally showed.

When Daric signaled he was also ready, Huldar gave him the nod. *You first, since the modifications are largely yours.*

The Enna bowed. He studied the surface of the rocks intently, then turned to the opening. His sweet yet resonant voice cut through the din of the falls with ease. After several seconds, the illusion formed, then he sang the notes that would tie it all together and stepped back.

There was no sense of a charm's presence, or even that one had been sung. Huldar examined where he knew the opening to be with every sense he had, but the disguise was seamless. He tapped it with his knuckles and it felt like rock, but it was a one-way effect. From inside there would be no evidence of the charm and nothing to stop one from leaving.

Song of the Breath! Malena exclaimed.

He gestured to Daric. *Now release it.*

Obligingly the opening re-appeared. He felt for the shoring, but there was no evidence of any charm whatsoever.

Remarkable! he said. *Now, if you would remove the whole thing and let Malena try?*

Malena stepped back. *You first. They're your babies.*

He turned to the cave mouth. As he plied his voice, he felt the notes resonate and gel where they should, then the end-notes slid into place and his creation set solid. Visual charms had always been a part of his storytelling technique, but this was definitely taking things a few steps further. Could any illusion be solidified this way? His mind reeled with possibilities.

My turn, Malena said.

Yes. Sorry! He sang the unlocking sequence and waved her forward. *All set?*

She gave him a mocking smile. *Navigator – remember? I sing for a living.* But moments after she opened her voice, the rocks around the cave-mouth began to tremble. Huldar and Daric jumped sideways as several rolled down the hillside.

She stopped in confusion. *I know I sang it right.*

Maybe the sound of the waterfall interfered? Huldar said.

I don't think so! Malena said indignantly.

Daric shrugged.

Try again? Huldar asked.

She opened her mouth, then hesitated. Confusion rippled her veil. *I know I should. I have the thing right there ... but – something is wrong. I ... I don't know. It's odd.*

Maybe you should ask one of the healers to look you over when we get back?

She shook her head. *You finish up.*

Huldar sealed the cave, but his mood had changed. The planet's bell tolled inside him as if counting his heartbeats.

What is it? Andel enquired. She was far away to the north of the inner sea. He sent a smile of reassurance.

The trio walked in silence until the clamor of the cascades faded.

"You must be excited about Kandät Enna's arrival," Huldar said. "Perhaps that's it."

"Maybe ... Although we've never gotten on." Malena answered.

"Would you like me to find out who took the berries?" Daric asked him. "Once Kandät's left us, they'll be gone."

"You think they'll send them back to the Realm?" Huldar asked.

"All navigators check their cargo thoroughly," Malena said sharply.

Daric snorted. "Think of the profit they'd bring. If it's the Faythan ..."

"Very well. See what you can find out," Huldar said. "They should be returned as soon as possible, at least until we understand better what they are."

AT THE SACRED SHORES

With the tops of the long dunes in view, Hnarse Stargazer stood close by Neetha's side and allowed the sight of the sacred shore to fill its eyes. The herd raised their noses and droned to the winds to announce their arrival, then lowered their heads and sounded a soft thrum of thankfulness to the Heart. They had arrived in good time. Now Grassmovers would watch for the Circle of Winds, waiting for the time when it would reach down to sniff the sand and bring about the engenderment.

"Do you ever wonder how it happens?" Neetha asked. "How the touch of the wind makes the circles combine? How it forms the New Purpose?"

"The touch of the wind does not form the New Purpose," Hnarse replied. "The Circle of Winds merely sniffs the New Purpose out, like Went detecting fruit. It is the finding that engenders. The New Purpose is defined by the Wind's discovery."

Neetha's hair waved in airy disagreement. "Without the Wind's touch, New Purpose remain unborn, but it requires the involvement of Wind, Sun and Sea. All know it. This has been observed through cycles incalculable. You yourself have seen it."

"Then why ask?" the Stargazer retorted. "Consider the aliens, the stilted ones. They came from somewhere. Did the Circle of Wind, Sun and Sea combine to engender them also?"

Neetha aimed its attention as if it observed the waves, but those eyes that held Hnarse in view seemed brighter.

"When the stilted ones came during the end of the last trail," Hnarse added, "I wanted to examine them more fully, but like all, I longed yet more for the tunnels of home."

Neetha's head tilted to observe a fading scrap of colorful alien skin. Caught on a spiky seaside flower, the remnant fluttered toward the endless curve of the beach.

Hnarse watched the wind move in Neetha's coat and formed a song about how the Grassmover's silken voice resembled the waves it observed. Alien remains on the sacred shore were unnerving, but could not alter the reason they were there.

Eventually, the hair on Neetha's head crinkled. "The Circle begins anew. Today is the day."

"And afterward, I wonder how many lost souls the Last Mother will find?"

"All of them, I hope. There will be New Mothers to instruct in this duty, all eager to assist, then next cycle, one of them will become the Last Mother ..."

"... and so on," Hnarse said. "The circle unbroken."

"Circle unbroken," Neetha repeated.

Side by side two Went watched and waited. When it saw the storm approaching, Hnarse bumped its companion playfully. They joined voices to bugle the news and other Went hurried to form lines on the dunes, some high on grassy hummocks, some in the valleys between. Turgid waves slumped against the shore as if afraid of what they might find. Towering clouds darkened and swelled into an edifice that blocked the light of the sun.

When a wind-snout joined sea to sky in a snaking silver rope, the Went's joyful welcome droned basso into the rising gale.

As if drawn by the sound, another waterspout was spawned, then yet more came to dance through the waves. Each sniffed deeply, blasting water aside as the search for New Purpose began.

Neetha Grassmover stood and displayed its colors. Other elders followed, lifting their noses in salute.

"The Circle of Winds approaches!" they chorused. "The time of engenderment is upon us!"

The news passed in a ripple of hair and posture. Noses swirled upward in the traditional gesture to summon the twisting ropes to shore.

Like roving tentacles, the waterspouts came nearer. All was as it should be ... but before the first could reach shore, it dissipated in a crash of waters.

The next also passed by, but still the Went swayed and sang. The spiraling winds would find the New Purpose. It had always been so.

Hnarse's heart surged with excitement as a towering spout touched shore at last. Sand and water exploded skyward. The air grew thick. The dunes vibrated. The moment of engenderment had come! Stinging sand blasted their exposed underbellies, but the Elder Went remained steadfast.

When the circle of winds withdrew, Hnarse looked to the skies for the next, but was shocked to see the remaining waterspouts dissipating. The Eldest Stargazer's eyes found Neetha's.

Among dunes, small lumps could be seen emerging from the sand, but where there would normally be a hive of young Went jostling for space, this time there were but few.

"Maybe more will come tomorrow," Neetha said. "The season lasts for more than just one day."

The New Purpose gained strength after hatching and stood in isolated groups, too young to understand there might be anything wrong.

Eventually the herd began to move among them, rounding up those who shared their clan's coat color and encouraging them to leave the shore and find food.

Through the following weeks, fresh storms came. Several waterspouts swept the dunes and more Wentlings emerged, but still in numbers far fewer than expected.

On a bright afternoon, Hnarse stared out to sea. The skies were blue and clear right to the horizon, and the brisk aroma of growing dune-grass mixed pleasantly with the smell of the ocean. The scene was beautiful to observe, but Hnarse would have liked it more if there had been clouds. For three days, there had been no storm activity at all. Neetha was convinced the season of engenderment had passed, and the stars above concurred.

The Last Mother shook her fine blue coat in sorrow, and accompanied by the small group of newly hatched mothers, began to gather the souls of those who had died during transition. There were many to find. As Last Mother, this was the first time she had collected since her predecessor's demise, but her stomach soon grew so distended it almost touched the ground. The new mothers merely followed and observed. Their capacity was to be reserved for the migration to come.

After selecting a favorite among them to gather her own soul when her duty was done, the Last Mother and her acolyte began their return to the sacred caves. There she would lay the lost lives to continue their path as part of the Great Circle. Then the new Last Mother would return to the herd and the migration would begin.

Hnarse stood with the other elders under the dappled light of the coastal forest and displayed its colors in honor of their departure. The Mother's gait was slow and labored. Laden with so many souls, her journey would be hard. If neither Went returned, a new Last Mother would be selected, and the two lost souls would not be collected until the next cycle. He hoped their journey would be successful.

It caught a strange look from Rangaara, the Eldest Singteller. As yet, the subject of prophecies had not been broached, but Hnarse was aware of a song about a time such as this when the circle would be broken. There was another tale, one from the far histories. When so few young Went survive the transformation, it warned of a rain of fire and a darkness that would plunge the Heart into purification too soon.

On the green lands beyond the dunes, sparse groups of young and old fed and learned.

It was not for a Stargazer to prompt a Singteller, and Hnarse shared no friendship with Rangaara as it did with Neetha, but over the coming weeks while each clan instructed their Wentlings in preparation for the journey ahead, it seemed to Hnarse that there were many more teachers than pupils.

Was this the time of the Broken Circle? Had their kind reached trail's end at last? Attrition during the migration was harsh. Many Went, both old and new, would be lost – maybe even Hnarse itself. As a veteran of five trails, it knew there was a possibility that not enough would survive. It recalled Fesneeth Singteller's rendition of the prophecy, always performed in the final days before they entered their tunnels for the long sleep. Hnarse recited the song to itself. Although it was sad, to see it at all was a mark of achievement – of having lived to see the end of another season – and of hope to wake again for the next. At that time, the notion of the end of days held a certain, distant poignancy, but the dread of their current situation was not poetic at all.

Fesneeth had not survived the last purification and was greatly missed. Would Rangaara Singteller be alive to sing the prophecy at the conclusion of this cycle?

Hnarse's thoughts wavered as a trickle of sand dribbled from a neighboring dune. Its coat stilled as more sand moved, then it watched in astonishment as a last New Purpose split its cocoon and floundered into the evening air.

Hnarse's nose outstretched in welcome, but the Wentling seemed unable to move. Its strange coat mingled patches of Stargazer with the russet of a Singteller. Stripes of blue crossed its head and back – the blue of a Mother. But beneath its legs was skin of indigo and Hnarse knew that, whatever else it might be, this last newcomer belonged to the Stargazers.

With a swell of happiness in its heart, the Elder moved closer and repeated the greeting.

Nothing happened.

When Hnarse brushed it with its trunk, the late one started as if noticing the Elder's presence for the first time, but its young coat, still damp from hatching, remained oddly silent.

Hnarse waited. It recalled the shock of wakefulness and the flood of memories that followed. If this one needed some time ...

At last, the wentling took a tentative step forward but then it halted once more, quiet and forlorn.

Hnarse made a soothing sound. It pushed closer.

When they touched again, the Wentling gave a squeak, then blundered into Hnarse's legs and huddled there.

Hnarse smiled. "I know this is strange ..." But when it touched the young one's head, its hair flattened with shock. Panic moved its soul. It looked around for Neetha, but the elders had moved on and the sacred shores were empty.

Oblivious, the Wentling's nose wandered over Hnarse's chest, examining its coat with the lightest of touches.

Hnarse forced itself to looked down again. It searched the hair of the youngster's head – gently at first, then with increasing urgency.

There had been a mistake, a terrible mistake.

A slow tear dribbled to the sand.

How could this little one be a Stargazer?

It had no eyes.

BLESSINGS

"Going out to help Casco? Of course I'm going out to help Casco!" Malena snapped. "Stupid kalla! Are you going to repeat that too? Stupid kalla? Stupid, stupid?"

With a stricken cry, Sari bolted from the tent.

Andel stood up. "Malena! How could you!"

The tall Maatu rounded on her with an icy green glare.

Huldar stepped forward. "Apologize, Maatu, and be quick about it!"

Malena's gaze wavered. Her eyes flooded with tears.

Andel's outrage softened. "Malena?"

"I'm so horrible!" she sobbed, then she too raced from the tent. "Sari! Sari, I'm sorry ..."

Andel and Huldar looked at each other.

"What's gotten into her?" Tam asked.

"Half the Host by now," Arko murmured snidely.

"I'll have a chat with her," Huldar said. "Maybe the strain of isolation's getting too much."

"I saw her talking to Alis yesterday," Andel said.

Huldar sensed his wife's concern and countered it with a smile. She'd stood up to Malena without a second thought – and that was no mean accomplishment. "Whatever it may be, if she's talking to the Naghari, I'm sure all's in hand." But he remembered her failure to sing the charm.

Let's head out to the valley, if you've got time? I want to show you something.

Is it important? she replied. *I have to get over to the tin mine. I think there might be another seam close by.*

I'll take you there as soon as we're done.

I can take myself there, thank you!

He winked. *All right, Malena.*

She glared at him. He could feel her indignation.

His eyebrows gave an enquiring flicker. *It's a joke?*

Jokes are meant to be funny, she snapped.

When they reached the lake, it was still flooded and soggy as when he was there with Daric and Malena, but the flowers had spread to cover the entire surface in shining white blooms. He was relieved to see the emerald lizards had grown in size and number and felt a belated stab of guilt for not considering whether the cave he'd sealed played a part in their reproduction.

"Now, what was it you wanted to show me?" Andel said.

Thoughts of alien creatures faded as he took her in his arms. *How much I love you.*

Her smile was wry. She pushed him back. *There are other ways to show appreciation.*

I know, he grinned, *but this way is quite enjoyable …*

Her look was fond, but her inner landscape gusted between exasperation and plain annoyance. He released her.

What is it? I thought you liked surprises?

"This will be my third 'surprise' this week."

"I'm sorry." He turned to look at the lake. What was he thinking? She was busy and so was he – and they shared a bed more nights than not. "I guess it was a bit … It's just that …" He shared an impression of her aroma tied with the way he felt when she pushed aside the wayward lock of hair on her forehead … her wrist turned and the sun caught her eyes – just so. "It's driving me wild," he admitted.

Wild?

There was a quickening of interest. He turned to face her. *Completely.*

She nestled back into his arms and purred, "Wild is good."

They kissed and enjoyed the tingle as their hazes interacted. He touched her breast and she arched to meet him. When their bodies merged, it felt as wonderful as ever, but it was as if her mind had changed color without him noticing. Eventually, he paused. *What is it?*

Tears came to her eyes. *I don't know,* she said.

He wiped her tears with the edge of his thumbs … *I know you want me* … and tucked those loose hairs behind her ear. *But it's as if another part of you doesn't. You make me feel like … I'm unwelcome.*

No! The tears started in earnest. *I want you – I do. I'm so sorry. It's my fault. I don't know what's wrong with me.*

At once, he was sorry he'd spoken. His wife was fragile in ways he was only beginning to understand.

I'm the one at fault, he said. *It's me that's turned into Malena, not you.*

She chuckled through tears. *So that's what you're doing all that time you're away!*

He kissed her forehead. "Perhaps a trip to the Naghari is in order?"

"It's only a feeling," she said slowly. Her hand migrated to the smooth skin below her belly-button. A welter of new emotions bubbled in her chest. "But ..." *What if we've been blessed?*

Blessed? He looked at her stupidly. His heart raced. It was certainly possible. He got to his feet and reached to help her up. "Let's go see them now."

Alis watched while Ubaid placed his hands lightly over Andel's abdomen. He paused, his expression mystifying.

"Well?" Huldar asked. "Should we be celebrating?"

The Naghari glanced quickly at each other, then Ubaid kissed Andel's cheek.

"Congratulations," he said. "You are blessed indeed."

Elation bubbled between Huldar and his wife. He swam in the love of her tawny gaze and kissed away tears of joy.

"It is too early for you to feel it directly, Huldar, but Andel? If you would allow me?"

Through their marriage bond, he followed as Ubaid showed his wife the tiny life-spark inside her womb. His heart churned. They were Blessed! Then he glimpsed something odd.

"Is that a second one?"

Ubaid shook his head. "An echo. As you know, twins are extremely rare. But look, can you see this?"

Huldar strained his senses.

See what? Andel asked.

"I believe our new little soul will be female."

"A girl …!"

Huldar's imagination saw a miniature version of Andel in his arms, a tiny miracle with hair maybe a bit more his color, but eyes tawny and deep like her mother's …

And hopefully not with your nose, she laughed.

They turned to share their excitement with the healers, but although Alis smiled, her veil was somber.

"Is something wrong?" Andel asked cautiously.

Ubaid's eyebrows wrinkled. "Not *wrong*, exactly." He looked at Alis again. "As you know, it is not customary to celebrate an impending birth until the beginning of the second trimester. At that time, the pregnancy can be confirmed …"

Alis cut in softly: "I am also blessed."

Andel's hands clasped. "That's amazing! How wonderful!"

"Then there *will* be twins, in a manner of speaking!" Huldar laughed. "The Uri'madu will be quite a busy group in eighteen months' time. Two babies? We'll have to have those extra healers shipped in now, won't we? The sooner the better."

Ubaid rubbed his forehead. "A little girl also, and we're delighted, of course – but Huldar, there's more."

"What, more babies?" he joked.

"Oh, darling!" Andel laughed. "Such a thing is impossible. Two at the same time in the same small group must already be nearly so ... Ubaid?"

Huldar took Andel's hand. The bell inside him tolled as if marking his heartbeats.

"I don't know how to say this," Ubaid said at last. "We've had trouble coming to terms with it ourselves." He glanced at Alis again. "Malena – is also Blessed."

Huldar gave a short huff. "That's impossible."

"Malena is pregnant?" Andel repeated.

"She came to us after her failure at the cave. I'm afraid there can be no doubt."

"Unmarried?" Huldar sat down. "But she is unmarried!"

"It is true she has not exchanged her bond," Ubaid said. "Yet she *is* Blessed. Also with a daughter."

"But how can that be?" Andel asked.

"We are as puzzled as you," Alis said softly. "It seems to have stemmed from the picnic. We are all at exactly the same stage of pregnancy."

"Something in the water?" Huldar suggested. "The lilies? No ..." Then he remembered the rich sensations he'd felt after crushing a certain small kernel between his teeth. "The berries? But you tested them."

"Yes – and there were unusual compounds present. I knew they would cause some euphoria, the strong desire for sex. How was I to know they would alter our very physiology?"

"There's no precedent," Alis added defensively. "Nothing like this has ever happened."

"Anyone else?" Huldar asked faintly.

He shrugged. "We'll have to check every female who was present, but given what's happened here, it seems likely"

Andel glanced his way. *Sari ...?*

"Unobtrusively, if you can." Huldar looked skyward. "We don't want a panic." He knew Andel could sense his confusion – he could sense hers. For a brief few moments their joy had been complete, but now?

Alis took Andel's hands. "A blessing is a blessing, dear one. The gift is a gift, no matter the path it takes to reach you."

"No wonder Malena has been acting so strangely," Andel said. "She was awful to Sari this morning."

Huldar recalled her distress when her song went awry. "If she is pregnant she can no longer navigate, did you know?"

Ubaid nodded. "Vibrational balance is most critical when traveling between worlds. Pregnancy alters the synergy between voice and mind." He turned to Andel. "As a Tsemkar, you will have no impediment, but it is best not to perform anything too intense. As the pregnancy progresses, over-strong use of your power may damage your unborn child."

"Will I be able to travel?"

"Of course, but Malena won't be plying the Chime for a good while to come. Even after her baby is born, it could take three or four years before her body has realigned itself, and many more before the child's psychic dependence reduces enough so she can leave it behind."

Andel looked at him, uncomprehending.

"Adults become accustomed," Alis said. "But for a little one? Every time Malena enters Qalān, it will seem to her daughter as if she has died."

"Will we be able to get home?"

"Yes, of course," said Ubaid. "But with another navigator."

"Malena was supposed to carry us home again at the end of our contract, leaving Kandät Enna to concentrate on carrying cargo. I hope he understands," Huldar said thoughtfully.

"There's plenty of time to worry about that. A new navigator will surely be found to take her place. But unmarried yet Blessed? Malena's state of mind may be more difficult to resolve."

MEETING

Set in the foothills above the endless plains, the Uri'madu's base on the Eastern Continent was an island of warmth in a landscape still gripped by winter. Inside the marquee, a predominantly female gathering clustered in small knots around the central hearth.

Huldar raised his hand. "A little quiet, please?"

Slowly, conversation died.

"Thank you." He turned to the healer. "Ubaid?"

Ubaid stepped forward. Outside. the thin wind made an eerie song in the guy-ropes. Further away, he could hear the arrhythmic slap of an unsecured doorway.

"Many of you are scared right now," he began. "I know I am … a little. Nothing like this has happened in all the long history of the annangi. This situation is absolutely unique, so it's hard to know how to proceed."

"But what happened?" someone asked.

"And what are we supposed to do?"

"I have work to do! I can't be blessed. How can I be?"

Ubaid grimaced understandingly. "What answers I can, I will give. This is what happened – the series of events. All of you, bar Tisha and Caine, were at the picnic by the lake, yes?"

Heads nodded.

"And you each ate one of those berries – is that right?"

"And had sex afterward," Malena said. "Rather awesome sex."

"That's right," said Ubaid. He turned to two Cantori miners. "And you, Tisha and Caine, ate one soon after?"

"The next day. We didn't know this would happen!" cried Tisha.

Caine rounded on her. "Farrel said they were a new thing, that they'd make us feel good. I knew he was lying about something! Some friend you are!"

"We didn't know!"

Huldar interjected, "Friends – please?"

Still glowering, the miners returned their attention to Ubaid.

"For reasons we have yet to deduce," the healer continued, "each of you has been blessed – regardless of your marital status. The catalyst here seems to have been the purple berries. Now, you have been fully examined by either me or Alis, and your pregnancies seem quite normal at this stage. We will continue to monitor each of you closely, but there is no reason to expect complications."

"Can Alis still heal if she's pregnant?"

"Yes. The ability to heal is unaffected, although as with anyone else, her use of Shamkar to augment various processes will be unreliable at best. This effect will pass soon after the birth, but until then, except for the most basic of functions, I suggest that those among you who are singers not even try."

"And if we can't complete our contracts?"

"Both the Overlord and the Faythan have been advised of the situation and extra workers will be requested to arrive at the mid-way transfer."

"But what will happen?"

Kira rolled her eyes. "You'll have a baby!"

"No need for sarcasm," said Ubaid. "The situation is difficult enough as it is."

"I'm sorry, it's just that I already have children – two of them."

"And your husband?"

"Rejoined the Breath. I know what it's like to rear a child on your own, and it's not fun."

"Then you'll be an invaluable help to those who know nothing. I know it's a strange situation – the unknown is always frightening – but at least we have each other. That said, if any of you wish to return to the Realm on the mid-point rotation, that's no problem, but I've been informed that for the transfer coming up, it won't be possible."

"Why not?" said Tisha.

"You want to leave?" said Calen. "Face the Realm like this? As Ubaid said – at least here we have each other." She returned to the healer. "Can the pregnancies be … stopped?"

Ubaid studied his boots for a moment, then lifted his head to face the anxious gathering. "Yes, it's possible. If you really feel that that is what you must do, then Alis and I will help.

But think carefully before you ask, and don't leave it too long. A life is a life, after all, and sacred."

There was a short silence, then everyone started speaking at once.

"We'll take a break," Ubaid announced, but Huldar was not sure anyone had heard him. The healer took a mug of tea and headed for the rear of the tent. Huldar followed.

"Going well so far?"

"Better than I expected, anyway," Ubaid replied. "As you know, I'm not used to speaking to crowds."

"You've handled it very well."

"With your help." Ubaid rubbed his chin. "I've a favor to ask. Alis just prompted me. I know they're off limits now, but would it be possible to have a single berry to study? I'd dearly like to know how they've caused this … bizarre situation. Can you imagine the furor back in the Realm?"

"Furor?"

"Blessings to order? Think of our God-Emperor, for one! Ishät Ashik's desire for a second child is driving him mad. He needs proof of El's favor." He shook his head. "I can't imagine how the Empress feels."

"I hadn't thought of it that way."

"Alis and I have spent time in the Imperial City's chapter house. Seen the aftermath of his rages far too often."

"I'll get one for you as soon as I can," Huldar said, then he rubbed his forehead. "You've reminded me of something. There were corpses in the adjoining cave – Went corpses. I know the area is special to them. We saw a group – we assumed them to be female – heading that way."

"You're worried the berries killed them?"

"Or it could have just been old age. I've said nothing to Andel."

Ubaid nodded. "Wise. No need to alarm anyone any more than they are already. But you're correct in thinking we should go there as soon as possible. I can examine the bodies – just to be sure."

"How about tomorrow, if the weather holds? Meet me in the morning." He looked at the group around the fire. Some were still in conversation while others simply stared into the flames. "Time to wrap it up?" he suggested.

Ubaid gave a thoughtful nod.

As they headed back to the fire, an anxious hush spread around them.

"This has been a difficult day," Ubaid began. "And I'm sure there will be plenty more to come. But a baby is a wonderful thing, a new life, a blessing indeed, and whatever difficulties you face, I am certain they will be forgotten in the joy new life will bring."

Kira snorted. "Well, we're about to find out, aren't we, girls?"

"Stick together. Help each other where you can." He paused, then continued, "Now there's one more thing before you all go back to your lives. Olatu of Faytha has requested that, as far as possible, we take a 'business as usual' approach. Those of you who can no longer perform your duties will be assigned fresh, more appropriate tasks. There will be no pay-penalties since the aberrant circumstances occurred through no fault of your own."

"Well, that's something I suppose," Calen mumbled.

Huldar stepped forward. "Eighteen months' gestation can seem a long time, but it will be upon us before we know it."

"And when the time comes, we'll need to be highly organized," Ubaid continued. "Please, some of you have partners in mind, but for those who do not, or are unsure, don't leave it too late to ask someone you trust to be your birth-guardian. Our next meeting will be for them also, and Alis and I will be running classes to teach these trusted ones how to support you and your babies both psychically and physically through the birth. It's a very important role and quite taxing. When Alis's time comes, I must be available to assist her – but if you can't find anyone suitable, I will do my best to help."

Andel turned to Sari. "You could ask Casco."

"Casco?" Her smile glowed from somewhere deep and soft. "Do you think he would?"

"I'm sure he would."

While the blessed filtered from the tent, Andel waited as Huldar resumed his conversation with Ubaid. There was some urgency to their discussion, but the content was hidden. She turned toward a peculiar sound from the rear of the tent and saw Malena seated on her favorite cushion with her legs drawn up tight. Her forehead rested upon her knees in a gesture strangely reminiscent of Lind.

"Sari, I think some tea might be required."

While Sari busied herself in the kitchen, Andel went to kneel beside the navigator.

"I can't sing," Malena sobbed. "I can't go home."

"I wish there was something I could do ..."

"Well there isn't," Malena snapped. "And if I'm not a navigator, what am I? What use a Shamkarun who can't sing?"

"It's not forever," Andel soothed. "Your baby will be born. You'll be able to sing again."

"Terrific!" she retorted. "This contract was supposed to be a punishment for not agreeing to marry. Can you believe it? I should have accepted a husband when I had the chance. Who would want me now? A navigator who can't navigate, with a child that shouldn't be!" She searched Andel's face. "I could ask the Naghari to send it back to the Breath, but it's a blessing, a gift from El ... isn't it?"

"Malena ... I don't know. Of course it is."

The navigator's haze showed her caught between anguish and fear. "It's all right for you," she said angrily. "You're married. You have Huldar. I have no one!"

"No one?" echoed Sari. She settled a tray with three cups between them. "That's not true. You have us. And don't forget Ariben. We are your family now – for as long as forever, and we will never let you down, isn't that right, Andel?"

Andel cupped her galano between two hands. "Yes, it is," she said with certainty.

Malena relinquished her knees. Hesitantly, she reached for her tea. She took a sip and tried to smile, but her eyes were red from weeping. "Forever is a long time. I don't think we can be family forever."

"Forever? Maybe not," said Sari. "Maybe it will just seem like forever – but we'll be there for you if you need us."

"Here." A slim form hovered over them. "I brought cakes."

Malena smiled up at Tala, one of her spinners. "Thank you," she said, and gave the offering a guilty look. "I am being a bit silly, I suppose. I'm not the only one, am I?"

"No," said Tala firmly. "We are all struggling. If this is what you need to do, Malena, then do it all you want – but don't forget – family works both ways."

―――――――――

Olatu rubbed his hands together. The God-Emperor's problem was solved. His rise within the Imperium was assured. And later on, with a bit of careful planning, he could sell blessings to order without compromising the God-Emperor's good will – after the Imperial pregnancy was safely fulfilled, of course. Faytha had blessed him indeed.

He must ensure the God-Emperor would be first to receive the opportunity to be blessed. There must be no rumors. All correspondence must be censored. Kandät Enna and his crew must be kept away from the Host, the mothers stowed out of sight, and, ideally, the berries delivered personally by the navigator or by Lucaät of Faytha himself.

But the Emperor would realize there were other pregnancies, of course, or how else would one know about the fruit's properties …?

Olatu considered this. Perhaps it would be best if he did not know … only that they were a powerful aphrodisiac. That way he would believe the pregnancy to be entirely natural and proof of El's favor at last, and maybe his rages would subside. Though if he discovered the truth for himself –he envisioned the terrifying spectacle of the God-Emperor's tentacles in action. That would not be good. Far safer to give them to Kandät Enna as a special delivery with a short explanatory note. The Imperial couple would try them, they would be blessed, he would be rewarded, and all would be excellent indeed.

But what if the baby is abnormal ... his subconscious whispered. *Surely you should wait?*

No! he replied. *If I am not the first, the opportunity will be lost. Ishät Ashik is not stupid, far from it! He will understand the risks. The decision will be his. I am merely providing him with an amazing opportunity at the first possible moment, as is my duty.*

THE TRUTH OF THE BERRIES

Huldar gazed out over the prairies of the Eastern Continent, their wide expanse still bare of vegetation. A stiff breeze whistled in his ears. Cumulous clouds piled high above the rim of the horizon – more storms on the way. Dark shadows scudded over the last tenacious snow, yet he could see in his mind's eye how it would be in a few months' time, covered in a floral carpet.

He pulled his jacket firmly around him and set off to meet Ubaid. Since he'd found out about the blessings, the bell inside him had tolled continuously and, gift-of-the-planet or no, he wished there was some way he could turn it off.

When he stepped back to their original Central Continent campsite, wisps of steam dissipated skyward from tents still damp from thunderstorms the night before. He smiled to himself, imagining how Andel would draw a contrast of their pale fragility presaging another round of violence to come.

His scan for Ubaid was fruitless, but others of the team still used this as a base-camp; Calen and Van were assigned to Flying Slug Reef for a routine ongoing environmental impact assessment – a task they could perform without the necessity to sing. Malena and her spinners had also chosen to remain there, as had Casco and Daric.

Calen and Van were preparing for their day. Malena and her spinners had already gone. But he could sense Casco and Daric inside the marquee, tidying up after breakfast. He wondered whose turn it had been to cook.

He knew it shouldn't worry him to speak to Casco, but still he hesitated … and while he gathered his nerve, the two came outside.

Casco gave him a nod before turning for the stores.

Daric paused as he passed on his way to the western portal. "Still on for this afternoon?"

"Sky-step cliffs," Huldar said. "There's a link to an unexplored island."

With a jaunty tilt of his head, Daric continued on just as a tingle from the south gate announced Ubaid's arrival.

The healer searched him with knowing eyes. "Something wrong?"

Huldar glanced briefly at the stores tent then shook his head. "Let's go. I think you'll be interested to see this."

"The undetectable charm?"

"I'd prefer you kept all knowledge of it to yourself."

Ubaid tilted his head. "Any special reason?"

"Instinct."

Ubaid paused as they exited the first portal. "Are you sure there's nothing wrong?"

"There's nothing wrong," Huldar said sharply.

Ubaid's eyebrows lifted.

Huldar looked away. "Something's amiss," he admitted. "I can't place it, and it's gnawing at me."

"Something to do with Andel?"

He shook his head.

"It's normal to have trepidation," Ubaid said. "You're about to face irrevocable change."

"There is that, of course," Huldar agreed, "but this is different." He hesitated. "It's the planet. When I spoke to her, it changed me."

Ubaid's gaze returned to the horizon. "I'd almost forgotten. Strange how one becomes accustomed to the extraordinary – and of course, you're not one to sing your own song. Let's hope our mothers-to-be adapt as well to their astonishing new status."

They stepped through the portal in silence, then made the short trek to the next. The path through the miniature strap-trees was easily seen, its terminus an island of bare dirt.

"Last step?" Ubaid said.

"It is." Huldar examined the bare ground. "I wonder if they will regenerate?"

"I think they will – if ever we stop using it. Otherwise ..."

Huldar grunted affably and stepped them through to the valley of the lake. The pressure inside him expanded. Ubaid gave him a suspicious glance, but said nothing. Feelings of distress grew with each stride he took.

When they rounded the knoll, not only was the entire lake cloaked in brilliant white blooms, he saw they'd continued up the mountainside as well.

Look! He pointed out two shapes partially obscured by the falls. *Went. I thought they were all camped by the inland sea.* Within him, the bell came to life, tolling every heartbeat like a gong. It was so loud he wondered why Ubaid couldn't hear it.

They look troubled, Ubaid noted. *They're usually slower, calmer, yes?*

Certainly are, Huldar agreed. *We should hurry.*

By the time they gained the path, both were breathing heavily. As they neared the Went, Huldar's inner clamor subsided somewhat. He put his hand out for caution.

We don't want to distress them further.

That one is so much bigger than the other, stomach quite distended. Ubaid noted. *Pregnant, maybe?*

Huldar winced. *We have no idea of their breeding cycle as yet ... although I have my suspicions.*

Perhaps the berries are essential to the process? They seem anxious to reach them.

I had no idea they would return. From a safe distance, he sang the sequence to open the cave, and with a bugle of relief both Went pushed inside.

Huldar hurried to follow.

He observed that the smaller one's nose stayed in constant contact with the larger one's bloated body – like a caress. – as she made her way to the back of the cave. She examined the berry piles, but did not eat any. As if satisfied all was in order, they moved away and young and old circled each other as if in a dance.

Huldar started, as with a scream of pain, the elder reared up.

Her bloated abdomen was shiny and taut, the patterns on it vivid. Although there was no breeze, her hair rippled in waves.

There was another scream and a tearing sound and he gasped as the Went's enormous belly began to rip open. Small purple objects poured from the jagged wound and landed in a squelching pile.

Breath! Ubaid exclaimed. *They're not berries, they're eggs!*

Huldar envisioned the pregnancies. *What have we done?*

As the last egg fell, the mother lowered herself to the ground. The rip in her abdomen dripped blue ichor. She staggered and leaned against the younger one for support. They turned and shuffled for the entrance, but despite the young one's soft calls of encouragement, it was clear the other's strength was fading.

The two archangels followed as the Went reached the path and turned toward the adjacent cave. The ripped one struggled to reach it. Huldar shared a sense of foreboding. Suddenly the bodies he had seen on his earlier visit made sense.

Within the second cave, the sound of crashing water was deafening. Step by step, the wounded Went made her way toward the precipice. When she collapsed, it was almost a relief. Her mouth lay open. Her breathing was slow and labored. Her trunk trailed like a thick strand of blue-grey weed in the water.

Strings of moisture dribbled from the young one's nose. It bowed its forehead to the ground before the fallen Mother and droned, then stood and hurried for the exit, seeming oblivious to the annangi's presence. By the edge of the path it kneeled to pick a bunch of blooms with its nose, then came back into the cave and arranged them on top of the dying Went. When that was done, it returned to the mountainside for more.

Ubaid squatted gently beside the injured Went and stroked her head. She gave a moan and tried to move her trunk toward him, but the effort was too much. Shortly afterward, she gave a final shudder and lay still. He pushed his fingers through the fur on her side and looked up. There were tears on his cheek. *She's gone.*

Huldar joined him. The Went's coat was as silken to the touch as he'd imagined it would be. He looked toward the cave with the eggs. *What does this mean?*

The young one hurried in with a fresh load of flowers.

They were quick to step back, but it paid them no attention and soon left to get more. When the body was completely covered, the smaller Went made a few short pokes to adjust the arrangement, then reared up in a posture of display. For a short time, its nose waved in circles, then with a plaintive call it came down and bent its forehead to the ground. Its drone increased in fervor – hair rippling with effort, then faded sadly away.

It gave a last whimper, then got to its feet and surveyed the body. With its long nose, it searched beneath the limp hair on the old one's head, then with a delicate tug removed the central eye.

Cradling the eye in its two front pads, it rose to its hind legs. The orb flared, and for a moment the cave was bathed in light, then with a loud cry, the young Went swallowed it.

With effort, it pushed the body toward the cataract until it fell with a splash. Flowers scattered across the water and were swallowed by the falls. Strong currents carried the old Went toward the precipice. For a moment it seemed it would be wedged against the rocks like the bodies Huldar had first seen, but the increased flow pulled it free and it slipped over the edge.

The young one stood still, watching the place where the body had vanished. Then, with a last cry, it turned for the exit.

The cataract's roar continued unchanged.

Huldar left the caves to sit in the free air and motioned Ubaid to sit with him, their backs to the mountain side.

He envisaged the mounds of soft, purple orbs. *Eggs*, he repeated. *We didn't know.*

Ubaid shrugged apologetically. *I'm sorry, Huldar. I did examine them. If I'd realized I would have said.*

I know. The reproductive cylces on this planet are so strange, and we've had little time for study – and now? We have trouble indeed.

It's not wrong to eat eggs, said Ubaid. *We do it all the time – when the donor population density permits.*

Huldar sighed. *Went are egg-layers, and they lay them here, in these caves*, he thought aloud. "So where did the young on the beach come from?"

"The beach?"

"Andel and I saw them. Every morning at daybreak we spend what time we can to watch what the Went are doing." He shared a scene of young and old standing in clumps on the dunes above the long foreshore and feeding on fruit in the forest behind it. "They seemed to appear overnight."

"Isn't that the beach where Duvät ...?"

"It is. I strongly suspect the Bel Nishani are larval Went, a developmental stage between these eggs and the six-legged young we've been watching over the past month or so. How that can be I don't know. Their reproductive strategies must be complex indeed."

Memories of the stricken mother's gaping wound and painful death filled him with sadness. His heart went out to the young one who paid the dying mother such respect. Would it be next season's sacrifice?

The images replayed in mind. His thoughts slowed. *Honoring the dead?* The planet's bell clanged. Excitement warred with alarm. He blasted a montage of evidence at the healer. *Ubaid! This is incredible!*

Ubaid looked at him blankly.

They are sentient! Huldar turned toward the trail of the departing Went. *Self-aware! Not creatures, but citizens of the Realm.*

Citizens?

Yes! He leaped to his feet. *This is the most important day of my – well, my working life at least! Of all our lives!* He paced up and down the track, trying to sort the implications, remember the protocols. *I don't know what to do. How to respond. The God-Emperor must be told!*

The Went must be protected at all cost. We must suspend all other investigations until their life-cycle is understood. There must be no interference. All mining must cease until the situation is fully understood.

Another thought bubbled to the surface ... were these the "watchers" the planet spoke of? But curiously, his inner bell had gone quiet.

Ubaid touched his arm. *Huldar, wait. There is more to this.* He passed a thought.

Huldar's elation paused. *Hosts?* His brow furrowed. *What do you mean? The pregnancies are normal. You and Alis – you both said so.*

Yes, but it's early days, Ubaid replied. *We ate these things, were consumed with the need for sex, then our females became pregnant?* "You said yourself that their cycle must be complex. There are other aphrodisiacs, some few even parasitic, but none that result in pregnancy. And this despite the female's reproductive statuses? I must admit, the thought concerns me more now than it did."

Huldar's brow furrowed. "Just to be clear … you are worried that the fetuses our blessed carry may not be of our own species?"

Ubaid nodded slowly.

He pictured Andel and the spark of life inside her. What was it if not annangi? Would it have six legs and hair? How would they cope? He visioned the Went-mother again, ripped open and dying. What if the same thing happened to his wife?

How can we tell? he asked.

How would I know? Ubaid said sharply, and Huldar was reminded that Alis was pregnant too. "We need to think this through," the healer continued. "We need to have a plan in place before the panic sets in. As soon as we tell them those were eggs, not berries, someone will start wondering, and it will begin."

"We should tell them," Huldar said. *They have a right to know.*

"I think it would be best to wait," Ubaid countered. He took a breath. "If there are abnormalities, we'll notice soon enough. Alis certainly will.' He winced. 'We can tell them then – when we know. If the pregnancies seem normal, it would be best for all concerned if the mothers looked forward to parturition. Fear, hatred, alarm … if experienced with intensity these emotions may negatively affect an unborn child – even scar it for life."

"But how can we keep this from our wives? From the other mothers-to-be? My people trust me."

"I know … but from a medical point of view, I think it necessary that we try."

Huldar grimaced as another thought struck him. "If I can't share what just happened, how can I explain to Olatu of Faytha that these are sentient beings? It is our obligation to protect them. This planet is theirs. Their rights must be observed."

"You must find a way," Ubaid said. "The discovery is only delayed. The health and wellbeing of the mothers is at stake and we are far from home – far from help. I say that to err on the side of caution is advisable."

Huldar put his head in his hands. Only moments earlier he'd felt the greatest excitement he thought possible, greater even than the moment he'd discovered his wife was blessed. Now, he didn't know. Every choice was laden with consequence.

Ubaid watched him. "Nothing that has happened can be changed," he said. "Knowledge can't help in this instance because as yet we have none. Please, let's just wait until we know more. Start no further panic until we are certain there are grounds."

"Very well," said Huldar at last. "But we must monitor every mother closely … please … and at the first signs there may be something amiss, they must be told. Agreed?"

"Agreed." Ubaid held his gaze. "I'm convinced it's for the best."

Huldar looked away. "As for the Overlord – and the Faythan – I will tell them that I strongly suspect the Went's sentience, and that more study is needed."

"Based on your observations of their behavior?"

"Exactly. But not every observation …" He shook his head. "I don't like it, Ubaid, but I do see your point. I doubt that Andel, or Alis, or anyone else would take the news well that she may be host to an alien life-form."

Ubaid rubbed his fingers firmly back through his hair. "Or that she may die in the birthing."

"Should the pregnancies be terminated?"

"What if they are annangi? What if they are genuine blessings?" Ubaid took a deep breath and let it out slowly. "If it becomes clear they are not of our own species, I'll put it to the mothers then. In that case, yes, may be best that they end their pregnancies, especially in the light of what we've just witnessed. Calen already has, and so has Caine, one of the Host."

Huldar stared at the ground beneath his feet. He moved a small rock with the toe of his boot, then moved it back the same way. Ninjay had seen Andel's child, a daughter … was this new life the one she'd spoken of? There was no way to tell – but even if it wasn't, if the vision was true, Andel must survive. He felt a sudden urgency to see her.

"Let's go," he said.

Ubaid nodded and started down the bank as if equally anxious to return and leave the troubling truth behind them, but a few steps into their descent, Huldar said, "Wait! I haven't re-sealed the cave."

"But you can't close it off again," Ubaid replied. "What if more Went come back?"

"But we can't leave the eggs unsecured," Huldar insisted. "We've lost enough already."

"An alarm perhaps?"

"I'm not good with alarms," he admitted.

"And I'm a healer ..."

Huldar nodded. "But even my poor effort will be better than none. I can set it to trigger if an annangi enters – that much I am capable of."

.

CONFRONTATION

Huldar set the alarm on the Went-cave as best he could, then started for the sprawling base-camp of the Host. It was mid-afternoon when stepped through the ridge-top portal and made his way down the muddy slope to the tent city. His senses sought and found Olatu as he emerged from the dining hall. The Faythan turned left along a tent-lined street of raised boards to where the supervisory staff resided. Huldar took a shortcut through the Cantori encampment, intent on catching him quickly.

He entered the street immediately behind the Faythan, but before he could say anything, Olatu paused and turned to face him.

Huldar gave him a cursory bow. "I need to speak with you. The matter is urgent."

"Urgent?" Olatu's brows arched. They were less manicured than when they had first arrived. "What could be important enough to bring the great Huldar of Leth to my doorstep unannounced?" He gave an oily smile. "Perhaps there are there more bugs to be evacuated?"

Olatu's tent was marked by fluttering banners with the rune of Faytha. Huldar nodded its way. "Perhaps we could speak privately?"

Olatu glanced sunward. "Very well, but I have quite a schedule to keep."

They ducked through the doorway into startlingly opulent surroundings.

"You seem excited by something," Olatu said.

Huldar took a deep breath. "I have amazing news."

"Another nacrite deposit?" Olatu said hopefully.

He shook his head. "Better than that. I believe the Went to be Citizens."

Olatu frowned. "Citizens? Those – hairy lumps?"

"Far more than hairy lumps!"

"Why would you think that?"

Huldar envisioned the greeting postures of the elders. "These are meaningful communications." He added a glimpse of the flowers the attendant Went had arranged on the dead Mother. "And even more telling – they honor their dead. They understand the concept of life – of being alive, and what it means when life ends. The floral shroud indicates they may even believe in an afterlife."

The Faythan sat heavily on the nearest chair. His tongue moved behind his lips as if examining the sharpness of his teeth. He looked up at Huldar. "And what do you *believe* we should do about it?"

"The protocols are clear," Huldar said. "All mining must cease, as I'm sure you are aware, until we fully understand the Went, their society, and their life-cycle. This planet belongs to them. We must negotiate our presence."

"Negotiate?" Olatu said scathingly. "With whom?"

"The Went."

Olatu burst into raucous laughter.

Huldar looked on incredulously as the Faythan waved his arm up and down in parody of a Went's nose. "This is no joke," he said flatly.

"It is to me," the Faythan sputtered.

"How will the God-Emperor react when he discovers your contempt for a new sentient creature? A new Citizen of the Realm?"

"The God-Emperor?" Olatu's hilarity vanished. "As if I'd bother him with this rubbish."

Huldar tried again. "Olatu of Faytha, you are leader of this Host. I must ask you to respect these protocols. Quite clearly, if normal procedures had been observed in the first place, we would not be in this position."

Olatu stood up. "And I'm asking you to return to work." He brushed down his tunic. "Our quotas are nowhere near filled and the navigator's arrival is imminent."

"Quotas?"

"The nacrite deposits are priceless."

He moved as if to leave. Huldar stayed put, barring the door.

Olatu scowled. "Get out of my way."

"Priceless?" Huldar said. "You would put coin before life?"

"What planet have you been living on?" the Faythan snapped. "The Realm runs on coin, not conversation with bizarre new species that may or may not be sentient. If they're so intelligent and concerned, let them come to us."

"Then stop mining this continent at least. There's no nacrite here."

Olatu pushed past him. "Out of the question."

Huldar reached for his arm, intent on showing him more of what he'd seen, but the Faythan wrenched away.

"How dare you?" Olatu exclaimed. "Your wife's touch sends people mad. How do I know you won't do the same to me?"

Huldar stopped, nonplussed.

"It's bad enough that half our staff are pregnant through your lack of care. Now this?" Olatu snarled.

Huldar followed him onto the street. "I have spoken to this planet," he said firmly. "I am sacred to Leth!"

The Faythan glanced over his shoulder. "Good for you. I've spoken to Ishät Ashik, tentacles and all. He wants nacrite. God-Emperor wins, every time."

Huldar strode behind him. "There is another matter," he started.

"No time," replied the Faythan. "I have profit to make."

"There'll be less coin if more miners get pregnant! Berries have been stolen. We must find them."

The Faythan gave a cursory nod and kept walking. When he encountered Farushael of Cantori, he stopped. "Have you examined the files I gave you?" he asked him.

Huldar pushed between them. "You can't ignore me! These matters must be discussed and acted upon."

Farushael bowed hurriedly and backed away.

"You! Stay!" Olatu barked. Farushael halted, his veil a study in neutrality. Olatu returned to Huldar. "There is nothing to discuss. Go count bugs, or whatever it is you do to fill your days. Here, we have real work to do. People rely on us for employment – for survival. Should we kill them now? Or send them home empty handed just so you Lethians can play with your pretty animals?"

"Of course not!"

"There you have it."

"But procedures must be followed."

"Yes, by all means! Just leave us out of it."

"I can't."

Olatu squinted directly into Huldar's face. "What are you going to do about it?"

Their hazes crackled with animosity. An unwelcome image of Olatu's face close to his during the episode by the lake flitted through Huldar's mind. How could he have found the Faythan attractive? He glanced pointedly at his un-Marked cheek. "I am *Shamkarun* Huldar of Leth. Listen to me! If you disobey these protocols you will lose your job. The guild will strip you of your assets –"

"The Guild?" Olatu rolled his eyes.

"The God-Emperor may even cast you from your clan!"

The Faythan snorted pityingly. "If your chicanery leads me to return empty handed, it's you who'll face El's Chosen – and believe me, no threat could be more terrifying." He half turned to the cringing archangel he'd ordered to wait, then added, "As for the missing berries, if I find any, I'll let you know."

Huldar stormed through several steps to reach Andel's side.

"He wouldn't even listen!" he cried. "I couldn't reason with him. It was like talking to a stone. In the end, I just stood there. I didn't know what to say!"

"Oh dear," Andel replied.

"I keep thinking," Huldar continued. "I should have said this, or done that. How can he be so ignorant?!"

Cobar and Ronin looked at each other. "We'll leave you to it, then ..."

Andel watched them head back to their campsite.

"Find more proof," she said.

He threw his hands in the air. "How?"

"Follow them. You'll find a way."

He tried to stop himself pacing. "But who will keep track of our study program? Keep the miners in check? And berries are missing!" *Why won't he listen?* He thrust his finger in the direction of the Host's base-camp. *Why won't he stop them like he should?*

Ask Casco to help – or Daric. Maybe Ariben ... perhaps not Calen.

I can't ask Casco. They treat him with such disdain – I can't bear it.

Then Daric or Ariben. I challenge anyone to treat either of those two with disrespect! ... Except for Malena, of course. It's a pity she's not taken more of an interest in our ways. And she's in such a state about her pregnancy. I feel for her, I really do. She took his hand. "Perhaps a new mission would lift her spirits. She is used to being in charge, after all."

A good thought. He felt tense muscles relax a little. "I'll ask her, see if I can convince her to take my place while I study the Went."

"Good. That's one problem solved, at least." *What would you do without me?*

I don't know. For a moment his grip around her fingers tightened. *I honestly don't know.*

WENT STORY

After the new Last Mother's return, the great migration of the Went began in earnest. Massive rains eased as they travelled south, following the slow curve of the shore-line. Hnarse Stargazer touched the blind one on the shoulder, signaling to it to follow. Nielli, they had named it, and its success so far was a mystery. Although deformed it seemed the youngster had senses others lacked.

The herd paused. Their heads lowered to the ground to communicate with the Heart. A deep drone vibrated up through Hnarse's feet.

Hnarse turned to Neetha. "Again? I have noticed nothing that couldn't wait for the evening circle."

Neetha's hair rippled primly. "If we had noted our surroundings more diligently during the previous cycle …" It glanced Nielli's way. "There can be no more mistakes. Maybe our numbers will be restored next time round."

Hnarse moved its follicles stiffly, indignant about the reference to Nielli but at the same time forced to acknowledge that Neetha may be correct. It glanced at the two-legged alien. As usual, it was shrouded in its own personal blurriness. "I know we should have spent more time observing them, but so close to cycle's end ..."

"And this is the result!"

"But it is good that this one has made itself available for study," Hnarse pointed out. "Perhaps it realizes we have wronged the Heart by not recording them adequately and is giving us an opportunity to restore the balance."

"Perhaps," Neetha said doubtfully, then it bent its knees to join the others, voicing fresh observations of the world above to the Heart below.

When little Nielli's head touched the ground also, Hnarse's heart clenched. One could hear so much in its simple drone: emotion so deep it was as if it had opened a new dimension of being, yet how did it know what to do? No one had told it – no one could.

Hnarse moved its nose over Nielli's side. Despite the blind one's tenacity, the trail's first true challenge, the sinking sands, must soon be faced. The gorge ahead filled it with fear. That was where the danger began. Those trapped would surrender their souls to the mothers. Only the strongest could continue.

It glanced at Nielli again. Other Wentlings would have foreknowledge and advice and could see the terrain ahead, but the blind one could not receive the songs of caution sung in the Herd's coats and must negotiate the danger alone. Without these advantages, how could it succeed? Dread flattened Hnarse's hair, and for a guilty moment, it was glad Nielli could not see.

At the entrance to the gorge, Hnarse paused and let the Herd brush past. It caressed Nielli's silken hair one last time and breathed deeply of its essence. The time had come to follow, but how could it leave the blind one alone?

Nielli shuffled restlessly.

Gently yet firmly, Hnarse pushed its trunk away. The path was different for each individual, and if they remained together, Nielli could be led into danger as likely as kept safe.

It made the small sneeze Hnarse had come to associate with a question. Hnarse answered with a sound it hoped would encourage caution, then moved forward with the herd.

When it looked back it saw Nielli had been left behind. All alone, its nose swayed as if searching for contact. Time and again, one foot would lift as if to follow, then it would hesitate and call, each time more loudly.

Hnarse forced another step through the pitfalls of the sinking sands, and tried to concentrate on survival.

After many exhausting hours and more than a few near misses, the path firmed and Hnarse realized it would live to face the next challenge. Even as it turned, another young one was claimed by the final test and vanished beneath the quicksand.

A blue-coated Mother started forward. She fished cautiously around the edge of the trap, then plunged head and forelegs beneath the sand.

For the longest time, her hind limbs clutched and shuffled, resisting the tug of the pit. Others began to notice. How could she hold her breath for so long? Then she surged upright. Her coat swirled in sorrow. Clasped in the end of her nose was the soul of Wentling lost to the sands. After holding it up for all to see, she swallowed it.

Hnarse's hair rippled with conflicting tides. Such losses were expected. The trail was hard. This lost one's life would continue in cycles to come, but no Mother watched over Nielli.

It waited with the other Elders as the stragglers came through. "Congratulations, young one," it said as the last visible Went passed by.

A wave of thanks crossed the survivor's coat, but it seemed too drained to express anything more.

Hnarse peered between the gorges again. High on the top of the cliff, the watcher seemed prepared to wait also.

As the shadows lengthened, Neetha brushed Hnarse's shoulder. Its hair movements were respectful, yet Hnarse could tell it was annoyed by its refusal to move on.

"The Mothers have agreed to search for Nielli's soul on the next cycle," Neetha soothed. "It will not be lost forever. You have done your best, and my comfort goes out to you."

But Hnarse stared back toward the sands. Its hair moved stubbornly. "Nielli will complete the trial."

"But how? It is blind. It observes nothing. Songs of instruction are meaningless. How can such a one be of benefit to the Circle's rhythm? How could the next New Purpose be entrusted to such a one?"

"Vision is not everything!" Hnarse retorted. "Nielli feels, smells, senses. Such observations must share equal importance, or what does it mean to have them at all? Maybe their absence in our observations has caused all the changes, and Nielli is here to teach us."

Neetha seemed stunned by its outburst.

"Nielli does understand," Hnarse continued more calmly. "It will complete the trial of sands. I will wait. Go if you must."

Neetha Grassmover's hair lifted in a silken sigh. It moved to the shadow of a rock to wait with the Stargazer.

The sun was low on the horizon when Hnarse lifted its nose to sample the air currents once more. Its hair quivered. Was that the blind one's scent? Another waft reached them and at last it was certain.

"Do you see?" it cried. "Nielli comes. I was right!"

Neetha lifted its trunk and took a polite sniff. "There is nothing," it said.

Despite its friend's negativity, Hnarse bugled a call.

It strained its eyes toward the empty sands, certain of its senses. It was said the nose could not lie, and after four successful migrations Hnarse was sure that was true.

The scent came again, more definite this time. Hnarse called as loudly as it could and was answered at last. It turned to Neetha in triumph.

Soon, Nielli shuffled into view, nose low to the ground, one careful step at a time.

Hnarse bugled again, and was thrilled when Neetha called too.

They ran forward together as Nielli reached safety. Hnarse caught the little one's nose and placed it soft and warm against its side. A great pain constricted its chest. Its nose stung with tears.

As they started back toward the herd, Nielli's warmth seemed more precious than the sun and Hnarse smiled to see Neetha behind them, close enough so that the blind one would not fall behind again.

COLLAPSE

Jalen of Cantori, site manager of the tin-mining operation, looked at Sari then turned to Casco with a nasty sneer. "No splitters."

Sari stood as tall as she could. "No *sp*–?" she fumed. "I can't even say it. You are so rude!"

"Come on, Sari," Casco said stiffly. "Can't reason with stupid."

They retreated to the outskirts of the camp while the miners got on with their day and ignored them completely.

"What do we do now?" Sari's eyes were moist with unshed tears. "How can she say such things? It's horrible."

Casco shrugged. "She's expanded her vocabulary since last time, hasn't she? Maybe she's thinking to impress the rest of the Host when they arrive."

"Last time they let us do our job."

"Let's see what our new coordinator can do," he suggested. "Water and waste must be checked."

He closed his eyes for a moment, then gave Sari a speculative look. *She's on her way.*

Casco could've sworn the air chilled as Malena stormed through the portal.

"What's happening here?" she snapped.

"They won't let us on-site to check their water and hygiene," said Sari.

"Why not?"

"Because of me," Casco said.

Malena looked him up and down, her expression shrewd. "This isn't the first time this has happened."

"The first time? They're horrible to him," Sari said. She pointed to Jalen who now watched their conversation intently. "That one in particular. Calls him a – a splitter. Says his kind aren't good enough to eat their … refuse, let alone check it."

Malena's eyes blazed. "Right!"

She strode in the direction of the miners' camp and loomed over the site manager, stabbing her finger first at the archangel's chest, then at himself and Sari.

The interlude was over in short order. The summons she sent them was brusque.

"Not quite how Huldar would've handled things," Sari murmured.

"But effective all the same," Casco replied.

Malena smiled brightly as they approached. "Jalen of Cantori, here, was just saying how much she appreciates your care for the health of their environment," she said firmly. "Weren't you, Jalen?"

"Please, be welcome," Jalen said stiffly.

"Go on," Malena prompted.

"Take all the time you need. Do what you must. There will be refreshments available in the mess-tent."

"And?"

Jalen gritted her teeth, then made an awkward bow. "I am sorry, Casco of the Uri'madu, and Sari of the Uri'madu, if my comments gave offence."

"There." Malena slapped her on the back with a little more force than was necessary. "That wasn't so hard, was it?"

She turned to wave Casco toward the cisterns. "If you would? Let me know if there's any further trouble." To Jalen she added, "but I'm sure there'll be no need, will there?"

Jalen shook her head.

"Good. And while I'm here, I need to check on your mining operations. It's on my list for tomorrow, but we can do it today, can't we? If you would be so kind as to lead the way?"

Casco watched them walk off. He turned to Sari. "Do you think this has helped her? Filling in for Huldar?"

"For Huldar?" Sari cocked her head. "She seems happier in herself – but I'm glad I'm not Jalen."

Casco grinned, thinking how Daric would enjoy the story. "Let's get to it then, if you would be so kind as to lead the way?"

They headed across to the outer edge of the campsite, where two hemi-spherical bubbles of water awaited the miner's use.

Casco peered into the smaller one. "Clarity's good."

Sari handed him a small glass. He sang a few melodious notes to construct a filter, then swirled the contents through it.

"Is that one of Bush's charms?" Sari asked.

"A new version."

"New version? Must've been Daric then," she teased.

"Actually no. It came from …" he'd been about to say Shen.
"… Someone back home. A chef. Water filters are part of their
job."

He turned as a cloud of insects screeched into flight and saw
a flash of light from the direction of the mine.

Sari frowned.

"Did you see –?" Casco started, but his words were cut off as
a deep rumble shook their feet. A wave of panic surged
outward. Malena's cry for help seemed to come with the puff
of dust from the mine's mouth.

He sprinted for the entrance.

Other miners emerged from their tents.

Malena! he cried.

There was no answer. He called out to Huldar, *Mine collapse.
We need a rescue team. Malena's trapped!*

A wail went up in the camp. Workmates gathered around
one stricken by his husband's death, offering what comfort
they could.

He felt a brief tickle as Huldar pinpointed his location.

Send an overview of what we're up against, Huldar said. *How
many trapped? Keep trying to make contact with them. We'll be
there as quick as we can.*

Keep trying to reach Malena, Casco said to Sari. *Let's hope it's
only that she's too deep underground.*

He turned to the twenty or so who'd clustered by the mine.
Behind them, fine dust still issued like smoke.

"Emergency team?" he asked loudly. "Who is your disaster coordinator?"

"What would you know, filthy splitter?" one said angrily. "Stay out of it!"

A stocky Cantori stepped forward. "Jalen. She's in the mine."

"Our own rescue team is on its way," Casco said. "How many are in there? Has there been any contact?"

"Ten ..."

"Miko's dead!" someone wailed.

"How could this happen?"

"When will your lot get here?" another demanded.

"They're on their way. Anyone with farsight? Has anyone taken a look?"

No one answered.

"No? ... I'll go then." He motioned Sari closer. *Watch my back.*

She nodded. *Still no contact with Malena.*

He pushed the worry aside, closed his eyes and set his vision free. The blockage was only ten paces or so inside the tunnel. It seemed like a pile of loose rubble, but without the skills of a diviner, he struggled to worm his way through. At last he made out the twisted leg of someone crushed beneath the debris. An arm protruded close by. He couldn't be sure it was from the same person. Another miner lay beyond the major fall, pinned by a rock between his shoulders. Red trickled from his mouth and nose. His eyes stared into oblivion.

Malena was clear of the rubble, but unconscious. Blood seeped from a wound on her head.

Two more sat propped against the wall, eyes stared blankly ahead, too dazed to move. One's lips were moving. Casco strained to hear.

"…two … three … four," he whispered.

The other began to mumble as well. Her hands fumbled blindly for her feet.

Casco recoiled in shock.

She's awake, Sari said. *Can you see her?*

As if on cue, Malena groaned.

Yes, he replied. *Tell her not to move. Don't even try to move! Help is on the way.*

He rushed back to himself but kept his eyes closed as he tried to steady his pulse.

What's wrong? Sari asked, but before he could explain, Huldar called, *Casco! Update please.*

With the ease of their long association, he opened a link to show him what he'd seen.

Huldar paused, then sent, *I've rounded up Cobar, Daric, Ubaid and Banga. Andel is with me also. We're on our way now.*

Lady Andel? Casco said doubtfully. *What about the counting?*

We need her skills as a diviner. Show no one else what you've seen. Ubaid can deal with it. Get a team to start hauling rock from your side.

He opened his eyes to a crowd of anxious faces.

"There are injuries," he said loudly. "It's not pretty down there. I need a team to shift rock and make a start from this side."

Miners looked at him blankly.

He singled out the stocky one who'd stepped forward earlier. "What's your name?"

"Arden."

"Thanks," he nodded. "I'm Casco. We have to be ready to act as soon as the rescue team get here. You know these people. Can you pick a crew?"

Arden gave a wry twist of his head. "No problem."

"Let me know when you're set." He waved the others back. "Can we clear a space here? If you're not part of Arden's gang, please return to your tents. We need room to work."

A surly miner raised her fist. "We don't take orders from the likes of you!" But before Casco could respond, Arden turned on them. "You heard im! If you're not gonna help, take your shit and fuck off!"

Still muttering, the crowd began to turn away. Of twenty or so onlookers, only seven gathered to Arden's side.

"Bastards!" Arden yelled. "Our mates es trapped!"

Two more had second thoughts, but the remainder retreated to a safe distance.

"What's wrong with you people?" Arden called after them.

"Where's the kitchen?" Casco asked him.

The miner pointed to the heart of the campsite. "Grub tent."

Sari, could you make sure there's food and drink available? You know what we need. Then come back. We'll need your help – and don't lose touch with Malena.

She nodded and started in that direction.

Arden's group gathered behind him and looked up expectantly.

How much longer? Casco asked Huldar.

Minutes, no more.

"Let's start with what we can," he said to Arden. "We need to clear rubble out of the way so our people can get in."

Arden and his gang started for the mine entrance, but paused when Huldar and the rescue team strode into camp. Andel seemed particularly pale and tense.

Huldar heard his unspoken question. *They know what to expect*, he assured him. *Andel too.*

I'll be all right, she said quietly.

"This is your operation," Huldar said to him. "You have the skills. You and Sari were here when it happened. We're here to assist and advise. So, where should we start?"

Casco took a deep breath. This was not what he'd expected.

"Malena is badly injured," he said. "Some have already died of their injuries. We need to clear the entrance and reach the trapped miners before any more are lost."

"Will she be all right?" Daric asked. "Why was she even here? I thought she was in the southern sector."

"Sari is in contact," Casco told him. He indicated Arden and his crew. "These miners are ready to help."

Ubaid tipped his head toward the kitchens. Casco nodded and the healer left to find Sari.

"What can I do?" Daric said. His eyes were wild. "We have to get to her before it's too late."

Casco moved his hand to indicate that he and Huldar should stand by. He turned to Andel. "Are you all right?"

"I'll be fine," she said firmly.

He gave a tight smile. "Can you stabilize the mine's ceiling, please?"

She nodded and started for the disaster zone. When she was closer she closed her eyes and the mark on her forehead flared to life.

"Banga," Casco said, "you and Cobar start clearing the way. Arden?" He beckoned the miner. "Banga's a spinner and used to lifting cargo, and Cobar here," he indicated the Rukh, "is strong in tsemkar. If you and your team could work with them? They'll tackle the heavier material."

After a brief round of introductions, the small group turned for the mine.

Casco turned to Huldar and Daric. "This is my idea, but I'm not sure if it's a good one." He looked at Daric. "Is there some way you and Huldar can make a portal into the mine itself? I know it's a concept you've been playing with," he hurried to add.

Huldar turned. "Is this true?"

"Maybe …" Daric looked into Huldar's face. There was a quick exchange, then they nodded. "We'll get onto it."

They strode to the outskirts of the camp, not far from the cisterns. He could feel the urgency in their discussion, but he could also sense the smooth professionalism of Andel's ceiling containment charm and the complex energy of Cobar's first lift. It was tricky, but with Banga's help, the massive boulder sailed from the darkness and landed gently by the entryway. The old spinner's connection with him wasn't so smooth, and he was reminded of the first time he and Andel had linked in this way. Maybe Malena's crew still hadn't fully accepted their place in the Uri'madu.

He looked up as the portal behind them activated. Radätel Gok stepped briskly through and made his way straight to Huldar. "What's happening here?" he demanded.

Casco felt his private flash of annoyance as he extricated himself from his work with Daric. "Casco is managing this incident," he said briskly. "I'm sure he'll be happy to give you an update."

"Casco?" Radätel's eyebrows raised, but Huldar offered nothing further.

The Overlord turned and started toward him.

Casco, we need help here, Cobar said. *Someone to work with lighting.*

"Casco, what's the situation?" Radätel said.

"One moment," Casco replied. "I have a problem in the tunnel."

"What problem?"

He glanced toward the campsite, hoping there was someone who could help. Maybe if he delegated the Overlord to ask … "I need a lightsinger."

"I am a lightsinger," Radätel said. He frowned. "My family are lightsingers."

Casco blinked when he realized his level of surprise may have been unseemly. "You'll be under my direction," he said, *and you'll have to go inside the mine.*

Radätel glanced Huldar's way then nodded sharply. *If it will help save lives, I will do it,* he said.

Then link with me, sir. Casco extended his hand. *But I feel we should hurry.*

Radätel joined his grip, offering a connection that was light and practiced, but here was no time for Casco to wonder. He sent Cobar the message, *Lightsinger coming through.*

Moments later, he felt Cobar bottle his surprise.

I happen to have these with me, Radätel said. *Gently does it ... Where should they go?*

A soft, even, glow fell through the dust from the tunnel mouth. With this improvement, the outward flow of debris continued more smoothly, but even so, the blockage would take hours to clear. He hoped his suggestion to Daric and Huldar had been the right thing to do.

Sari, he asked, *how is Malena?*

Ubaid is trying, she replied, *but without actual touch, it's difficult. Alis is ... oh! Here she is now.*

The slim Naghari hurried into camp, accompanied by four more spinners.

While Alis turned toward Sari and Ubaid, Kira and the spinners headed for him. After a heartfelt thanks, Casco waved them on to join Banga and Cobar.

He turned to a burst of excitement from Huldar.

I think we've solved it! Huldar said. *Daric is brilliant.*

Daric sent a virtual wink. *Make sure we are undisturbed for the next few moments.*

Huldar watched intently as Daric's hands made contact with the ground. His eyes closed in deep concentration, notes were sung, then there was a slight flash as the new portal came into being.

The Enna got to his feet and dusted his hands off, then after a determined nod, the two stepped through.

We're in!

The exclamation came in eerie stereo. Light bloomed from two separate globes. Twin views of the inner tunnel filled his mind.

One at a time, please? he asked.

The vision returned to a single viewpoint – Huldar's, as he hurried toward Malena.

Seconds later, Daric stepped back into the campsite. His expression was troubled. "Reactivation of some quite ancient threads, but that's not important now. Malena can't be moved, so I'll sing healers through to her."

"Into the mine?" Casco thought of the crushed bodies he'd seen. "What if there's another cave-in?"

"There won't be," Daric said.

He sounded very confident. Casco frowned. "Have you tested it?" he insisted. "I can't send our healers into danger. They're all we have."

"Malena needs help now!" Daric snapped. "There's no time for this. You're team leader. Get the healers so I can sing them through."

Casco bit back a retort and signaled Ubaid. *The way is open. Daric will take you both now.*

Without another word, Daric strode to meet them.

Casco fought the urge to apologize.

Through Huldar, he saw them arrive in the tunnel. While Ubaid turned to the counting miners, Alis hurried to Malena. After a few soft words, she moved her fingers down the navigator's spine, vertebra by careful vertebra. When she reached a certain point, the mark on her hand flared to life.

Malena screamed.

What's happening? Ariben cried. Casco had barely sensed his arrival. Now he and Gento stood expecting answers.

"Don't worry," Casco said. "She's in the best of hands."

She's tough, Banga said. *A Maatu, you know ... just tough.*

Ariben stared toward the mine as if willing it to clear. "I want to go to her!"

"You can't reach her that way," Casco said. "You'll just have to wait like the rest of us." *Sari,* he called privately. *I need you!*

Need me? Yes. Tam and I have been busy in the kitchen. If you could get them to organize something?

Casco nodded and turned back to Ariben. "We have enough help to clear the mine, but Sari and Tam need a trestle for some food – and we'll need a sturdy hospital tent with a table for the healers to work on, and beds for the injured when they're evacuated." He looked around as thunder cracked nearby. "And cover for us as well. Can you do that?"

Gento placed his hand on Ariben's shoulder and they left in search of tables and tents.

Casco gazed around the site. It felt odd not to be physically involved in the rescue, but the clearance team worked smoothly, piling rock after rock by the mine entrance. Gento and Ariben soon returned with a trestle, and, while they went to look for a spare tent, Sari and Tam brought hot food, snacks and drinks and started running orders for those in the tunnel.

The next time he saw Ariben, he and Gento carried a large box between them.

It's a couple of tents, Gento told him.

Near the new portal? Ariben asked.

Casco sent his approval. Miners arrived with a table and beds.

He looked up at the sky and a grey veil of rain that sped toward them. *Hurry! It's on its way!*

A second tent covered the food just in time. Leathers billowed as the squall struck. Rain sluiced in sheets. Lightning flashed. He ran to help lash down the hospital tent. Had he forgotten anything? He didn't think so. Then Huldar and Ubaid arrived with the first of the victims and there was no more time for doubts.

DEBRIEF

It was dark and cold. Heavy rain beat against the tent. Ubaid turned as Malena whimpered in her sleep, a deep, drug and song induced stupor she would not wake from until late next morning. He hoped her dreams were kind. Three more beds lined the walls, but only two were occupied. In the distance he could hear the miners' dirge for their dead and was glad it was not the Uri'madu singing for their navigator on this unforgiving night.

Alis settled closer, attuned as ever to his moods. Too tired for conversation, they sat staring into the fire. The cups of broth held loosely in their hands smelled comfortingly plain.

Ubaid looked up as the door flap parted and Daric came to sit with them. The Enna's haze drooped with exhaustion.

"Thank you for your efforts today," Ubaid said. He mustered a heartfelt smile. "Your flexibility never ceases to amaze. The portal into the mine was a masterful thing on its own, but then, to join with Alis and be her voice in healing? Remarkable."

"It was the least I could do. Will she be all right?"

"Malena? Yes, I believe so."

"And her pregnancy?"

"All's well. She'll be up and about in a few days – a week and she'll have forgotten how fondly the Breath caressed her."

Daric grimaced a little. "She's been more assertive than ever since Huldar gave her license."

Ubaid smiled again, but Daric's head dropped into his hands. "I tried with that miner, but we couldn't hold him, and he just … slipped away."

"We did our best," Alis murmured, "but sometimes the call of the Breath is too strong."

"I can't even remember their names …"

"Halmät," Ubaid reminded him. "The one you're thinking of was called Halmät." He studied the wiry Enna with concern. Why would this death in particular affect him so?

"His friends," Daric murmured. "They're genuinely upset. I've been out there just now …"

"Sad, I know," Ubaid agreed. "But Malena and the others you helped save will thank you. Without the portal, maybe none would have made it."

Daric's head remained bowed. He massaged his scalp with deliberate fingers. "Even Malena?"

Ubaid glanced again at the tall navigator, remembering the struggle they'd had to save her. If not for Casco's quick thinking, knowing she should be kept still … "With both skull and spinal fractures I doubt she could've held on much longer."

Alis watched Daric closely, as concerned as he was about the fluctuations in his psychic emanations.

Guilt? She gave a slight lift of her brows.

Ubaid gave a minute shrug. Whatever the truth of Daric's deeper emotions, such depths were completely opaque, held firm by an impenetrable web of screens. However, his outer state was almost readable for trained empaths such as Alis and himself.

"Huldar helped with the portal," Daric said. "It wasn't just me. I just stretched what we already knew."

"And your work with me?" Alis said.

He looked up. The glow of the coals reflected in his tawny eyes. "I have some small healing ability of my own, as you know."

The calmness of his voice contrasted steeply with what they could see beneath his haze.

"When I realized you couldn't sing – because of your condition … I … it made sense to do it that way."

Ubaid snorted softly. "Sense to you." He took a mouthful of broth and nodded. "Well, Daric Enna, whatever you are – or have been – we are most grateful."

Daric's sudden stillness seemed to capture time. Ubaid swallowed. He gave his wife a covert warning. *I may have made a mistake …*

The Enna's head turned slowly. "Or have been?"

Outwardly, nothing about Alis's appeared to change, but Ubaid knew her defenses were ready for anything. He studied Daric for a moment, as much to assess the danger as to gather his thoughts. His reply must be delicately balanced. "We are healers," he said at last. "Empathic. It's part of our job to observe."

"We've known for some time," Alis added quietly.

Daric looked at them each in turn. "You knew?" The roil of his psyche became more visible.

"We're not just repairers of broken bodies."

Ubaid's alarm grew when he saw Daric's eyes glisten with the hint of tears. Was he about to break?

Get out. Quickly! he said to his wife.

I'm not leaving you, she replied.

He tensed when Daric's hand moved, but breathed again when he saw it was only to cover his face. Moisture bled between the assassin's fingers. A single drop escaped and fell glittering to the ground.

Alis, please!

He'll be all right, she assured him. *He's adjusting. It hurts to grow a soul. It frightens him.*

Daric snarled as he turned to her. "You knew, and yet you trusted me? We were so enmeshed. I could've killed you … easily."

Her face softened. He looked on incredulously as she took his hand and held it.

"I could have killed you," he repeated, but now, the tremor in his voice was heartbreaking. Gracefully, formally, he put Alis's hand to his mouth and kissed it.

Tension dissipated. Time flowed on.

Ubaid sighed. Despite layer upon layer of sublimation, his wife had seen the truth of this one's tortured heart and understood it. How had that happened? His love for her flowed like a river. They were a good team, but she was the mainstay.

"I've ears for ye, Daric Enna," she said, "un bein so minded."

Daric's eyes widened. "How did you know?" His head slowly tilted. "But of course you would." He closed his eyes as if in great pain. "I've never healed anyone before – not like that. And to try to save someone's life ... and lose ..."

Alis squeezed his fingers gently.

He looked into her eyes. "I have something to tell you ..."

Ubaid looked up, sensing Huldar's approach.

Alis flinched as Daric's defenses slammed back into place. He pulled away like a child caught stealing.

Her expression seemed troubled, but she wouldn't say why.

Huldar poked his head through the door. "Are you up to joining us? Debrief. I think it's important you're there."

Daric glanced back at Malena. "I don't think ..."

"I'll stay," Alis assured him.

Daric looked down. For a moment, Ubaid thought he would refuse, but then he stood up and, after a low bow to Alis, turned to face the door as if ready to leave. As he started back into the rain, he showed no sign that anything out of the ordinary had happened, only that he was fatigued. Ubaid guessed assassins had to be good at compartmentalizing, but now Daric had discovered they knew what he was, it seemed he was taking the exercise to new levels.

Inside the mining camp's kitchen/dining tent Huldar gazed over the dispirited gathering. The song for the dead was over, souls returned to their keeper and ashes to nourish the ground they'd defiled, he thought sourly. Miners and Uri'madu mingled as if they were part of the same team ...

and at a very important level they were. But at another, they were enemies, and that saddened him as much as anything on this dreary night.

The Overlord gave him the nod to proceed.

"Jalen of Cantori, Halmät and Miko," he started. "Basät, Cissael and Dase. Six souls have rejoined the Breath."

He paused as Miko's husband was overcome once more by the pain of a bond broken.

Ubaid threaded through to the miner's side. *I'll shift him into the hospital*, he said.

Huldar waited while the stretcher-bearers got organized. As they departed, those who remained turned to him again.

"I do not presume to know much about them and cannot lead you in mourning," he continued. "I only ask that those who grieve take extra care in the weeks and months to come, and that friends and workmates are especially kind to those who suffer." He nodded toward Ubaid. "Our healers are also experienced counsellors. They will stay for as long as the survivors need them. Please, do not be afraid to ask for their support should you need it."

He singled out Jalen's second-in-charge. "Brit, I understand you are to take Jalen of Cantori's place as supervisor?"

The sturdy Cantori nodded.

"It will be your job to get this site operational once more. I ask this crew to respect you as they would Jalen."

He turned to Casco.

"Is the shaft now clear?"

"Almost," Casco replied. "Arden and his crew will continue the tidy-up in the morning, but we've still no clue as to what triggered the cave-in."

Radätel stepped forward. "Lord Olatu assures me he will order an investigation as soon as possible."

"I have examined the internal structure of the rock-face," Andel said, "and found no weakness that might have caused such a thing to happen, but until we investigate more fully I recommend heavy shoring throughout."

"Farushael of Cantori is highly skilled in such charms," Radätel said. "He will be made available."

"Thank you, Overlord." Huldar turned to the miners. "Are there any questions?"

Arden stood up. "I've got one." He looked around. "Where's Olatu of Faytha?"

"Doesn't he care?" a voice called out.

"Faythan!" someone spat in reply. "Care for nothin but coin."

"Navigator's due any day," Arden went on, "and we have quotas yet to fill – but what if it happens again?"

"The navigator will be here the day after tomorrow," Radätel replied. "Your quotas have been relaxed. There's to be no work in this mine until Farushael of Cantori comes to help with shoring and our diviner, Lady Andel, gives the all-clear."

There was an angry snort from the crowd. "She what gave the all-clear in the first place?"

"I beg your pardon?" she said.

This is not your fault, Huldar said privately. *It was an accident.*

But what if it was? she replied to him. *What if I missed something?*

"Tsemkarun Andel of Trianog is highly skilled and experienced," Casco said hotly. "This has nothing to do with her."

"Yeah, but ..." The speaker rounded her belly in a suggestion of pregnancy.

Andel stood up. "How dare you!"

"The Tsemkarun's skills are unaffected by her condition," Ubaid said firmly. "I suggest your immediate apology."

The speaker paused as if just realizing her mistake. The gathering looked on in varying degrees of shock.

Brit got to his feet. "We're waiting!"

"But Miko, Dase, even Jalen – they're all dead ..."

"And my wife is not to blame," said Huldar.

"We will discover what has happened," Radätel said. "But we must acknowledge that ours is a dangerous occupation. Breath blows as it will, and we, its creations, merely roll in its path."

The speaker bowed half-heartedly. "My apologies, Tsemkarun Andel."

Andel nodded and resumed her seat, but Huldar was well aware of her tumbling emotions.

"Please, Lady Andel, forgive young Renlät's outburst," Radätel said. "Grief has spoken here. Grief and isolation." He faced the crowd. "We should thank the Uri'madu for their rapid response, their skill and bravery in conducting this rescue, and for the lives they helped save."

"And the enquiry?" asked Brit.

"Will commence as soon as possible," Radätel Gok replied.

CONSCIENCE

Casco looked around as Sari and Tam served another round of hot food. The atmosphere among the miners was somber. Although the debrief was over, many seemed reluctant to leave, almost as if the tent was shielding them from the reality of so many deaths.

Sari took a steaming mug to Renlät who sat alone toward the back of the tent. As he looked up to thank her, she saw tears streaming down the rugged young miner's face.

On the other side of the room, Arden and the Overlord stood in discussion.

"And when will that be?" Arden said sharply.

"As I have said, he has promised," Radätel Gok replied. "I can do no more."

Arden's scowl deepened. "No? Well we want answers. I want answers! What happened here?"

Huldar moved toward them to break it up.

Ariben paused in the doorway and gave Casco a wave. *Was going to sleep in the hospital tent, but Ubaid said best not.*

Malena's safe now, Casco assured him. *Ubaid and Alis won't let anything happen to her.*

Daric's expression grew a touch wistful as he watched Ariben depart. Casco was aware that gatherings, especially among strangers, were hard for him, but he seemed particularly uncomfortable at this one.

Gento came over and held out a long-necked bottle. "S'not besh," he said, "but it's got kick."

Casco smiled his thanks then turned again as Brit approached him, also with a bottle in hand.

"I see you already have one," Brit said. "Perhaps another for later?"

"Thank you," Casco said, wary of the miner's turn of goodwill.

Brit gave a rueful smile. "Some of us may have been rude to you in the past," he said. "Maybe even me. I apologize. It won't happen again."

Gento's eyebrows raised. He took a swig of ale as if enjoying the entertainment.

"I'm glad to hear it," Casco responded.

"You worked hard to save us, even though ... Anyways, I'm sorry." With a short bow, the new mine boss left them and headed for Daric.

Clasping the neck of the second bottle in his free hand Casco looked after him in surprise.

"That's one for your report," Gento said.

Casco overheard Brit say something about portals, and Daric's unease reached new heights. He guessed he was being congratulated on his latest act of brilliance. His Gaze found Casco's. *Can we leave now?* One corner of his mouth twitched as if he was in genuine pain.

Soon. Casco suppressed a yawn. The rigors of the day were catching up and he was more than ready to call it a night. Even so, it was hours past midnight by the time they made it back to their tent at Eastern Base-camp. Casco sank beneath the furs, grateful for the chance to rest. Even thoughts of dazed miners counting their toes was not enough to keep his eyes from closing. But the same was not true for Daric.

The night wore on. Casco groaned as he was jolted from yet another doze.

Wha kennin? He asked crossly.

Daric replied with a whiff of annoyance.

Casco shoved him. *Un tossin a turnin – canna sleep!*

There was a long silence. Daric shared something of the way he was feeling, the edges of the tumult in his soul, but gave no explanation. *The way you took over the rescue, managed everyone ...* he said at last. *You're a natural leader.*

Job to be done. I's be dere, sho la, no more.

That's a lie, and you know it. But I'm surprised Huldar let you keep the reins. He must ... trust you ... very much.

An Arden dere, be a warrin de hecklers true. An Brit, ja? Starry prize ... Casco gave a short huff as he savored the memory, then became serious again. *Be starry leader or no, beint whas needlin.*

Daric withdrew. Evidence of his inner storm was barely enough to ruffle the still depths of his deepest screen. Casco reached over and ran his palm down his shoulder in a long caress. Beneath the smooth skin was lean muscle even harder now than when they'd first arrived. Whatever troubled his lover, he was glad to have him by his side.

Daric turned to face him. Dark pupils enlarged until they resembled eclipsed moons ringed by tawny sunlight. They moved slowly, studying every plane of his face, then settled on his lips.

Their kiss was long and sensual, but Daric's emotions remained as remote as the real moons in the dark skies above.

A wave of sadness swept him.

I'll be all right, Daric assured him. *Dinna fash yerself.*

Something in the tone of his thoughts reminded Casco of Alis. He remembered the bolt of alarm he'd felt shortly after Daric returned to the hospital tent.

They know, Daric admitted.

Know what?

Daric envisaged him as a lumbering shuna. *Thick as a half-breed?*

Deflection will get you nowhere, he replied. *So, they know. What of it? You promised you'd tell everyone.*

That was then, he admitted, *before I knew them.*

So, your promise? He imaged a smashed gem in a muddy puddle. *Lyin Kishlak?*

Daric flinched. *No! It's just that ...*

That what?

Daric sighed, then kissed him again. *Just leave it for now – please?*

Casco rolled away. "Funny thing," he murmured. "Jalen ... she was always rude to me. Just routine checks, but this time she wouldn't even let me and Sari in." He shared the scene as he'd seen it. "Malena gave her such a serve! Bin gannin to say. Starry queer! Huge Maatu balin oor. Jalen – ye's visin?

She be near pissin unsel, ja? Den dat scapin wid grittin fang.
Be funny den, sho la. Now jus sad." He paused. Six dead. Six
souls at one with the Breath. It seemed unreal, except that he
was so tired. "Then, right before it happened," he continued,
"a cloud of bugs flew up and I thought I saw a flash of light."

"Haters," Daric snarled. "That's one gone. You going to miss
her?"

"No," he admitted. "But –"

"There you go! One less bigot to darken your day. You
should thank … Breath's design."

"She wasn't my favorite person," Casco said, "but sad she's
dead – and the others. Maybe with Malena's help she could
have changed."

"They never do."

"I think you're wrong," Casco ventured. "Take Malena
herself, for instance. You two didn't get along at first. She
hated you because you're Tiamäti. But you like each other
now." He visioned the statuesque Maatu and her green eyes
flashing as the two of them laughed together. At first, even he
had found her brash ways grating, but when she let her
guard down he'd discovered a well-read individual with an
interest in ancient language, a gift for unarmed combat and,
even more so than Lind, an uncanny ability to cheat at ashut.
"She's quite something, isn't she?"

"Hmm," Daric murmured in a non-committal way.

"When she was trapped … It's funny how you don't realize
how important someone is until something happens. Sad,
really. We're so lucky to have Alis and Ubaid," he continued.
"They never hesitated – even with the counters. Ubaid knew
exactly what to do. And as for you …"

He thought of the two feats his remarkable friend had performed on the one day – a portal to somewhere underground, and then to link with Alis in healing? How could so much brilliance reside in one single individual?

To be another's voice – how did that feel?

Daric's shutters came down hard.

His brow skewed. *What did I say?*

The silence was so complete he could almost hear the frost settling on their tent.

Is it Halmät? You did your best … everyone knows it.

At last, Daric released his breath. *The inspection wasn't supposed to be until tomorrow.*

I know. Casco nodded. *Breath blows …*

"Fuck the Breath!" Daric snarled.

"You don't think it's my fault!?"

Of course not!

With a savage movement Daric rolled away and pulled the furs up over his ears. Casco's urge to reach out was so strong it almost hurt – but his thinking mind said no. Coiled like a wisp of smoke inside him, a dreadful suspicion had taken root.

Other miners had died. Each the victim of an accident, but each, now he thought of it, someone who had insulted him for the heritage of his birth. He had shared that pain with Daric – something he would in the past have kept to himself. Slowly, slowly he increased the density of his inner screens – just as Daric had taught him. Such dire misgivings should never see light – not unless he had proof absolute. Maybe it *was* just chance. He felt Daric's warmth next to him, the glow of his presence, his care, his love. Despite his strange mood, that had not changed.

But something had.

LOST AND FOUND

Daric raised his collar against the driving rain and made his way to the eastern portal. His mood softened somewhat at the thought of Casco, finally asleep, but the horrible mistake he'd made denied him that respite and so he'd appointed himself a mission – to find the missing berries before the navigator arrived. Once the rest of the Host exited the Chime, there would be chaos. He wanted the issue solved before any new problems arose. It was one thing he thought he could deal with. One thing he might be credited for when credit became scarce.

He stepped through the portal toward the service end of the Host's encampment and wrapped himself in screens. It was one hour until daybreak and Shen was already at work, alone by the cookfire. He looked up as Daric stepped inside, shuddered as if he'd felt a draft, then shrugged and returned to his mixing bowl.

Daric crept as close as he could without alerting him and whispered, "Seen anything out of the ordinary?"

A spoonful of broth flew skyward. *Breat!*

With agile tsemkar, Daric captured the spill mid-air and returned it to the bowl. He chuckled at the cook's expression.

Droppin skin or what? Shen demanded.

Mebee somat. He eased his cover.

Shen tipped his head in a sarcastic bow and returned to his cooking.

So, what news? Daric asked.

Apart from tragedy at mine? Shen replied.

Old to me.

So I heard. Place be hummin for navigator's arrival, sho la. Be doublin de numbers den, ja. Fresh stores ud be cheery.

Daric looked around. The menu seemed undiminished. *What else?*

Ah – now dis be de starry ride! Shen scowled at him. *Woulda said sooner beint for de scare tactics.*

"One takes joy in small things," Daric said softly. He gestured for Shen to continue.

Seen Olatu talkin to Farushael, ja. Looken shifty – well, shiftier than usual. Left here burdened wid a calcite chest. He tipped his head to the western escarpment. *Mebee stashed in de rocks dere. It's not in his tent. He was away most yesterday. I looked.*

What about his screens? You didn't set off any alarms, did you?

Shen frowned. *Don't think so.*

Daric paused to consider. Shen had come a long way with screens and covert operations, but did he have the skills to penetrate the Faythan's premises and leave no trace?

Why didn't you tell me this? he asked.

It was only yesterday arvo, Shen said patiently, *and you's flat workin de miracles, ja? Olatu, he stepped out for a good while – I got the feeling he went snooping around while yous were all distracted. Mebee even checkin out your'un.*

Not mine, but I'll make sure the others are safe. Anything else?

Whole Host's chatten on Casco. Starry skies ya?

Starry indeed.

You feature pretty solidly too, in case you wondered. How is he?

Fine.

Shen's expression grew wistful. *He's right there, but I miss him, ja? It's harder than I thought to pretend I don't know him. Every time I see him I want to shout out in de lingo, be knowin?*

Daric nodded. *Be knowin, sho la.*

Keep un tidy, ja? Keep un safe.

Casco ... He'd tried to keep him safe. He wanted to keep him from harm, but was that the right thing to do? The smell of fresh baking, tangled scents of caluma and cilfra took him back to Giahn, to his childhood home in the mountains. He remembered an early morning, the light similar to the light here now. He saw again his mother's smile as she pulled a tray from the oven, heard her cry as she burned her hand. The tray fell. Father scolded her for playing in the kitchen when they had a perfectly good cook. Savory cakes spilled to the floor like so many round, brown fruits ...

He shook his head. *Seen any of those berries?*

Those berries? Shen replied innocently, but Daric noted the minute flutter of deceit.

Where are they? he asked firmly.

To Daric's surprise, the cook reached into his pocket. *Only one.* He shrugged and held it out.

One of the most valuable items in the known, and you kept it in your pocket?

I tried to hide it in Qalān, but it wouldn't go.

Daric retrieved a small blue box from Qalān. *Here, put it in this.*

Shen turned the container over. *Calcite?*

The lid slides open, Daric told him. *Here's the song.*

Shen slid the lid back and put the purple fruit inside. He weighed the small casket thoughtfully in his hands, then offered it back to Daric.

I don't want it, he said. *Do you know how to turn the calcite invisible?*

The cook shook his head.

Daric passed him another song, this one with a subtle tsemkar twist that made Shen's eyes widen.

Try it, he said. *You're more than capable.*

What if I get it wrong?

Don't.

Shen paused to rehearse, and after a breath to steady his nerves, voiced the charm. The box vanished. A slight indent on his palm was the only evidence of its existence. He gave a small squeak of triumph and looked up, almost disbelieving.

Keep it on you at all times.

Shen placed the box solemnly in his pocket. *I will.*

All times, Daric emphasized, then a new aroma caught his attention. A thin wisp of smoke issued from the oven.

Shit! Shen cried.

As the Kareski sprinted to save his cakes, Daric slipped from the tent and headed for the bluff. Soon the camp would begin to stir. He wanted to find his quarry before then. After, it would be a simple matter of covering his tracks – *Maybe another small explosion*, he thought ironically. If he could find the missing berries, the Uri'madu might forgive him when he told them what he'd done … because he knew if he really wanted to be part of the team, genuinely change his life, he had to. His interaction with Alis had made this very clear to him, and he treasured her now as dearly as a sister – if rating such emotion made sense at all. And if so, where did Casco fit in? He shook his head and focused on finding the berries. Even if calcite was rendered invisible, it was possible for the ultra-sensitive to trace the faint harmonic produced by the charm.

Loose footing was no challenge to his nimble feet. With barely a scrabble, he scaled the ridge and searched for a suitable place to position himself. Below, the first shadows of dawn drew detail from the city of tents. The dark shape of an early riser clumped along the boarded streets, heading for the kitchen.

He closed his eyes and began. Steadily, he filtered through small natural vibrations, the movement of leaf and frond, furtive footfalls of tiny creatures, the far-away clamor of clicker-bugs striving for dominance, but the sought-after resonance was not there. Aware that time was short, he abandoned that particular quest and employed his farsight. If the box was there as Shen believed, perhaps it was not disguised after all – merely hidden.

Wildlife chirruped as the morning light grew stronger. Mist lifted from bedewed greenery. His vision cut through fog to flit over and between stones. Unfamiliar plant-forms vied for his attention, but he let them be. Blue – he must find something blue. His mind shot toward furtive movement at the foot of a crevasse. There was an azure flash and he swore. He had found the calcite box, and Olatu of Faytha with it.

Olatu rubbed the back of his neck and looked around.

Daric withdrew to a position high above where his awareness would be more difficult to detect. He prodded a group of foraging clickers toward the Faythan and the ensuing din gave him his hoped-for distraction.

Olatu's attention returned to the box. He slid the lid open – just enough for Daric to glimpse the purple mounds inside, then, with a look of satisfaction, he pulled it firmly shut. With another quick look around, he tucked the box beneath his coat and turned to pick his way back downslope. Daric followed him as far as his tent, but didn't go to the trouble of breaking through the Faythan's screens and alarms. Such a wealthy person would have anti-surveillance charms of the highest standard. Daric couldn't see the need to spend the time. Instead, he dusted himself off and went to give Huldar the news.

―――――――――

"Yes, I understand," Radätel Gok was saying. "But you must see my point of view? Reports should be delivered on time."

Huldar sighed. Gok could be pedantic to the point of idiocy. "Malena is in recovery," he explained patiently, "and will be for the next week at least. I'm sure she will complete her paperwork as soon as she is able. You were there, Radätel," he said with some exasperation. "We are all tired."

"But she was already behind."

"Only by a day or two."

He looked up with some relief as Daric stepped into camp.

Radätel turned expectantly.

Daric's bow was perfunctory at best. "Huldar, I need to speak with you."

"I *am* your Overlord," Radätel said pointedly.

Daric shook his head so minutely Huldar almost missed it.

He gestured Daric to the side. "If you would give us a moment?" he said politely to the Overlord. "I'm sure this won't take long."

I know who has them – the berries. Daric said. *It's Olatu, as we suspected. I saw him with them. I believe he means to send them with the navigator back to Giahn.*

That must not happen!

"Excuse me?" Radätel lifted his palms. "I'm still here."

"Of course, Overlord." Huldar said. "My apologies. Daric's news ..."

"I can see it's important. Whatever it is, I assure you, if it is sensitive, it will go no further."

"Just give us a minute more?" Huldar asked.

Daric answered his unspoken question about Radätel's allegiance with uncertainty of his own. *I've not seen him socializing with the Faythan since the picnic. My instinct says there's definitely a rift – But he is the Overlord ... Your call.*

Huldar's mind tumbled through options and outcomes. He remembered Radätel's genuine efforts as part of the team the day before, and hoped he wasn't about to make a mistake.

"Daric's news is dire," he said. He heard Daric let out a breath through his nose. "He has discovered the missing berries. They are with Olatu of Faytha. They are vital to the Went's existence."

"Vital? You know this?"

Huldar nodded.

"This has not been mentioned in any of your reports."

"No. The information is sensitive indeed. The berries must be recovered and returned to the cave."

Radätel turned to Daric. "You are certain?"

"Absolutely," he replied.

Radätel shrugged. "Then we will speak with him. Huldar, if you would sing us through?"

"Shouldn't we make some sort of plan?" Daric said. "Have breakfast at least?"

"Olatu is Lord of the Host," Radätel said. "He should lead by example!"

With that, he strode toward the portal, leaving Huldar and Daric to follow in his wake.

They arrived at the edge of the Host's plateau. Their footsteps marched in time as they made their way along the main street of the city of tents.

Huldar closed his eyes briefly then indicated the southern end of the settlement. "He's over by the Djan'rū."

"That's not good," Daric muttered.

"Why not?" Radätel asked.

"He may be hiding them there so he can slip them past the navigator."

"Surely the leader of the Host would not behave so badly," said Radätel. "We will ask. There must be an explanation."

"I hope you're right," Daric muttered, "but I doubt it."

They found the Faythan by a clump of dwarf strap trees. He gave a guilty start as he sensed their approach.

"Olatu of Faytha? A word please," said Huldar.

Olatu narrowed his gaze and directed it over each of them in turn. No one bowed.

"We believe you have stolen berries in your custody," Radätel said. "If this is the case, they must be surrendered immediately."

"Who told you this?"

"That's irrelevant," Huldar said. "What is important is that no more of those things are eaten. I cannot stress how important this is. The long-term effects are not properly studied. Please, if you return them to me now, I'll take them back to the cave and no more need be said."

Daric closed his eyes for a moment then tapped Huldar's arm. "Behind the strap trees."

Olatu saw Huldar's look and blanched. "I need time to consider!" he said. "These are valuable items – the property of our God-Emperor."

"They are the property of the Went," Huldar countered, "and you risk responsibility for the genocide of an entire species."

"In that case, it may be preferable to keep them!" Olatu snapped. "At least there would be no further hindrance to my mining operations."

Huldar opened his mouth to retort, but no words came.

"Ha! Look at your faces!" Olatu sneered. "Well, if they mean so much, by all means." He stepped aside and fixed Radätel in an imperious glare. "A warning. You are supposed to be Overlord of this rabble. Keep them out of my way or the Went may not be the only species in danger of extermination."

At that, he turned on his heel and walked away.

While Radätel glared after him, Huldar bottled his anger. Deep in a hollow between the diminutive tree trunks, half-hidden beneath a layer of seemingly natural detritus, was a glint of blue. He bent to pick up the box.

"Wait!" Daric said. "It's a trap. Allow me …"

There was a small snap as the Enna defused the nasty little surprise Olatu had left. Huldar shook his head. He should have seen it, but he had to admit, this whole business had him rattled. Secrets and lies – he had no head for politics.

"You carry them," he said to Daric. "Let's get them back where they belong." He turned to Radätel. "Thanks for your help, Overlord. Have you business elsewhere?"

"I know where they come from," Radätel replied shortly.

No you don't, Huldar thought to himself. *You don't at all.* "Daric and I will safeguard the site. The fewer who know what measures we take, the safer the … berries will be."

Daric's attention flitted over him and he wondered how much longer the secret of the eggs could be kept.

"You are right of course. Huldar." Radätel scowled after the Faythan. "How dare he threaten us? We were warned of this: the personal dangers of living in isolation from the Realm." With a drawn-out sigh he turned to face them. "My tent is here with the Host, but I no longer feel welcome. May I move over to your campsite? Perhaps there I could do something more useful than remind you of the tardiness of reports?"

"Of course," Huldar said. "There's no need to ask. You are one of us."

He stepped them through to soggy ground above the vast waterways of the northern delta, and from there, directly to the Eastern Continent.

"Bring the main part of your belongings to Central Base-camp," Huldar said to Radätel. "There's always been a tent there for you – unoccupied until now. Then, if you have time, could you check on the progress of the mine victims, make sure Alis and Ubaid have all they need and see that the debris is being disposed of in an ecologically sensitive way?"

"Of course!" Radätel replied.

"There's plenty to do, I assure you. Meanwhile, Daric and I will attend to this particular problem."

Radätel straightened his shoulders. "Don't take the Faythan's threats to heart, Huldar. There are a few Ashik scheduled to arrive, but they are merely peacekeepers, or so I was assured, assigned to help keep order when the camp expands."

"I'm sure that's the case," Huldar replied, but inside him, the planet's bell tolled otherwise.

GRAND THEFT

With their precious cargo in tow, Huldar and Daric trudged along the faint path that led from the portal to the lake. Already the deep thunder of the falls vibrated through their feet. As they rounded the bend above the lake, the thunder became a roar. Huldar paused, as usual, to admire the expanse of white blooms that vanished into the mist at the base of the massive cascade, and the small flashes of green as the flying lizards combed the falling waters for prey.

"The flowers don't have seeds," he said to Daric. "It's unusual. And watch while this cloud goes over … see?" With his hand he followed the shadow of a cloud as it scudded over the lake. Petals closed in a wave of brown, then opened again as it passed. "They work quite hard on days when clouds are intermittent, yet there are nights when they don't close at all."

"A mystery," Daric said. "Is it the variance in light they respond to, rather than its absence?"

"But why? We must always ask ourselves why, and what is the outcome."

"Perhaps there is no reason."

"There is always a reason," Huldar assured him. "Nothing is wasted in the natural world."

As they continued around the shore to the mountainside, the noise from the cascade grew deafening. Huldar looked at the steep slope before them, now completely covered in the same white flowers as grew in the lake, thriving in the sodden conditions.

As they started upward, he tried to position his feet between the blossoms, but the ground was slippery and there were casualties. *Do you know, the Went follow that trail on and on wherever it leads? I watched them cross a flooded lake – much like this one. It was deep, and there were underwater predators waiting for them.*

Did they make it?

Some died. The blue ones, 'the Mothers' I call them, searched for the bodies – even underwater. When they found one, they'd take the central eye from its head and swallow it. He thought of the first time he's seen this happen – the shroud of flowers and the young Mother swallowing the dead one's eye.

Ritual?

Maybe.

After they'd heaved themselves onto the path, Huldar looked back the way they'd come. It always seemed much further than he expected.

So what are these? Daric hefted the calcite box. *More than just berries.*

Are you sure you're not secretly Trianogi? Huldar asked. *You seem intuitive to an unnatural degree.*

It's the way you look at them, Daric said. *As if you don't really want to see them. You and Ubaid – something happened here. Am I right?*

Huldar stalled for a moment, then decided to tell the truth. The canny assassin would work it out eventually anyway. *They are eggs, Daric. The eggs of the Went. That's why they are so precious. I don't know when or how they'll hatch, but we saw them laid.*

... So ... the pregnancies?

We've said nothing.

You should let them know. Daric frowned.

Ubaid thought it best to wait, Huldar said quickly. *There's more to it, I'm afraid – but if we tell one thing it will be harder not to tell everything. We'll let them know if there's cause for alarm.*

Daric gazed out at the lake. *The mothers died. I can hear it in your voice.*

In my voice? His brows furrowed. How could Daric could sense so much just from the tone of his thought? It was no use telling him he was mistaken.

I see why you're reluctant, Daric went on. *This is a terrible thing, a great burden on yourself and Ubaid.*

Huldar started for the caves. *Not if nothing happens.* Daric walked behind him, perplexing as ever. He wondered what else he knew about them – but he could see such hyper-acute observational powers would be as much a curse as a gift. Was it an aspect of his healing ability? Could he hear the din of whatever it was the planet had set inside him? He wished it would stop. *We'll just have to wait and see,* he continued. *Ubaid seems satisfied that all is proceeding as it should, although the babies are growing more rapidly than expected.*

And they appear annangi?

So far.

Although it was not intended, the comment was laden with doubt. The planet's bell clanged loudly – was it warning or censure? He shook his head and continued up the slippery bank. *There is something else I need your help with,* he said to Daric. *I set an alarm on the cave mouth – it didn't seem right to close it again after what happened, but my skill with wards is minimal I'm afraid.*

Daric's wry inner smile was felt rather than seen. *I'll do what I can.*

By the time they reached the falls, the clangor of his inner bell filled his mind. He blinked heavily and tried to carry on as if nothing was wrong.

Beneath the torrent, the air was cold and thick with spray. He kept one hand against the cliff to steady himself. Cool water trickled over his fingers. The smell of water and damp stone filled his nose. Moss squelched beneath his feet. Debris from a fresh rock-fall by the entrance caused him to stumble. His recovery step peeled the moss from slick rock below and he fell to his knees, triggering the alarm. The jangle competed with the noise in his head until his thoughts cleared enough to turn it off.

I see what you mean, Daric said. *But don't worry, I know a thing or two about alarms.*

Thought you might.

In the near-complete darkness, he was glad of the sandy floor. The heavy scent of damp soil was all-pervading. He waited for his eyes to adjust then moved toward the rear of the cavern, but the familiar mounds were gone. He pushed through the clamor in his head and looked again.

Daric came up behind him. *Where are they?*

Shock made Huldar slow to respond. Had they hatched? If so, no evidence remained.

Daric stopped him from moving further forward and bent to examine the ground. *Boot marks – see?* He traced a pattern of arcing trails. *Not yours … too small.*

Whose then?

Olatu, I'd say. I can tell by the tread – they're not standard issue. Shen said he'd been out somewhere yesterday, and … yes. I can feel his residue. He tampered with your alarm. Sorry, but it really is quite primitive.

Huldar imagined the Faythan smirking at his efforts. Despair pushed him to his knees. The banging in his head would not stop. Daric set the calcite container beside him. He bowed his head. *No wonder he gave these up without a fight.*

I'll find them, Daric said.

It won't be so easy now he knows we're coming, Huldar pointed out. *And there's no time. The navigator will be here tomorrow.*

He opened the lid on the remaining eggs – about forty in all. Not enough to ensure the Went's survival. *Let's put these back. I'll get you to ward the cave again.* He glowered at the box. *Even if I knew a better way, It's as well you're here. I'm too angry to sing straight.*

Daric's head tilted. *And you think I'm not?*

Huldar looked at him for a moment, unsure what to say. Why had he assumed that Daric would be less affected? He sent a wordless apology. *Your feelings are seldom shown – and because you have not been with us for long, I …*

An Enna and an assassin? Which is worse? Daric said bitterly.

Forgive me, Daric. I made a thoughtless assumption. He battled to keep his tone even.

Of course, Daric replied. *And vocals under duress was part of my training.* But his mien had more than a hint of stone.

Huldar placed the eggs where he thought they'd once been, although they made a much smaller pile now. As he turned to close the box, his companion softened a little.

I could teach you … if you're interested.

The techniques of an assassin? Huldar replied sharply. He stood up, unable to quell his flare of anger.

Daric raised his shoulders. *Singing under duress …? With the greatest of respect, if Lind had known …*

Huldar paused. At first, it was all too much to process, but it only took a moment to see Daric was right. He opened his hand in capitulation. *Go on then. But time is short.*

Daric reached for his bare forearm. *If I may*

After the slightest of hesitations, he agreed.

The assassin's palm was warm against his skin. It closed around his arm in a firm but gentle contact.

Do you realize this soft spot inside your elbow is the weakest part of your defenses? Daric said. *There's nothing you can do about it – it's the same for everyone. Even me. Now, pay attention. This may feel strange, but it won't hurt.* He put his other palm to Huldar's forehead. *Try not to resist.*

Huldar blinked as a series of ideas materialized in his head.

Doesn't matter if you don't understand, Daric said. *Let your mind work through the shapes on its own. It won't take long. You should feel a difference in your larynx as soon as the patterns take hold.* He paused as if puzzled by something, then asked, *What's that noise?*

You can hear it?

How could I not? Daric answered, unaware he was the only other who could. Even Andel was immune. *What is it?*

The planet gave it to me, he explained. *A gift. She said the sound would guide me, but … I don't really understand it yet. It's not always this bad.*

A gift? Daric's tone was skeptical. He relinquished their deeper link. *I'll leave you to it. Let me know when you feel it working.*

Huldar pushed the noise aside and tried to give his mind room – the implantation of ideas was a sophisticated method of training he'd read about but not encountered before. He hoped there were no inbuilt traps, but it was too late to worry now. Then, like a silken glove, peace flowed through his throat. The absence of pain struck him most. He hadn't noticed how much his vocal chords hurt until the ache vanished.

We store tension in strange places, said Daric. He pointed to Huldar's neck and chest. *This structure alleviates those repositories. The stress may manifest elsewhere, but your throat will work to sing.*

Would it help the others?

Not with pregnancy. Daric's head moved slightly. *It's a little-known device …*

Assassin's secret?

Daric nodded reluctantly. *But I'm happy to share with any of the Uri'madu who wish it.*

Huldar bowed his thanks. *The difference is amazing. Shall we?* He indicated the cave mouth.

If you like, I could also teach you a more complex alarm?

His head was too full to absorb a new and complex charm.

A powerful gust of wind blasted them with spray and the light beneath the falls dimmed as outside, a torrential downpour began.

Daric's series of charms was soon complete and set to alert either one of them if breached.

They turned to contemplate the driving rain. Huldar was determined to confront Olatu as soon as possible.

Daric touched his arm. *What of that … gong in your head?* he asked. *Can you ask the planet for help? Surely it's not a deliberate torment. Maybe she knows where the eggs are. If they have hatched or vanished due to natural causes, it won't help to accuse Olatu.*

Huldar shook his head. *You're right again. I just can't seem to think straight.*

Quite understandable, given the circumstances, said Daric. *But if I might say – you've gone into a reactive state. Easiest for any enemy to control. Olatu will know that.*

Don't tell me – training?

Indeed. There's more to my former occupation than knowing how to wield a knife, and my one-time boss is an excellent strategist. Try to step back and see things through Olatu's eyes. What does he want? What will he give for it? When you know that, you can reclaim control. It doesn't take an army – or an Ashik for that matter – to win a war.

And we are at war, Huldar acknowledged. *The Bel Nishani have yet to arrive, but I've noticed activity in the portal that leads to their beach.*

Daric bowed his head. *Let's cross that hurdle when it comes. For now, would it help to return to the volcano? Ask the planet where the eggs are?*

It may. She has helped before, he said, but inside, he quailed at the thought. Each time he'd tried, the contact seemed easier, the escape more taxing.

They headed into the beating downpour and skidded down the bank, stumbling as lilies caught their feet. By the time they were far enough from the falls to hear each other speak, Huldar had come to a decision.

He raised his voice to compensate for the rain. "I'll do it. I'll go to the volcano. You go to the Overlord and warn him what has happened. I'll give you the verdict as soon as I can, theft or natural causes. If Olatu has the eggs, you must be ready to take action immediately without waiting for me."

"Who will watch over you?"

"Andel." He took the last few steps to the portal. "I'll tell her what I'm doing. She'll know where I am." He extended his senses, seeking a break in the weather, but the cloud and sheeting rain seemed endless. "Warn as many as you can of the danger of flooding," he added. "Especially the miners. We want no more emergency rescues."

"What about you?"

"I'll be fine," he replied, but in his heart he doubted it. "And don't forget, no one else but Ubaid knows they are eggs, not berries."

"If anyone can keep a secret, it's me," Daric said wryly. With a short bow, he stepped through the portal, leaving Huldar to tune it to the destination he required.

HIDDEN DEPTHS

Huldar peered out from under his small shelter and shivered. Flooding rain carved jagged erosion gullies in the volcano's most recent layer of ash. Andel and Cobar were on their way, but he knew he should wait no longer.

With a single long breath he stilled himself and sent his awareness into the now familiar depths, but this time he let the bell guide him.

As if she'd been waiting, the planet rushed to fill his consciousness and he was consumed by frustration too vast to comprehend.

Why won't they leave me? she whispered. Her voice filled him to capacity, like water filled a glass. *New bones for old. The trap is set. They seek like worms, gouging deeper.*

Huldar fought to make room for himself. *What trap?* he asked, but his voice seemed small and insignificant.

My watchers blind, their voices gone ... She wavered between frustration and sadness. *The sacrifice guides until the guide is sacrificed ... when will we know? You must seek the truth, find the way, hidden until the day of restitution comes ...*

I seek the truth, Huldar forced, but were her words even about him? He focused on the eggs of the Went. *I want to help.*

The planet seemed to step back. At last he had room to think.

Ahh, achaar, it is you, she said. *Too soon is the day we will know each other … What is it you require? You believe there is time but time is gone. The trap is set.*

Achaar? I don't understand. What trap? he asked again. *Does Olatu have the eggs? How can I get them back?*

Blessed and blown, the blessed wait in darkness until the spear of purpose finds them. Stolen they flee, but will they return? You cannot help them …

The eggs are stolen? He could barely make sense of her words. It was as if she spoke about future events, but how could he be sure? He wished there was some way he could understand, but it was like blundering through thick fog.

Her voice faded. She seemed to hold him in her gaze. As if time raced forward, a kaleidoscope of change filled his vision. The thaw was late, then later still. The once vibrant planet became a wilted husk. Its ring of moons collapsed and fell in a fiery rain. Volcanos belched. Ash and soot darkened the skies. Went's orbit lengthened until finally it slipped its bonds and drifted into the void. As if he were a scryer, he saw other planets around other suns. Each star in the Wentish sky had its own family of satellites, some with life and some without, but all were doomed.

Why? he railed. *How could this be? Does Breath no longer blow?* The bell inside him clanged with intolerable intensity. *What can I do?* he cried. *How can this be stopped?*

You must give yourself freely … Love is the one true beacon …

I don't understand. The pain was too much. *I never understand. Where are the eggs? What must I do?*

The watchers must return. Love lost is love's gain … The guide will be reborn. Only then will you be free.

From far away he heard someone call, *Come back! Please, my love! You must come back!*

He screamed in frustration, and as if the bell had been caught mid-swing by unseen hands, there was silence.

It is long since I walked among Annan's children, the planet said at last. *Strength housed by frailty. The guide comes with power, falls to power, hides from power then with the Wings of the Breath breeds hope for all …*

Who is the guide?

When you see him, she said sadly, *it will already be too late. Come to me then, achaar. You will know what must be done.*

The far-away voice reached him again. It seemed familiar … *I am not giving up! You must come back. I love you. Please!* He listened more closely. *Please, Huldar. I need you to come back to me now! Our baby needs you!*

Like the slow stretch of molten glass, he slid toward it.

His eyes opened to Andel's.

"Haven't we done this before?" he croaked.

Tears fell against his cheek. "I thought I'd lost you!"

He raised his hand weakly to her beloved face and wiped the tears away. *Tell Daric it's theft*, he said. *He knows what to do.*

───────────

Despite the continuing downpour, Daric's mouth twitched into an almost smile. The shadowless dusk had turned the Host's encampment into a perfect hunting ground.

Radätel pulled out a sodden cloth and wiped rain from his face. Elevated breathing betrayed his nervousness. With a small extension of his senses, Daric could feel the overlord's rapid heartbeat.

"Give me a minute or so to fully gain his attention," Radätel murmured. "If he sees reason and surrenders the goods, I'll let you know. Otherwise …"

"Remember to commit every corner of his room to memory," Daric prompted him.

"So I can share it with you if needs be," he said impatiently. "Yes. Understood."

"This is not a game, Radätel Gok."

"Of course not!"

Daric returned to surveying the camp. "I should be the one to tackle Olatu."

"As Overlord, I represent the Imperium. You asked my opinion and this is the correct way to proceed. Protocols must be observed … where possible – especially here in the wilderness. You have no rank. Olatu wouldn't listen to you in such a matter."

"Neither do you," Daric pointed out, "… have rank, that is." But neither did Olatu, for that matter. Technically, between Huldar, Andel and Malena, all the weight was with the Uri'madu – but the Marked were unavailable and, rank-wise, Radätel's appointment was the only political advantage they had. Flutters of uncertainty threatened his seamless veil. "I hate crowds," he admitted.

"Too bad," said Radätel. "I'm sure you'll manage. Speak to them honestly. Show them your outrage. Tell them what's at stake. They'll listen."

"Easier said than done. Until I came here, my life was a study in isolation."

They made their way down the bank and split up at the outskirts. Radätel's chest inflated, and with importance marking every stride, he started for the Faythan's tent.

Daric paused in the shelter of a dripping awning and followed with his mind's eye.

Olatu flicked aside his door. "What is it?" he said coldly. "You can see I'm very busy."

Daric used this moment to seamlessly infiltrate the Faythan's screens. He kept his touch as light as possible so as not to arouse suspicion and watched Radätel track muddy footprints over Olatu's rug.

"Where are they?" Radätel said boldly. "We know you have them. They must be returned immediately."

"What must be returned?" Olatu made a convincing picture of puzzlement. "What are you talking about?"

"The berries," Radätel said. "Where are they?"

"I returned them to Huldar this morning."

"The rest of them," Radätel said patiently. "As I said, we know you have them."

Daric watched fleeting changes progress through Olatu's veil before he settled on an answer. "And even if I did, what could you do about it?" His lip curled. "Write a report?"

"What function do we have here?" Radätel asked in desperation. "What authority? If the station granted us by the laws of the Imperium means nothing to you, what of Huldar's own status? His Mark sets him above every one of us. He requires that you return those berries. That should be enough!"

Olatu lifted his hands in appeal. "Those things are valuable beyond calculation. Think of your debt to my House," he added slyly. "Perhaps we could –?"

"Beyond calculation?" Radätel retorted. "The value they have to the species that needs them to survive – that is beyond calculation. My financial situation will be resolved when we return." He started to look around as Daric had requested, even peering beneath the bed. "Where are they?"

The distraction they had planned was under way. Daric gave a single nod and started for the dining area, but his listening ear remained with the Overlord's conversation.

"More berries will grow …" said Olatu.

"You can't know that," the Overlord responded.

There was a short silence. The Faythan's tone shifted. "Look around all you like, you won't find them here."

"Then where?"

"Stay out of my way, little Gok," Olatu said menacingly, "I am lord here."

Daric eased his awareness away from Radätel's conversation. It was time for him to do his part and he wanted no distractions. He already suspected how dangerous Olatu might be, but doubted he'd harm the Overlord.

He lowered his screens and entered the kitchens through the back door.

Shen looked up in surprise.

Daric tipped his chin at a quiet corner and sent the idea of secrecy. With simple farsight, he glanced through the canvas wall into the mess tent. Rows of rowdy diners, mostly angels, sat along trestle tables not dissimilar to a navigators refectory. The atmosphere was boisterous, anticipation of the navigator's arrival was high. He swallowed nervously, then chided himself for showing weakness.

"How many in there?" he asked discreetly.

"Fifty or sixty," Shen said. "Changes all the time. There's others outside getting things ready. Hope Shamkarun Kandät Enna brings them through easier than Malena did. Why do you want to know?"

"I have to speak to these people. I don't know how."

Shen frowned. *Whose idea was that?*

Not mine, Daric admitted, welcoming the change to mind-speech. *Radätel Gok thought if we could get to them while the Faythan's not around, maybe they would tell us something. Malena's still weak, Huldar's recovering from his latest adventure, Ariben doesn't know enough about what's going on. Calen's the only other archangel, but she said no.*

And that left you. What do you have to speak to them about?

That's the thing. All the berries are missing. Stolen. We have to get them back.

What about Lady Andel?

She's with Huldar and the healers.

Shen frowned. *He needed healing? Why?*

Daric shook his head. *It's a long and complicated story.* He thought of happier times with Casco in Haaseen, before all this madness began, and gravitated to a bottle of ale at the end of the bench. With a wave of his hand a mug slid toward him.

Shen gave him a dubious look.

You'd be surprised, Daric told him.

The alcohol was stronger than expected. He shuddered as it went down and grimaced at its rawness.

He looked again at the miners. "This is a bad idea."

Shen snorted. "You're admitting you were wrong?"

"There's a first time for everything," Daric murmured sourly, "or so they say."

He finished the ale and stilled his nerves. There was no plan. There was nothing he could give that these people would want, but he'd agreed to try and so he would. With Shen's eyes on his back, and Huldar's bravery on his mind, he went into the dining area and jumped nimbly onto the servery bench.

"Listen up!"

"Whoo hoo!" someone whistled.

"Listen up," another echoed in an exaggerated Enna accent.

"Should ah say it laak theis?" Daric retorted in low-class Cantori.

The heckler's mates ribbed him. "Gotcha, Carsa."

"We have a problem," Daric continued. "No doubt you all heard about those berries?" He nodded. "Yes, *those* berries. Well, they're not as much fun as you might think, but what they *are* is essential to the survival of one of the major species here."

"So what?"

"They've been stolen," he said. "We want them back. I'm here to ask if any of you can help me."

"Fuck off!"

"No, he's right," another countered. "If they're that important …"

"Heard they're the greatest bonk since arra-kanth."

"Really?" Daric's voice cut through the buzz. "That's what you heard? Well, the truth is, we don't know enough about them. Pregnancy might be the least of it. Please, if any of you know anything – I can't stress enough how important this is."

A buxom Cantori leaned back on her chair. "And we're guessin you want em back afore that coin-grubber sends em off as cargo?"

"Huh! That's if the navigator even makes it," said the miner beside her.

"Uh-ah!" Another of her companions waggled her finger. "Don't ever want to do that again."

Daric slid from the bench and strode toward the ring-leader. "Coin-grubber, eh?" He tried to bury his eagerness. "What do you know?"

She licked her lips and looked him up and down. "The Lady Malena says you'd be fit for it, if you weren't as cold as Went's blue arsehole. Gonna make it worth my while?"

Daric's anger caught even him by surprise. "Sure … I'll make it worth your while," he grated.

The angel fell from her chair and scuttled backward.

Daric advanced.

Someone ran up behind him. "Hey! That's enough!"

Daric didn't turn. With a tiny gesture, the interloper fell. His focus on the Cantori remained unshaken. A small part of him registered the agonized gasps behind him. Another part enjoyed it.

The Cantori backed into a creaking wall of empty crates. She cringed as Daric leaned over her.

"Tell me what you know," he said quietly. "It would be better if you did."

"I saw him leave," she stammered. "Then he came back. Bags – he put them in stone boxes. Calcite. I don't know where they are! I don't know any more!"

"Lay off, fancy-pants," someone said. "She doesn't know any more!"

He sensed distress from those who'd gathered round the writhing archangel.

"What have you done to him?" one of them cried. "Call the healer!"

Then there was a cold draft as the Faythan entered the tent. Rain dripped from his coat. People stopped talking.

"You!" he barked. "What's going on?"

"He come in," someone said, "makin a scene. Says you got something that belongs to him."

"Oh does he now?" Olatu said coldly.

Daric turned from the terrified Cantori, resentful of Olatu's interference. "Yes, I do," he said coldly. His fingers contracted as he prepared another attack.

"It's a lie!" Olatu said to the crowd. "Whatever he said, it's a lie. This lot want the famous fun-pills all for themselves." He returned to Daric. With an imperious lift of his nose he pointed to the dying archangel. "Fix this, and get out!"

Daric held his gaze, noting the weakness of his defenses. How satisfying it would be to see this pompous windbag writhe. How quickly he would break and tell him anything he wanted to know. Berries would be the least of it.

Fear shadowed the Faythan's haze.

The assassin's charm hovered on the brink of delivery, just a simple clench of mind, and …

Daric! Stop it!

Should he obey, or should he just get the information and end this self-important blowhard's life. They would thank him for it later …

Don't do it! Casco pleaded. *A fresh start. A new life, remember?*

He saw Radätel, motionless in the doorway, his face ashen. He could feel Casco's fear – for him, not of him … Without another word, he released his hold on the stricken archangel. In silence, the miners parted before him – a passageway of confusion. He brushed past Olatu and, with Radätel Gok at his side, strode back into the pouring rain.

On the Eastern Continent, the weather was dry. Radätel took a small white towel from Qalān. "My career is over," he said to him, "and that's sad enough – but I'm afraid, Daric Enna, that I will rejoin the Breath still wishing you had delivered that blow."

Daric's eyes crinkled at the Overlord's unexpected support. His last shreds of anger were corralled.

"I never was very good at public speaking," he said, then Huldar's attention raked him. *Daric. A word, please.*

He tidied his clothing, straightened his back, and bowed deeply as he entered Huldar's tent. "My apologies," he started. "I don't know what came over me –"

Huldar waved him to stop. *I'm too tired for this.* "We know Olatu has the eggs," he said. "We may not be able to get them back, but we must at least try."

"I shouldn't have –"

"No, you shouldn't," Huldar snapped, "but this isn't about you."

Daric paused. He noticed the strain in Huldar's eyes, and his haze, ragged with exhaustion.

"What happened?" he asked.

Huldar shook his head. "Many things I don't rightly understand. I want you to scour that camp. Go alone. Use every sneaking, spying skill you have, but no one gets hurt or killed," he said firmly. "The eggs may be more important than we understand, and it's tempting, believe me, to allow you to force people to answer, but don't. There are long-term ramifications for every move, every decision."

Daric nodded.

"If you find them," Huldar continued, "mark their location, retreat to a safe position and call me. If you don't find them … I know you will have done your utmost." He paused. Daric stood firm beneath his gaze. "I trust you," he said at last. "Don't make me regret it."

Thankful for his reprieve, Daric bowed again and slipped back into the darkness.

A LAST ATTEMPT

As the night deepened, the Overlord shifted uncomfortably in his bed. He couldn't communicate directly with his wife – a peculiarity of this planet he found increasingly trying, but he could feel her with him.

Olatu's scornful manner lingered in his mind. Had she seen that? The questions he'd asked still rang in his brain – what function did he have there? What authority? If he could not compel the leader of the Host to obey an environmental imperative, what use was he? The Imperium had made him its representative, yet he had been treated with contempt. Did Olatu spurn the God-Emperor by his actions, or was he merely the obedient, if terrified, servant he claimed to be?

It was equally distressing that, initially, he'd thought of Olatu as a friend. Allies in the wilderness. How wrong he'd been. The Faythan called no one friend. His cold heart was wrapped firmly around perceived profit and nothing more. Even the great beauty of El's unsullied creation could not sway him to a single empathic shred.

He turned over again, then, with a sigh of exasperation, threw the covers aside. He would confront the Faythan once more. Perhaps now he'd had time to think …? There was no need to tell anyone what he was going to do. If he assured him there would be no repercussions for his disrespect, no fingers pointed, maybe there was a chance he'd be more inclined to do the right thing.

He pulled on his clothes, tidied his hair into a suitable braid and headed back to the Central Continent.

Even though it was past midnight, the Host's encampment bustled with activity.

Near the outskirts of the Djan'rū, dwarfed by containers with the first of the refined ores, a crew of miners maneuvered smaller boxes filled with opal and precious stones. Above them, tethered bags of nacrite floated like lumpy brown clouds.

Other teams moved through streets of new tents, ensuring all was in readiness to welcome the remainder of the Host. He noted the pennant of Tiamät above a long, narrow structure – a dormitory for the expected Ashik.

Light bled from the seams around Olatu's door. It seemed he was also still hard at work. Perhaps that was something Radätel could respect him for.

He scratched on the leather. "Lord Olatu? May I come in?"

"One moment!" He heard the rustle of papers. The door pulled ajar. Tight screens prickled as he stepped inside.

The Faythan stepped out from behind his desk. "What is it?" he demanded. "Have you changed your mind?"

Radätel bowed politely. "Greetings, Olatu of Faytha. No. In fact, I was rather hoping you had changed yours."

Olatu grunted scathingly and waved his hand at the door. "If you've come to waste more of my time, leave now."

"I have no intention of wasting your time. I've come to make a counter-offer," Radätel said.

Olatu rolled his eyes. "Spit it out."

"Amnesty."

"For what?" Olatu tilted his head. "I don't know that you fully grasp the situation. I have done nothing wrong, and even if I had – there will be no repercussions."

"But I know you plan to take those berries back to Giahn and sell them to the highest bidder," Radätel said. "I know you intend to present some to our God-Emperor, and on the face of it, that seems like a good plan. No doubt you expect to be showered with favor for having solved his ongoing problem. But you must not give them to him under any circumstances. We have no idea what the after-effects might be, or even if the pregnancies are normal."

Olatu studied him carefully. "What do you mean?"

"I have overheard discussions. There are fears."

"Are there any actual problems? Have you proof?"

"Not yet, but it would be wise –"

"Fool!" He flinched as Olatu's hand slammed onto the desk. "I warned you!"

Frustration bubbled beneath Radätel's screens. Could his wife could see this? He remembered her voice, gentle yet strong. "If one desires respect, one must sing the song ..." He stood tall in her honor and lifted his chin. "I am the God-Emperor's chosen representative on this planet. If you disobey me, you disobey the Imperium, and I will be sure to inform him of your insubordination."

Olatu glanced at some papers on his desk. Radätel noticed familiar handwriting. "Those are my reports!" he said. "Why have they been opened?"

"So naïve," Olatu sneered. "As if I'd let your babble get in the way of my operations!"

Radätel snatched the papers from the desk and turned his back to look at them in private. On page after page, words, sentences, even whole lines of his painstakingly accurate work had been erased. He felt such anger as he'd never thought possible.

"You have no right –" He started, but something hit his head with brutal force.

He toppled slowly to the carpet.

"Oh dear!" Olatu said theatrically. "Radätel? Radätel Gok? You've had an accident. Can you hear me?"

The Faythan's shiny slippers were vague blobs by his face. The smell of dust and blood filled his nose. A cold hand touched his neck and an even colder force invaded his mind. Helpless to resist, his soul floated free, and Radätel was shocked to realize that Olatu's feet were the last things he would see in this lifetime.

Hidden beneath powerful screens, Daric looked up from the crate he'd just examined and sighed. Maintaining such cover was exhausting. He had been over every inch of the encampment, every hiding place he could think of, inside and out. Now the night was nearly over, he had no result, and his energies were running low.

He was alerted as Farushael of Cantori left the campsite and headed for the latrines. As Olatu's favorite archangel, Daric was fairly certain Farushael didn't feel so much favored as tyrannized, a situation he might be able to use to his advantage if necessary.

Careful to make no sound on the loose litter beneath his feet, he stalked his mark.

After a quick glance over his shoulder, Farushael went behind the thick screen of woven strap-tree fronds. When he leaned forward as if to study the contents of the trench, Daric stationed his mind's eye at an unobtrusive distance and peered over his shoulder.

After a first timid foray beneath the muck, Farushael wiped clean the lid of a calcite box.

Daric shook his head and almost laughed aloud. The oldest trick in the book and he'd overlooked it.

By the time the first fingers of dawn stirred the air, Farushael's simple cleaning charm had brought the outside of five such containers back to shiny blue.

Daric knew he should contact Huldar, but was reluctant to do so until he'd seen where the chests were to be taken. A short time later his patience was rewarded by the arrival of two angels.

"Follow me," Farushael said to them quietly.

With careful footing, Daric trailed the small party as they took the boxes back into the camp and delivered them to the Djan'rū site. Farushael lifted the lid of a large, non-descript crate and reburied the boxes within a load of granular pebbles. The lid was resealed, and the container positioned amid a stack of equally unremarkable cargo.

Daric memorized the location and turned for the nearest portal, determined to report his findings to Huldar as promised, but after only two strides he heard a familiar sound and looked back.

The air above the Djan'rū distorted, there was a chime, and Shamkarun Kandät Enna stepped from a shimmering field.

People scattered and, seconds later, the envelope collapsed, revealing a mountain of stores spread over an improbably large area. Seven tired spinners stood back from the second wave of the Host – one hundred and sixty-two battered souls.

Still fighting his way into an ostentatious jacket, Olatu rushed from his tent to greet them. He sighted Farushael and barked loudly, "Summon the Overlord!"

Shamkarun Kandät Enna returned the Faythan's grandiose bow with a slight inclination of his head. It gave Daric a strange feeling to hear the navigator speak. No one else on Went was of his clan, and the high-Enna accent echoed his own long-dead father's.

"So glad you made it safely," the Faythan said. "Our own passage was fraught with the most terrible danger."

"This was no picnic either," the navigator said dryly.

"Any losses?"

"Three."

"Terrible," said Olatu. "No one important, I hope?"

Kandät Enna tilted his head as if unsure how to answer.

"We lost one to the trip and ten to injuries sustained," the Faythan continued. "It was much colder when we arrived – much, much colder."

Kandät looked around, then up at the sullen dawn skies. "Well, I'm glad it's warmed up for you now."

He signaled his spinners and while they organized into a loose bunch behind him, he returned his attention to Olatu. "Our entry was harrowing to say the least. I must speak with Shamkarun Malena of Maatu as soon as possible – but first we must eat. Our reserves are exhausted."

"Of course!" The Faythan gestured them toward the dining hall. "Right this way."

"Shamkarun Malena?" Kandät asked. "I trust she is well?"

Before the Faythan could answer, nine Ashik formed a line and blocked their path.

Their leader stepped forward and bowed stiffly. "Commander Elmät Ashik, reporting for duty."

Kandät Enna and his crew detoured around them, sights set on the dining hall.

Olatu looked for Farushael and snapped, "Show them to their quarters!" then hurried to catch up to the navigator.

Daric closed his eyes and reached out for Huldar. *I've found them*, he said, *but you'd best hurry. The navigator has arrived.*

DUPED

Moist winds accompanied a dawn obscured by heavy cloud. The rain seemed over for the moment, but securely wrapped in his expert screens, Daric barely noticed. He chose a vantage point where he could continue his observation of the Host's encampment yet be ready to greet Huldar when he arrived.

Below him, the aftermath of the navigator's arrival continued. Miners shepherded shell-shocked newcomers toward food and accommodation while others examined damaged crates, dealing with everything from broken corners to splintered panels. Excited onlookers bustled like insects over a corpse. At the heart of the melee, a single Naghari tended those who'd been injured during entry, five so badly they were unable to walk. Beside them the bodies of the deceased lay covered in blankets like so many parcels – three who could now taste the Breath for themselves but would never enjoy the revitalizing air of Went. Daric shook his head as Alis and Ubaid hurried onto the scene. One more healer was nowhere near enough.

The portal beside him shivered and he stood to greet Huldar and Malena.

Malena smiled. "You look tired."

"You're not so flash yourself," he said, and gave her a small bow. "Good to see you up and about." He gestured toward the Djan'rū. "I overheard Kandät asking after you."

She snorted. "I can hardly wait."

He gave her midriff a surreptitious glance. It was far too early to see a bulge and her personal screens could still hide the changes to her vibration, but that would alter as the little-one grew and began to exert more presence. "What will you tell him?"

"Don't worry, little Enna," she replied. "I'll make it up as I go along."

"Where are they, Daric?" Huldar asked.

He passed images of the crate's current position, where the calcite boxes were placed within it, and a full account of what he'd seen of Farushael's activities.

Huldar nodded his thanks. "Stay put, but remain hidden and keep an eye on us – if you don't mind? I'm sorry to work you so hard, but …"

"I'll be fine. Until now, Went has been a comparative holiday."

"Radätel is already here, I take it?"

Daric shook his head. "Haven't seen him, but I've been otherwise occupied."

"Of course." Huldar turned to Malena. "Ready?"

While the two started for the Host encampment, Daric scanned for Radätel, but he was nowhere nearby, nor was he at Central Base-camp. Huldar had come from the Eastern Continent, and it seemed the Overlord wasn't there either.

This worried him, but when Huldar and Malena entered the dining hall, training took over and he settled his attention on them.

The navigator and his crew were seated at the kitchen end. Several mounds of pies, a pot of rich, thick stew and a basket of seasoned flat-bread were lined up down the center of their long table. Kandät sat at the head, while Olatu sat alongside the spinners, eyes slightly wide as he watched them eat.

Kandät stood when he saw Huldar and Malena and beckoned them over. "Shamkarun Huldar of Leth, Shamkarun Malena of Maatu! It is a pleasure to see you."

"Shamkarun Kandät Enna," Malena said politely. They gave each other a small but decorous bow. "How are things in the Realm?"

"Greetings, Kandät Enna, Olatu. Where is Radätel Gok?" Huldar asked. "It was my belief he was already here."

Olatu frowned. "How should I know?" He peered at the doorway and shrugged.

Huldar tilted his head toward the Overlord. "In the meantime, I have a matter to discuss."

Kandät Enna resumed his seat and lifted another pie from the pile. "I hope you don't mind?" He took an enthusiastic mouthful and poured himself a drink from a steaming pot of tea. "Our approach was difficult in the extreme."

"No, of course, go ahead," Huldar said.

The navigator waved the dripping pastry at Olatu. "So, how has this one offended you?"

"Offended? Ridiculous!" Olatu blustered. "It is the Uri'madu who offend. They have been nothing but trouble, hampering my mining operations with their ridiculous sentimentality –"

"I seriously doubt that," Kandät said evenly. "Go on, Shamkarun Huldar. Do you have a grievance?"

Huldar inclined his head. "We have discovered a very special species on this planet – the Went –"

"Nothing more than shaggy lumps," Olatu interjected.

"You forget yourself, Faythan," the navigator said sharply. "Speak when you're required to. Time in the wilderness has addled your perceptions."

Olatu's mouth opened, then closed again. Daric was amused until he noticed a flash of true hatred escape the Faythan's veils. An image of Radätel Gok pushed forward and a slight memory of furtive movement outside Olatu's tent in the pre-dawn gloom … had the Faythan just arrived back from somewhere? Why hadn't he noticed him leaving? The pictures disturbed him.

With masterful calm, Huldar resumed speaking. "We believe that the Went, the creatures for whom this planet is named, should be honored as true Citizens."

The navigator lowered his pie. "Citizens?" He poured tea for himself and Huldar "Intriguing! Do you have proof?"

"We are working as hard as we can," Huldar said. "I anticipate presenting a successful case by the mid-term communication point." A smile flitted across his face. "It is by far the most exciting study I've made."

"Indeed!" Kandät eyed the Faythan shrewdly. "And I'll bet our little friend here's none too thrilled by your findings?"

"Nor helpful, I'm afraid." Huldar also glanced the Faythan's way. "Which brings me to my second, and most urgent point. These beings, the Went, are absolutely reliant on certain berries for their survival. The berries have several remarkable effects on annangi – outcomes which we are still studying. No doubt you'll hear more. With these properties in mind, Olatu has taken the entire cache."

The Faythan began to splutter, but was silenced by Kandät's glare.

"Although he has returned a small number," Huldar continued, "he refuses to surrender the remainder. I believe he intends to ship them back to the Realm as cargo, hidden among the ores."

Kandät Enna frowned. "This is a serious accusation, Shamkarun Huldar, and knowing you as I do, I am sure it's not unfounded." He turned to the Faythan. "What do you have to say?"

"It's rubbish!" Olatu shook his finger at Huldar. "He is the one who's addled. And where is the Overlord?" He looked toward the door. "We cannot proceed in our resolution of this … this baseless allegation until the Imperium is correctly represented."

Kandät Enna snorted in amusement. "Now I know you're up to something!" He turned to include his crew. "We will not knowingly be involved in ecological crime. No cargo will be loaded before the content is thoroughly checked." He leaned closer to Huldar. "But if you don't mind, and I'm certain you'll understand, we'll finish our meal before we begin any investigations. Agreed?"

Huldar bowed. "Agreed."

The navigator smiled good-naturedly and stood to bow even lower in return. "There's no need for you to bow to me, Shamkarun Huldar of Leth, as I'm sure we are all well aware."

Olatu's face twitched, but he said nothing more.

"Please, won't you sit down?" At Kandät's gesture, Olatu was shuffled aside to make room. Huldar smiled as Shen arrived with fresh tea and even more food.

Malena pushed in on the other side between Kandät and his spinners. "Kaliga, Manse!" she said. "Great to see you."

The two glanced at each other. "Things must be tough," said one.

The other nodded. "She's remembered our names."

"Ha, ha," she said dryly, and turned to Kandät. "How long are you staying?"

He spoke around another huge mouthful. "We'll have a good sleep, a few more meals and be on our way tomorrow. We must leave at first light. I hope your crew have time to help with the lading? Keep them in practice."

"We have all the practice we need, thanks just the same," Malena replied, then she seemed to reconsider. "Time is tight, but I'll ask around."

"I'm sure your new duties keep you quite busy," Kandät said. "But I really would appreciate any assistance you could spare. We'll need all our strength if the escape is as difficult as the entry. It would be ideal if we could stay a few days and rest, but problems on Parsay left us behind schedule."

"Parsay?"

"An eruption. Perturbations in Qalān."

"Rotten luck." She gave a tight smile. "As I said, I'll ask around."

"And I'll send Bush and Topper over," Huldar assured him.

Kandät smiled in thanks. "Those two certainly know what they're doing."

From his position in the strap-tree scrub, Daric watched the mounds of food disappear while his own stomach rumbled. Finally, Kandät and Huldar started for the Djan'rū.

His heart beat fast as Huldar indicated the crate he'd been shown, but as it was pulled aside, he noticed Olatu's sly smile.

There's something wrong, he said to Huldar. *Olatu's not worried.*

Huldar glanced his way. *What do you mean?*

I don't know – but there's a problem! He could feel his work unravelling.

With little ceremony, the first of the calcite boxes was revealed.

Kandät opened his hand and the lid slid back. Inside the box was empty. Daric's heart plummeted. Huldar leaned forward, then backed off in confusion.

"Not what you expected?" Kandät enquired.

"Not at all," Huldar said quietly.

"Try the next one," Kandät suggested.

Each box they opened proved empty. Huldar's shoulders slumped.

"You see? It was all lies," Olatu said angrily.

"One must ask why it is you've buried empty boxes among the ores," Kandät Enna said.

Huldar turned on him. "You did steal them," he snarled, "and I *will* find them."

"I doubt it," Olatu retorted, but he flinched as Huldar stepped closer.

"Where are they? You have no idea what's at stake!"

"Be assured we will check anything that seems out of the ordinary," Kandät said, "but in the meantime?"

With a shudder, Huldar pulled his anger back and bowed to the navigator. "My apologies, Shamkarun Kandät Enna."

"I have no doubt your claims are genuine," Kandät replied. "But there is little else I can do except have each item checked for anomalies and inform you if we find anything suspicious."

Daric's heart twisted as Huldar and Malena turned to leave. He should have known they'd been had. He'd been certain Olatu had had no inkling of his presence, yet he must have done, else why spring the trap? Then he remembered Shen's attempt at snooping – perhaps not as successful as he'd believed. He watched Huldar and Malena walk up the hill – Huldar supported her elbow as she struggled with the rise. As they came within talking distance he turned and pretended to study a break in the clouds.

Come on, Daric, Huldar said tiredly. *You did your best. You need food and sleep.*

They haven't left yet, Malena said stoutly. *There's still time. I'll get Banga and some of the others to help load the cargo as Kandät suggested – males only of course. I'll keep the blessed away as best I can.*

Thank you, Malena, said Huldar. *And as for Radätel Gok, his absence worries me indeed. We'll get started with a search party while you rest, Daric. Join us when you're ready and we'll decide what our next move should be.*

He felt Huldar's eyes on him but couldn't bear to meet his gaze.

"Please, don't blame yourself," Huldar said. "Sleep on it. Sometimes answers come in the logic of dreams rather than this world of trial by obstruction."

Daric looked up at last. "Lady Andel's words?"

Huldar's expression softened. "Her father's."

A QUIET CHAT

It was late-afternoon on the same day when Malena walked toward the Host's encampment again. Her entrance through the western portal gave an easy, if zig-zagging, downward path, but also an extensive view of what they were up against in the search for Radätel Gok. Days of torrential rain had accelerated the melt. Sheets of fast-moving water covered the plains below the settlement and further on the delta was now a wide brown ocean. But thankfully, the sun had made an appearance, insects clattered, small creatures chirped and a cool breeze kept the humidity at bay.

She set off down the trail. Thanks to Ubaid's excellent abilities, she could revel in the free movement of her body and the long, rhythmic stride she'd developed since becoming a Planet Walker. But her confidence was short-lived. A small stumble rocketed pain through her still-fragile back and she was forced to pause.

After a few minutes, when her breathing had returned to normal, she felt able to move on – just with a bit more care.

Kandät Enna was seated on a rock overlooking the encampment. He slid to his feet as she came closer and gave a rakish bow. "Kattíst?"

"Bai'ah," she replied. "You've rested? I never thought I'd say it, but it's good to see you."

His gaze travelled up and down her torso and came to rest on her face. "And I hate to admit it, but … you look radiant. Perhaps you've found your true calling at last?"

"And I see you have yet to discover the secrets of humor," she retorted.

"If I didn't know you better I'd think you didn't like me." His mouth twitched in a shallow grin. "I hear you are in recovery from a nasty accident. Given the serious nature of your injuries, I didn't expect to see you up and about again so soon – or is that just Maatu bloody-mindedness?"

Malena sighed, resisting the urge to massage her paining back. "I don't like you, Kandät, and you don't like me – but look, the sun is shining and I've survived something that should have killed me. Can't we just be nice to each other? It's only for a few hours, then you'll be back in the Chime and I'll be left behind."

Kandät turned to study the workers below. Crates and boxes floated in ever-changing lines and patterns as they were ordered for the out-bound trip. At length, he nodded. "I suppose it's not too much to ask. How are you getting on with the other Enna – Shamkarun Dasai's secretive little brother?"

"Rocky at first, but we're all Uri'madu here. A team. It makes a pleasant change. He's actually something of a hero. Saved my life – or helped to."

"Dasai Enna will be pleased to know. I'll tell her if I see her." He looked at the skies. "The silence is unnerving. Cut off from everything? It's not natural."

"It took some getting used to," she admitted. "But now? I like it. Liberating."

"Liberating?" Kandät snorted. "Olatu of Faytha would no doubt agree with you. Perhaps a poor choice for leadership under these circumstances."

"Power's gone to his head," Malena said. "I avoid him at every opportunity. Bai'ah, this thing with the berries – it's very important that they're found."

"They must be extraordinary if Olatu's willing to go to such lengths."

"They are a potent aphrodisiac … among other things."

"Then no wonder he wants them. Probably plans to sell them to the God-Emperor."

"He mustn't!" she said strongly. "We don't know enough about them."

"I can't stop him," Kandät replied.

She heard a touch of bitterness, and for the first time wondered what Kandät's relationship with the Imperial family might be like. She turned to examine his features: neat and handsome, she supposed – in an Enna-ish way.

"Can you get a message to Mael for me?" she asked.

"What message?"

She held his gaze. "Swear to me you'll tell no one else, Bai'ah."

His head tilted a little. "Swear? But I'm Tiamäti." He examined his blue-painted nails. "How can you trust a pretentious bimbo such as me?"

"Now's not the time," she snapped. "I know you. If you swear, you'll keep your promise. So swear!"

He bowed. "Kattíst, I swear I will release your words to no one except Shamkarun Mael of Maatu until my vow is released by your word."

"And the rest," she insisted.

"Bey et El a'sien," he said solemnly, and bowed again. "Now, what is it?"

"Thank you, Bai'ah," she said, but when she went to tell him, the words would not come. Moisture welled in her eyes.

Kattíst?

His sending of genuine concern only made things worse. She bowed her head, powerless to stop her tears.

"You seem tired," he said. "Perhaps food would help? Some things are expressed more easily with a pot of tea to keep them company."

She nodded, and tried again for self-control.

"That cook is a master," he continued lightly. "Best talemgal pies I've had, and the seafood parcels rival even Mirashael of Cantori's. Ever tried them?"

She smiled through tears. "Finest in the Realm."

He gestured toward the encampment. "When you're ready?"

"The injury – you know?"

"Of course," he replied.

She focused on her breathing as she'd been taught and allowed the primal in-out patterns of life to reassert themselves. Slowly her psyche stabilized, at least enough to be seen in public.

"Thank you," she breathed.

Kandät nodded, and they started down the bank.

She shivered as cloud sent the light into hiding. Mud clung to her boots as they picked their way toward the encampment. But as they got closer, the smell of cooking lifted her spirits.

"The search for Radätel Gok continues?" Kandät said conversationally.

"No luck as yet," she replied. "The situation is very hard on Huldar. They almost lost someone to Qalān last time they were here. But he's a tough one in his own way. Stubborn as only a Leth can be."

"A fascinating individual, I'll admit. Disarmingly humble."

"Well, he never stopped trying and, somehow, he saved her."

Kandät slowed to negotiate a twist in the path. "Yet despite their efforts, that particular story had a tragic ending."

"Oh, of course!" She nodded. "You were there."

"It was very sad."

"And along with everything else there's been the mine collapse, the missing berries – now Radätel … and that Faythan? Arrogant kalla! Huldar should've hit him when he had the chance."

"Kattíst!"

"You have no idea!" *I'd happily pay someone to send him to the Breath.*

"Kattíst! I can't believe you said that."

"Listen, Bai'ah, whatever properties the berries have for us, the Went themselves are beyond amazing. I have seen them for myself – only at a distance, but from what he and Andel have shared, I have no doubt Huldar is correct regarding their citizenship. It hurts my heart to think anyone would endanger such gentle and fascinating creatures."

Kandät Enna glanced her way, his slender eyebrows raised. "An ecologist now?"

"Waking up, I think. Maybe there's more to life than navigating."

"Well, you're welcome to it," he said good-humoredly. "And besides, small-group politics drive me insane. Everyone arguing over the slightest infractions. For me, the Chime is all, and I definitely prefer the luxuries of civilization. But you're right about Olatu. Reprehensible, even for a Faythan."

He pushed aside the dining room door. She ducked beneath it as if nothing was wrong, but the pain in her back forced a small gasp and for once she wished she was smaller in stature.

They chose a seat in a private corner and almost before they'd had time to settle Shen arrived with tea and a serving of fresh omosa.

Fragrant steam wafted from the bowl between them. Tea gurgled softly as they poured. Kandät selected a morsel and chewed with his eyes closed, but she was happy just to sip from her mug and appreciate the warmth between her hands.

"Now, Kattíst, you've done a marvelous job with the new Djan'rū – for a Maatu."

She rolled her eyes. Would he never let it go?

"I had no trouble finding it," he continued, "and it has a strong, smooth connection. Quite commendable." He raised his tea in salute. "But the entry-zone was appalling. I'm sure it was nowhere near as turbulent when I came here last. I don't mind admitting, it was one of the most difficult I've experienced." He paused to take another omosa from the bowl. "This may sound peculiar, but it was as if the planet itself fought against us."

"Strange you should say that," Malena said. It was odd but vindicating to hear her own impressions repeated by another – especially one so well credentialed. "At the time, I thought the notion somewhat fanciful, but that was before ... Do you know she's sentient? Huldar can speak with her."

"He can? You know this to be factual?"

She nodded. "But each time he does, he comes closer to death."

"No wonder this world feels strange beneath my boots. I don't think she welcomes us."

Malena thought of her life now, and the new life within her. The joy she felt while walking, surrounded by energy so vital, as if she was a part of it. Something had happened to her while she was in the mine; she felt she'd been examined and found acceptable at last.

"I feel quite the opposite," she told him, "as if I've found a home I never knew I had. As if we are part of each other. I know that must sound strange. Ekeridu is my true home and always will be ... and that brings me to Mael. I think I'm ready."

She released her warm mug and whispered her navigator's seal from Qalān before offering her hand. Blue polish glinted on Kandät's nails as his fingers closed over it. His eyebrows dipped as he felt the cool metal in her palm and its distinctive signature.

Remember your vow ... she started.

OVERLORD NO MORE

Some time that night, the rain started again. Huldar hunkered beneath his heavy coat and listened. His tiredness was through to the bone. Cold water dripped from his hood. Memories of the search for Lind intruded on his concentration.

He felt his wife's return from farsight and closed his eyes to listen.

Nothing yet, she reported. *That's the western links done.*

Try doubling back toward the Host. I can't help thinking that's where he went – or tried to go.

We're on it. Kira feels guilty because we're here by the fire.

No need for you to be out here too.

Or you.

It's easier for me. Ether's more receptive.

She sent a skeptical smile then slipped back into tandem with the spinner.

He could sense other teams and hear their calls, but hope of an answer from Radätel Gok had faded.

Casco searched alone. Under Daric's tutelage his ability with farsight had improved immensely, but despite this, Huldar wished he hadn't agreed to it.

His friend vanished briefly as he stepped through a portal, then seconds later rejoined the wider net. Huldar had a sense of his movement somewhere in the mountains behind the Host's plateau, where the terrain was difficult and the weather worse. Then something caught Casco's attention.

His read of the others receded as Huldar waited, hoping against hope that if it was the Overlord, he was still alive.

Over here! Casco cried. His shaken tone said the news was not good.

Huldar's heart fell. His coat was heavy and stiff as he stood to receive the news. Seconds later, shared imagery of a body in the water confirmed his fears.

I'll contact the Naghari, he said sadly. Another quick telepathic shout called off the search, then he alerted those waiting in the base-camps to heat up food and drink ready for the other teams' returns.

I've a feeling Daric should see this, Casco said. *There's something not right. What would he be doing way out here? And the nearest gate happens to be just one step away from the Host.*

I've thought all along that was where he was going, Huldar replied, *but you're right. It makes no sense. Do you want to wake Daric or should I?*

Reluctant to go near the Host at this time, Huldar found another portal and picked his way toward Casco's location. The night was so dark it was hard to see. Jagged outcrops and thick scrub hampered his progress and the roar of water was everywhere. Then a flicker of light glimmered through the downpour and he found Casco beneath a sheltered overhang.

373

Although he was beyond the reach of the weather, Huldar was sure the small flame he'd conjured gave more psychological comfort than actual warmth.

Casco stood to greet him. *It's bad*, he said.

Huldar nodded, and from long habit opened his heart to his friend.

I'm sorry, Casco said guardedly. *I didn't mean those things I said.*

You were angry, and rightly so, Huldar replied. *I took you for granted. Gave too little in return.*

Casco lifted his shoulders. *It wasn't you I was angry with. It was just … everything. The whole thing at home, fighting, hiding, arranging emigration, permits, rules, so unfair – but like Daric says, any Kareski who expects fairness from the Imperium is in for disappointment.*

But others have helped?

So many others. He shook his head. *I'm sorry. You've always stood by me.*

I've missed you.

Casco smiled a little. *So you should.* He took a small globe from Qalān and held it for Huldar to see. *He was one of them, Radätel was, a Tiamäti, but a good heart. A light-singer*, he said brokenly. *He'd been showing me … since the cave-in. Afraid of caves, but he went in. Just wanted to help.*

He paused before whispering the crystal to life. Warm light held the night at bay.

Huldar nodded. *Better take a look then.*

The glow preceded them down a rocky bank into a long gully filled with rushing water. Across the stream they saw the glimmer of foaming rapids, but closer to shore a dark eddy held a pale shape trapped between rocks.

Huldar shuddered. He didn't want to look, but he knew he must. *How did you find him?*

There was a break in the cloud-cover. I saw something shining – the remains of his overcoat. Casco glanced upriver. *Two hundred paces that way.*

Huldar went on alone.

Radätel's face was turned up. He was naked but for a torn undershirt. Tangled limbs gave testament to the violence of their journey. Huldar's head tilted as he tried to absorb what he saw. Bent flat beneath his shoulders, the Overlord's right arm looked as if it should belong to someone else. His legs bobbed and tugged in the current. One foot faced the wrong way. Jagged white bone poked like fangs from his shin.

He squatted beside the body and smoothed bedraggled hair from Radätel's face. The expression on it seemed trapped in shock.

Casco still faced upstream.

"Are you all right?" Huldar asked him, but his voice was no match for the roar of the water. He tried again, *Are you all right?*

Recognized the red trim. It's a bit torn about.

Any sign he slipped?

Casco shook his head. *Not that I could see. Could've gone in anywhere.* He turned toward the portal, although Huldar sensed nothing. "It's Daric," he yelled.

Huldar nodded. "Ubaid won't be far behind," he yelled back. *Not that there's anything he could do for him now.*

After a few minutes, Daric arrived. He stood with them and studied the body in silence. "Perhaps he tripped and fell," he said at last. "But he's been dead for some time – a day at least. What was he doing out here in the middle of the night?"

Come to meet someone? Huldar suggested, although the notion seemed far-fetched.

"If so, whoever it was didn't raise the alarm," said Daric.

"And although the closest portal leads to the Host, we're a fair way from it," Casco added. "It's not like him to have wandered off, especially in such bad weather."

Huldar glanced at the eastern sky. "Be light soon. Maybe we'll see more then." It was tempting to retreat to the overhang while they waited for Ubaid, but it seemed disrespectful to leave the body.

Casco nodded. "We could take it in turns to stand with him."

I'll take first watch, Huldar said. *You two get out of the weather.*

"Tea?"

"I'd appreciate it," Huldar said thankfully.

By the time the clatter of dislodged stones announced Ubaid's arrival, a warm mug had relieved the chill in his fingers, and the woody taste of Urmahji had settled his stomach.

The Naghari surveyed the body with a clinical eye. "Accident?"

"Look more closely," Daric suggested. "No water in his lungs."

With his fingertips resting on Radätel's chest, Ubaid half-closed his eyes. "You're right." He pointed out marks on the corpse's ribs. "And this discoloration happened after death."

"The wound on his head?" Huldar asked.

Ubaid parted the hair with gentle fingers, then looked up. "Not enough to kill him outright."

"Could have happened after he fell?"

"Might have," Ubaid replied doubtfully. "If he hit a rock while he was caught in the rapids, or tumbled head-first, it could've stunned him – but surely he'd have called for help?"

"And there's no water in his lungs," Daric repeated.

Huldar frowned. "So, not an accident?"

Ubaid and Daric studied the body for a moment longer.

Ubaid shook his head. "Huldar, this death is unlikely to have been the result of natural causes."

"Who would want Radätel dead?" Huldar asked.

"Duvät Gok, I could understand," Ubaid muttered, "but this one was a decent sort."

Huldar looked at him.

"You think because I'm a healer I don't have opinions?"

Casco glanced at Daric. There was a rapid subliminal exchange.

"I overheard something," Daric said.

"Of course you did," Huldar said tiredly, but the flicker of hurt across Daric's veil made him regret his words. "Sorry, Daric. It's just that –"

"You're running on bare nerves," Daric said. "No need to apologize. I've been sleeping while you and Casco have worked through the night."

"No more than you did for us the night before." Huldar inclined his head in a bow of respect. "What did you hear?"

"Olatu threatened Radätel. Said he – and the Uri'madu – should get out of his way. He seemed quite serious, but I didn't think he'd actually hurt him."

"With Ashik now to back him, he'll be unstoppable."

"That doesn't prove he killed him," said Ubaid. "Deliberate murder is a terrible thing."

Daric tipped his head to look at the corpse again. "And sadly, something I know a bit about," he admitted.

Huldar raised his eyebrows. This was the first time he'd heard Daric openly reference his career as an assassin.

"Radätel was stunned then sent," Daric said confidently. "Evidence of the psychic injury is slight and easily overlooked, even by so skilled a healer as yourself," he said to Ubaid. *But see here on the neck?*

Ubaid nodded. *Ahh ... yes indeed.*

"Indicators fade within thirty-six hours or so – a timeframe of sorts. Only an archangel, and one with some skill, would have the power to do this."

"He was last seen ... when?" Huldar asked.

"We returned together from the Host encampment," Daric recounted. "You asked me to resume the search for the berries and I left straight away."

"Did anyone see him after that?" Huldar looked at Casco and Ubaid, then returned to Daric.

"I didn't kill him!" Daric said. "I even liked him ... sort of. He was on our side – the Uri'madu. I made a promise!"

"I'm not suggesting you did," Huldar said soothingly, although privately, the thought had entered his mind. But if it was Daric ... why would he? As he'd said, he and Radätel seemed to have developed a certain rapport, especially since the cave-in. Casco had obviously been fond of him, and neither Daric's haze nor veil showed the slightest perturbation ... but would it?

"Someone must have done it." Casco said. "Daric might be able to help us find out who."

"Better you than the Ashik," Ubaid said to Daric. "I don't want them anywhere near our camp or our mothers."

"Neither do I," Daric said vehemently.

"Their involvement may be unavoidable," Huldar pointed out. "This is the Overlord, after all."

"Whatever we do, we must hurry," Daric said. "The navigator leaves soon, and the eggs – I mean *berries*, with him."

Casco looked at Daric. "Eggs?"

"I'm sorry, Casco," Huldar said. "He was ordered to tell no one, not even you."

"Eggs – of the Went?" Casco said. His eyes widened. "And now, our friends are pregnant?"

"I promise I'll explain," Huldar said shortly, "but unlikely as it seems, we have more pressing matters to deal with."

"I suggest we report the death as accidental," Ubaid said. "Sad, but not at all suspicious. We investigate more fully in our own time."

"You're good at this," Daric remarked.

"Many centuries of dealing with annangi in confined and isolated conditions," Ubaid replied dryly. "Our poor victim has rejoined the Breath. Nothing we do will bring him back."

"Another secret," Huldar said sourly. Water swirled at their feet. He looked down at Radätel's broken body. Anger surged against his battered walls. "But I think you're right. This is what we must do." *I mean no disrespect*, he whispered, and hoped that wherever he was their Overlord would understand.

"What of his cry?" asked Casco. "He has a wife ..."

"I presume that's where it went," said Daric, "but even if she alerts the Guild, it will be many months before we know their response."

A chorus of creaks and trills announced a grey dawn. Vague new light made a transparent shroud over the broken body. The dank smell of over-wet forest did nothing to lift Huldar's sense of doom.

"We should take him back to Central," Casco said. "He liked it there."

Huldar nodded slowly. He shared a glance with Daric and asked Casco, "Have you finalized your order for the Guild?"

"With Daric's help. But I haven't given it to Olatu. You asked me not to."

"Best it should be given directly to Shamkarun Kandät," Huldar said.

"Wise move," said Ubaid. "All our reports should've been handled the same way."

"Too late now," Huldar said. "But this one at least may get through un-censored." He turned back to Casco. "Can you add news of Radätel's death to the list?"

Casco nodded. "But who'll get it? The list will go to Mirashael of Cantori ..."

"I can help you there," Daric said. "He is someone we can trust."

"We can only hope."

"It's at Eastern," Casco said. "I don't have it with me."

"Good. Make the changes and bring it back to Central as quick as you can. Ubaid and Daric, if you could prepare the body, I'll help take it through. Then Casco and I will go to see the navigator off and make sure he gets the order in person."

"And the eggs?" Daric asked.

Huldar's shoulders slumped. "Unless Kandät Enna somehow stumbles upon them ..."

Casco frowned. "You're giving up?"

"Of course not! Olatu is playing a complicated game. It may be that they're hidden elsewhere and not in the manifest at all."

"Let me get it out of him," Daric said. "There's still time."

Huldar paused. The offer was tempting. He recalled the planet's warning. There was more at stake here even than the continuance of a sentient species.

In that moment's hesitation, a dark ferocity bloomed in Daric's gaze.

He looked the assassin in the face. Almost, he agreed, but the planet's bell tolled sharply and with great reluctance, he shook his head.

Like oil over water, Daric's usual aspect resurfaced. Casco gave him the slightest of nods. Although he'd made no protest about Daric's offer, his relief was clear.

"Then we'd best get moving," Daric said. He turned to Ubaid. "If you could spread a blanket on the bank, I'll lift him free."

As Daric turned his agile mind to the task of extricating the body, the Overlord's hand moved as if in farewell.

Casco turned away.

Huldar thought again about what might have happened. Had he been on his way to confront the Faythan? It could only have been about the eggs. One way or another, Radätel Gok had lost his life over his passion to do the right thing.

He recalled Olatu's fake outrage, his ostentatious demand for Radätel's presence, and his anger was amplified. How could he look such a monster in the face and keep his rage contained?

You must try, Andel sent to him, and he bowed his head. He'd forgotten she would share his emotions.

Held secure in the grip of Daric's mind, Radätel's body lay suspended above the eddy where it had washed up. Water dripped from his flaccid fingertips.

"And we're only at the first quarter, not even to the halfway mark yet," said Ubaid.

NIELLI AND HNARSE

Hnarse Stargazer moved its trunk absently over a clump of small red flowers. In a landscape of scent, theirs was reminiscent of busy wasps. When its nose-end grazed too close, the blooms released a cloud of little stinging barbs – another kinship to wasps. Hnarse sneezed. Nielli bumped its side, its coat fluffed in amusement.

When the sneezing stopped, Hnarse returned its attention to the observation of the stars. Directly above, the blue star would soon eclipse the red. In three days, a shower of sparks would herald the season of fires. The herd must be through the trial of black pits and far from the forest before that happened. Also, the path of the blue star mirrored the most favorable path through the pits, and it was up to Hnarse, the Eldest Stargazer, to ensure that all young ones were taught to observe its movement before entering the trial.

Still as a moss-covered boulder, Hnarse aimed its eyes upward. Bright-edged clouds raced across the skies, obscuring then revealing the patterns that told of the season's progress. Once the constellations were clearly held in its mind's eye, Hnarse Stargazer kept the memory foremost and lowered its head to drone against Nielli's side.

The blind one's breathing pushed in and out. Hnarse's follicles twisted and twirled against the brindled coat, singing the story of the stars to Nielli's heart as if it were the Heart of the world.

It was more than possible its pupil wouldn't understand, but it felt it had to try.

Nielli shuffled aside, breaking contact. One small foot-pad came deliberately to rest by the end of Hnarse's nose, and the elder's droning ceased.

The small one shuffled again then draped its trunk awkwardly across Hnarse's face and began a song of its own. Its hair moved in patterns with meaning known only to itself, but Hnarse watched anyway. Sometimes, the movement rippled like storm across its body, and if Hnarse looked closely, it could see the dance of grasses bending to the tune of the clouds above. This movement was gentle, and Hnarse knew Nielli was at peace within its soul.

The drone continued. It seemed to have purpose. Hnarse focused inward. To its joy, it began to sense Nielli's emotions, happiness and frustration, just as it had read in the little one's outer voice. It listened even more closely, as if there was nothing else in the world but the two of them – and, to its astonishment, words came into its head.

I hear you inside … You make pictures in my heart.

Hnarse jumped back with shock and the contact was gone. Hurriedly it grabbed Nielli's nose and tried to drape it over its face again. Finally Nielli seemed to understand and the trunk stayed put.

What do you see? Hnarse said, but Nielli's trunk slid downward, leaving a cold echo where the contact had been.

It pushed under Nielli's nose again, desperate to warm the empty space. Nielli seemed to gain confidence. The trunk stayed put and, tentatively, the small voice came once more into Hnarse's heart.

Shapes, Nielli said. *I see many small points swirling in darkness. You think of them as ... stars.*

Excitement was replaced by stillness as Hnarse wondered what to do. Then it pushed its head against Nielli's chest and droned again. *Those are indeed stars. You are a Stargazer, Nielli!*

Nielli swayed thoughtfully from side to side. *Nielli? Is me?*

Yes! You, it bumped it, *are Nielli. That is your name.*

And star is different? It moves among the others, showing the way.

Yes! Yes it does! Hnarse Stargazer's nose stung with tears. *This one, the blue one, shows the way.* It imaged the constellation more closely. *That star is blue. You are Nielli Stargazer, a Stargazer like me!*

Stargazer ... It rolled the word through its mind. *But where are they, the stars? What is blue? How can I gaze?*

Hnarse sneezed away its tears. Nielli should know only confidence. *I will show you and you will learn. Then we will help other Went hear your Heart as I have!*

Nielli thought for a moment, then said, *Nielli is tired now*, and the contact dropped away.

Hnarse stroked its protégée's face. The sound of its voice had filled it with more emotion than could be processed all at one time. It bugled for Neetha to come to them.

"Friend of my cycles," Hnarse cried, "I have heard Nielli's voice. It spoke to me!"

"Heard it?" Neetha's crown tufts flattened. "One does not hear words."

"But I did hear them!" It pointed the end of its nose to its head, then its chest. "In my mind and in my heart."

Neetha moved its head from side to side as if it needed to see Hnarse through different eyes. "Nielli is blind," it said patiently. "Nielli has no words and cannot see ours."

Beyond them, where Neetha had been, young Grassmovers wandered among fruiting vines. Hnarse knew Neetha had been teaching them of the trial to come.

The Stargazer's follicles moved stiffly. "Nielli has a voice, if you will listen." But Neetha's crown-tufts remained stubbornly smooth.

"Nielli is sweet," Neetha's hair flowed with small signs of sympathy, "and has somehow survived the trials so far, but there are many more challenges to come." Its voice firmed. "Nielli has no eyes, Hnarse. It cannot see. Accept it. There are other Stargazers who would benefit from your instruction – especially now."

Neetha pointed to a small knot of young Stargazers, frighteningly few, who were gathered around Meahar, the second-eldest Stargazer.

Had it neglected its duties? But Meahar would most likely be Eldest one day and was a good teacher.

"Friend of many trials, Neetha, dearest to my heart, please see me."

Neetha's head swayed slowly back and forth. "Now Nielli is dearest to your heart."

Hnarse's coat rippled unevenly. "Nielli needs my care. If you would touch noses with it," it pressed, "you might hear words too."

With a skeptical sigh, Neetha moved closer to the Wentling.

Nielli stood very still as Neetha reached for its nose and twined it in its own. "What now?"

"Sing to it as if you were singing to the Heart."

"This seems very odd," Neetha said, but nevertheless it butted gently into Nielli's side and began to drone. As sound came from its nose, its hair related details of the smell of the swamplands as if speaking to a young Grassmover. The song explained how the scents would change as the season of fires advanced and made the forest dangerous.

When it stopped, Nielli remained still, as if still waiting for something to happen.

Neetha turned away. "See? It is useless."

Its stance was condescending, but Hnarse saw disappointment in the lay of its hair.

"I will help you care for the blind one in any way I can," Neetha continued, "but hope has drowned your truth, Hnarse. I heard no words in my head."

"I am sorry, Neetha," Hnarse whispered, and as it watched Neetha turn to leave, it wondered if its friend was right.

After several steps, the Grassmover paused. Its hair glimmered grey-green in the fading starlight. "Will you come now and share observations of the approaching dawn? Stand beside me and mingle thoughts as we used to – in the normal way?"

Hnarse's coat crinkled stubbornly. "First I must finish telling Nielli of the wandering moon. When it grazes on the net of cloud the weather will be unpredictable. The trial of swamps must be concluded before that time or too many will be lost."

Neetha turned away.

"It is important," he rippled after her.

The Grassmover slowed a little. "I will wait by the trees of selly farn. We may never see them again."

Hnarse Stargazer bubbled with relief. "That is true, I know – and it is one of your favorite places. I will come there soon."

Alone again, Hnarse brushed its nose along Nielli's side. The stillness of the young one's hair was absolute. Steady breathing moved its sides. Hesitantly, the Elder rested its trunk over Nielli's head. Instinctively, the sensitive tip ruffled empty spaces where eyes should be. Had their exchange been imaginary, as Neetha suggested?

Are you there? it asked.

Nielli bumped against the pressure of its trunk and nestled closer.

Selly Farn, a grove of massive green trunks crisscrossed with sagging vines, was a favorite landmark, especially for the older members of the herd. Fragrant purple fruit, sweet and full of energy, hung in clusters from the roping branches.

Neetha saw Hnarse and lifted a dark-stained trunk in greeting. It picked a fat bunch and held it in offering, but although the scent was enticing, Hnarse had little appetite.

"Not hungry? How can you resist?" Neetha slurped the fruit noisily. "What troubles you? I am sorry if it is my words about Nielli, but those are my thoughts."

Hnarse swirled its crown tufts in negation. "Your thoughts are what you are, and you are my friend," it said. "No, it is my own thought which troubles me. The question must be asked so the Great Circle might bring answer."

"What question?"

"Should I sing of Nielli to the Heart? Should I sing of Nielli's achievements?"

Neetha's hair rippled slowly as it considered. "There has never been such a one," it said eventually. "I know of no songs to describe the blind one's condition, and would not know how to make one, yet I believe the Heart should know."

"But you do not cherish Nielli Stargazer as I do."

"I do cherish Nielli, Hnarse, but I pine for our time together. Your actions in guiding the blind one are praiseworthy. This, the Heart should know also. So few New Purpose came to us, and now even fewer survive. Each of them is to be treasured."

Hnarse aimed its eyes at the glowing dawn, but the shining display could not hold its attention.

Neetha butted it gently from the side. "What now?"

"You know me too well," Hnarse said.

When it said no more, the Eldest Grassmover picked more fruit and ate patiently.

"How could Nielli's engenderment have been mistaken?" Hnarse blurted. "How could the Circle of Winds have forgotten to give a Went eyes? Have we been so remiss in our duty to the Heart?"

Neetha leaned its warm bulk against Hnarse's side and rippled, "The Heart cannot be mistaken. Hnarse, you must sing Nielli's praises at every opportunity. Nielli's every success is an achievement all should learn from. Maybe Nielli has purpose only the Heart can fathom."

"A purpose only the Heart can fathom …" Hnarse paused. It felt its spirit lighten. "You are most wise, Neetha Grassmover."

As the new day's sun poured over the land, a chill breeze riffled exposed areas of Hnarse's coat, but where Neetha stood close all was warm and still. Behind them, Nielli snuffled among the fruiting vines, seeming relaxed and happy. The blind one's unusual coat and odd mannerisms stood out, but Hnarse now understood that it was right for them to do so. Nielli *was* different, and to its eyes, the Wentling glowed as a treasured flower among dull stones.

SOME TRUTH

In the crisp morning sunshine at the Host's Settlement, seven spinners waited in position, ready to sing the envelope of translation around their cargo and propel it into the Chime. Beyond the circle of the Djan'rū, Kandät Enna glanced skyward, then turned to face the Host's leader.

"Where is Shamkarun Huldar?"

"No need to wait," Olatu replied irritably. "His reports are sealed and packed alongside those of the Overlord and everyone else's."

"And if the Overlord is dead?"

"I have no doubt he'll turn up somewhere. But as to how long that –"

The navigator raised his hand as Farushael of Cantori hurried toward them.

"He's been found," Farushael said. "In the water – drowned."

Olatu gave an extravagant gasp. "Another death? Such carelessness! Mirashael of Cantori is at fault here for his consistently poor choice of personnel. I've said as much in my report!"

"Mirashael of Cantori had nothing to do with Radätel Gok's appointment," Kandät Enna said stiffly.

"Well, someone is to blame! I've lost worker after worker to similar ineptitude. It's all there. No doubt Lucaät of Faytha will have plenty to say about the matter, and I expect some Imperial compensation may well be in order."

"Don't worry." Kandät's mouth moved in the slightest of sneers. "The God-Emperor will also have my full account when I return to Giahn, and it will be comprehensive."

Olatu's eyes narrowed. This hadn't occurred to him. But whatever the navigator reported, here on Went they were well beyond even Imperial reach, and by the time they returned to Giahn, there was little chance anyone would remember – or care, if his plan for the God-Emperor bore fruit.

"Lord Huldar has asked that you wait, Shamkarun Kandät Enna." Farushael bowed.

The Faythan scowled. "As I said, there is no need."

"We *will* wait for Lord Huldar," Kandät Enna snapped. "Olatu of Faytha, you have repeatedly spoken out of turn and above your station. Your personal rank is insignificant in comparison to Shamkarun Huldar of Leth's, mine, Lady Malena's, and nearly every other archangel on this world – including that of your aide, Farushael of Cantori, who is great grand-nephew to the Cantori himself. Your insubordination will also be included prominently in my report. I suggest your manners improve before my next return."

Olatu bowed, as if submissive. Maybe he had been a little overly assertive, but after flitting through the heavens all his life, how could this popinjay appreciate the rigors of controlling such a diverse and lucrative operation?

They waited in awkward silence. After what seemed an age, Huldar came into view. When Olatu saw he'd brought his pet half-breed with him, he found it hard to smile as pleasantly as he should. The navigator's frown prompted him to bow.

Kandät bowed also. "Shamkarun Huldar of Leth and Casco, I bid you farewell. Huldar, I am sorry not to have had opportunity to speak with your wife, Tsemkarun Andel. I hear she has been blessed?"

Huldar replied with a thin smile. "Early days yet. By the time of your next arrival we may have true cause to celebrate."

"And time," Kandät added, "but such is my schedule. The Guild drives me hard."

"The best are always in demand, Shamkarun Kandät Enna." Huldar tipped his head.

"The Overlord? A tragic outcome," Kandät said.

"We try our best to be careful," Huldar replied, "and to ensure the safety of all, but accidents are unavoidable. I have detailed a team to return him to Central Base-camp, where his song will be sung." He turned to Olatu. "You are free to attend, of course."

Olatu made a small bow, but had no intention of seeing Radätel's body again. "Terrible," he said. "Here in the wilderness, one misstep and ..." he shrugged "... it's all over."

Huldar's gaze narrowed. For a chilling moment Olatu wondered if he knew, but he said no more.

"His belongings?" he asked.

"Will be kept safe until we return to the Realm," Huldar replied. He looked at the navigator. "If I may have a word?"

Olatu stood by while the two luminaries spoke in secret, and held any incriminating thoughts deeply hidden. Huldar's shrewd gaze had unnerved him, but there was nothing in his haze to say he believed anything but that the Overlord's death had been accidental. To occupy his mind, he envisaged a bag of shiny gold imperials – a soft leather purse filled to the brim.

He glanced at Farushael, then at Casco – still as a statue, screens tighter than any splitter's had a right to be. He felt his gorge rising. If it wasn't for those eyes, the mongrel could almost pass for pure. He was just about to look away when he noticed Casco's neutrality slipping. Those angel eyes looked slowly up and came to rest on the bags of nacrite.

Olatu fought to control his nerves. Sweat started on his face.

Huldar half-turned as if Casco had said something to him, then continued his exchange with Kandät. Both glanced up as Casco had. At the navigator's signal the volume of the spinner's voices decreased.

Casco watched keenly as the navigator led Huldar toward the bag's tether-point.

Farushael stood calmly beside him, unaware of any problem. With regard to the calcite chests, he had followed orders admirably; he had asked no questions, and still hadn't.

Hit the half-breed! Olatu ordered him. *Hit him now!*

Startled by this request, Farushael hesitated.

Casco noticed Farushael's change in stance and gave a warning glance.

Olatu looked up. Huldar was about to open the sack.

Do it! he shrieked.

Farushael's intent firmed, but Casco fixed the archangel in a blinkless gaze.

Fool! Olatu screamed. How could a half-breed intimidate anyone? He stepped around to hit the mongrel himself, but as he lifted his fist, Casco caught it, and before he could retaliate or even think to break free, the splitter was behind him with his arm clamped across his throat.

"Help!" he gasped. *Help me, Farushael!* He could feel his consciousness slipping. Too far away, Ashik boots pounded. He glanced in desperation at the activity by the sacks, but it was too late. Huldar held up a purple globe, his gaze triumphant.

Olatu ceased struggling, thinking maybe if he slumped, his neck would break and he would not have to face such a humiliating defeat.

The navigator shook his head as another nacrite bag was opened at the base, and the Faythan's dreams of profit spilled with his contraband. Only the berries hidden among his reports remained undiscovered: the pair set aside for the God-Emperor. He hoped Lucaät would follow his instructions ... surely they were clear enough.

Followed by several of her troop, the Ashik commander finally rounded the corner.

Kandät Enna held up his hand.

The troop halted in confusion.

"Ready to be civil?" Casco said into his ear.

"Let me go, you insolent mo–!"

He gasped as Casco's grip tightened.

"What is the meaning of this?" the Ashik demanded.

"You really should release him," said Farushael.

"And you're going to make me?" Casco said nastily. "Why don't you give it a try?"

Huldar and the navigator left the Djan'rū with several loaded sacks. Behind them, the now even lighter bags of nacrite were re-tied.

"Let him go now, Casco," Huldar said. He glanced at the Ashik as if they were there to support him. "There's nowhere for him to run."

For a moment, Olatu thought the Ashik commander would remain loyal to him, but she looked first at Huldar, then Kandät, then bowed and formed a cordon as if to contain him.

He stumbled as Casco pushed him away. He couldn't catch his breath. His neck felt bruised.

Fully cloaked in the hauteur of his lineage, Kandät Enna looked him up and down.

Pinned beneath that gaze, fear crept into bed with his shame. This was not just a simple navigator he'd tried to trick. It was quite possible there *would* be repercussions. He buried the taint of Radätel Gok's demise so deep he almost believed the accident story himself.

"As I said," Kandät said coldly, "I do not take environmental crime lightly. This is a serious misdemeanor and should be judged before I depart."

Olatu looked at Farushael, but the Cantori had taken a step back. A small crowd began to gather. "Please forgive me, Shamkarun Kandät Enna ... I ..."

The navigator tilted his head. "The chance for increased wealth blinded you?"

Under the circumstances, Olatu saw abasement as his best chance – an appeal to his obvious ego. With his inner eye trained on the Enna's haze, he got to his knees. "I am sorry. It is as you say," he said to the ground. "Please accept my apology."

The navigator's haze softened enough for him to know he was on the right path, but his performance was ruined as Huldar stepped forward.

"Stop this farce! You stole items you knew to be necessary for the survival of an entire species. Caught in the act! You are a disgrace. No amount of groveling can change that!"

"Please don't send me home," Olatu said humbly. If they did, his career would be over. Again, he appealed to Kandät. "I've done well in every other way. The camp is clean and ordered. Quotas met. In every other environmental issue I have bowed to the will of the Uri'madu."

"Is this the case?" Kandät asked Huldar.

"It has been a struggle at times," Huldar said sourly. "The matter of the new Citizens has been the greatest sticking point."

Olatu cringed. Perhaps he should have done more to appease the ecologists, but to halt operations while geeks who'd never worked a day in their lives examined a herd of hairy behemoths for potential self-awareness ... Even as he said the words to himself, it almost made him laugh.

"I must confer with my team," Huldar said.

The navigator bobbed his head. "I understand. Please, go ahead, but remember, time is short."

Both Huldar and Casco closed their eyes. Huldar's lifted his face toward the skies as if he communed with the sun. He glanced back to Casco, who was clearly engaged in the same long-distance conversation.

While his silent trial went on, Olatu remained kneeling in the dirt. To take his mind from his discomfort, he wondered who the spy had been. Since the screens that shielded his tent had been breached, he'd been aware there was someone of skill in the camp, and whoever it was, they'd played right into his hands. Maybe the Maatu, he mused. She was powerful enough and had certainly familiarized herself with the camp … or that snide Enna, so adept with his charms. He'd been the one alongside Huldar when the calcite boxes were unmasked – but who in their right mind brings their spy along for the reveal? He glanced at the half-breed with hatred. If not for him, the heist would have proceeded and he would have won. Now the best he could look forward to was the eventual smile of Imperial good-will, a shaky asset at best.

Casco opened his eyes and returned his hate-filled glance with one of his own.

Huldar shook his head as if freeing it from entanglement and turned to Kandät Enna.

"Are you ready?" the navigator asked. He peered anxiously at the sky. "The decision is yours, Shamkarun Huldar, but the stolen goods have been recovered and I must leave soon."

Huldar bowed. "A shawl, please?"

Kandät returned his bow with a brief one of his own and beckoned to one of his spinners. A snowy-white length of cloth was passed to Casco, who arranged it over Huldar's shoulders.

Olatu watched as the two shared an unreadable glance, then Huldar's penetrating blue eyes came to rest on him.

His knees ached, his mouth went dry. What should he do? He had not planned for this.

"Olatu of Faytha," Huldar began.

Olatu held his breath. To be caught in the act was an inconceivable mistake for one of his standing. He must have the chance to redeem himself to Lucaät – he must!

"You may remain here on probation until the next rotation."

Olatu closed his eyes in relief.

"During that time," Huldar continued, "you shall make Farushael of Cantori familiar with all aspects of leadership of the Host. Also, you will order the Host to assist my investigation of the Went in every way I deem appropriate. If I am unsatisfied with your performance, you will be returned to the Realm on the next rotation and Farushael of Cantori will take your place. Do you understand?"

Olatu let out a breath. It was a reprieve of sorts, but what had sparked it? Huldar's impeccable haze and veils held no clue. "I understand," he said, but he was not sure he did.

"Before these witnesses – myself as leader of the Uri'madu and representative of the Explorer's guild, Shamkarun Kandät Enna of the Navigator's Guild, Farushael of Cantori, representative of the Host, and Casco of the Uri'madu – do you agree to my terms?"

He nodded. What choice did he have?

"Say it!" Huldar barked.

"Yes. I agree."

Huldar paused.

Olatu held himself very still. Surely he would not retract his verdict? "I agree!" he said again. "I do! I will do my best."

"Very well, the matter is closed," Huldar said.

Kandät Enna bowed. "Bey et El a'sien."

Casco took the shawl from Huldar's shoulders and returned it.

Olatu's knees were on fire, but he dared not take it upon himself to stand – not while the navigator was still there. The half-breed studied him with narrowed gaze, then turned to look at the Djan'rū.

At Kandät Enna's gesture, the spinners raised their voices. The broad envelope rippled and reformed, shielding the vast amount of cargo from view.

Huldar and the navigator left him kneeling in the dust and walked toward it, then Casco hurried after them and handed the navigator a sealed scroll.

Moments later, the chord firmed, swelled, and in a blink the space emptied.

Huldar glanced Olatu's way. Just discernable beneath his perfect veil was a glint of bitterness.

His shame was intense. No doubt Huldar regretted his leniency, but the navigator was gone, and despite his embarrassment, the Host and the Ashik were his. He looked the tall Lethian in the eye and climbed to his feet. He doubted he'd have the guts to have him dismissed on the next rotation.

"You think you've won?" he said angrily. "We'll see who the God-Emperor thanks when his wife is blessed."

Huldar's look of shock was satisfying.

"You didn't get them all," Olatu said.

Huldar's eyes blazed.

For a moment, he thought Huldar would actually hit him. But the leader of the Uri'madu gave the empty Djan'rū a last look, then he and Casco picked up their precious berries and turned away.

Olatu massaged his neck. Damp fabric stuck to his knees. His slippers were ruined.

"Get back to work!" he snapped to the onlookers, then to Farushael, "I want a drink. Now!"

―――――――――

Huldar and Casco started for the portal, the precious cargo suspended between them. Huldar frowned as he walked. The eggs of the Went were saved, no one had been tortured, but the planet still tolled its distress.

A chill northeasterly stole across the ground. Damp fronds rustled in sullen acknowledgement. *Breath Blows* ... he thought he heard her say. *The sacrifice begins as foretold.*

He should be delighted with the outcome, but he wanted to cry. What was the great loss she warned him of? Was Olatu's small victory such a disaster? If only there was a sign, a clear path to follow, something to show him where the danger lay ... but the fronds just rustled, and the bell merely tolled.

He thought of the Uri'madu – each worth so much more than one bigoted, over-inflated Faythan. Andel, Malena, Daric, Casco and the Naghari ... The impromptu council had convinced him to keep the Faythan there, but he could only hope the rest of the team would understand. If Olatu returned to the Realm without the testimony of the Uri'madu, it was likely he would evade the Explorer's Guild and never face justice. They wanted certainty he'd pay for his crimes.

"We did it!" Casco crowed. "We got them back – well, most of them."

"Thanks to you!" He smiled to see his friend's elation. "What made you think of the nacrite?"

"The lumps in the bottom of the bags," he said. "It struck me that nacrite floats."

Very clever! Huldar congratulated him. "Even Daric never thought to look there."

"And I got to squeeze the Faythan's neck," he added. "That's a keeper."

"Certainly is," Huldar said. *The Rukh will love it!* He forced the darkness back. They had won a great victory. Casco had earned his right to celebrate.

So what's wrong? Casco glanced at him from the corner of his eye.

He frowned a little. He thought he'd covered his concerns quite well.

I know you, he insisted. *Is it Radätel?*

Huldar pictured the Overlord's body, wrapped beneath his favorite coverlet, waiting to be sung to its rest. *It will be difficult to face him*, he admitted.

"The others don't know it was murder," Casco said. "Are you going to tell them?"

"Daric and Ubaid advised against it. What do you think?"

"I agree with Daric. It doesn't have to be common knowledge just yet. If it gets back to the Faythan that we know, it should be at the right time ..." *For maximum impact. Information can be a weapon. It's all about timing.*

Huldar nodded, although taken aback by this new, strategic bent to Casco's thinking.

As they stepped through to Central, he paused to take in the scene. The sides of the marquee were open. Some of the Uri'madu were gathered around Tam's kitchen, while others waited by Radätel's bier – keeping him company. Soon he would sing the body clear, empty its Qalān and set the effects aside for his family, then the entire company would join him in singing the body back to the elements which formed it.

Andel's face turned to him, tilted in understanding. Warmth channeled through their link.

A cheer went up as their arrival was noticed. He pushed Casco forward. "Here's the real hero," he said. "If it hadn't been for Casco, Olatu would've gotten away with it."

"Berry commendable," Daric said solemnly.

"One eye on the food, as usual," said Tam.

Casco patted one of the bags. "Well these little beauties are definitely off limits." He laughed.

"And the choke's on Olatu!" cried Bush.

"Yes, I think you acted for all of us there," said Banga. "Malena was watching. She showed us the best bits!"

While the others joined Casco at the campfire, Huldar ferried the eggs into his tent. Andel came beside him and took his hand and out they flowed – anger and sorrow for Radätel's murder, the frustration of the double-blind, the joy of victory, then the nagging doubt of his judgement concerning Olatu. When all that remained was the warm glow of love between them, he sighed, more relaxed than he'd been for weeks.

She leaned against him. *Such things are easier to bear when shared. And there's no need to worry: they understand why you allowed him to stay. Daric and Malena made it quite clear.*

A spark of alarm threatened his peace. *Radätel's death?*

A terrible accident, she reassured him. *It must have happened while he was on his way to talk to the Faythan alone. He was so adamant that the berries be returned. That's the only reason we could think of that he'd be out there … and in a way it's true.*

Just enough truth …

Exactly.

I'd be lost without you.

Exactly.

At last he felt able to attend to Radätel Gok with the honor he was due, but as they stepped back into the campsite the weight of his responsibility seemed heavy. There has been too many such ceremonies in recent times. He looked at the faces around him, his beloved Uri'madu, as the planet's warning tolled. *The trap is set … You cannot help them.*

MEETING OF MINDS

With his back to the night, Casco sat cross-legged and stared into the flames. Beside him, a mug of besh stood forgotten. When the Overlord's body had been sung and the last mist claimed by the breeze, Huldar had presented Radätel's precious globes to him for safekeeping. They would be returned to his family when they got back to the Realm, but in the meantime he was sure the practical Gok wouldn't object to their use.

He sighed. The Went were saved and their eggs already replaced in the cave. They had re-sealed it, this time with a small space left open for lizards or any other small creature that might need access, and an all but unbreakable alarm should anything larger try to get in. But despite their success, Huldar still seemed worried. And as for the blessed ... made pregnant by the eggs of another species? What did it mean?

In that moment, he wished more than anything to be sitting in his favorite corner at the Weyfal with a pot of besh on a stained table, the smell of greasy omosa warring with the odor of sour ale, and Huldar beside him listening to his woes, or the two of them swapping an image back and forth, each embellishment more ridiculous than the last.

He stifled those thoughts as Daric came closer. Casco didn't have to turn around to know exactly where he was, but he recalled times when he'd been hidden. Times when he could have done things he didn't want anyone to know of.

With inborn elegance, his lover settled beside him. Their knees touched with a jolt of warmth. Daric leaned across him to pick up his drink and held it up to peer at him through the swirling brown fluid before handing it over.

Looks like you could use it, he said.

The invitation was there for Casco to come closer, but he put the mug to his lips and let it go.

You're the hero of the hour – again! Why aren't you celebrating with the others?

He shrugged and drank more ale. *Takes some getting used to, and to tell the truth, I'm exhausted.*

Shen's on his way, Daric said.

He nodded. It would be good to see his old friend, but it irked him that their charade of being strangers must be maintained. It was hard work.

It was a good idea to give Kandät your list in person, Daric said. *Mirashael will receive it as you wrote it. Yours and Shen's will be the few uncensored documents to leave this planet.*

He nodded again. Daric seemed expectant. He realized he should say something, but, "I want to go home," was all that would come.

"Home?" Daric spluttered, then pretended to cough. "But it's just getting interesting, thanks to you."

"Interesting?" Casco frowned into his ale. He glanced at Lady Andel, Sari and Malena sitting around a second fire with the rest of the Uri'madu's blessed. Even Alis had joined them. "Things will never be the same again. Never be normal."

"What's normal?" Daric retorted.

He visioned Sari's belly, already a little thickened. *We don't even know for sure what they're carrying. Ubaid says the pregnancies are progressing too fast. That means something's wrong.*

As if succumbing to Casco's mood at last, Daric's energy dimmed. *I spoke with Ubaid after the song,* he said. *The Hara it's called in the old language ... the farewell. I don't like it that the Faythan censored our mail – for more reasons than one. I'll bet that some reports, even some personal letters, didn't get sent at all. That worries me.*

Why do you think he did it? Casco shrugged. *Why would he kill Radätel? It doesn't make sense.*

If I was Olatu, Daric mused. *What would I want?*

They looked up as Shen joined them.

"What does Olatu want?" Casco asked him.

"That's easy," Shen replied. "Coin. Wealth. Prestige. It's what Faythans live for."

"What was he going to do with the berries?"

"Highest bidder," Shen said.

"No. He's not that stupid," Daric countered.

"Very unpleasant, though ..."

"Granted!" Daric grinned, then grew thoughtful again. "But the ones he has, they'll go straight to the Imperial couple."

Casco looked at him. "That's what you told me to say in my list ... in code of course."

"Me too," said Shen. "How did you know? What if we'd found them all?"

A picture of Mirashael of Cantori, florid shirt and all, popped from Daric's mind into theirs. "There's no one smarter," he assured them. "He would've worked it out – still will."

"But what will the information mean to him?" asked Casco.

Shen snorted. "Stock up on Imperial Blessing souvenirs?"

Daric put down his ale. "And that's our problem, right there," he said slowly. "The Imperial couple will be blessed ..." Casco started as his lover's alarm flashed through him. "Why didn't I think of it before!" Daric murmured. "We have to tell Huldar. We must begin to take steps now – right now."

"What do you mean?" Casco asked. "Tell him what?"

Daric got to his feet. "You don't think the God-Emperor will let us live, do you? Even you aren't that naïve."

Naïve? Casco frowned. Was that how Daric saw him? *I don't think so!*

Shen stood up beside Daric. Even in the firelight, his face was pale. "He's right. We have to do something."

"Why?" Casco frowned up at them, still confused. "Why will he kill us?"

"Because we know," Daric hissed. "If Olatu had returned, there may have been a chance. Now all knowledge of the eggs is confined to this one, isolated planet. We'll be the only ones who'll know how he's cheated."

A TALL ORDER

A river of street sounds drifted into the well-lit sitting room above Mirashael's café. Engrossed in her ledgers, Leahät marked the passage of time by the way the shadows fell across her desk. She looked up as her senses alerted to a particular, almost dancing tread, and smiled. Those same footfalls continued between the tables and chairs in the café below, through the kitchen, then bounced up the stairs. She opened the door before they reached the top.

A flash of garish pink and yellow filled the doorway as Mirashael of Cantori paused to take in the sight of her, then hurried over.

"Ah! My love, my love, my love! I have found you."

"Of course you have," she replied fondly. "Really, you do say the silliest things."

"Yes, yes, sometimes it does seem so. But your comment about *saying* is pertinent because ..." He reached into Qalān to extract a sheaf of papers and waved them with a flourish *... here in my hand I have correspondence most longed for.*

From Shen!

His eyes sparkled. *Indeed, dear lady. Delivered just now by Hermes from the Guild.*

Leahät pushed aside her books and reached for the letter. Mirashael dangled it in front of her, then teased her by lifting it just beyond reach.

What does he say? She tried for the letter again and failed. *Is he well?*

Mirashael went to the divan and patted the space beside him. *I brought it straight here so you and I may read and enjoy it together.*

The elderly couch creaked as she sat beside him. At first glance the letter seemed nothing but a lengthy list of supplies to be ordered, but Leahät was becoming proficient at reading Mirashael's code.

Greetings my dear friends ... she deciphered. *I hope you do not miss me too much. I am well and no one suspects, but if this list finds you intact, it may well be the only uncensored information to leave here. The atmosphere is strained. There have been troubles with personnel and ...* "Many deaths?"

She looked up. Mirashael's smile had evaporated. His eyes were intent on the remainder of the page.

Strange things ... I have seen many strange things, she corrected, *but strangest of all are the ...* she hesitated, unsure of what she was reading. "Is that, 'pregnancies'?" *Several miners and all female Uri'madu have been blessed, even unmarried.* She looked at Mirashael again. "Unmarried? That can't be right."

"That is what it says, dearest Lady," he said thoughtfully. "You have read correctly."

"But that can't be."

"Yet this is what he says, so it must be true."

She returned to the list. *The God-Emperor has been sent some berries. If she eats one, the Empress will also be blessed. Cause for celebration? Please tell no one what I tell you.*

"The Empress blessed?" She looked up. "That's good, isn't it?"

Mirashael frowned. "No, no, my Lady. Shen is astute. The blessing will not be El's. This cannot bode well. And look here ..." He pointed to some symbols in the lower margins that looked for all the world like a last-minute alteration to the amount of talemgal needed.

Leahät's fingers came to her mouth. "Radätel Gok?"

"See the way he has hooked this flourish? Far from merely missing, I fear our clever Shen believes him to be dead."

"But his wife ... I seem to remember bad news?"

"Yes, she is also at one with the Breath these three weeks since. Three weeks," he repeated slowly. "They would have reached Mecca. Lucaät has a new outpost there ..."

"She was killed? Murdered? But surely it was Radätel's death – they were close. She couldn't deal with the pain."

My contact did not believe her death to be of her own design.

There was a pause. She remembered Radätel Gok and his wife. They had eaten together at the café. He had been excited by his selection as Overlord. "And the other papers?" she asked.

"Olatu of Faytha," he said absently. She could sense his thoughts whirring, deep and busy. "Complaints about the quality of the staff, the tea, the food, demanding more alcohol, and replacements for the twenty-six miners who have died – apparently he blames our poor initial selection criteria."

"That's outrageous! And twenty-six dead? That's terrible! I thought Went was a peaceable planet."

"Indeed, I believed so too. It says here he also wants two more archangels with deep ore extraction and refinement skills, and one with experience in under-sea extraction."

"More archangels? They weren't included in the original contract."

"No. But he wants them now."

"Has Lucaät agreed to pay for them?"

"We are meeting with him tomorrow."

She'd always been aware that Lucaät was a dangerous opponent, but knowing he had killed, or had had someone kill, Radätel Gok's wife – someone she knew to have no political value or aspiration … She remembered her own brush with Lucaät's Ashik. How lucky she'd been to have Mirashael come to her rescue. No one had come to save the new Overlord's wife.

Mirashael went to lean by the window, but he didn't see the street below. She sat in silence, unwilling to interrupt. Eventually, he turned.

We must make arrangements to leave here, my love, and soon.

What? "Why?"

It has occurred to me – "Linkages …" He passed her an image of Radätel Gok.

"Radätel Gok?"

He put his finger to his lips. *He's dead. I am absolutely certain of it.* He turned to her. *We must warn Shen, even if he won't receive it until the next delivery. If the Empress is indeed blessed, I fear his suspicions will be proved correct. There will be no true cause for celebration. His return to us – indeed, the safety of everyone on that planet – will be in grave doubt. And we will be in danger also. If we are not already.*

She looked at him in shock.

Prepare quietly. Alert no suspicion. I must stay somewhat longer – my other duties, you understand? But as much as we love our Pannias coast, it is to Cantor we should return.

But this is my home!

Do you trust me, my beloved? Do you?

Yes.

Then believe me: you, at least, must be gone before news of the Imperial Blessing is even announced

IMPERIAL JOY

The God-Emperor Tsemkarun Ishät Ashik, 36th Chosen of El, swept into the Empress's favorite sun-lit chambers.

There was a quiet patter of feet as servants and slaves pressed themselves against the walls and averted their gazes.

Ishiquel clasped her hands together. This must be the special gift from house Faytha – some rare berries from the planet Went. Her husband was quite besotted by the place, and the prospect of possessing more of the exquisite Eyes of Bel Nishani was certainly engaging.

"Do you have them?" she asked.

"Indeed." From behind his back he presented a finely figured wooden platter edged and filigreed with their House Rune in bright silver. Two unremarkable fruits, dull purplish in color, reposed in its hollow.

Ishiquel stroked this offering mysteriously. The skins were smooth but not slippery. "They don't look like much."

Her husband studied them with her. "Yet I am assured of their exceptional power."

He placed them on the small table at her side. The Empress smoothed the front of her silken gown. "And I will be blessed … by a berry?"

Ishät chuckled good-humoredly. "They are to be eaten, my glorious one, not inserted." He let his robe fall open. "I have some very fine equipment designed for *that* function. The berries merely – open the way."

His eyes glittered in invitation. Tiamät lay quiescent. She felt herself warm to the idea.

Leave! she commanded her attendants.

There was a scurry of feet, then silence.

Ishät's powerful mind coiled into hers. He lifted the berries with long, strong fingers and pushed one between her parted lips. The globe filled her mouth. She rolled it with her tongue, feeling the tingle of life inside, and bit down hard.

At the same time, his teeth closed decisively on his own berry. Their shared sensation of the pulp and kernel entranced her. His yellow gaze consumed her. He reached for her breasts with an urgency rarely felt after millennia of marriage.

Only you, my Chosen, he whispered as his mouth covered hers. *There is no one else in my heart – Only you.*

And at that moment, she almost believed it to be true.